The Animals of Farthing Wood
OMNIBUS

Colin Dann

The Animals of Farthing Wood OMNIBUS

In the Grip of Winter
Fox's Feud
The Fox Cub Bold

Illustrated by Terry Riley

LEOPARD

This edition first published in 1995 by Leopard Books
An imprint of the Random House Group
20 Vauxhall Bridge Road
London SW1V 2SA

First published in the United Kingdom in 1994
by Hutchinson Children's Books

ISBN 0 7529 0130 3

Printed and bound in Great Britain by
Mackays of Chatham PLC, Chatham, Kent

Contents

In the Grip of Winter

Colin Dann

In the Grip
of Winter

Illustrated by Terry Riley

Contents

For Kathy

—1—
First Signs

It was soon time for the animals and birds to face their first winter in White Deer Park. They had moved in a group from their old homes in Farthing Wood when it was destroyed by Man, and the strong links of friendship and the spirit of community forged during their long journey had caused them to build their new homes close to one another. So a certain corner of the White Deer Park Nature Reserve became almost a new Farthing Wood for them, and every creature found conditions exactly right for his particular requirements.

In the centre of this area lay the Hollow which, from their earliest arrival in the Park, had formed their meeting-place. In the autumn months they met less often and, eventually, as the evenings grew colder, both Adder and Toad knew it was time for them to go underground for the winter.

It was late October when Adder ceased to lie in wait at the edge of the Edible Frogs' pond, a feat of patience that had not brought him its hoped-for reward. 'This cool weather makes me feel so sleepy,' he remarked to Toad, whom he sometimes saw going for a swim.

'Me too,' replied Toad. 'I've been busy fattening up while food is still available. I must confess that now I really feel ready for a nice long snooze.'

'Where will you go?' Adder enquired.

'Oh, hereabouts. The earth is soft in this bank and I've noticed quite a few holes remaining that must have been dug in earlier years.'

'Mmm,' Adder mused. 'That would suit me admirably. Those frogs would then have the benefit of my presence in spirit throughout the winter.'

Toad chuckled. 'I'm sure they won't be aware of it,' he said. 'They're digging themselves into the mud on the pond bottom. Once they've settled, they'll be quite oblivious of everything.'

'I shall, too,' admitted the snake. 'My only interest at the moment is in sleep.'

'Er – have you made your farewells?' Toad asked him hesitantly.

'Farewells? Stuff and nonsense!' Adder rasped. 'No-one cares to seek me out when I'm around, so they'll hardly miss me when I'm not.'

Toad felt embarrassed. 'Oh, I don't know,' he said awkwardly. 'I think it's just that most of us feel you prefer to be alone.'

'I *do*,' said Adder a little too quickly, as if trying to dispel any doubts at all about the matter. 'However, Toad, I've no objection to your company,' he added not uncourteously.

'Thank you, Adder. Er – when do you plan to begin hibernation?'

'Straight away, of course. No point in hanging around above ground in these sort of temperatures.'

'If you can wait until tomorrow I'll join you,' Toad suggested. 'Just leave me time to call on Fox and Badger, and Owl, perhaps.'

'Oh, I can't sit here waiting for the frost to bite me while you go making social visits,' said Adder impatiently. 'I'm going underground tonight.'

'Very well,' said Toad. 'As you wish. But I really don't see what difference one more day would make.'

Adder made a gesture. 'I'll tell you what,' he offered. 'Let's choose a comfortable hole now, and then you'll know where to find me.'

Toad considered this was about the closest Adder was ever likely to come to being companionable, so he accepted readily.

Having chosen the best site, Adder promptly disappeared into the earth with a hastily lisped, 'Try not to wake me.' Toad wryly shook his head and set off to find his friends.

As he approached the Hollow, the sky was darkening fast, and a cold wind was whipping through the grass. Toad almost wished he had followed Adder into the shelter of the hole, but he felt he just could not have been so unfriendly. No movement could be discerned in or around the Hollow, so Toad sat down to wait, amusing himself by flicking up a stray beetle here and there. Presently a ghostly form could be seen lumbering towards him through the gloom. Toad made out Badger's grey outline.

'Hallo, my dear friend,' said Badger warmly. 'I'm surprised to see you out on a cold night like this.'

'It'll be the last time,' commented Toad. 'Before the Spring.'

'I see, I see,' Badger nodded. 'You've come to say goodbye. Well, it could be for quite some time, you know.' He paused and snuffled in the brisk air.

'Do you think it will be a hard winter?' Toad asked.

'Every winter is hard for some,' Badger answered. 'The weakest among us always suffer the most. The small creatures: the mice, the shrews, the voles and, particularly, the small birds – every winter takes its toll of them. But yes – I sense that this winter will be one to reckon with. There's something in that wind. . . .'

'I felt it, too,' Toad nodded. 'And Adder – he's already settled.'

'Just like him to disappear without trace,' Badger muttered. 'Well, at least it'll put an end to that nonsense of his with the Edible Frogs.'

'Yes, until next year,' Toad remarked drily. 'But, d'you know, Badger, he actually invited me to join him in his sleeping quarters – at least, in a roundabout sort of way.'

'Oh, he's all right really,' Badger granted. 'After all, you can't expect a great deal of warm feeling from a snake.'

While they were talking, they saw Fox and Vixen slip stealthily past in the moonlight, intent upon hunting. Toad was disappointed. 'They could have stopped for a word,' he complained, 'when I've made a point of coming to see you all. And in this wind, too.'

'Don't feel slighted, old friend,' Badger said earnestly. 'I'm sure they don't realize you're about to go underground. It wouldn't be like Fox.'

'No, I suppose not,' Toad assented. 'But he's not the close friend he used to be before Vixen came – at least not to me. Ah well, that's the feminine influence for you.'

Badger nodded his striped head, smiling gently. 'We old bachelors have little experience of such things, I'm afraid,' he said softly. 'We live out our solitary lives in rather a narrow way by comparison.'

Toad was touched by the note of wistfulness in Badger's voice. 'I – I never realized you felt that way about it, Badger,' he said in a low croak. 'But there are lady badgers in the park, surely?'

'Oh yes, it's different from Farthing Wood in that respect,' Badger agreed. 'But I've been living alone for too long now. I couldn't adjust.'

Toad was silent. He felt it was best not to add anything. There was a long pause and Toad shuffled a trifle uncomfortably. 'Hallo,' he said suddenly, 'here's another old bachelor,' as Tawny Owl fluttered to the ground beside them.

Owl nodded to them both, then said, 'I hope you weren't speaking derisively, Toad. I can't answer for you two, but I'm single from choice alone.'

'*Your* choice – or the choice of the lady owls?' Toad asked innocently. Badger muffled a laugh.

'Very amusing, I'm sure,' Owl snorted. 'I'd better go. I didn't come here to be insulted.'

Badger, so often the peacemaker, stepped in. 'Now, Owl, don't be so hasty. No offence was intended. Toad's come to see us because he's going into hibernation soon.'

'Humph!' Tawny Owl grunted, ruffling his feathers. But he did not go.

'Yes, tomorrow to be exact,' Toad informed him. 'And I shan't be sorry. I sympathize with you fellows who have to face whatever comes: ice, frost or snow. It's marvellous just to fall asleep and forget all about it – and then, simply wake up as soon as it's warm again.'

'There's certainly a lot to be said for it,' Badger remarked.

'But it takes months off your life,' Tawny Owl pointed out. 'You may as well be dead for six months of the year.'

'Not quite as long as that,' Toad corrected him. 'Anyway, it depends on the weather. In a mild winter, I might be out again in February.'

'Mark my words, Toad,' Tawny Owl said with emphasis. 'This is going to be a difficult one.'

'Then my heartfelt good wishes go with you,' Toad said sincerely. 'I hope you all come through.'

The three friends remained talking a while longer, while the cold wind continued to blow. Finally Tawny Owl declared he was hungry and flew off in search of prey. Something struck Toad at his departure and he fell to musing.

'You know, Badger,' he said presently, 'we shake our heads over old Adder and his designs on my cousins the frogs, but really he's not so much a threat to the denizens of White Deer Park as Fox or Owl, who go hunting here every night.'

'A thought that had also occurred to me,' Badger acknowledged. 'But there were foxes and owls – and other predators – in the park before we arrived. So in the same way the voles and fieldmice and rabbits of the Farthing Wood party run the same risk from the enemies already here.'

Toad nodded and sighed. 'My idea of the Nature Reserve as a new and safe home for all has not proved quite true,' he said ruefully.

'Nowhere is completely safe,' Badger assured him. 'But the Park is about as safe as anywhere could be for wild creatures, for there is no presence of Man. And in that respect it is a veritable haven compared with Farthing Wood.'

Toad grinned. 'You've soothed my mind as usual,' he

said. 'Well, Badger, I shall not delay you any longer. Farewell till Spring.' He turned to make his way back to the bank where Adder was already asleep. On his way he encountered Fox again. This time Fox stopped. Toad explained where he was going.

'You could perhaps give a message to Adder for me,' Fox requested. 'Tell him to go down deep. And you too, Toad,' he finished enigmatically.

'How deep?' queried Toad.

'As deep as it takes to escape the frost.' Fox shivered in the wind as if illustrating his warning.

'We shall take heed, Fox,' Toad answered. 'Have no fear.'

They parted and Toad crawled on towards his objective. Fox stood and watched him a long time. Then he shook himself vigorously and went to rejoin Vixen. Winter, he knew, was hovering just around the corner, waiting to pounce.

―――2―――
First Snow

During the next few weeks, as October passed into November and the leaves fell thick and fast in White Deer Park, the animals kept very much to themselves. Their main preoccupation was food.

Nature had provided an abundance of berries and nuts which, as all wild creatures know, is a sure sign of severe weather to come. So the squirrels and the voles and the fieldmice were able to feast themselves for a short period. There was a spell of heavy rain which brought out the slugs and worms, and Hedgehog and his friends fattened themselves up nicely before they made their winter homes under thick piles of leaves and brush in the undergrowth. As they disappeared to hibernate, the other animals knew that time was running out, and renewed their efforts. All ate well for a space.

The first heavy frost descended at the end of November and Mole, whose tremendous appetite was undimmed, found an abundance of earthworms deep underground. Their movements were restricted by the frozen ground near the surface and he amassed a large collection against emergencies. He was so proud of his efforts that he was bursting to tell someone about them. So he tunnelled his way through to Badger's set which was close by, and woke him from a late afternoon snooze.

'It's me! Mole!' he cried unnecessarily. 'Wake up, Badger. I want to tell you what I've been doing.'

Badger sat up slowly and sniffed at his small friend. 'You smell of worms,' he said abruptly.

'Of course I do,' Mole replied importantly. 'I've been harvesting them.'

'Harvesting them?'

'Yes, you know, collecting – er – gathering them. I've never known it to be so easy to catch so many. They're all securely stowed away in a nice big pile of earth where my nest is.'

'I didn't realize it was possible to stow away slippery things like worms,' Badger remarked. 'By the time you get back they'll all have wriggled away.'

'Oh no, they won't,' declared Mole. 'They can't,' he added mysteriously.

'Why, what have you done to them?'

'I've tied them up in knots!' cried Mole excitedly. 'And they can't undo themselves.' He began to giggle as he saw Badger's stupefied expression, and he was still giggling when Badger received another guest, in the shape of Fox.

'Have you been outside?' he asked, after greeting them.

They shook their heads.

'It's snowing,' he stated.

They followed him up Badger's exit tunnel to look. It was dusk, but the sloping ground in the little copse Badger had favoured as his new home was gleaming white. The trees themselves glowed mysteriously in their soft new clothing. They watched the large flat flakes drift silently downward. There was no wind. Everything seemed completely still save what was dropping steadily from the sky.

'It's already quite thick,' Fox told them. 'I can't see my tracks.'

'I've never seen snow falling before,' Mole said as he watched with fascination. His eyes, used to darkness, blinked rapidly in the brightness of the white carpet spread before them. 'Will it cover everything?'

'Not quite everything,' answered Badger. 'But it makes movement very difficult for small creatures. The birds don't have to worry, of course. Except in so far as feeding is concerned.'

'I can only remember one winter in Farthing Wood when it snowed,' said Fox. 'That was when I was very young. But there was only a light fall, and it didn't really hamper anyone's movements.'

'Oh yes,' nodded Badger. 'Of latter years there's not been a great deal of bad weather. But I recall the times when Winter meant Winter, and we had snow every year. Of course, my memory goes farther back than yours, Fox.'

Fox smiled slightly. He knew Badger loved to indulge in reminiscences, and he was aware of his proneness to exaggerate about 'life in the old days'.

'I remember one winter in particular,' Badger continued, delighted to have an audience. 'You hadn't appeared on the scene then, either of you, and I'm pretty certain Tawny Owl wasn't around at that time either.

Anyway, the snow lay on the ground for months, and I had to dig a regular track through it for foraging purposes. Everything was frozen hard – the pond, the stream, every small puddle. My father was still alive then and he taught us how to munch the snow for water. Otherwise we couldn't have drunk and we should have died.'

'What does it taste like? What does it taste like?' shrilled Mole.

'Oh, well – er – like water, I suppose,' replied Badger. 'Yes, and I shall never forget the number of birds and small creatures who perished from the cold.'

'Oh dear, oh dear!' Mole cried. 'I hope you don't mean moles?'

'Well, possibly not moles,' said Badger hurriedly. 'Mostly songbirds really. They couldn't find enough to eat and, naturally, their little bodies weren't able to withstand the bitter weather.'

'Poor things,' said Mole in a subdued tone. 'It's a pity they can't hibernate like Adder and Toad.'

The snow seemed to fall more thickly as they watched. Mole shivered.

'Go back inside,' the kindly Badger said at once. 'It's warm in my sleeping-chamber.'

'I'm not cold,' Mole told him, 'but thank you, Badger. No, it's just the eeriness that made me shiver. It's so quiet and still – it's uncanny.'

Through the ghostly trees they spotted a dark figure stepping through the snow. They all knew at once it was the Warden of the Nature Reserve on his rounds. They watched him stop periodically by a tree and tie something on to a low-hanging branch.

'What's he doing?' Mole asked, whose short-sightedness could only distinguish a tall blur of movement.

'I don't know for sure,' answered Badger. 'But it's my

guess he's leaving some sort of food for the birds.'

'Then that's bad news for us,' Fox said at once. 'Humans never do such things without a particular reason. It is well-known they can tell in advance what sort of weather is approaching. We must be in for some severe times.' He trotted over to look at the objects the Warden had left behind.

'You're right, Badger,' he called back. 'It *is* bird food. Nuts and fat and so on. I hope our feathered friends are up early,' he continued to himself, 'otherwise Squirrel and his pals will be having a feast at their expense.' He said as much to Badger on his return.

'Well, we must stop them,' said that thoughtful animal resolutely. 'The squirrels have buried enough acorns and beech-nuts to feed the whole of White Deer Park.'

'You'll be asleep when *they* get up,' Fox reminded him with a smile. 'You'd better leave it to me to have a word.'

'Will you and Vixen be warm enough in your den?' Badger asked suddenly. 'I've collected plenty of extra bedding for my set, and you're welcome to share it.'

'You're very kind,' replied Fox, 'but I think we're all right. We keep each other warm, you know,' he added.

Badger smiled. 'That must be a great comfort,' he remarked. He looked around. 'Well, I feel like a bit of a ramble. Coming, Fox?'

'With pleasure. Er – see you later, Mole?'

'No, I'll go back to my nest,' said the little animal. 'I'm sure to feel peckish again soon – you know what I'm like.'

'We do indeed,' laughed Fox. 'Shall we go, Badger?'

The two friends ambled off through the snowy wood. For some time neither spoke. Badger felt that Fox had something on his mind, so he remained quiet until his friend should be ready to talk. He watched the snowflakes settle on Fox's lithe chestnut body, grizzling his fur and making him appear prematurely aged.

At length Fox said, 'If we do have a long spell of snow, I shall have to start making plans for a food supply.'

'I don't think that will be necessary just yet,' Badger said calmly. 'We can see how things develop. The animals will make shift for themselves.'

'Of course they will,' said Fox hurriedly. 'They'll have to. But I have a feeling in my bones about this winter and – well, quite frankly, Badger, I'm more than a little concerned.'

Badger felt he should allay his companion's fears if he could. 'Don't go worrying yourself,' he told him. 'After all, to begin with Toad and Adder and the hedgehogs are not involved. I can look after myself and so can Weasel, Tawny Owl and Kestrel. Of the smaller creatures, the squirrels have only to dig up a fraction of their buried treasure to survive, and Mole has never been so well supplied. So who does that leave? Hare and his family, the rabbits, the voles and the fieldmice. All of *them* eat seeds and vegetation. You're a carnivore. You couldn't begin to be as proficient at finding stores of their food as they are themselves.'

'Yes, I suppose you're right,' Fox agreed. 'It's just that if any of them do get into difficulties I shall feel responsible for getting them out.'

'It's early days yet,' said Badger. 'You just think about Vixen for the time being. The others will manage, you'll see.'

'You're always a comforting chap,' Fox said warmly, 'and I'm truly grateful, Badger.'

They reached the Hollow together and Fox's next words made it clear that Badger had not succeeded in putting his mind at rest.

'This is where our new life began last summer,' he said, looking down at the familiar meeting-place of the Farthing Wood community. 'Let's hope the next few months won't see the end of it for some of us.'

3

First Losses

The first signs were not good for wild creatures as the old year drew to a close. December came in with a blizzard, and over the next few weeks a cruel, bitter frost held the Park in its grip night after night. During the daylight hours the sun gleamed fitfully but snow clouds blotted it out for most of the day, and so very little of the frost disappeared. The ground became as hard as iron, and ice coated the Edible Frogs' pond to a thickness of two inches.

A stream ran through most of the Reserve and, some distance from where the Farthing Wood animals had set up home, Whistler the heron could be found. He had chosen an area under some overhanging alder trees where fish abounded in the shallow reaches. Now each

day he and his mate watched the slower-moving water
by the stream's banks gather more ice. Soon only the
centre of the stream, where it rippled swiftly over the
tinkling pebbles, continued to flow. Whistler had to step
on to the ice to be able to continue his hunting, but the
fish were less plentiful further out in the water and the
heron and his mate began to notice their diet suffering.

'It looks, my dear, as if we shall have to be rather less
choosy in our fare,' Whistler observed in his slow, precise
manner. 'From your greater knowledge of the Park, can
you suggest any fresh avenues of approach?'

The female heron nodded. 'I told you long ago of a
place upstream, where the water runs very fast, and
which abounds in crayfish. But you told me you had no
liking for shellfish.'

Whistler shrugged his great wings. 'Obviously I shall
have to overcome my aversion, at least temporarily.
Show me the way, if you please.'

The two water birds rose into the air together, their
long, thin legs trailing beneath them like pairs of stilts.
From the air, the Park was one vast expanse of rolling
white, pierced by clumps of bare, snowclad trees. Whistler's damaged wing shrilled musically with its every
beat, and his eyes began to water in the freezing
temperature.

They landed after a brief flight, and Whistler's mate
began to search the stream-bed. Here the water was
completely free of ice. Suddenly her pointed beak
stabbed downwards, and then re-emerged firmly clench-
ing a feebly moving crayfish, which she swallowed at a
gulp. Whistler joined the hunt and was soon successful.
His mate watched for his reaction. 'Hm,' he murmured,
swallowing hard. 'Not at all bad. It's surprising how an
empty stomach may overcome the most rooted
prejudice.'

As there were fish also to be had in this stretch of water, the two birds made an excellent meal. His satisfaction made Whistler call his friends from Farthing Wood to mind. He wondered what difficulties they might be experiencing.

'We mustn't be selfish,' he told his mate. 'This food source might well be of benefit to others. While you return to the roost, my clever one, I think I'll search out Fox and see if I can be of use to him.'

Accordingly he flew off in the direction of Fox's earth. As it was daylight he did not expect to find his friend above ground, and was surprised to see a very lean Vixen sitting by one of the entrance holes when he arrived. She appeared to be very disconsolate, but bravely tried to look cheerful as she greeted the heron.

'Is Fox below?' Whistler asked her.

'No,' she replied. 'Things have been getting rather hard, and he decided to go and see for himself how everyone else is coping.'

'The very reason I came to see you,' Whistler explained, and went on to describe his earlier success in the stream.

Despite her efforts at control, Vixen's mouth began to water freely as she heard of the fish Whistler and his mate had enjoyed.

'It would be more than a pleasure for me to help you catch some,' Whistler offered.

'I'm sure Fox would be most grateful,' Vixen said appreciatively. 'I think I should wait for him to return before we go. There might be one or two other animals who would like to join us.'

'I wonder how long he will be?' Whistler asked.

'I don't know exactly,' answered Vixen, 'but he's already been gone some hours.'

While they waited, she explained how their hunting

trips had become steadily less fruitful and how their diet had become one of carrion, insects and even snails when they had discovered a hibernating colony. 'But they tasted so good,' she added.

'Oh yes,' agreed the heron. 'I myself have made some adjustments in my eating pattern,' and he went on to tell her of the crayfish he had eaten.

Presently they saw the familiar figure of Fox approaching them, accompanied by a smaller one they could not at first distinguish. It turned out to be Weasel.

Whistler and the two animals greeted each other with pleasure. But Fox's expression returned to one of deep concern when Vixen questioned him on his discoveries.

'It's even worse than I'd expected,' he informed her miserably. 'The voles and fieldmice have already lost a considerable number of their party, and some of the older rabbits have died of the severe cold. If this weather continues for a long spell the mice, in particular, are going to be decimated.'

Whistler expressed his sympathy but, privately, was more alarmed at Fox's own appearance. Gone was the vigorous, supple body of the resourceful leader the animals had come to rely on during their long trek to the Nature Reserve. Gone was the bright-eyed, healthful expression of his face. And gone was the rich lustre of his coat, that had marked Fox as a creature in his prime. Now his eyes were downcast, his fur dull and staring, his movements slow and hesitant, while his body was not so much lean as distinctly bony. By comparison Weasel's much smaller form, always as slim as a sapling, looked in much better shape.

Whistler hurriedly told Fox about the proposed fishing. Without a great deal of interest, Fox agreed. Then he said, 'But of what use are fish to voles and fieldmice? They are hungry too.'

'Of course they are,' said Vixen. 'But you must keep
your strength up if you wish to help them, even though
that is going to be difficult.'

'Rabbits and fieldmice soon replace their numbers,'
Whistler pointed out in an attempt to ease Fox's mind.

'Yes, but there may be no stock of fieldmice to replace
numbers from,' Fox muttered. 'Their community has
lost more in the last week than during the whole of our
journey across the countryside. And the voles haven't
fared much better.'

'Did you see Hare?' Vixen asked him.

'Yes. His family are all reasonably well though, like
everyone else, they've taken on a lean look. The leverets
are almost up to his size now, and quite independent.'

'How is Badger?' Whistler wanted to know.

'He wasn't at home,' replied Fox. 'But I've no fears
on his account. He has more experience of life than any
of us. He'll survive.'

'I'm sure we'll see a thaw soon,' said Weasel optimistically. 'The winter has a long way to go yet, and a cold
spell like this rarely lasts for more than a few weeks.'

Fox did not reply, but they all knew he was wondering
what could be done if it lasted through to the spring.

Whistler gave them directions to the fishing area and
told them he would meet them there. When they arrived,
they found he had wasted no time. Four reasonably sized
fish and a couple of crayfish awaited them. The three
animals fell to at once and made short work of the meal.
Whistler enquired if they had had enough.

'Better to save some for another day,' remarked Vixen,
'than to feast now and starve tomorrow.'

Whistler acknowledged her wisdom. Then he said,
'I've seen nothing of the other birds. Has anyone encountered them recently?'

'Oh, Tawny Owl can always be found in his beech

coppice,' Weasel answered. 'He was dozing when we
came past just now. He's found himself a snug hollow
trunk out of this biting air. As to Kestrel, he flies so far
afield you would be lucky to catch a glimpse of him.'

The animals enquired after the health of Whistler's
mate. As she was the favourite topic of the heron's conversation, he answered enthusiastically. 'Oh, she is such
a wonderful creature,' he told them. 'It was she, of
course, who knew where to find the crayfish and showed
me the spot. I'm sure I never shall be able to express
sufficient gratitude to you all for allowing me to accompany you on your journey to the Park. Had I not met
you, I should still be patrolling the waterside in that
quarry, with no more company than a lot of raucous
mallards and coots. Now I'm living in that perfect con-
tentment of a paired wild creature which I'm sure you,
Fox, also enjoy.'

Fox and Vixen smiled at each other and Weasel chuckled. 'Hold on,' he said. 'Some of us still opt for the
single state, you know.'

'Ah, not for long, Weasel, if you are a wise beast,'
Whistler admonished him. 'There is no comparison, I
assure you.'

Weasel laughed again. 'Perhaps you're right,' he said.
'But, on the other hand, "better the devil you know"
and so forth.'

This little exchange served to lighten their mood, and
provided a welcome relief from their troubles. The
animals thanked Whistler heartily for his generosity and,
telling him to keep in touch, began to make their way
back along the bank of the stream towards their homes.
Dusk fell early at that time of year, and the cloud-covered sky hastened the darkness. Weasel left the fox couple for his den, and as Fox and Vixen approached the
earth, they could see an agitated Mole waiting for them.

'Whatever is the matter?' Fox asked at once.

'Badger's disappeared,' said the distraught little creature, and broke into a sob.

'Now, now, calm down, Mole,' Fox said soothingly. 'He always leaves his set at this time in the evening. You know that.'

'Yes, but he hasn't been in it all day either,' wailed Mole. 'I've been along my connecting tunnel half a dozen times today to see him, and the set has been empty all along.'

Fox looked at Vixen. 'Hm,' he mused. 'That does seem strange.'

'I'm sure there's some simple explanation for his absence,' said Vixen. 'He may be on a visit or – '

'He wouldn't be likely to go visiting in this weather,' interrupted Mole. 'I'm so worried. Badger's habits never change. He sleeps during the day, and only wakes up in the evening.'

'When did you last see him?' Fox asked.

'Yesterday. We talked about the shortage of food, and I offered him some of my worms because he said *I* was looking plumper than usual. Then he started to talk about you, Fox, saying that it wasn't fair for you alone to feel responsible for all the animals' welfare, and that he was sure you were getting thinner and thinner because of it, and you needed some help.'

'That's Badger all over, the dear kind creature,' Vixen observed.

'Yes, and it makes the picture much clearer,' announced Fox. 'He's obviously gone off on some venture of his own with the idea of helping us in one way or another, though Heaven knows what he can possibly do. Don't be too alarmed, Mole. I think we shall see him back by the morning, and I'll ask Tawny Owl to keep an eye open for him tonight.'

'But what if he doesn't return?' persisted Mole. 'I know I shan't be comfortable until I know he's all right.'

'If he doesn't return,' replied Fox, 'I shall personally go out tomorrow to search for him, even if it means combing the entire Park.'

'Oh, thank you, Fox,' said Mole. 'I knew you would. I'll go home and stop bothering you now, and I'll look into Badger's set in the morning and let you know.'

Fox trotted off to speak to Tawny Owl, leaving Vixen and Mole to return to the comparative warmth of their underground shelters.

—4—

The Search for Badger

Mole went straight to Badger's set before he ate a single worm the next day which, in his case, was the strongest possible measure of his anxiety. The set was, again, empty. He emerged from one of Badger's exit tunnels and made his way as fast as his short legs would allow him to Fox, cursing his slowness as he did so. But his journey proved unnecessary for, when he reached the earth, Vixen informed him that Fox had already set off on his search. He had wasted no time on hearing from Tawny Owl that Badger had not been seen returning home, and all that they could do now was to wait for news.

It was not long before Fox realized that, if he did not find Badger within the area of the Reserve settled by the

Farthing Wood animals, or at least close by, he would
never have the strength to travel the confines of the
whole of White Deer Park. In addition to his own weaker
state, there was the powdery snow, which in places had
formed thick drifts, and was very tiring to walk through
as he frequently sank in it as deep as his shoulders. Even
as he trudged along it again began to snow heavily, so
that visibility became very poor too.

Skirting the Hollow, he made a tour of the perimeter
of their home area. The falling snow covered any tracks
or scent that might have been useful, and Fox knew he
was on an impossible task. He must recruit some assistance. A swifter and less heavy animal such as Hare
would be able to cover a greater distance more easily,
but most of all Fox wished for a sight of Kestrel. His
piercing eyesight from high above the ground could locate the lumbering form of Badger faster than anyone's.
For the moment, however, he must make do with Hare.

Luckily Hare was to be found sheltering with his mate
in a scooped-out 'form' of snow behind a hawthorn tree.
The leverets were elsewhere. Fox explained why he had
come again so soon.

'That *is* surprising,' Hare said afterwards, 'old Badger
going off like that. I wonder what he intended to do?'

'We've no way of knowing, at the moment,' answered
Fox. 'The thing I'm afraid of is that he might have met
with some accident. He doesn't normally wander far
afield.'

'How can I help?' Hare asked.

'You're much fleeter of foot than me,' replied Fox,
'and can cover greater distances more easily. If I comb
this side of the Park, could you investigate a bit further
afield?'

Hare was silent for a time. Eventually he said cautiously, 'I *could*. But I don't relish the idea of going too

far away from the home area. After all, there are other
foxes in the Park beside yourself and Vixen, and I'm fair
game for all of them.'

Fox nodded. 'I know,' he said. 'But I've never yet met
a fox who could outrun a hare.'

Hare's mate had pricked up her ears at this latter turn
in the conversation. 'Don't put his life too much at risk,'
she begged Fox. 'He's the father of a family, you know.
Badger is a loner and would leave behind no mate to
mourn.'

'No, but the number of creatures who would mourn
the loss of Badger would be far greater,' Fox pointed
out.

Hare looked from one to the other, torn between con-
flicting loyalties.

'Well, I shan't press you,' Fox said finally. 'It may be
that your duty to your family should come first, after all.'
He started to move away, but Hare called him back.

'I *will* go,' he announced. 'I should never forgive myself if I turned down such a request for help.'

'Thank you,' said Fox simply. He described where he
wanted Hare to go – the area beyond the Edible Frogs'
pond. 'We'll confer later at the Hollow,' he added. 'I
shall be there at dusk. Good luck.'

He left the two animals but did not fail to hear Hare
being up-braided by his mate as he went – 'Why did
you let him talk you into it like that?' and Hare's quiet
reply, 'For the sake of Farthing Wood.' Now as Fox
plodded on through the relentless snowfall, his spirits
rose a little and some of the tiredness left him. He found
some harder patches of snow, where it had begun to
thaw and then frozen over, and he was able to increase
his speed, all the time casting about for his old friend.

He came out into the open expanse of parkland where
the White Deer herd usually roamed, and it was not

long before he spotted a group of them feeding from bales of hay specially provided by the conscientious Warden. One of their number was the Great Stag himself, a huge figure who now did not look so imposing as before. The hard winter was taking its toll of all creatures, from the highest to the lowest. Against the dazzling snow carpet, the white hides of the deer looked duller than Fox had remembered. The Stag noticed him and stepped elegantly towards him.

'How do things go with you and yours?' he asked.

'Not well,' Fox answered. 'Food is hard to come by and the cold very cruel.'

'Yes, I don't recall many winters such as this,' said the Stag. 'For some reason this year *we* are not to be expected to fend entirely for ourselves. The humans, in their wisdom, have decided to buffer us against extreme hardship.'

'I understand your herd is unique,' said Fox, 'so it isn't surprising that your numbers are not allowed to become too depleted.'

The Stag nodded sagely. 'I'm only sorry you don't eat hay,' he said. 'We have more than enough.'

Fox thought of the rabbits and mice. 'There is something you could do,' he said, 'if you are so willing. My smaller, weaker friends are suffering particularly. If you didn't object, perhaps some stray stalks could be left aside for their use?'

'Of course. Certainly,' the Great Stag agreed readily. 'But you don't often come to these parts, do you? It would be a really difficult undertaking for creatures smaller than yourself.'

'That's true,' Fox answered. 'But if they are sufficiently hungry I'm sure they will come.'

The Great Stag pondered a moment. 'It is most unusual,' he observed, 'this mutual co-operation and concern your band of animals feels for each other. Normally, in the wild, each animal goes his own way and – well, the strongest survive. I find the idea of helping one another most interesting – even appealing. Perhaps we deer should also show a willingness to assist our brother creatures. Supposing I arrange it that each member of my herd carries a mouthful of hay and deposits it at a point more conveniently close to your friends?'

'That would indeed be kind,' Fox told him, and added that the best place to leave the food would be by the Hollow.

'It shall be done today,' the Stag said. 'But tell me, my friend, what brought you this way in the first place?'

'One of our party – Badger – has disappeared,' said Fox. 'I'm looking for him.'

'Hm, again this concern for others. Most interesting,' intoned the doyen of the deer herd. 'Well, if I hear of his whereabouts I shall most certainly come and tell you. I wish you all well.' He rejoined the rest of the herd and Fox continued on his way.

Presently he came within sight of the Warden's cottage and garden area beyond the fence and here he struck lucky again, for Kestrel was perched on top of one of the palings. The hawk called joyfully to him and flew over, wheeling playfully over Fox's head.

'Come down, Kestrel, I want your help,' shouted Fox.

The bird was at once all seriousness, and landed beside him. 'What is it?' he asked.

Fox told him.

'I'll go now – at once. Earlier today I was flying over the Park, but I had no sign of Badger.'

Fox told him of the rendezvous at dusk in the Hollow with Hare; then he said, 'Before you go, can I ask you to stay closer at hand for the next few days? You might be needed again.'

Kestrel agreed and swooped off to begin his exploration.

For the rest of the day, Fox methodically combed every part of the Reserve he could before he felt exhaustion to be imminent. With the last reserves of his strength he made his slow way back towards the meeting point. The snow had ceased by the time he reached the Hollow, where he discovered Vixen, Mole, Weasel and Tawny Owl waiting for news. He merely shook his head as he saw them.

Mole said nothing, almost as if he dare not speak.

'I asked Hare and Kestrel to help me,' Fox said wearily. 'I'm more hopeful of their news.'

Hare was the next to arrive, but he had no comfort for them. However they tried not to feel too disheartened until Kestrel had come.

'If anyone can find Badger that hawk can do it,' Weasel said encouragingly.

'Unfortunately that remark implies,' Tawny Owl pointed out, 'that if Kestrel can't find him the rest of us don't have a chance.'

They fell silent again, shifting their feet in the bitter cold. At last Kestrel arrived.

'I've searched every corner of the Reserve twice over,' he told them, 'and found not a trace of Badger anywhere. He seems to have disappeared into thin air.'

Mole broke down at this appalling news of his beloved Badger, and it was left to Vixen to try and console him.

'He can't just have vanished,' muttered Fox. 'There's something very odd about this.'

'Perhaps he's been adopted into another set,' suggested Hare.

'Never – not our Badger,' declared Weasel.

'Unless he were coerced?' Tawny Owl added.

'This is what is worrying me,' Fox admitted. 'It seems

the only solution: that **Badger** has somehow managed to get himself captured and taken underground, or at any rate carried off by something. But no, no ... it's incredible.'

'Well, there's nothing any of us can do for the moment,' remarked Tawny Owl. 'I'm famished, and I need longer than usual to hunt up my supper these days. I'll bid you farewell till tomorrow.'

He had not been long gone, when the animals espied a group of deer coming towards them. Fox told of his talk with the Great White Stag, and they all watched as each deer dropped its mouthful of hay by the Hollow and quietly retreated. This put other thoughts into Fox's mind.

'Hare, on your way home, will you inform your cousins the rabbits about this?'

'I'll have a mouthful or two myself first,' he answered.

'I'll go and tell those poor mice,' Fox continued.

'No,' said Weasel. 'You're far too tired. You go and rest. *I'll* tell them.'

Fox was about to relate the Great Stag's comments on their mutual help for each other, but he was simply too worn out, and allowed Vixen to lead him back to their den.

Mole was the last to leave the Hollow. 'I won't believe it,' he kept muttering to himself. 'He *hasn't* disappeared. I'll find him. I'll find him.'

——5——
What had Happened to Badger

Badger had thought long and hard about the animals' difficulties, and it had occurred to him that none of them had any idea how the original inhabitants of the Reserve were coping with the winter. As they would know the resources of the Park far better than the recent arrivals from Farthing Wood, he decided there would be no harm done if he went to seek out advice where he could.

Saying nothing to any of his friends, he left his home at his usual time in the evening and set off on his quest. The night air was still and the moon glowed from a clear sky. It was intensely cold and Badger hurried along as quickly as he could with his rather shambling gait.

He had left the familiar region of the Park far behind
before he encountered another creature. Under some
shrubbery he surprised a stoat who was feeding from the
carcase of a rabbit. The two strangers eyed each other
warily.

'It's a bitter night,' Badger said at length.

'There's not enough for two,' the stoat replied, who
obviously thought he had a competitor for his meal.

'I'm not after your food,' Badger told him. 'I can see
you are very hungry.'

'Famished,' answered the stoat bluntly. 'Haven't eat-
en for three days.'

'Hunting difficult?' Badger asked unnecessarily.

'That's an understatement,' came the reply. 'There's
nothing about. This rabbit died from the cold, I should
say. Of course, it's frozen solid. But you have to eat
what you can these days.' The animal wrenched off
another mouthful and appeared to find it of great relish.
'What about you?' the stoat enquired. 'I don't think I've
seen you around before.'

'No, you wouldn't have,' Badger told him. 'I don't
usually wander as far as this. I'm one of the newcomers
to the Park.'

'Oh, you're one of the great travellers, are you?' the
stoat said with a touch of cynicism. 'Well, you've found
no garden of abundance here, I'll bet.'

'Who could have expected weather like this?' Badger
answered. 'In any case, the whole countryside must be
affected.'

'Of course,' agreed the stoat. 'This winter will halve
the population of this Reserve, though.'

'Do you think so? As bad as that?'

'Bound to,' the animal said shortly. 'Very little food
means very few survive.'

Badger nodded. 'Yes, I suppose so.'

The stoat seemed to be waiting to be left alone again. Badger eventually noticed. 'Er – I'm sorry to have interrupted you,' he said. 'I'll leave you in peace.' He moved away and called back a hesitant, 'Good luck!' over his shoulder, but the stoat was too busy with his meal to respond.

However, the remarks he had made to Badger had made it pretty evident that none of the creatures in the Park was faring very well. He thought of the Great Stag, whose wisdom could perhaps serve the animals' interests in their hardship. But where was he to be found? Not in the woods, at any rate. He would be in open country. Badger continued on his way.

But he never reached the deer herd, though they were in his sights before the accident happened. He was descending a slight slope which was very slippery with ice. His feet skidded and he went hurtling down, unable to stop himself, just like a toboggan. At the bottom of the slope was a large rock. Badger was completely powerless to avoid it. One side of his body and one hind leg struck the rock heavily. Badly winded, he let out a cry of pain at the blow on his leg. When he could breathe freely again, he tried to hoist himself upright, but such a searing agony shot through the injured hind leg that he merely collapsed on his side once more.

There he lay for the rest of the night. He knew there was no possibility of walking, and the dreadful cold seemed to penetrate every inch of his fur. He wondered what would ever become of him. 'What hope have I got?' he asked himself. 'I'm a long way from my friends, I've no food, no shelter, and I can't move.' He fell into an uneasy doze.

When morning came, Badger awoke so cold and stiff he could barely even raise his head. But salvation was on the way, although he did not know it. The Warden

of the Park had been out distributing the bales of hay
for the White Deer herd, and was doing a general round
of the Reserve in his Land Rover. Stopping periodically
to view an area through his field-glasses, he spotted the
almost inert form of Badger and went to investigate. In
no time Badger found himself being lifted, taken to the
vehicle where he was laid gently down amongst some
old rugs, and transported back to the warmth and comfort of the Warden's cottage kitchen.

The Warden fetched an old dog basket, lined it with
sacking and old cloths and deposited the uncomplaining
Badger inside. Then he stood contemplating the animal
thoughtfully for a minute, before beginning to prepare
some food. Badger fell into another doze, induced by his
weakness and the warmth of the room.

When he next sleepily raised his eyelids, he found
some raw mince and warm milk placed in front of him.
He was able to move his body sufficiently to feed and he
ate greedily. His rescuer appeared to be delighted with
this, for Badger sensed eyes on him and looked up. The
man was smiling broadly, and Badger was astonished,
almost numbed by the brightness of the human face.
Never had he been so close to humankind before. There
was something mysterious – awe-inspiring – there: something quite beyond his own experience and
understanding.

But the Warden did not linger. Badger was left to
finish his meal and rest in peace. As he sank back on
the bed provided for him, he thought of his friends in
the Park that he had wanted to help. A lot of help *he*
had been to them. They were still suffering in the bleak
winter weather – battling against elements that soon
could overwhelm them entirely. He knew that his
absence would be noticed. The animals would be ignorant of his fate, and he as ignorant of theirs. Would he

be able to walk again? He realized the Warden wished to aid his recovery. But how long would he be kept here? He despised feeling so helpless.

Eventually his very helplessness overcame him, and in his weak state he fell asleep again. He did not know that, on several occasions while he slept, the Warden looked in, and was amused by his snoring. But there was a fresh supply of mince and water to drink when he woke at his usual hour in the evening.

When he had finished eating again, he became aware of a presence in the room, although he had heard nothing moving. In the gloom that he was so used to he soon noticed a pair of green eyes watching him unblinkingly from the doorway. They belonged to a large ginger cat, the Warden's pet.

'You're in a bad way,' the animal remarked, and walked on noiseless feet towards him in an elaborately unhurried way. By the basket the cat bent and sniffed curiously at Badger for a long time. 'You have the rank smell of a wild creature,' he announced.

The creature's coolness nonplussed Badger. He was not a mouse or a pigeon, but a large untamed animal whose normal strength must be totally unknown to the cat.

'Have you been eating my meat?' was the next question.

'Your master fed me,' Badger replied.

'I have no master,' the cat responded at once. 'I am my own master. I do as I choose.'

'Then why do you choose to eat meat provided by a human?' Badger asked subtly.

'Why ever not?' the cat wanted to know, flicking his tail slightly in irritation. 'It saves me the trouble of finding it for myself.'

Badger was silent.

'I've no objection to your eating it, anyway,' the cat said nonchalantly. 'There's plenty more where that came from, and all sorts of other things as well. Do you like fish?'

'I've eaten fish on occasion, yes,' Badger answered.

'Hm. What do you usually eat?'

'Grubs, roots, bulbs, small creatures. . . .'

'Rats?'

'Sometimes.'

'Good. Then we have something in common. My chief pleasure is hunting rats.'

'Are there many around here?' Badger asked, immediately thinking of their value to Fox and Vixen and Tawny Owl, too.

'Not since I arrived on the scene,' replied the cat boastfully, flexing his claws. 'The man brought me here as a kitten two winters ago.'

Their conversation was cut short by the sound of human steps. The Warden came into the room, and Badger was astounded to see a complete change of character come over the domestic animal. Running to its owner, it became at once the playful and affectionate pet, rubbing itself round his legs and purring noisily; then scampering off to a corner before returning to repeat the performance. The man spoke to his pet which increased the volume of purring instantly.

Badger soon understood it was the cat's mealtime now and the leg-rubbing ritual, together with stretching and mewing, continued until the food was ready. It then abruptly stopped while the more important task of eating was taken care of.

Badger came in for a word or two from the Warden also, though of course he understood nothing. Yet the sounds were very pleasing to him and comforting, too, and he was quite sure that had been the intention.

When the Warden left the kitchen again, the cat followed him. A short time afterwards he returned to put his ginger head round the door. 'I'm going to spend the rest of the evening in front of the fire,' he informed Badger. 'I feel very sleepy. But we'll talk again later. I hope you're comfortable for now?'

Badger assured him he was, and found himself alone again. He was soon musing over the strange mixture of his new acquaintance's personality: semi-domesticated and yet semi-independent. Despite himself, he felt drawn to the animal. He promised to be an interesting source of information.

Outside it was snowing again. In the warmth and security of the basket, Badger felt distinctly guilty as he thought again of his old companions. How he wished they could be sharing his new-found comfort with him now.

—6—

Conversations

The next day Badger felt a good deal stronger after plenty of rest and food. He particularly enjoyed a couple of apples the Warden thoughtfully gave him. With his returning strength, he began to look forward to being active again, and was pleased to receive another visit from the cat as a relief from the monotony.

The cat came running into the kitchen, his ginger fur glistening where the snowflakes were melting. 'It's really quite dreadfully cold out there,' he announced. 'Far too cold for me. I bet you'd sooner be in here too.'

'It's certainly warm here,' Badger admitted. 'But my set was always quite cosy, you know. There was plenty of dried bracken and leaves and grass and so on to pull round oneself.'

'But didn't the snow cover you?' asked the cat.

'No, no, my home's underground,' Badger explained.

The cat looked surprised. 'Underground? How extraordinary,' he said.

'Not extraordinary at all,' Badger said a little defensively. 'A lot of wild creatures live underground. It's a lot safer and, as I said, very comfortable.'

'Who are your enemies?' whispered the cat.

'Humans principally,' Badger replied. 'And dogs.'

'Well, you've no fear from humans hereabouts,' the cat reassured him in a well-meaning way. 'There aren't any, except the man here, and he loves all wild creatures.'

'I know there's nothing to fear here,' Badger replied. 'That's why we all came to the Reserve in the first place. For safety.'

'Where did you come from, then?'

'Oh, a long, long way away. A place called Farthing Wood. We had to leave, because the humans were destroying the wood. Our homes were threatened, and if we had stayed we would have been killed.'

'How many other badgers were with you?' asked the cat.

'None. We were a motley party. Fox, Weasel, Tawny Owl, Mole, Toad, Kestrel, along with hedgehogs and rabbits and hares and squirrels and voles and fieldmice and even a snake.'

'This is most interesting,' declared the cat. 'It sounds as if half the countryside was on the march.'

'It wasn't really like that,' Badger smiled. 'We were only a small band and, naturally, we lost some of our number on the way. Considering the hazards we encountered, we were fortunate not to lose more.'

'I see,' said the cat, who did not at all. 'The mice were taken to provide food for you on the way.'

'No, no, no,' Badger cried in horror. 'They were companions on our journey. Before we set out, we all swore an oath to protect each other's safety – not to molest one another.'

'But surely,' persisted the cat, 'in the wild it is common for stronger animals to prey on the weak?'

Badger nodded. 'But we are no common group of animals,' he said with the greatest satisfaction.

'I'm beginning to understand that,' remarked the cat. 'Tell me about your adventures.'

'With pleasure,' said Badger. 'And the only way to do that is to begin at the beginning.'

So the cat sat perfectly still while he heard about the animals' escape from Farthing Wood and their journey across country, with all the dangers they had faced of the fire, the river crossing, the Hunt and the motorway. He also heard how the animals had seen the Warden before arriving at the Park. 'Well, well,' he said afterwards, 'quite a story. Makes my life seem very dull.'

'Each to his own,' Badger said sagely. 'I imagine you're content with your lot?'

'Oh yes, I have everything I want. Food, warmth – and I can come and go as I please. A cat can be happy with very little.'

'Have you never felt the desire to be completely free, completely in charge of your own life?' Badger enquired.

'But I am,' the cat protested. 'As I told you, I please myself.'

'It's not what we wild creatures would call really free,' Badger said provokingly. 'I rather think you're more attached to the man than you care to admit. I was interested to see the way you responded to him yesterday – you made quite a fuss of him.'

'Oh well,' the cat answered, beginning to lick his chest fur as a diversion, 'they expect something for their pains, don't they? The man likes to think I'm dependent on him.'

'Perhaps you are?'

'Not at all,' the cat said huffily. 'I can survive perfectly well on my own if I have to. You're just trying to rile me.'

'I certainly am not,' Badger said at once. 'But I'll tell you what. Once I can walk again I shall leave here. Why don't you come with me and prove to the human you don't really need him?'

The cat did not take up the challenge. 'How *is* your leg?' he asked. 'Still painful?'

Badger indicated that it was. The cat began to lick the wound sympathetically. But Badger had to call out to him to stop. 'Your tongue is so rough,' he explained. 'But you're very kind.'

There were human voices outside. The cat jumped up to the window-sill to look. 'Ah,' he said. 'The man who makes animals well is coming. He often comes here when a wild creature has been found in trouble. He will help you.'

The Warden came in with another human who was, indeed, a vet. Badger found himself quite unalarmed at being closely examined and tested, and then having his bad leg bound tightly with some materials. The two men then talked for a period, and the Warden seemed to be quite satisfied with what he was told. The vet made a fuss of the cat, calling him by his name, 'Ginger', and tickling his chin. Badger's new friend responded in the way expected, by purring very loudly and nuzzling the proffered finger. Then the animals were left alone again. Badger was amused, and decided to persist with his suggestion of the cat's adopting the wild way of life.

'Well, perhaps I may,' the cat said evasively, 'but I

think it will be quite a while yet before you're fit enough
for the man to release you.'

'Release me?' said Badger sharply. 'I'm not to be kept
here, am I?'

'Oh no,' said the cat. 'As soon as you are considered
to be quite well enough to return to the wild, you'll be
taken outside to run away freely.'

'I shouldn't have doubted really,' said Badger. 'I know
that man really wants the best for wild creatures. If only
all humans were of his type, there would be no need for
any beast or bird to fear them. But I believe they are
few and far between.'

'Oh, there's not many like him,' the cat averred. 'He's
about the best you can hope for from their race.'

Badger noted the enthusiasm in the cat's voice, which
certainly did suggest there was a bond of attachment
between him and the Warden, despite the animal's claim
to be independent. Then he thought of his own attach-
ments. He wished he knew how his old friends were. By
now they were sure to be concerned about his disappearance. He dared not think too much about how Mole
might be feeling. He watched the cat washing himself
meticulously, preparatory to curling up in his own bed.
A thought struck him. He himself was unable to go to
them, but he could send a messenger. The cat could be
his legs.

'I wonder if I could ask you to do me quite a large
favour?' Badger asked rather nervously, for he suspected
the cat's reaction.

The cat paused in the middle of his toilet, the tip of
his tongue protruding from his mouth and one hind leg
raised into the air from his squatting position.

'I'm getting increasingly worried about my friends in
the Reserve. They don't know where I am,' Badger went
on. 'I know they'll be out looking for me, and they've

more than enough to cope with just staying alive at the moment, without bothering about me.'

'I think I know what the request is to be,' the cat remarked, lying down.

'*Would* you be able to be so obliging as to carry a message of my safety to them?'

'To be perfectly honest,' the cat said, 'I don't think it is possible. Your friends are meat-eaters, or some of them are. They don't know me, and they're very hungry. Don't you think I would be exposing myself to more than a reasonable risk of attack by a fox or an owl?'

'I'm sure you would be too large a morsel for an owl,' Badger said reassuringly. 'As for Fox and Vixen they, like Tawny Owl, are mostly inactive in the daytime. You would be quite safe then, even if they might pose a threat after dark, which I personally don't believe. You are a reasonably large animal yourself, and sure to be beyond their scope. In any case, you showed no fear of *me* from the outset.'

'But I knew you were sick,' the cat pointed out, 'otherwise you wouldn't have been here. And, even if I am safe in daytime, I don't know the terrain. The Park is enormous, and completely covered by snow. I'd sink up to my neck at the first step.'

'No, you're too light-footed for that. You've been outside the cottage, anyway, in the snow.'

'Yes, but most of it has been cleared by the man where *we* want to walk. If I went into the depths of the Park where would I shelter? It would be a long trek to where your friends live, and then to come back again.'

'You could shelter in my set and be quite warm and safe,' Badger offered unrealistically. 'Any of them would show you where it is.'

'Impossible,' the cat declared roundly. 'I couldn't go

underground. No, I'm sorry, my friend, because I would like to help. But I really don't see that I can.'

Badger resorted to a final means of persuasion. Affecting a slightly malicious tone he said, 'So I was right. You couldn't survive alone, without human assistance.'

The cat looked at him angrily for a second. 'You seem to forget I wasn't born in the wild like you and your friends,' he snapped. 'I haven't the long experience of the lore of survival you have acquired from birth. You tell me you wild creatures are literally battling for life in what are, after all, exceptionally bad conditions. How well do you think I will manage, without the knowledge you are armed with?'

Badger felt this was an honest enough answer and that it would not be seemly to pursue the argument. But his friends *must* be informed. 'Then there's no alternative,' he told the cat quietly. 'I accept what you say as reasonable, and so it means I shall have to go myself.'

'Don't be so ridiculous!' cried the cat impatiently. 'I can understand you are fond of your friends, but you are taking unselfishness too far. They will just have to get along without you for a bit. You *can't* walk now, but it shouldn't be too long before you are able to return to them – perhaps a couple of weeks. I don't know how serious the damage is. Who knows? Perhaps the worst of the winter will be over by then.'

Badger shook his head. 'I couldn't possibly leave them in ignorance for a matter of weeks,' he persisted doggedly. 'You don't seem to understand. That oath we swore back in Farthing Wood – it hasn't lapsed. My friends won't just accept that I've vanished away. They will be risking their necks to find me.'

'Humph!' the cat snorted irritably. 'You seem to have a very high opinion of yourself.'

'Don't be absurd,' retorted Badger. 'Oh, you can say

what you like, but I've got to get word to them. If you won't go I mean what I say. I shall go myself even if it means crawling all the way.'

The cat realized he was in a corner. He could not possibly allow the crippled Badger to throw his life away, for that was what it would mean. So he had to relent.

'Very well, you've convinced me,' he said with reluctance. 'I'll start tomorrow if it isn't snowing. You'd better describe your friends to me in detail, so that I can recognize them.'

'I shall never forget this, Ginger Cat,' Badger said warmly. 'And, believe me, neither will the other animals. You've just made yourself a host of new friends.'

'Well, Badger' – the cat smiled – 'you're a very persuasive fellow.'

'You are now party to the Oath that binds all the creatures of Farthing Wood, Vixen and Whistler,' Badger reminded him. 'That means, if ever you yourself are in danger or difficulties – well, I think you understand me?'

'We understand each other,' said Ginger Cat.

——7——
A Meeting

No snow was falling in the morning and two very different animals, who were destined to meet that very day, were preparing to set out from opposite ends of the Park on behalf of Badger.

From the Warden's cottage Ginger Cat, having bade farewell to his new friend, was emerging. He jumped over the fence and looked with foreboding at the great white expanse before him over which he would have to travel. His first faltering steps found the snow surface reasonably firm, and his courage rose slightly. But he knew it was a long way in difficult conditions to Badger's companions.

Meanwhile in Badger's own set, Mole had determined to begin his search. He had formed the idea that Badger

had somehow got lost or injured underground as he was
not to be seen anywhere on the surface. So he had
decided that, as he, Mole, was quite the kingpin among
subterranean travellers, it should be he who must search
this new area. He began by investigating all of Badger's
tunnels in case he had had an accident while digging
close to home. Of course he found no sign of any mishap.
His next task was to surface and look for any other holes
in the neighbourhood where Badger might have entered.
This labour of love was as doomed to failure as it was
devoted. But Mole kept trying, his stout little heart
allowing him to emerge undismayed at every fresh disappointment. Each time he plunged down into the bar-
ren, frozen ground he thought that perhaps this time he
was going to rescue his poor friend, and it was this idea
which made his persevere.

Ginger Cat continued on his way, his silent footsteps
taking him slowly, but steadily, towards his goal. He
was beginning to feel very chilled and longed for the
bright fireside of the cottage, where he basked content
in the company of his human companion. As the morning wore on he got colder and colder and regretted his
foolhardy mission. After all, what was an injured badger
to him? For all the fine words about this wonderful Oath
of theirs, he was an outsider, an individual. He was no
member of a party. Why should he concern himself with
whether Fox or Mole or Weasel or any of the rest of
Badger's precious friends should lose their lives looking
for him? They were all total strangers to Ginger Cat.
Whatever he might have boasted to Badger, he was not
a wild creature like they were, having to make shift
through the seasons as best they could, come sun, wind,
rain, snow and ice. He had an alternative – the alternative of keeping warm and comfortable all day if he felt
like it; of sleeping by a blazing fire with a full stomach,

ignorant of the raging elements of Nature. It had been his pride alone that had sent him on this absurd journey. Oh, how cold he felt!

All the time the cat was cursing his own misfortune, he was nearing Badger's home area. He passed by the Hollow without knowing its significance and then, suddenly, his senses were alert again as at last he saw movement ahead. He increased his speed and found a small black animal with a long snout crawling out of a hole. It was, of course, Mole.

Mole saw a large unknown animal approaching him and instantly ducked back underground.

'Don't go!' called Ginger Cat down the hole. 'You may be who I'm looking for. I have news of Badger.'

Mole reappeared at once. 'Badger? Where is he? Is he all right? Who are you?'

'He was injured,' Ginger Cat said. 'He's been rescued by the human you call the Naturalist, who is caring for him. Don't worry, he will soon be well.'

Mole did a little jig. 'Thank heaven he's still alive,' he said joyfully. 'But tell me who you are?'

Ginger Cat explained. Then, 'You must be Mole?' he enquired. 'Badger told me you lived underground.'

Mole confessed. 'We've all been so worried,' he said. 'No sign of him for three days. But you are our good friend. You've been very brave.'

'Badger told me about your long journey here from your old home,' said Ginger Cat.

'Will you come and meet the others?' Mole said enthusiastically. 'They'll be so grateful for your news.'

'No, I'm afraid I must decline. I want to be back before it gets dark, and it's a long way.'

'Of course. Tell me, when does Badger think he can come back to us?'

'Oh, Badger would come now if he could,' Ginger Cat

said with a smile. 'But he would be very wise, in my opinion, if he waits for the man to decide. Then he will be sure to be fully well again.'

Mole noticed this tribute to humankind, and realized the cat stood in a different relationship. 'Tell him we are all well,' Mole said. 'At least, tell him we are managing, and that we are missing him terribly.'

'I will, certainly. I hope I may see you again some time,' said Ginger Cat politely.

'Thank you again from all of Farthing Wood,' Mole answered importantly. 'There will always be a greeting for you here.'

Ginger Cat turned to make his way back. Mole watched him go. As the representative of the Farthing Wood community, he wondered if he had handled the meeting correctly. With a start, he remembered he had not offered the cat any refreshment. The animal had made a long journey, and now had the same distance to retrace. There were an abundance of worms in his larder. He called out.

The cat heard the noise and looked round. He could not make out Mole's words for he was a small creature and did not have a strong voice. Mole called again, but Ginger Cat still failed to understand and started to run back.

At that moment Kestrel, who had been patrolling the Park all day from the air for signs of Badger, spotted the two animals on the ground. He saw a large cat running towards his friend Mole, and naturally assumed it was an attack. Wheeling quickly, he dived earthwards and struck Ginger Cat like an arrow, his talons digging deep into the creature's flesh.

The cat howled and lashed out at the bird, but Kestrel was already ascending again for another plunge.

'Stop, Kestrel, stop!' called Mole frantically. 'He's a

friend!' But the hawk was too high to hear and was preparing to launch another strike. 'Quickly, into the hole,' Mole said desperately as the cat was instinctively flattening its body against the ground. Ginger Cat heard, but it was too late to move. Down swooped Kestrel again and Mole hurled himself against the ginger body, so that the hawk hesitated and lost the impetus of the descent. This time he heard Mole's pleas, 'No, no! Keep away, Kestrel! He's a friend – a friend!'

Kestrel landed and looked at Mole questioningly with his piercing eyes. Ginger Cat arched his wounded back and hissed aggressively.

'He came with news of Badger,' Mole explained lamely. 'All the way from the Naturalist's house. He wasn't pouncing on me.' He described the news the cat had brought.

Kestrel apologised inadequately for his actions, and told Mole what he had surmised from the air. He and Mole looked at Ginger Cat's back. The blood was flowing freely from the two large lacerations, dyeing the ginger fur and making it sticky.

'You and your confounded Oath,' muttered Ginger Cat weakly.

'We can't stay here,' said Mole. 'Kestrel, will you fetch Fox? I don't know what to do.'

Fox was not long in arriving on the scene, accompanied by Vixen. Without much difficulty, they persuaded Ginger Cat to go to shelter in their earth. He was too feeble now to argue. As they made their way along, Mole acquainted Fox with Badger's plight and of the cat's journey to see them.

'What a reward for such a good deed,' said Fox bitterly.

'I acted with the best intentions,' Kestrel hastened to

assure them. 'I thought only of Mole. How could I have known?'

'No-one's blaming you,' Fox replied. 'It's just a very unfortunate incident.'

Once inside the earth, Vixen took it upon herself to lick the wounds on the cat's back and to clean his fur. 'They are nasty cuts,' she observed, 'but they aren't bleeding any more. I hope you will share our meal later? When it is dark Fox and I will go out to see what we can find.'

Ginger Cat expressed his thanks and, himself convinced that his feebleness was more due to excessive tiredness than his wounds, fell gratefully asleep.

Mole stayed with him when the foxes went off on their foray and, before they returned, Ginger Cat awoke with a start in even pitcher blackness than before. 'It's all right,' said Mole. 'You're not alone.' The cat was amused at his tiny companion's effort at reassurance. He could have killed Mole with one paw, but of course had no desire to do so.

'You needn't stay, Mole,' he said smoothly. 'I'm a lot better for that nap. I'll be quite happy to wait on my own for my promised supper.'

'Just as you like,' said Mole readily. 'I'm as hungry as can be myself. I think I'll pay a visit to my own food store.' They exchanged farewells and Mole departed.

As soon as Ginger Cat was sure Mole had got right away, he himself stood up, stretched carefully, and shook his coat daintily. Despite himself, he winced at the pain that throbbed in his back. But he was ready to leave. He had no intention of waiting for Fox and Vixen to return. He would go hungry, but at least before morning he would be back in the warmth and cosiness of the cottage.

He emerged into the starlight, shivering in the bitter

cold, but was thankful to see no further snow had fallen. So his mission had been accomplished and he was gratified to have met Mole, Fox and Vixen. But he cherished a hope for revenge on the other of Badger's friends he had encountered. Was he, a cat, to allow himself to be bested by a bird – his natural prey? Hawk or no hawk, should the opportunity ever arise Kestrel would find he had made an error of judgement if he believed he could inflict any harm on an equally cunning hunter without redress.

—8—
Recovery

It was almost dawn when Ginger Cat limped back through his special flap into the Warden's lodge. Never before in his life had he felt so weary. He knew Badger would be agog for his news, but he was too tired to face his questions. So he lay down on the hall carpet where he was and dropped into an immediate sleep.

It was the noise of the Warden's rising that woke him. He stood up stiffly to greet the man's arrival. The Warden, of course, was overjoyed to see him but very concerned to find the wounds inflicted by Kestrel. These were attended to in no time and a large saucer of warm milk proffered while a well-deserved meal was prepared.

Badger could barely restrain his impatience for the man to leave the kitchen, but as soon as he did he started eagerly to demand to know all that had happened.

'I met your friends Mole and Fox and Vixen,' said Ginger Cat. 'They were relieved to hear of your safety. I also met Kestrel who is responsible for this,' he added in a hard voice, indicating his newly-bandaged back, and he went on to describe the incident.

'Oh dear, I really am so sorry,' Badger was most contrite. 'I can see exactly how it happened. He won't be able to forgive himself for injuring you.'

'Really?' hissed the cat sarcastically. 'I think he recovered his presence of mind fairly swiftly. It may be news to you that there is no love lost between cats and birds.'

'But I hope you won't hold this mistake against Kestrel,' Badger said worriedly.

Ginger Cat did not reply. Badger looked hard at him, but his bland expression was totally inscrutable.

'I will tell you one thing,' said the cat. 'You have lost your battle to persuade me to live wild. At the risk of appearing soft – and I don't care a jot – I would never leave this comfortable life to join you out there. I have had my taste now. I've experienced the worst weather I've known. I've been into one of your underground homes and pronounce it to be the most cheerless place I've ever seen or, rather, felt. I've seen the reality of what lack of food and poor shelter can do to an animal, and for that I had to look no further than the skinny, underfed bodies of your fox friends. But I'm going to turn the tables on you now. I say to you, Badger, that if you give up your cosy new home here to return to those appalling conditions amongst your friends you are absolutely mad.'

'But this isn't a home,' Badger pointed out. 'I'm merely being tended while I'm hurt. Once I'm on my feet again, whether I wish it or not, I shall be removed to the Park.'

Ginger Cat shrugged. 'You've seen how I behave and remarked on it,' he said. 'I'm quite sure a little feigned affection from you for your human benefactor would be very well received. That seems to be the only reward he expects for doing almost everything for us.'

'No, no,' Badger shook his head, smiling. 'I haven't the necessary technique. It's inbred in you cats to make yourself ingratiating. It's natural to you.'

'Well, I'm sure it wasn't always so,' Ginger Cat responded. 'It must have begun for a definite purpose. Why don't you decide to become the first domesticated badger?'

'No, it wouldn't be appropriate,' Badger replied. 'I'm too old to change my ways now. And, besides, I'm used to living underground, and tunnelling, and sleeping on beds of leaves and grass and moss and so on – not curled up in a basket like a lap dog.'

'Well, at least stay until the warmer weather,' Ginger Cat wheedled. He had become genuinely fond of Badger and was sincere in wishing him to be comfortable.

'Well, well,' nodded Badger, 'we'll see. But I hope you won't forget all about me if I do go. For my part, I can never repay your kindness in making that journey. And then you come back hurt! It's most distressing.'

'You may rest assured I should keep in touch,' declared Ginger Cat. 'But, tell me, is your home any better appointed than Fox's?'

'Oh yes,' Badger laughed. 'He and Vixen live very simply. But you went underground! I'm most impressed.' He chuckled as he thought of it.

Ginger Cat almost laughed. 'It's a topsy-turvy world,' he said. 'We'll have you curled up in front of the ·fire next.'

The days passed and Badger's leg grew stronger. He was able to limp a little way around the kitchen to begin with, and then the cat introduced him to the main room of the cottage and he practised walking backwards and forwards from one room to the other. After about a fortnight in the Warden's home Badger had become quite accustomed to his new life. Well-fed and well cared for, he looked sleeker and fitter than at any time since leaving Farthing Wood. He looked a new animal, and he began to dread the appearance of his longsuffering friends when he should return to them. He knew they would look haggard by comparison, and he felt they might look at him accusingly, envying his new-found health.

But he had to acknowledge that that was not all he was dubious about. There had been an element of truth in Ginger Cat's words. Perhaps he *had* grown too used to comfort now. He certainly did not relish the prospect of scraping a living again in the freezing desolation of the Park. He was worse equipped to do so now than before his accident. To adjust now to searching once more for his food, to learn again to live on less than he needed to eat and to adapt to those wicked temperatures from which there was no relief, was indeed a daunting thought.

He felt sure that the Warden would not simply turf him out into the cold once he was walking normally again, if there were still no sign of improvement in the weather. The change would be too sudden. So the temptation to stay on where he was, was constantly with him. Yet he knew he would feel guilty if he did stay unnecessarily long. How could he rest content in such luxury while all the time his old companions continued to suffer the worst sort of discomfort? But what if they were to join *him*? Was it possible?

Day after day the same thoughts went through his mind until the time finally arrived when he knew that his injured leg was completely well again. The strapping and bandages had been removed a week before, at the same time as those on Ginger Cat's back. Now he could shuffle around quite normally once more at his old pace. Now he must decide what he should do.

When he next saw Ginger Cat he told him he was completely recovered. The cat looked at him long and straight. 'Well?' he asked at length. 'What are your plans?'

Badger mentioned his idea of his friends joining them under the care of the Warden. 'Would the man take them in? Would he be able to, would he want to?' he kept asking.

'I don't know,' replied Ginger Cat. 'I don't know if he would have room for all. I *am* sure he would do his best for the animals who seemed most in need of help. But will they wish to come here?'

'Now it's my turn to say I don't know,' Badger confessed. 'But I could try persuading them.'

'You would have to exclude the birds,' Ginger Cat said pointedly.

Badger knew what was in his mind. 'I had already ruled them out,' he agreed.

'When will you leave?' the cat asked next.

'As soon as the man lets me go.'

'That will be when you make it apparent you are eager to return to the Park. You'd better make it obvious you want to follow him when he next goes outside.'

The opportunity eventually arose and, the Warden showing willingness, Badger stood once more on the borders of the Park, sniffing the air in all directions. The snow still lay packed on the ground, and the icy temperature cut at his pampered body like a knife. He half turned back, looking towards the open cottage door that symbolized the way through to comfort. Ginger Cat was sitting on the threshold. He stood up. 'I'll come with you part of the way,' he offered.

'Gladly,' replied Badger.

The Warden watched the two animals that had become fast friends walk slowly off. His job was done.

They skirted the Edible Frogs' pond and Badger remembered Toad and Adder were sleeping nearby, deep down in a bankside away from the weather. All they would know of the winter would be from the stories they would hear from their friends.

'I wonder how *they've* been?' Badger muttered to himself. Fox and Vixen, Mole, Weasel, Tawny Owl . . . his friends seemed as strangers. He had become more familiar of late with a human's pet than with his companions of old.

A little way further on Ginger Cat stopped. 'I'll turn back now,' he said. 'Go carefully. And my best wishes to Mole and the foxes.'

'Farewell,' said Badger. 'Your company has been delightful. I know we shall meet again.'

'Until then,' responded the cat.

Badger watched his sinewy form retrace its steps through the snow. The sky was leaden above the Park; the air still and threatening. A snowstorm was imminent. He must reach his set as quickly as possible. There would be plenty of time to see his friends tomorrow.

—9—
Old Friends, New Friends

The reticence Badger was feeling for re-adopting his old life and friends he himself would never had admitted – even if he had been conscious of it. But those same old friends noticed the change in him at once from *their* unchanged world. Mole, who had been haunting Badger's set regularly ever since the animals had heard of his whereabouts, entered the set through his connecting tunnel. At first he thought a strange badger had commandeered the place, his old friend looked – and smelt – so different.

'Oh! hallo, Mole,' Badger greeted him unenthusiastically, as his little friend stood hesitantly. 'Yes, it *is* me.'

'I've been keeping a look-out for your return for days,' Mole said. 'We've missed you so much. But it *was* kind of the Warden's cat to come all this way to put our minds at rest. I'm only sorry about the accident that occurred.'

'He certainly deserved a better reception,' Badger remarked rather coldly, to Mole's consternation. 'He only made the journey at all because I forced him into it, really. However, he asked to be remembered to you.'

'Thank you,' said Mole in a small voice. He did not like this new, gruff individual.

There was a silence for some moments. Badger did not seem at all disposed to carry on a conversation, and Mole was becoming timid.

'You – you look d-different,' he stammered. 'Sort of fatter.'

'I probably am,' Badger agreed shortly. 'I was fed well.'

'I'm g-glad,' Mole whispered. 'I'll go and tell Fox you're here,' he added, and moved away in a confused way.

'Don't bother yourself,' said Badger. 'I suppose I ought to go. Er – I'll see you later, Mole.'

The crestfallen Mole watched his friend disappear up the exit tunnel without so much as a backward glance.

Outside it was dark and a fresh fall of snow had covered the Park. Badger's face became grim and he gritted his teeth. The contrast between the stark world of the wild and the comfort of human habitation was heightened still further in his mind. On his way to Fox's earth he was spied by Tawny Owl, who skimmed down from an oak branch.

'Welcome back, old friend,' the bird said, eyeing Badger openly. 'You seem to have prospered during your spell under the Warden's roof. You've got plump – and soft.'

Badger shrugged. 'It was a welcome relief from staring starvation in the face,' he said.

'I can see that,' Tawny Owl responded sarcastically. 'It must make it all the more difficult to adjust back again.'

'Why do I have to?' Badger asked bluntly.

Tawny Owl feigned ignorance. 'What *do* you mean, Badger?'

'Come along with me to see Fox,' Badger told him, 'and I'll put you both in the picture.'

'Hm,' Tawny Owl muttered. 'This should prove to be a most interesting meeting.'

Fox's earth was deserted when they arrived, and Badger said he would wait for Fox and Vixen's return. So he made himself as comfortable as he could underground while Tawny Owl perched in a nearby holly tree. He found his thoughts straying back to that warm kitchen in the Lodge. He imagined his friend Ginger Cat curled up in his basket, secure in the knowledge that he could depend on being fed without even stirring out of doors, and quite oblivious of the icy clutch of Winter that still held imprisoned every inhabitant of the Park.

Yes, the ways of the Wild could be dreadfully hard, and the arrival of Fox and Vixen at that juncture gave an emphasis to Badger's conclusion. Their emaciated frames, rimed with frost from the freezing air, slunk into the den and slumped, exhausted, on the hard ground. Badger, shocked beyond his expectation, was speechless. Presently the pair of foxes revived sufficiently to greet him. Of the two, Fox seemed thinnest and the most spent, which suggested that the best of the pickings of their nightly forays were going to Vixen. That would be Fox's way, Badger knew.

But Fox had lost none of his shrewdness. There was a look in his eyes that seemed to penetrate to Badger's

most secret thoughts. His words, too, went straight to
the heart of the matter. 'Well, are you back with us now
for good?' he asked.

The question made Badger feel ashamed – ashamed
of his well-fed appearance, his spotless coat. He felt as
if he had betrayed Fox in a way, even if only in his
thoughts. He did not know how to answer.

'The other way of life seems to agree with you,' Fox
continued in a parallel of Tawny Owl's remark.

'Well, Fox, you know, I *was* injured,' Badger said
defensively, almost apologetically.

'Of course you were,' Fox said. 'I'm sorry. How is
your leg? Are you fully recovered?'

'Absolutely, thank you,' Badger replied a little more
brightly. 'But, my dear Fox – and Vixen – you look as
if you are suffering dreadfully.'

'Things are very, very hard,' Fox admitted, shaking
his head slowly from side to side. 'Each day is harder.
Only two of the voles are still alive, and scarcely more
of the fieldmice. Rabbit and his friends have lost four of
their number, too. And the squirrels find it almost impossible to dig through this never-ending snow to reach
their buried nuts and berries so, they too, are dwindling.
I really don't know what's to become of us all. We shall
all die, Badger, if this weather doesn't lift soon, I'm sure
of it.'

Badger felt that now was the time to play his trump
card. 'There *is* an answer,' he said quietly.

'Well, let's have it. We're at our wits' end.'

'You don't *have* to live in the Park,' Badger explained.
'Come back with me to the Warden's cottage.'

Fox and Vixen looked at him in amazement.

'You can't mean it, Badger?' Vixen spoke for the first
time.

'Of course I mean it,' Badger insisted. 'Why are you looking at me in that way? I was looked after, fed properly, and restored to health – and now I'm fitter than I've been for ages.'

'But you were injured and found by the Warden,' Fox repeated to himself uncomprehendingly. 'The welfare of the creatures of the Park is his concern so, naturally, he nursed you until you were better.'

'Exactly!' cried Badger. 'You've said it yourself. So isn't *your* welfare, and the rabbits' welfare, and the voles' welfare, and everyone else's welfare also of interest to him?'

At this point Tawny Owl poked his head down the hole. He felt he was missing an interesting discussion and wanted to hear. Fox's voice was audible next.

'Are you suggesting, then,' he was saying in an incredulous tone, 'that all of us band together and follow you to the Warden's Lodge?'

'Yes, I am.'

'And then what would we do? All rush inside the next time he appears at the door?'

'I don't know exactly what plan we could make,' Badger allowed. 'But we could work something out. Ginger Cat might help us think of something. Don't you see, Fox, your worries about food would be over? You would have no need even to think about it. It would be provided for you automatically.'

Tawny Owl stepped into the den. He could not resist participating any longer. 'I think our friend Badger has spent a little too much time amongst domestic creatures like cats,' he said drily. 'He's beginning to talk like one of them.'

'I can't believe it's our Badger talking,' Vixen said. 'Whatever has happened to him?'

'Oh, why can't you understand?' Badger wailed. 'I'm thinking of your good. Look at you – you're half-starved. A few more weeks and there may not be any trace left of the animals of Farthing Wood. Is that what you want?'

'Badger, your wits have become softened by your dependence on human aid,' Tawny Owl told him. 'I believe you've forgotten how to think for yourself. How could all the creatures from Farthing Wood be accommodated in your precious Warden's house? Squirrels, rabbits, hares, foxes . . . he isn't running a zoo.'

'He would find a way, I'm sure,' Badger replied vaguely. 'He would *have* to, once he sees the pitiful state of you all. It's his job, isn't it?'

'You're not making sense, Badger. You seem to have forgotten all the *original* inhabitants of White Deer Park,' Fox reminded him. 'We're just a small part of the fauna here. What if they all decided to come too?'

'The whole idea is the most absurd thing I've ever heard,' Tawny Owl said bluntly. 'I'm sorry you were injured, Badger, but I'm more sorry you were ever taken into captivity. It seems to have turned your brain.'

'I didn't say anything about *you* coming,' Badger snapped irritably. 'You and Kestrel wouldn't be welcome. Ginger Cat will vouch for that.'

Fox and Tawny Owl exchanged glances. It really did seem as if Badger had undergone a change of character. Vixen tried to smooth things over. 'You'll feel differently when you've got used to your old life again, Badger,' she said soothingly. 'I can see you're finding it difficult to pick up the threads again, and that's understandable. We'll win through yet, if we all pull together. Think what you Farthing Wood animals have survived before. If any creatures can see it through, you can.'

Badger was furious at the rejection of his idea. He rounded on his old friends angrily. 'You don't understand,' he fumed. 'I don't want my old life anymore. I didn't have to come back, but I did – for you. If you won't join me, I'll go back alone.'

'Back to your new friend the cat, no doubt,' Tawny Owl said. 'He's really got to work on you, hasn't he?'

'The Warden is my friend, too,' Badger barked.

'Well, it's quite obviously a clear case of preference,' Tawny Owl told him. 'You must go where your inclinations direct you.'

'Sssh, Owl,' Fox warned him. 'This is getting out of hand.' He turned to Badger. 'My dear friend, you can't mean what you say. We've been inseparable. You can't turn your back on us now?'

'*You* turned your back on *me*,' Badger insisted with a glare. 'My suggestion was made in good faith. I can't force you to come. It's your choice. As far as I'm concerned, *I* have no intention of starving to death. If you all want to die together, I must leave you to it.' With that he turned and left the earth.

His three prior companions were stunned. None of them ventured a word. Fox went to the exit and peered out at the retreating figure. He wanted to call out, to bring him back, but he could think of nothing more to say. A cold shiver ran along his body. It had begun to snow again.

—— 10 ——

A Question of Loyalties

In the morning Mole arrived at the foxes' earth in a
very piteous state. He had remained in the set where
Badger had left him, hoping to see him again. But after
the talk with Fox, Vixen and Tawny Owl, Badger had
returned to his set in an unpleasant mood and had been
very unkind to Mole.

'He told me I was a confounded nuisance and a sni-
veller, and that I must leave him in peace or suffer the
consequences,' he sobbed to Fox.

Vixen intervened. 'You must accept that Badger's
simply not himself at the moment, Mole,' she counselled.
'None of us understands exactly what's happened. But
if he's still our Badger, sooner or later his real feelings
will show through. I know they will.'

'Oh, do you think so, Vixen?' Mole wept. 'Oh, I hope so, I hope so . . . . '

'Has Badger gone back?' Fox asked Mole.

'Gone back where?' queried Mole who, of course, was unaware of the scene of the previous night.

Fox was obliged to explain. 'He wants to go back to the Warden. He can't face his old life any more.' He described the meeting with Badger in his earth.

'What ever can we do?' Mole shrilled. 'We can't just let him go.'

'Perhaps it's the best thing for us to do, at present,' Vixen said. 'Then he can get this new way of life out of his system. If I know Badger, very soon he will begin to feel very guilty indeed, and then he'll come to his senses.'

'I think we should inform everyone of this business,' said Fox, 'and the best way to do it is for us all to meet – everyone – in Badger's empty set. I'll get Tawny Owl and Kestrel to round all the animals up. It's too cold to meet in the Hollow.'

'When do we meet?' Mole wanted to know.

'This very day,' said Fox. 'You go to the set now, Mole. I'll contact Kestrel. Vixen, will you speak to Owl? There must be no delay.'

While preparations were being made, Badger was well on his way across the Park to his destination. Already a slight sense of shame hung over him as he turned his back on the Farthing Wood animals' home area. But he also felt resentment of his treatment by Fox and Tawny Owl, and looked forward to Ginger Cat's commiserations.

He had not bothered to hunt for any food, because he knew the Warden could be relied on to look after his stomach. He saw Kestrel flying over the Park and hoped he would not notice him. In the case of Kestrel this was a vain hope, for the hawk did not miss much that moved on the ground. Badger watched him swoop down.

'Well, what do you want?' Badger grunted ungraciously. 'I suppose you've come to insult me as well?'

'Not at all, not at all,' Kestrel declared indignantly. 'Fox has sent me to round up all our friends. I'm still looking for Weasel.'

'What for? A meeting?' Badger asked uninterestedly.

'Yes. No need to guess what it's about.'

'Me, I suppose? Well, I'm not surprised. But listen, Kestrel, tell Fox from me not to interfere. I can live where I choose. You must know as well as I do *they'll* all be dead inside a month the way things are going.'

'Not if I can help it,' Kestrel replied quickly. 'I hunt outside the Park every day and bring back what I can for them. And I know Whistler does too. Of course, at night Tawny Owl does what he can. *We* haven't forgotten the Oath.'

Badger looked away, a little shamefaced, at this pointed rejoinder. But he would not turn back. 'I wish you all well,' he said, 'but when the solution to your problems was offered it was refused. *I* can't be blamed.'

Kestrel directed one of his piercing glares at Badger and flew away resignedly. But later that day, he and Badger were due to meet again in very different circumstances.

Ginger Cat was sitting by the Warden's fence, blinking dozily in a few brief moments of sunlight that had managed to penetrate the clouds. Badger called him as he saw him. He expected the cat to come towards him, but he did not move. He called again. 'Hallo – it's me – Badger!'

Ginger Cat looked at him enigmatically. 'So I see,' he said coolly.

Badger stopped in his tracks, completely taken aback by this most unexpected lack of enthusiasm. 'Whatever's the matter?' he asked. 'I thought you would be pleased to see me.'

'I'm surprised to see you again at all so soon,' murmured Ginger Cat, yawning widely.

'But I've come back,' Badger explained. 'You know – for good.'

The cat looked at him long and steadily. 'What do you mean – for good?'

'I've made my decision, and I'm going to live with you.'

'What *are* you talking about? You live underground, you told me.'

'No, no, not any more. I'm finished with all that. I don't want that sort of existence. I've left my old friends because they wouldn't come with me.'

'Of course they wouldn't,' Ginger Cat said. 'I never expected them to. I thought all those pie-in-the-sky ideas of yours would be forgotten once you'd got back to your real home.'

These last words really jarred on Badger's sensibility. 'But I have a new home now . . . or I thought I had,' he faltered. 'Don't you remember, we talked about the Warden looking after Fox and Mole and everyone?'

'Indeed I do,' the cat answered. 'But I would have been astonished in the extreme if your wild friends chose of their own accord to leave their homes. Would *you* have come here if you hadn't been brought?'

'Er – no, I suppose not,' Badger admitted. 'But that doesn't matter. *I've* chosen this way of life.'

'How convenient for you,' Ginger Cat observed bitingly.

'*Aren't* you pleased to see me?' the bewildered Badger cried. 'I thought we were friends.'

'Oh yes,' the cat shrugged. 'But we were forced into each other's company, after all. One makes the most of a situation.'

'Well – er – aren't you going to invite me in?' Badger asked hesitantly.

'You're too bulky to go through my cat flap,' Ginger Cat pointed out. 'You'll have to wait for the man to find you. But I don't think you'll get the reaction you want from him. He looked after you until you were well again and, in his view, you should now be living in your natural state.'

'We'll see about that,' Badger answered hotly, but he was beginning to feel he had made a fool of himself. He went and sat by the front door and, as luck would have it, the Warden appeared soon after. A cry of amazement escaped him as he saw his old charge looking hopefully up at him. He bent down, examined the healed leg, patted Badger, and looked at him in a puzzled way for a moment. Then he seemed to think of something and turned back inside. Badger immediately tried to follow him, but the Warden kindly, but firmly, pushed him back and shut the door. Badger was heart-broken.

'You see,' Ginger Cat's soft voice purred at him. 'He doesn't want you any more. Oh, he'll probably bring you a bowl of food in a minute or two. He imagines you've come for that. But your home is not his cottage any more.'

The realization of his stupidity flashed into Badger's mind in a blinding flood of light. What a miscalculation he had made! *He* was not a domestic animal. How could he have thought he understood human ways? Both the cat and the human were on another plane of existence, in a world he could never comprehend. He had humiliated himself, and in the process he had lost the respect of the cat and, what was worse – far worse! – spurned his real friends.

The bowl of food predicted by Ginger Cat was brought out, and a dish of warm milk with it. More to save the Warden a disappointment than because of any feeling of appetite, Badger ate and drank. Then, with a wry look at the cat, he turned back without a further word – back to his waiting set.

A short distance from the cottage he looked behind him. The Warden was not to be seen, but Ginger Cat was still sitting, watching his retreat. Badger heard a flutter of wings above and Kestrel alighted beside him.

'Keep going, Badger,' he told him. 'You're going in the right direction this time.'

Badger knew the hawk had guessed what had happened and smiled sadly at him. 'Yes, Kestrel,' he whispered, 'I have indeed been a foolish creature.'

Behind them, unknown to them, Ginger Cat had spotted his enemy. Now, belly flat to the icy ground, he was creeping stealthily forward on his noiseless feet. With a tremendous spurt, he leapt on the unsuspecting hawk, teeth and claws as sharp as razors finding their mark. But Kestrel was no sparrow or blackbird. He was a hunter, a killer himself, and his powerful wings flailed, beating against his assailant, while his lethal beak darted in all directions in an attempt to strike.

Badger looked round in horror. The bird, taken unawares, was struggling desperately against the attack. Badger was hopelessly torn between his affection for the cat, albeit recently somewhat battered, and his loyalty to an old friend. He could see Kestrel's struggles weakening and, in a trice, it was as if a veil had been lifted from his eyes. The Oath!

Badger rushed into the fray. Bringing all his considerable weight and power into the attack he fell on Ginger Cat, lunging with bared teeth at his throat. The cat let out a scream and spat at him in fury. But the grip was loosened and Kestrel was able to free himself, flying up into the air instantly.

Now the fight was left to the two animals, and soon Badger's superior strength began to tell. He knew the cat was at his mercy and that one snap of his jaws could kill him. His instinct told him to do it, but he held back. Although he had made the cat party to the Oath, the animal had forfeited his right to protection by attacking another of its adherents. But Badger recalled the good turn Ginger Cat had done him and now he must repay it. He stepped away, his sides heaving, and, like an arrow, the cat sped away, back to safety.

The significance of Badger's rescue was not lost on Kestrel. 'Welcome back to the fold,' he screeched from the air.

'It's quite safe for you now,' Badger called back. 'Come down and let me see if you're injured.'

Kestrel did so and Badger noticed the marks of the cat's claws. He began to lick at his friend's body.

'Most obliged,' said the hawk. 'Thanks for your help. For just a moment I wondered if you were going to.'

'I know,' said Badger. 'Oh, what a supreme idiot I've been. I've entered unknown waters and found myself out of my depth. It's so absurd. I'd rather die *with* you all than live without you.'

'We *won't* die,' Kestrel insisted. 'It's going to be tough, but we are tough creatures.'

'They're not deep scratches,' Badger was saying. 'They'll soon heal.'

'Er – Badger – why did you let the cat go?'

Badger explained.

'I thought as much. That means I still have him after my blood.'

'Just stay in the air in this vicinity,' Badger told him. 'But the cat will know why I didn't kill him and that my debt is repaid. He has a fair nature. I don't think he will be out for revenge any more.'

'I hope you're right,' said Kestrel. 'Well, if you hurry, you will surprise the rest of them holding forth about you in your set.'

'I'll see you there,' Badger replied.

— 11 —

An Expedition

The meeting of the animals of Farthing Wood to discuss
Badger's strange behaviour and what should be done
about it had not long begun when Kestrel arrived. He
saw Whistler standing at the entrance to the set.

'Are you on guard?' he asked the heron.

'No. My legs are too long for me to go in there.' He
pointed with his long bill to the entrance tunnel.

'In that case,' said Kestrel, 'you'll be the first to know
that Badger is himself again.' He went on to describe
his rescue from Ginger Cat.

'That *will* delight everyone,' Whistler said. 'You go in
and tell them before Tawny Owl runs him down too
much.' He winked elaborately.

Kestrel walked into the set. As he joined the meeting,

it was evident that Tawny Owl was replying to a suggestion from someone that they should bring Badger back by force.

'What for?' he hooted. 'Leave him to his own devices. He turned his back on us. Why should we bother any longer?'

'You're beginning to talk just like Adder,' said Mole. 'It would be wrong of us to desert him.'

'That's just what he's done to us,' snorted Owl.

'Two wrongs don't make a right,' Mole replied, rather weakly.

'You can all save your breath,' Kestrel informed them. 'Badger's on his way back.'

They looked at him dumbfounded. Then he explained again about Badger's change of heart and his rescue.

'You see, Mole,' Vixen said kindly, 'I knew his real character would win through.'

'Oh, *I* never lost faith in him,' Mole declared proudly, while Tawny Owl looked rather abashed. 'Dear Badger! So he came to help you, Kestrel?'

'He saved my life,' Kestrel said honestly. 'No question about it.'

'I'm very happy,' said Fox. 'I feel that this heralds an improvement in our affairs. Well, Kestrel, should we stay for him?'

'Oh yes!' answered Kestrel emphatically. 'Now we're all together. He's depending on seeing us.'

'So be it,' said Fox and the animals settled down to wait patiently.

Late in the afternoon Badger greeted Whistler outside his home. He paused at the set entrance nervously, unsure of his other friends' reception.

'Oh, you're a hero again,' Whistler reassured him. 'Kestrel has told them all about it.'

Badger smiled and, taking a deep breath, went to meet his fate.

He need not have worried. Most of the animals had not seen him since his accident and received him like a long-lost friend. Mole was in raptures, Fox and Vixen relieved, and even Tawny Owl gave him a gruff, 'Glad to see you, Badger.'

A tacit understanding seemed to exist on both sides not to mention Badger's recent aberration, and all was forgotten. But Badger gloomily noticed the depletion in numbers of the little band that had set out the previous spring to look for their new home. Leaving aside the absence of the hibernating hedgehogs, Toad and Adder, there were gaps in the ranks of the squirrels and the rabbits, while Vole was accompanied only by his own mate and Fieldmouse by just two others of his family. Of the rest, lean bodies and hungry eyes told their tale. Only Mole, apart from himself, seemed unchanged.

Fox followed Badger's gaze. 'The winter has not left us unscathed,' he summarised.

'No.' Badger shook his head sadly. 'But perhaps we should turn the meeting towards a more positive course. Unscathed we are not, but we should now plan how we can emerge from the season undefeated.'

'For many of us that call is too late,' Vole said bitterly.

'Then let us resolve to lose no more,' Badger responded.

'There's not a lot that can be done,' Fox said with untypical pessimism. The winter had taken its toll of spirit, too.

'Fox has done everything possible for him to do,' Hare added loyally. 'But none of us can control the weather conditions. When the entire Park lies buried under two feet of snow, it needs more than animal ingenuity to cope with the situation.'

'Let me tell you,' said Badger quietly, 'I think we really do need help from another source.'

'Are you thinking again along the same lines we all think you are thinking?' asked Weasel cryptically.

'No.' Badger replied at once. 'Not the Warden. But I *am* thinking about human help.' He looked round at his companions whose faces had, for the most part, dropped.

'Only it would be help,' he intoned slowly to emphasize his words, 'that the humans wouldn't know they were giving.'

'Whatever can you mean, Badger?' Rabbit asked.

'Well, listen. Now it's well-known that humans waste as much of their food as they eat. Why, then, shouldn't we make use of what they don't want?'

'I could never bring myself to resort to scavenging,' Tawny Owl said, rustling his wings importantly.

'Don't be pompous, Owl,' Badger said. 'When the other choice is starvation you should be ready to resort to anything.'

'Badger's quite right,' agreed Fox. 'We must consider any plan that will keep us alive. Please explain further, Badger.'

'You'll remember that Toad told us the story of his travels. Well, on the other side of the Park, not far from the boundary fence, there are human habitations and gardens. It was from one of those very gardens that he actually began his long journey back to Farthing Wood. And somewhere in those gardens, you can count on it, we will come across some of those tall things they put their unwanted food in.'

'You've certainly hit on something,' Fox conceded. 'But it will be a great way, and few of us are now strong enough to travel great distances. For the smaller animals it is completely out of the question.'

'I'll go,' said Badger. 'I'm the fittest of all at present. And the birds can go with me. Then they can carry back anything of use I find. Of course, if anyone else feels able to join me, I'd be delighted.'

'I shall accompany you, naturally,' said Fox.

Badger looked at his wasted form with misgiving. He knew Fox felt that in any such venture it was his duty to attend. 'Well, Fox, you know,' Badger said awkwardly, 'are you sure that – '

'That I'm strong enough?' Fox anticipated him. 'Of course I am. I should never forgive myself if I stayed behind.'

'There is never any doubt about your being brave enough anyway,' Vixen said lovingly and nuzzled him.

So it was arranged that Fox, Badger, Tawny Owl, Kestrel and Whistler would form the expedition. It would be essential to travel in the dark, so they decided they must go at the very first opportunity, which was that very night.

'How I wish Toad was around to direct us,' Fox said.

'Couldn't we dig him up?' Mole suggested. 'I bet I could reach him.'

Badger laughed. 'Impossible, I'm afraid, Mole,' he told him. 'You'd get no sense out of him. He's in his winter sleep and nothing will wake him up except a rise in temperature. In fact, to expose him suddenly to these temperatures would probably kill him.'

'Oh dear, I hadn't thought of that,' said Mole.

'I remember he mentioned a ditch on the other side of the fence,' Fox mused. 'If we can find that, and then that first road he travelled down from his captor's garden, we should make it all right.'

'Leave it to me,' offered Tawny Owl. 'I'll find you your ditch – and the road.'

'How long will it take you to cross the Park?' asked Fieldmouse. 'It must be miles.'

'It would be no problem at all if it weren't for the fact that we are so hampered by snow,' said Fox. 'But we must reach the houses while it's still dark. It should be dusk now. I suggest we start straight away.'

The others agreed and, without further ado, Fox and Badger with Tawny Owl and Kestrel, made their way out of the chamber to assorted cries of 'Good luck!' Outside the set they acquainted Whistler with their idea, and he was delighted to be of use.

Fox and Badger went, shoulder to shoulder, across the snowy waste in the direction of the Reserve's far fence. Kestrel and Whistler fluttered slowly in the unaccustomed darkness for short distances while they waited for the two animals to catch them up. Tawny Owl the night bird flew on ahead on silent wings to locate the ditch that was their marker.

'What do you expect to find?' Fox asked Badger.

Badger found it strange to be in the role of leader, which at present he clearly was. 'Oh, I don't know. Meat and vegetable scraps – there could be all sorts of things,' he answered vaguely. Then he wished he had not spoken, for he saw the eager look in the famished Fox's eyes and his mouth begin to water.

'It really has hit you hard, hasn't it, old friend?' he whispered to him. For a time Fox did not answer, and Badger wondered if he had heard. Then Fox spoke.

'It's been the hardest trial I've ever faced,' he said wearily. 'Harder than anything we faced on our journey here, including the Hunt.'

'It is so sad that, after the triumph of overcoming

every hazard en route to reach our new home, so many of our friends have perished before they really had a chance to enjoy their new life.'

'It *is* sad,' agreed Fox, 'but there is no doubt that old age has played its part. The life span of a mouse is very short.'

'But the rabbits? The squirrels?'

'I know, I know. It's not the start to our new life I had envisaged,' Fox muttered. 'But then, how many would have survived staying behind in Farthing Wood? If we get through the rest of the winter without losing any more of our numbers, there will be a breeding stock, at any rate, of all the animals to ensure a permanent representation of the Farthing Wood party in the Park.'

'Except in one or two cases,' Badger said, smiling sadly.

'I'm sorry, Badger,' Fox said awkwardly. 'I really put my foot in it. I wasn't thinking.'

'Don't worry. I know what you meant. And it seems our priority must be to save Vole and Fieldmouse at all costs.'

'That is so,' said Fox. 'And that's where the difficulty lies. The White Deer herd have, on occasion, brought some of their hay for our vegetarians to eat. The problem is, the mice don't really like stalks. It's the seeds they want. And berries and insects. Of course, they're virtually unobtainable.'

'Well,' said Badger, 'perhaps we'll find something for them.'

When they next caught up with the birds, Tawny Owl was waiting as well. He told them he had found the ditch and the road down which they must go.

'Did you find the houses, too?' asked Badger.

'Er – yes,' he replied uncertainly.

'What's wrong?' asked Fox.

'Well, we shall all have to be cautious,' he explained. 'It seems there are others around on the same errand.'

—12—
A Raid

'Foxes?'

'Yes, a pair.'

'Where?'

'Along the road.'

'Well, we aren't the only creatures in the Park who are suffering. We sometimes tend to forget that.'

'How do we know they're from the Park?' Kestrel mentioned.

'True,' admitted Fox. 'But it's most likely.'

Before they reached the boundary of the Park, he asked to have a brief rest. Badger's concerned expression was unconcealed. 'I'll be all right,' Fox assured them all. 'I've lost a little of my strength, I'm afraid.'

Eventually they reached the fence and found a spot

where previous animals had scooped away the ground underneath in order to come and go as they pleased. Badger and Fox scrambled underneath and crossed the ditch. Tawny Owl led them to the road.

The surface was like glass where motor traffic had beaten down the falls of snow into a tight mass. But it was quiet now and empty. The animals padded slowly along it until the first of the human dwellings was reached.

'Wait here,' said Tawny Owl. 'I'll investigate.' Badger and Fox hid themselves in the darkest spot against the garden wall, while Whistler and Kestrel perched high up on a chimney pot.

'This one's no good,' Tawny Owl later informed them. 'The wall is too high for you and so are the gates.' They moved on to the next house to find the same problem. Fox looked at Badger significantly.

'Owl!' Badger called in a low voice. 'See if you can find the other foxes again. Perhaps they know something we don't.'

Tawny Owl returned with astonishing news. He had located the strange foxes in the grounds of a large house some distance away from the others. They had simply jumped the comparatively low fence and were nosing around a number of sheds and hutches. From sounds he had heard, Owl had discovered that one of these was a chicken coop, and this was obviously the foxes' target.

'Chickens!' exclaimed Fox.

'The same,' said Tawny Owl.

'But the racket! They'll wake the entire neighbourhood.' Despite his protestations, Fox was having the utmost difficulty in preventing himself from drooling. The thought of food had an overwhelming effect on him.

'There might be enough for all of us,' Badger hinted.

'What? You can't mean it, Badger. You wouldn't con-

done such – ' Fox broke off. He knew he was blustering;
playing a part – and so did Badger. For it had been the
first thought to cross his mind, too. After all, in strai-
tened circumstances, one has to consider any opening.

'I wonder how they get them out?' Badger muttered.

'Come and see,' Tawny Owl said.

They followed him further along the road, the other
birds accompanying. Owl perched on the fence he had
told them about.

'There's certainly a strong scent of fox,' said Badger.

'And also of chickens,' Fox whispered.

'Carefully now,' Tawny Owl warned the two animals
as he, Kestrel and Whistler fluttered into the grounds.

Fox and Badger looked at the fence. 'Can you jump
it?' Badger asked.

'If I were fully fit – nothing easier. But a lot of my
stamina's gone. However, I'll have a jolly good try.
What about you?'

'*I'm* no jumper,' answered Badger. 'You go ahead,
and I'll scout round the outside of the fence and see if
there's another way in. I'll join you inside.'

He watched Fox backing away from the fence in order
to give himself a good run up to it. Then he saw him
leap upwards, just scraping the fence-top, before he
landed the other side. Badger was now alone on the road
side of the fence. He shuffled along its length, looking
for a suitable opening. But there seemed to be no way
through. There was a gate halfway along one side which,
of course, was closed. He paused, wondering whether he
should call out. Just then there broke out the most appalling din. There was a loud crash, immediately followed
by the most frenzied squawks and a clattering of wings.
Badger correctly surmised that one of the foxes was
attempting to break in to the coop. The noise grew

absolutely deafening, and then he heard a barking and human shouts.

Cowering against the fence, not knowing if he should stay or run, Badger saw two foxes leap the fence into the road, a hen dangling from each of their pairs of jaws. Then they were off, racing down the road as fast as their burdens would allow them. Suddenly he heard three or four gunshots in quick succession and a very scared third fox – his own friend – leapt the fence almost on top of him.

'Quick!' Fox shouted hoarsely. 'This way!' And he raced away in the opposite direction to that taken by the two raiders. Badger sloped after him as fast as he could go – and in the nick of time. Out of the gate in the fence came a huge, ferocious and furious dog followed by two men – one young, one elderly – each with shotguns. The dog instantly set off after the foxes carrying the chickens. These animals were badly hampered by their heavy loads and the dog gained on them quickly. But the two men were taking aim with their guns. One called the dog, which checked its headlong rush, and then two more shots rang out. The two foxes dropped like stones and rolled over in the snow, the maimed chickens flapping helplessly in the gutter.

The men went to examine the fox carcasses, and seemed satisfied with their work. The younger one put the injured chickens out of their misery, and picked them up by their feet. The dog pranced around him, tongue lolling and tail wagging.

From their hiding-place under a parked car, Badger and Fox watched the men and their dog trudge back to the garden, their hearts beating wildly. Only when the gate in the fence had once again been fastened after them did they dare to move.

'Phew!' gasped Fox who really had felt in fear of his life. 'That was a little *too* close for my liking.'

'Yes,' Badger agreed. 'It's certainly a good thing we hadn't reached that garden first.'

'But I don't know if I should have tried what those poor devils did anyway,' Fox confessed. 'I've never been one for taking such prey.'

'Maybe they were desperate like us,' Badger suggested pointedly.'

Fox ignored him. 'Where are the birds?' he asked.

Tawny Owl was the first to find them. 'So much for your ideas of invading gardens,' he said to Badger crossly. 'Could have had us all killed.'

'*You* were the one to tell us about the chickens,' said Badger. 'We still haven't investigated my suggestion.'

'I don't think I could go back in there again,' Fox said. 'Is the coast clear now, Owl?'

'No,' he replied. 'Those foxes turned the coop over and the stupid hens are running all over the place. The men will have their work cut out collecting them together again.'

'Give them time,' said Badger. 'After coming all this way we can't go back with nothing.'

'Will you keep us informed please, Owl?' Fox asked. 'Badger and I will wait here.'

'Can't see the point,' muttered Tawny Owl. 'Badger can't get into the garden anyway.'

Badger looked at Fox. 'This garden is our only chance,' he said. 'It's the only one with a fence. Are you sure you couldn't make just one more jump?'

Fox wavered. It seemed as if he was fated always to be the one on whom everyone else depended.

'You know I would gladly go if I could get in,' Badger added. 'But I've looked all round for a hole and there's just nothing.'

Fox smiled a little smile of resignation. 'It looks as if I have no choice really, doesn't it?' he said.

So Tawny Owl flew back to watch the proceedings, and Fox and Badger huddled together under the car again to wait. Some time passed and they heard nothing. Badger was restless. 'I think I'll just wander a little further along this road just in case there's anything of interest,' he told his companion.

He had not been gone long when Fox heard a familiar whistle in the air, and then saw the long thin legs of Whistler standing by the car. He emerged from his hideaway.

'Ah, there you are,' said the heron. 'I've some excellent news for you. The men have hung the dead chickens up in a shed and I think, if you really make yourself as flat as possible you could get under the door. There's a gap just about wide enough for you.'

Fox's ears pricked up. 'Things are looking up,' he replied. 'Is all quiet again?'

'The men have set all to rights and returned inside,' Whistler answered.

'And the dog?'

'Er – chained to a kennel,' said Whistler. 'But I'm sure you can handle him.'

'What are you saying?' cried Fox in exasperation. 'Am I, in my state, a match for a dog of that size?'

'Not physically, of course,' said the heron calmly. 'But we all know of your powers of persuasion.'

'I'm afraid you must have too high an opinion of me,' Fox returned, shaking his head. 'You may have heard of a previous exploit of mine, regarding a bull-mastiff – a stupid dog. But this situation is altogether different. This dog, whatever it is, is twice the size with twice the strength whereas I – well, you have only to look at me.'

'You are indeed underweight,' Whistler acknowl-

edged. 'But that is to be expected. Are you saying your
mental faculties have been affected by the winter?'

'It's a question of spirit and courage – and the will to
do something,' Fox said wearily. 'I'm simply not the
same animal any more. On the journey from Farthing
Wood I had plenty of spirit. Determination, too. I had
a *purpose*. It's different now.

'But, my dear Fox,' Whistler said with a worried look.
'I can't bear to hear you talk like this. You, above all
my friends, have always been an example of tenacity
and resourcefulness and resolution to look up to. You
inspired the others – you still do. And surely you *still*
have a purpose. To survive. Think of Vixen if not of
yourself.'

For a moment something of the old look returned to
Fox's poor haggard face. He was thinking of what he
had been like when Vixen had first encountered him.
The pitiful shadow of himself that he now was would
never have won her regard and admiration as he had
then. Then his eyes glazed over again.

'No, it's no use, Whistler,' he said lamely. 'I'm sorry
if I'm letting you down but I'm beaten before I start.
I'll simply wilt in front of that monster.'

Whistler was really alarmed at Fox's lack of motiva-
tion. Even his mention of Vixen had not done the trick.
He flew back to Tawny Owl and Kestrel for advice.

'Yes, he's taken things very hard,' Kestrel said when
the heron had related his conversation.

'Humph!' snorted Tawny Owl. 'I believe in calling
things by their proper name. His spirit is completely
broken, and he's no longer the brave leader we once
knew.'

'How can we help him?' asked Whistler. 'It's awful to
see him cowering in the road under that car.'

'Only a full stomach and the arrival of Spring can help him now,' said Tawny Owl. 'He's a beaten animal.'

Unbeknown to the three birds, the subject of their discussion had crept up to the garden fence and could overhear every word. If the scene had been pre-arranged it could not have had a better result. Fox's pride, battered as it was, refused to accept the verdict of Tawny Owl, and his body visibly stiffened. He thought again of Vixen and what it would mean to her if he failed. He could not bear to sink in her estimation. He pulled himself more erect and backed away from the fence.

The birds were still talking when they saw him leap the fence for the third time, but with an added grace that made them fall silent. He went warily across the centre of the grounds of the house, giving the re-established chicken coop a wide berth. He saw the dog, half in and half out of the kennel, with its head on its paws, and he approached cautiously step by step. Having convinced himself that it was dozing, Fox looked around for the shed Whistler had described to him. He soon found it.

In his emaciated state it was no problem for him to crawl under the door. The chickens were hanging by the feet from nails in the side of the shed. Fox pulled one free and backed under the gap again. Here he met with a difficulty for the chicken got caught. However, with a backward tug, he wrenched it free and ran back to the fence.

The birds fully expected him to jump the fence and be satisfied with his good luck. But Fox had evidently decided to do things in style. He dropped the chicken, then loped back to the shed and scrambled under the door again. All this time the dog had not stirred a muscle. Fox found the second hen to be much larger and needed two pulls to bring it to the ground. Back he came under the shed door and then the larger hen became firmly wedged. Fox tugged it this way and that, but its plump body would not shift. Whistler was on the point of flying over to tell Fox that perhaps it would be best to be content with one and to get away while the going was good, when Badger's voice was heard calling beyond the fence.

'Fox! Owl! Are you there?' he was saying.

'We're here,' hissed Tawny Owl from his branch. 'Be quiet. The dog's asleep.'

'I've found a regular dump of food,' he called back excitedly, regardless of the warning. 'At the end of the road. Come and look.'

Kestrel flew over to the fence and perched on the top. 'Wait a moment, Badger,' he whispered. 'Fox is in the grounds collecting chickens.'

Badger's jaw dropped. He could not comprehend that Kestrel was referring to the two dead ones. 'He must be mad!' he cried. 'Does he want to commit suicide?'

Kestrel calmed him down. 'It's not what you think,' he said. 'We'll explain later.'

Fox had given the second chicken a particularly vicious wrench and it was almost free. But at that moment the dog awoke and yawned widely. It stood up, shaking its body vigorously. Fox heard the sound and froze. How far did that chain stretch? He peered round the side of the shed. The dog was some twenty feet away, but Fox had no idea if it could reach him if it made a lunge. He waited. The dog began to sniff the snow all round its kennel. It found something of interest and sniffed harder, running in looping patterns through the snow, its nose always on the ground. Fox watched it go to the full length of its chain in the direction opposite to where he was standing and gulped as he saw how far it stretched. If it came his way it could easily reach him. He waited no longer. He heaved the chicken free and ran almost in front of the dog as it was returning on the axis of the chain's length. It saw him and immediately started to bark again.

Fox raced for the fence and cleared it easily. 'Take this!' he cried as he dropped the chicken on the road side of the fence by Badger. Then, incredibly, in the teeth of danger he backed away for yet another jump. The dog was barking incessantly as Fox leapt the fence again to snap up the chicken he had left behind. Lights were appearing once more in the house. But Fox was up and over the fence for the last time with the second chicken in his jaws. Without hesitation he took the opposite direction to that taken by the first two foxes, leaving poor Badger to struggle after him with the heavier hen. Tawny Owl, Kestrel and Whistler swooped over the fence behind them.

'The Park's that way!' called Tawny Owl. 'You're going in the wrong direction!' But Fox did not seem to hear.

Badger had no idea what Fox had in mind, but he gamely followed him as quickly as he could, expecting every minute to find the huge dog bearing down on him from behind. But though the deafening barking continued, no dog – nor men – appeared. Then suddenly the noise ceased. It seemed as if this is what Fox had been expecting, for he immediately stopped running and dropped the chicken, the better to take some deep breaths while he waited for Badger to catch him up.

'Not a bad haul, eh?' he said coolly to his friends as they bunched together. He seemed his old self.

'I don't understand,' said Badger.

'Understand what?'

'Why we weren't chased,' Badger panted.

'It's obvious,' Fox confided. 'When the men came out

of the house the second time they expected to see their chicken coop overturned again. As soon as they saw it intact, with no more chickens missing, they assumed the dog's barking had driven off any further prowlers. How could they know I knew about the dead hens in the shed?'

'Bravo, Fox. You're to be congratulated,' said Whistler. 'And you've proved you're still a shade sharper than most of us.'

Tawny Owl disliked anyone to be overpraised when he considered he had exceptional abilities himself. 'Oh well,' he said huffily, 'when you're down as low as you can be, you can only go upwards.'

The others glared at him but Fox, in his new-found confidence, only chuckled.

'Yet a little cunning can go a long way,' he said.

—13—
Live and Let Live

Badger was delighted at Fox's reinstatement as the animals' resourceful leader, and Whistler politely failed to mention that the idea of stealing the dead chickens had been his.

'I also have found something of interest,' Badger then announced.

'Ah yes – your discovery,' murmured Kestrel. 'What is it?'

'I hope it's something of value to our smaller friends,' said Fox. 'We mustn't forget that we still have nothing for *them*, and that is why I didn't turn back for the Park.'

'Well, come and see,' said Badger excitedly. 'There's everything we need.'

'How far is it?' Fox wanted to know. 'I feel quite worn out.'

'Of course you are, jumping backwards and forwards over that fence all those times – without mentioning the journey here. But it's not far along the road. We've run most of the way already.'

'You take the others with you, and show them what you want them to carry back,' Fox suggested. 'I'll wait here and take a breather and look after the chickens.'

So Badger, accompanied by the three birds, proceeded to the end of the road, where in fact a small general store that served the neighbourhood was situated. To the rear of the shop was a yard where discarded cartons, packets and unwanted stocks abounded. Amongst this was enough greenstuff to feed all the rabbits and hares comfortably, wasted bags of mixed nuts left over from Christmas and even quantities of pet food such as millet sprays for cage birds. Badger seemed to think the voles and fieldmice might like the latter, while the squirrels would be delighted by the nuts.

What would have been the astonishment of any human awake at that hour and looking on, to see a small aerial procession of a hawk, an owl and a heron on their way back to the Nature Reserve carrying their assorted gifts? Kestrel led the way with a collection of millet sprays in his pointed beak, then came Tawny Owl, a little self-consciously, laden with string bags of nuts – one in his beak and one clutched in his talons – and finally Whistler, his huge bill stuffed with cabbage leaves and a selection of greenery.

Badger watched them on their way and then rejoined Fox. 'I thought you might have indulged in a mouthful or two while you were waiting,' he said, referring to the chickens, 'just to keep your strength up.'

'No,' said Fox. 'We shall all feast together when we

get back to the Park. You and I and Vixen and Weasel. And, of course, Owl and Kestrel, though I know Whistler prefers fish. But first we have a journey ahead of us.'

Dawn was threatening to break as they went back along the road, Fox now carrying the larger chicken. They passed the scene of the raid and then the two dead foxes. Now they were just stiff corpses in the snow, lying where they had dropped and staining its whiteness with their blood.

'These hens should have been theirs by rights,' Fox muttered as he paused briefly at the sight. 'It could have been Vixen and me.' Then they went on, crossed the ditch, and re-entered the Park at the same point.

It was well on into the morning when the two animals, after frequent stops to rest from their loads, arrived back at Badger's set.

'Will you eat with me?' Badger asked, 'or shall I come and join you and Vixen?'

'Just as you like,' Fox said wearily.

'May I suggest the set then?' said Badger, aware that it offered considerably more comfort than the sparseness of the foxes' earth.

'I must have a nap first,' Fox said decidedly. 'I'll help you take our quarry underground, and then I'll be back when it's dark, with Vixen.'

'I'm tired too,' agreed Badger as they deposited the chickens in a safe place. 'But it was well worth the effort, wasn't it?'

'Without a doubt,' replied Fox.

Later that day Fox, Badger, Vixen, Weasel, Tawny Owl and Kestrel were together in Badger's set. There was plenty to eat for all, and each of them felt it was the first good meal they had had in a long while. Kestrel informed Fox and Badger that he, Owl and Whistler had made several trips back and forth to the food dump

and that all the animals had eaten well and were feeling
a lot more cheerful.

'I really believe that Badger's brainwave will prove to
be our salvation,' Fox said optimistically. Vixen looked
at her mate lovingly. She had heard the tale of Fox's
courage and cunning from Kestrel and was prouder of
him than ever.

'It certainly seems that Badger's stay with humankind
has produced some useful thinking,' remarked Tawny
Owl.

'Owl and I and the heron can make regular flights to
pick up more supplies,' said Kestrel. 'With just a little
luck our depleted party should be around to welcome
the spring.'

'But what of all of *us*?' Weasel demanded. 'Where do
the supplies for the meat-eaters come from? Those small
birds killed by the cold we sometimes pick up don't
make a proper meal.'

All were silent, faced with a problem none of them
had really considered. Badger thought of Ginger Cat's
rats but diplomatically decided to say nothing.

'There can be no more raids on chicken coops,' said
Fox. 'That would be suicidal.'

'Was there no meat amongst the wasted food?' Vixen
asked.

'I have to admit we didn't really look,' said Kestrel.
'But that is easily remedied.'

'Perhaps, Owl, you could investigate tomorrow night?'
Fox suggested.

'Perhaps I could, perhaps I couldn't,' he answered
grumpily. 'I may have other plans.'

'Don't worry – I'll go,' said Kestrel in disgust. 'I can
fly there in the daytime. No-one will notice a hovering
hawk.'

'I didn't say I *wouldn't* go,' Tawny Owl rejoined. 'If you had waited, I no doubt would have offered.'

'Can't bear to be *asked* to do anything,' Kestrel muttered. 'Pompous old – '

He was interrupted by an unearthly scream outside the set.

'Whatever's that?' he cried.

'Have you never heard the scream of a captured hare?' Weasel asked.

'HARE!' they all shouted and Fox and Badger went racing for the exit. The others followed. Outside they smelt blood and Fox snuffled the crisp, icy air. 'This way!' he called. A little further off there was a patch of blood on the snow, and a trail of drops leading away from it. They followed and, eventually, found what they were looking for. Under a holly bush a stoat was devouring the limp body of a young hare. It looked up in alarm at the approaching group and quickly snatched up its prey, preparatory to flight.

'You needn't run,' said Fox. 'If that is one of our friends you have killed, we are too late. And, if not, we don't need the food.'

'I'm afraid it's one of the leverets, Hare's offspring,' Weasel announced.

'I have to eat, too, you know,' the stoat said defensively in a voice unnaturally shrill. 'I hunt what I can. N-no offence meant.'

'It's the law of the Wild,' said Badger. 'We mean you no harm.' He turned to the others. 'I met this fellow once before,' he said. 'Like us, he's finding it difficult to survive.'

'Of course,' said Fox. 'Who are we to complain?'

'What a strange world it is,' murmured Vixen. 'That poor little friend of ours came here, believing he had found safety, only to end up like this.'

The stoat was looking from one to the other, still unsure of its best action and half inclined to run.

'What's the difference?' Tawny Owl shrugged. 'He could as easily have been killed by the winter.'

'For most of us no home is without its dangers,' Fox observed. 'It's something we have to accept without question. However, my friend,' he continued, looking at the stoat, 'I wish you had hunted in another corner of the Park.'

The stoat seemed to sense it was safe now and increased in boldness. 'And you foxes – you hunt too. Where do you go in the Park to find food?'

'Yes, yes. We take the point,' answered Fox. 'Wherever we can find it – the same as you.'

'Never have I known such a winter,' the stoat went on. 'My mate has already died. I can see by your leanness you have suffered as well. But the badger seems very sleek.'

Badger shifted his stance a little uncomfortably.

'Yes, I saw you on another occasion,' the stoat said. 'You weren't so stout then. You must have been luckier than the rest of us.'

'If injuring myself severely can be called lucky, I have been,' Badger said enigmatically.

The stoat, of course, looked puzzled.

'He was discovered by the Warden and taken into care,' Weasel explained.

'A sort of fattening up process,' said Tawny Owl mischievously.

'All right, all right,' said Badger. 'Am I never to be allowed to forget it? Would you rather I hadn't been found and frozen to death?'

'Don't be absurd, Badger,' replied Tawny Owl. 'Nobody was more pleased than I at your recovery.'

'Well then, how much longer do I have to endure these carping comments?' Badger said irritably.

'Oh dear,' said the stoat grinning. 'The incident appears to be a bit of a bone of contention between you.'

'Let's drop the subject,' suggested Fox, 'and leave our friend here to eat in peace. And I sincerely hope Hare is nowhere at hand to overhear my remarks. He'd never forgive me.'

'I promise I'll endeavour to keep away from this area,' the stoat said agreeably. 'You've been more than polite.'

'Live and let live,' answered Fox. 'The Park belongs to all of us.'

He led the others away and they gradually dispersed to their own homes.

'H'm, quite a philosophical evening,' remarked Tawny Owl as he fluttered silently to his roost.

—14—
A New Danger

The winter wore relentlessly on, the old year fading into the new with no sign of change. The birds continued their trips to the food dump and were able to find a kind of meat – perhaps unwanted sausages or bacon or the like – to supplement what the meat-eaters were able to find in the Reserve. Now that the threat of imminent starvation had been lessened, the animals gritted their teeth, confident that it was now just a case of lasting out until the better weather came.

In other ways they were no more comfortable than before. They simply could not get used to the treacherous cold which never let up, nor the blizzards and snowfalls which occurred with monotonous regularity. But they had all learned to suffer in silence.

Then, when at last they had all begun to hope that they really must be approaching the end of the winter, an entirely new threat emerged. The Warden was taken ill and removed to hospital. Ginger Cat disappeared at the same time – presumably to a well-wisher. The Lodge fell empty and there was no longer any restriction to human access to the Nature Reserve. When the fact became known to the local human population, it was not long before gangs of boys with skates and toboggans were invading the Park, shattering its peace and quiet and destroying the freedom of its inhabitants. But, worse still, at night came poachers.

The first sounds of a gun came late one evening when Fox and Vixen were on the prowl. They stopped dead in their tracks, heads up sniffing the air, ears cocked for every slight sound.

'It can't be,' muttered Fox, looking at his mate. They waited. Then another bang convinced them of their suspicions and they dived for cover.

Under some shrubbery they listened with racing hearts, their bellies pressed to the frozen ground. They were a long way from their earth. As each second passed their nerves quivered in trepidation. There were no more shots, but then they saw two dark figures moving like shadows across the snow, not twenty yards from where they lay. Instinctively their heads went down in an attempt to render themselves even less conspicuous. But they could see what the figures were carrying and at the sight of it they both gasped.

'A deer!' they both hissed under their breath.

'And a large one, too,' said Fox, watching how the men were bent beneath its weight. 'Poor creature.'

'Is there nothing these humans won't stoop to?' Vixen said furiously. 'They know the very purpose of this Park is to preserve wildlife.'

'More to the point,' Fox reminded her, 'it was created a Nature Reserve to protect the very White Deer herd they are attacking.'

'Oh, where can our Warden have gone?' Vixen wailed.

'That we shan't know,' Fox said. 'But it is enough to know he is absent, and we are all unprotected.'

'The deer must be in a panic,' said Vixen. 'They've no experience of guns or of being hunted. And why *are* they hunted?'

'They're rare animals. Who knows what value the skin might have to a human who possesses one?'

'Then can *we* take that as some consolation? If the humans are only hunting the deer, maybe the other creatures here are not at risk.'

Fox laughed hollowly. 'It is my experience of such humans that all creatures are at risk as long as they have a gun in their hands.'

'Will they be back, do you think?' Vixen asked.

'As long as they know there is no Warden around, I think we can expect them,' Fox replied grimly.

His words were proved right. Although no guns were heard the next night, on the ensuing one they returned. The deer herd was frantic. Unlike their cousins in the unprotected wild and rugged areas of the country, they had nowhere to run to; no means of escape. What had been a haven of peace to them had now become a death-trap.

The other animals of the Park, who had always enjoyed a security from human intervention which was owed principally to the existence of the White Deer herd, forgot any obligation they should have felt. They only counted themselves lucky not to be the hunted ones. But the animals of Farthing Wood – the newcomers – were of a different mettle. From many different loyalties in their old home they had forged themselves into a unit

on their long march across country. They had learnt
during that period that the good of the individual usually
meant the good of the majority. The Park was now their
home, as it was the deer's, and they all of them felt some
responsibility towards their fellow inhabitants in fighting
their common enemy. But none of them could think of
anything they could do to prevent the poaching.

Fox and Vixen were again out foraging when the next
visit of the men with guns took place. This time they
were in a position to see everything. The deer herd were,
as usual, in the open part of the Park. In the absence of
the Warden they had lost their supplies of hay, and were
now reduced to digging beneath the snow with their
hooves as best they could to reach the grass and mosses
underneath. From the cover of a nearby clump of trees,
two men were creeping stealthily towards them.

The noble figure of the Great Stag himself towered
over the other deer, making a clear target for the guns.
Fox saw the men raising their weapons to take aim.
Without thinking, he commenced barking with an
abruptness that startled the already nervous deer. They
began to mill about, sensing danger again. When Vixen
joined in, Fox started to run towards the deer barking
as he went. He hoped the deer would take alarm and
run. The trick paid off. The more nervous of the deer
bolted, which alarmed the rest and they were soon running in all directions. Even the Great Stag ran, with a
backward glance at Fox over his shoulder. But, although
Fox may have saved the overlord of the Park, which had
been his main thought, he unconsciously hastened the
end of another. Unfortunately some of the deer ran
straight towards the trees where the men were hidden,
and so on to their guns. One was shot as they approached, causing the others to veer away. Then the
whole herd raced in panic as far as they could go, away

from the noise. But the men were satisfied with their stalking, and another white deer was removed from the Reserve.

'I hope my motives won't be misunderstood,' Fox said ruefully to Vixen. 'It might have looked as if I was in league with the killers.'

'Nonsense!' said Vixen. 'Is that likely? You aren't a man's pet but a creature of the Wild. You saved the Great Stag and he knows it.'

'But they still had their taste of blood. The herd is yet one fewer in number.'

'What can we do against the intelligence of humans?' Vixen asked. 'If they decided to slaughter every creature in the Park we could do nothing to stop it.'

'I'm not so pessimistic,' Fox said. 'All we have to do is to think of a way of preventing them getting into the Reserve.'

'Utterly impossible,' she replied flatly. 'How could we achieve that?'

'I don't know. Perhaps we could, at least, arrange a warning system at their approach so that we're not to be found when the men arrive.'

'And what would you do with the deer herd? Take them all underground?'

'All right,' Fox said wistfully. 'I suppose it's just wishful thinking, but there must be something that can be done to make them less vulnerable.'

'Oh, I know you when you're in this mood.' Vixen looked at him, and her great affection shone out of her eyes. 'You won't rest now. But thinking for a party of small animals that can hide themselves away is a far cry from causing a herd of deer to vanish.'

'I think I'll go and have a talk with the Great Stag,' Fox replied.

'I'll leave you then,' said Vixen. 'You won't want me around.'

'You couldn't be more wrong, my beloved Vixen,' he told her. 'I need you with me. You are my partner in everything.'

The Great Stag had not run far. He had been trying to muster the herd together again after the alarm. 'I am indebted to you,' he said to Fox at once. 'We only lost one. There was no scent of Man. We could have lost more.' He did not have the conceit to own that it was he who had been the prime target.

'We have to devise a way of preventing any more deaths,' Fox said earnestly.

'I spend all my waking hours trying to do so,' said the Stag. 'The fact is, without our supply of hay we may lose more animals from starvation than from the gun.'

'I can see it must be very difficult for the older and weaker among your herd to cope,' Fox agreed. 'But I am convinced we've seen the worst of the winter. The threat from Man, in my opinion, is far more severe.'

'You talk wisely,' said the Stag. 'I know you to be the intelligent animal who brought your friends here last summer from a great distance. But you didn't have large animals like us to contend with. I'm afraid the problem of ensuring our safety is well-nigh impossible.'

'You are repeating almost word for word what I've said to Fox,' Vixen remarked. 'Although our hearts are with you I don't believe we have the power to be of assistance.'

The Great Stag shook his noble head. 'If the Warden does not return I have decided there is only one course of action open to us.'

'I think I know what's in your mind,' said Fox quietly, 'for it has occurred to me also.'

'I fear we must leave the Park,' the Great Stag pronounced.

'Yes. It's as I expected. But outside you would run the same risk.'

'However, we could scatter over a wider area.'

Fox was silent for some moments. 'No,' he said finally in the determined manner that Vixen knew so well. 'It mustn't come to that. I won't admit defeat. I have the germ of an idea. Will you give me a day or so?'

'My dear friend,' the Stag said feelingly, 'you are under no obligation to do anything. You have your own problems. Of course I will give you whatever time you wish. I had not planned to leave our home just yet.'

'The men don't return every night,' Vixen said. 'You should be safe for the time being.'

Fox was deep in thought. 'I need to work things out,' he said presently. He turned to the Stag. 'We'll leave you now,' he said, 'and I will return to put my plan before you.'

'You are a gracious and clever animal,' replied the overlord of the Reserve. 'I shall await your coming again with the utmost eagerness.'

As Fox and Vixen turned after their farewells, she questioned him. 'May I ask what you have in mind?'

'I'll tell you all eventually,' he replied. 'It's the Pond, you see – that's the key to the whole thing.'

—15—
The Trap

The following afternoon the Park was invaded again by groups of young boys, most of them muffled to the chin to beat the cold, who had come to skate. The home of the Edible Frogs had been frozen over for months, but there were signs that a slight rise in temperature had occurred. In a few places the surface of the Pond had a little water on top of the ice. The youngsters, however, after inspecting thoroughly, donned their skates and proceeded to enjoy them selves.

From a snow-festooned bed of rushes Fox was watching their antics closely. He chuckled to himself as he thought of the many times Adder had waited at the waterside during the summer, patiently watching the

Edible Frogs disporting themselves. But his vigil was for a very different reason.

After an hour or so he had seen all he wanted to. Carefully avoiding any risk of being spotted by pairs of sharp young eyes, he made his way back to his earth. Vixen woke as he entered. She looked at him searchingly. 'Nothing yet,' was his only remark.

During the next couple of days the weather became noticeably milder, and for longer stretches the sun broke through the cloud formation that had loured upon the Park for so long. Each day Fox watched at the pondside. On the second night the men returned and another deer was shot. The Great Stag in this time had not seen Fox again. Once more he began to think in terms of leaving the reserve.

But the very next afternoon Fox saw what he had been waiting for. The children arrived, but found their skating restricted. Almost a third of the Pond now had to be avoided, and they soon left it altogether in favour of tobogganing. Fox knew it was time for him to re-visit the Stag.

The great beast listened silently while he unfolded his plan, then raised his head and bellowed a challenge to the air, 'Now let them come,' he roared. Fox waited no longer. There was much to do.

But first he wanted Vixen's approval. During the journey to the Park he had relied a good deal on her judgement and had learnt to value it. She heard his plan and looked at him in admiration. Her enthusiasm did not need to be expressed in words. The Fox gathered all his friends together and put them in the picture also. They were totally in agreement save, predictably, for Tawny Owl who only gave grudging support.

'Can't see why you want to bother so much with a

deer herd,' he muttered. 'As long as the humans are banging away at them, *we're* that much safer.'

'But safer still if they can't "bang away" at *anything*' Fox said coolly.

'Very well,' said Badger. 'Now we must arrange for the sentries.'

So a system was arranged by which the animals were to watch the place where the poachers entered, the boundary between the Park and the road, and give early warning of their approach. Tawny Owl, Kestrel and Whistler were stationed at intervals along the fence. Along the ground Weasel, Hare, Badger and Vixen waited. Midway between the boundary and the Pond, Fox was stationed, while in the region of the Pond itself the Great Stag was patrolling in readiness to play his part in the Plan.

The first night passed without event, and at dawn the animals and birds returned to their homes. On the second night they were back at their posts. Although it was still cold, there was no longer the viciousness in the wind that had cut through their fur and feathers like a knife-blade. The snow that had covered the ground for so long had softened and, on the road outside the Park, had been churned into slush by motor vehicles. It was the noise of the steady squelch of steps through this slush that was the first sign to the waiting animals of the men's approach.

Weasel's sharp ears were the first to detect the sound. His small body, so close to the ground, had not the stature to see into the road. He ran quickly to the fence-post on which sat Tawny Owl. 'I hear footsteps!' he cried. 'Is it them?'

'I can see something coming,' replied Owl. 'Wait – yes, two figures . . . Yes! Yes! Quickly! Tell the others! I'm off to Fox!' He flew up in a wide arc over the tree-tops and sped off in the direction of the waiting Fox. Weasel passed the word to the others and together they raced back through the Park. Fox saw Tawny Owl approaching him at speed and himself prepared to run.

'To the Pond!' cried Owl. 'They're on their way!'

At once Fox set off at a breakneck pace, his breath coming like small bursts of steam from his mouth. Whistler and Kestrel were first back to safety. Vixen, Weasel and Badger had a long run ahead of them to keep in front of the men. Only Hare was almost as swift overland as the birds through the air.

Fox had told them to hide themselves once he had received the message. Out of sight they were quite safe from the poachers' guns. The men had come for larger game. But it was not in the nature of the animals of Farthing Wood to disassociate themselves from such an important event – and one in which the leader was placing himself in danger. So the slower animals had condemned themselves to run across an exhausting stretch of parkland to be in on things. Of the three Vixen was by far the fastest and she outdistanced Weasel and Badger as quickly as Hare had outdistanced her. Weasel, although far smaller than Badger, was much more lithe and had a far more elastic and rippling running pace. But he moderated his speed to suit the older animal's comfort.

As his friends hastened back to join him, Fox was on his way to join the Stag. The scion of the deer herd had agreed to keep his station by the Pond each night until he saw Fox again. He lowered his head as he saw the familiar chestnut body racing towards him.

'Hold – yourself – ready,' gasped Fox, his tongue lolling painfully from his mouth. 'They're coming.'

'So tonight is to be the night,' the Stag intoned. 'Rest

awhile, my friend. You appear to be somewhat
distressed.'

'No, I – mustn't stop – I must complete the – task,'
Fox panted. 'I – have to make – sure they – find you.'
And he was off again, back in the direction from which
he had come – back towards the men with guns. He
passed a black poplar in whose boughs clustered Tawny
Owl, Kestrel and Whistler. But they did not interrupt
him and he did not see them. He did see Hare but there
was no time to stop and he went by without a glance.
Next he passed Vixen who gave him a longing look. He
half looked back as he ran, but even she had to be
ignored for the sake of the Plan. When he spotted Badger
and Weasel in the distance he dropped on all fours, for
behind them the two fateful shadows were approaching.

'Go to cover,' he told his friends as they reached him.
'No need to endanger more of us than necessary.' They
passed on and Fox waited to begin the gamble of his life.

Among the snow-coated sedges by the Pond lay Hare.
He was watching the White Stag nervously tossing his
head as he stood by the edge of the ice, his legs quivering.
Vixen found him and lay down. She was unable to speak.
Her heart was pounding unmercifully. Eventually
Badger and Weasel tottered in to join them. There they
waited and watched.

Twenty yards from the men, Fox stood up and yapped
loudly. The signal was heard and out from the nearby
copse came the White Deer herd, slowly, timidly, in
knots of three and four. The men stopped. One pointed
and their voices made themselves heard. They were looking among the herd and Fox knew who they were looking
for. But the one they wanted was missing. The human
voices were heard again – harsh, rough voices. The deer
paused. Fox yapped again and started towards them.
The deer scattered as instructed, running in the direction

of the Pond. The men shouted angrily, now pointing at the fox. This was the animal that had frustrated them before. Fox ran behind the herd as if driving them. His back was to the men, and every nerve-end along his neck, his spine and his haunches was strung as taut as a guitar string. The hackles rose on his coat for he knew he was courting death. At last he had to glance back. He saw one of the men raise his gun. It was aimed at him, the cause of their wrath. But Fox had no intention of being shot. He wheeled away at a right-angle, running fast, then twisted and swerved, twisted and swerved, like a hare followed by hounds. A shot rang out but the bullet found no mark.

Now the men were running, for their quarry was escaping. They would have one deer, if not the one they were after. The herd reached the brink of the Pond and spread out, screening its edge. In front of them, on to the ice itself, stepped the Great Stag. Cautiously he went, pausing at each step, until he reached the limit of safety. As the men came up, the herd swung away to the right, leaving the Stag exposed – solitary, undefended, alone on the ice. The men saw their passage was clear on the left side of the Pond. The Stag's head was turned away as if he were ignorant of their intention. They edged out, foot by foot, on the treacherous ice. They meant to have him this time. At the moment they raised their weapons Fox barked a third time. The Stag swung his great head round, saw the men and, with a tremendous bound leapt for the shore. But the poachers were committed now. They saw their target about to escape from their grip again. They ran forward to take aim at the retreating animal and then – crash! suddenly it was as if their feet were snatched from under them, and they were plunging down, down into black, icy water. Their guns were thrown away as they sought to save themselves, floundering and trying to find a handhold on something.

The Great Stag turned at the edge of the ice and saw the weapons meant for his death sink to the murky depths of the Pond's bottom, abandoned without a thought by their owners. At this clear evidence that Fox's plan had worked to perfection the Stag laid his head back and bellowed in triumph. Then Fox was surrounded by his jubilant friends – his old friends and the whole of the deer herd. The Great Stag joined them. 'That,' he boomed, 'is a piece of animal cunning never likely to be surpassed.'

While the animals were milling around, the men were striking out for the shore. The Pond was not deep and they were in no danger save that of a severe ducking and a bad chill. Their cries of anger had changed to cries of distress before they had pulled their frozen, dripping bodies clear of the water on to the shore. They cast one look at the bevy of wild creatures who had bested them, and then set off at an uncomfortable trot. Their misery would not be over for a while, for back they had to go across the Park and along the slushy road before there was any hope of being dry and warm again. At every step the icy coldness of their drenched clothing chafed at their bodies and neither of them could imagine a discomfort existed that could be more severe.

'I think we've seen the last of them,' said Hare. 'Fox, this is your greatest day. Even on our long journey you never reached these heights.'

Fox felt the admiration of all the creatures swell like a tide around him, but he was content to know that his plan had worked without mishap. Only Vixen, in all her fierce pride, felt a nagging doubt about what might be the reaction of two humans degraded and humiliated beyond belief by a fox.

— 16 —

One Good Turn...

Fox's courage and ingenuity were now the byword of the inhabitants of White Deer Park. It was no new discovery for his old friends from Farthing Wood, but he was the acknowledged hero of the deer herd, and even those creatures who had not been witness to the events at the Pond heard the story and marvelled. Once again he was brimful of confidence after his successes with the chickens and now the poachers. In both instances he had pitted his wits against humans and each time emerged triumphant.

So Fox had a special status in the Reserve and, although still underweight from the rigours of the winter, he carried his head more erect, his gait was looser and the sparkle had returned to his eyes. Vixen was delighted. 'You're your old self again,' she told him. Yet still that unnameable thought lurked in her mind.

For the next few weeks the weather fluctuated. Warm spells were followed by cold spells which then gave way to milder temperatures again. Most of the old snow had melted, but there were still heavy frosts at night and new, but slighter, falls of snow still occurred. But the Park no longer seemed to be deserted. The inhabitants were out and about again when it was safe, and all sensed the coming of Spring. Food was easier to find for all creatures and health and appearance improved.

One day in late February Whistler found Squirrel, Vole and Fieldmouse enjoying together some nuts which Squirrel had been able to dig up from the softer ground.

'I don't think you need me any more, do you?' he asked, referring to the trips the birds were still making to the general store's dump.

'Not really,' replied Squirrel. 'But we're most grateful. You may have kept us alive.'

'It's not quite Spring yet,' Vole pointed out, shaking his head. 'I wouldn't like to say for sure – '

'Nonsense,' cut in the more reasonable Fieldmouse. 'Whistler and Kestrel – and Tawny Owl too – have done more than enough for us. It's time they had a rest.'

Vole was outnumbered and conceded defeat. 'At any rate,' he persisted, 'if things should get difficult again I imagine we can still call on you?'

Whistler bowed elaborately and winked at the other two animals. 'Always at your service,' he answered with a hint of sarcasm. 'I'll tell Kestrel the news.'

The hawk had been on a similar errand to Rabbit and Hare. 'So we've both been released?' he said as Whistler concurred.

'I can't say I'm sorry,' Whistler admitted. 'The job

was definitely acquiring a considerable degree of tedium.'

'Well, I think we can say no-one ever heard a word of complaint from us,' Kestrel remarked. 'Though the same couldn't be said of Owl. His constant grumbling is enough to wear you down. Some days I simply can't bring myself to talk to him.'

'Oh, it's only his way,' laughed the good-natured heron. 'His heart's in the right place really.'

'D'you think so? I sometimes wonder. But I suppose you're right.' Kestrel gave Whistler a mischievous glance. 'Er – have you told Tawny Owl yet?' he asked.

'No,' replied Whistler. 'I suppose we'd better go and –' He broke off as he noticed Kestrel's expression. 'Are you thinking what I think you're thinking, Kestrel?'

Kestrel screeched with laughter. 'Undoubtedly,' he said.

'Well, I don't know. . . .' Whistler said hesitantly.

'Pah! Teach him a lesson!' Kestrel said shortly. 'He won't know we've stopped because he sleeps during the day.'

Whistler reluctantly agreed. He was not one for perpetrating jokes on others. 'But we mustn't let him continue for long,' he insisted.

So poor Tawny Owl carried on flying outside the Park at night to fetch what he could from the usual spot. The animals the food was destined for said nothing as they never saw him arrive with it, and assumed all the birds had changed their minds. Then one night, as he was flying over the road, Tawny Owl saw two figures which he thought he recognized. He paused with his load on a nearby bough to make sure. He did not need long to ascertain that it was the two poachers abroad again and seemingly on their way to the Park. He watched them long enough to see that they appeared to be unarmed, but decided to fly straight to Fox to warn him of their approach.

On his way he saw Badger ambling along. 'Good gracious!' Badger called up, seeing the bird with his load. 'Are you still doing that, Owl?'

Tawny Owl dropped what he was carrying at once and landed by Badger. '*What* did you say?' he demanded.

Badger unfortunately began to laugh. 'I think you've been the victim of someone's joke,' he chuckled. 'The other birds stopped flying to the dump days ago.'

Tawny Owl's beak dropped open. Then he snorted angrily. 'So that's it,' he said. 'That's how I'm treated for trying to help others.'

'Oh dear,' Badger muttered to himself. He thought quickly. 'No, no,' he said, 'they just forgot to tell you, I expect. Er – don't take it amiss,' he added hastily.

But Tawny Owl was in high dudgeon. He stalked round and round Badger, rustling his wings furiously and a hard glint came into his huge eyes. 'So they forgot, did they?' he hissed. 'We'll see how much forgetting *I* can do, then.' His last words were uttered with a menace that alarmed Badger, though he did not know that Tawny Owl was referring to the warning he had meant to bring. Then the bird flew off, climbing higher and higher in the sky until he was far away from any of his companions.

'Oh dear, oh dear,' wailed Badger. 'He's really angry now. I wish I hadn't laughed. Whatever did he mean by his last remark? I shall never know now, and it might have been important.'

'And after all,' he thought to himself as he trotted homeward, 'it wasn't a very nice trick. He *was* doing it for others. I wonder who's behind it?' He made his way to Fox's earth but Fox and Vixen were missing. Badger decided to wait.

When his friends eventually returned, Badger told them of Tawny Owl's feelings. Fox shook his head. 'He hates being made a fool of,' he said. 'He won't forget this for a long time. He's a very proud bird – and I think he's sensitive too, underneath. We've not been very kind to him.'

'*I* didn't know he was still collecting food,' Badger said.

'Neither did we,' said Vixen. 'It must be Kestrel's idea. He and Tawny Owl don't always see eye to eye.'

'But he'll be blaming *all* of us,' Fox said. 'He'll feel we've ganged up on him. I know him.'

'What can we do?' Badger asked. 'He flew a long way off. We may not see him for days.'

'Kestrel must apologise,' Fox said firmly. 'I shall tell him so.'

'Poor old Owl,' said kindly Vixen. 'It's not fair.'

As they conversed, none of them was aware that the poachers had entered the Park once again. It was Weasel who saw them approaching, but he stayed to watch. He knew where their guns lay and thought the men no longer posed a threat.

They seemed to be searching for *something* though, Weasel was sure, it could not be for the White Deer. He followed them, and was relieved to see they were going away from his and his friends' area of the Park. Suddenly one of the men nudged his companion and pointed. An animal was trotting briskly over the snowy patches only some ten yards away. Weasel could see plainly it was a fox. He knew it was not his fox because of the gait. Both men had pulled pistols from their pockets. One of them fired immediately at the animal but missed. The fox stopped in its tracks and, for a second, glanced back. It saw the men and started to run. But it was not quick enough. Another shot, this time from the other pistol, brought it down.

Weasel, keeping well out of sight and with a fiercely pounding heart, saw the men walk over to the stricken creature and examine it. One of them put a boot under its body and turned it over. It was quite dead. But the men were not satisfied. They did not turn back as if intending to leave the Park, but continued on their way in the same furtive, searching manner. Weasel followed them no longer. He needed to see no more to recognize the men's purpose. It was imperative to find Fox and Vixen.

Luckily the two distant cracks of the pistols had been heard by them and Badger, and they were debating what the new sounds of guns could mean when the breathless Weasel found them.

'It's the same two men,' he told them. 'But they're not after deer. They've got small guns and they've just shot a fox.'

Fox and Vixen both gulped nervously.

'You *must* take cover underground,' Weasel went on. 'They – ' he broke off as another shot was heard. The four animals looked at each other in horror.

'They're after all the foxes,' whispered Vixen. 'I dreaded this.'

'No,' said Fox grimly. 'They're after me. It's revenge they want for the trick I played them. They'll kill every fox they can in the hope that one of them will be me.'

Weasel nodded miserably. 'That's exactly the conclusion I came to,' he said. 'Please, Fox, take shelter.'

With a dazed expression, Fox allowed himself to be led to his earth where he numbly followed Vixen underground.

'We'd better make ourselves scarce, too,' Weasel said to Badger. 'We must have been seen at the pond-side along with Fox. We can't be too careful.'

In his den Fox was shaking his head and muttering, 'What have I done? What have I done?'

'You did what you thought best,' Vixen soothed him. 'And it was a brilliant plan.'

'But what have I achieved?' Fox demanded. 'I've set our enemies more firmly against us. The deer might be saved – they can't shoot *them* with pistols – but now I've brought even greater danger to *us*.'

'You weren't to know this would happen,' she assured him. 'You acted with the best intentions.'

Fox stood up. 'But how can I skulk around here while innocent creatures are being shot?' he cried. 'It's *me* they want. How many other foxes have to die while I hide away? I'm putting every other fox in the Park at risk.'

'And what do you intend to do?' Vixen asked angrily. 'Run up to the humans and offer yourself as a sacrifice?'

'At least if they killed me they would be satisfied. Then the Park *would* be safe again.'

'Don't talk such foolishness, Fox,' Vixen said in desperation, seeing the look on his face. 'Will they recognize you as the fox who made fools of them? To a human we all look the same. You would be killed and still they would hunt for others.'

'Then they *will* kill every fox,' he said. 'Only in that way can they be sure they have got rid of me.'

'Is it likely with the sounds of guns again, that any wild creature will stay abroad? By now they'll all be lying low,' Vixen said.

Fox looked at her and marvelled. '*You* are the wise one, dear Vixen,' he said, 'not I.'

'Pooh, you're merely blinded by your concern,' she replied.

'But what can I do?' he moaned.

Vixen knew how to handle her mate. 'You devised a

plan before. Now you must use your wits again,' she said. 'It's your brain that's our safety measure.'

Fox smiled and was already calmer as he settled down to think. 'Whatever did I do before we met?' he murmured. 'My brave counsellor.'

——17——
...Deserves Another

Tawny Owl, feeling very aggrieved, had flown as far away from his friends in the Park as he could without actually flying over its boundaries. His pride was hurt and, as he moodily munched his supper, his indignation grew with every mouthful.

'Serves them right if they never see me again,' he muttered. 'And a fat lot they'd care if they didn't.' He went and hunched himself up on a sycamore branch and brooded. With each minute he felt more and more unwanted. He had done the worst possible thing for himself by disassociating from all those he knew. For, on his own, he had nothing to do but brood over his misery; whereas in company a cheery word or two from someone would have made him forget his hurts far more quickly.

However, in his own company, he had no appearances to keep up; no risk of losing face. He began to wonder after a while if he had over-reacted. He sat and thought.

It was probably not true that all the animals had collaborated to make him look a fool. Fox, he was sure, would never be a party to such a thing. And neither would Badger, although he had chuckled at his discomfiture. The more he thought of Fox, of whom he was genuinely fond, the more guilty he felt. To what fate might he have consigned Fox and Vixen by not warning them of the return of the poachers? They surely had been cn the way to the Park, and who could say for what purpose? He shifted about on the branch, feeling more and morc uncomfortable and nervous. If anything had happened, he could never forgive himself. In the end he could stay put no longer. He leapt from the bough and sallied forth in the direction in which he had first spotted the men.

The darkness was fading as he flew over the Park, and he spied the poachers in the act of clambering back through the fence before they jumped the ditch. He was glad they were leaving, but was fearful of what they might have left behind them. A little further on he saw something that made his stomach turn over. The body of a fox lay crumpled on the snow, its red blood mingling with the white ground. Tawny Owl, of course, immediately thought the worst. He had murdered Fox. He fluttered to a tree and sank down, overcome by weakness. Drained of all feeling, he contemplated his own selfishness. It was a long time before he could force himself to approach the body. At length, with a heavy heart and wings of lead, he managed to fly over to it.

As he came close he knew it was not Fox; neither was it Vixen. His spirits lifted, but only for a few brief minutes. Because, not very much further away, a second fox corpse greeted his sight. This time he examined it at once. A second time he was relieved. But now he wondered how many deaths had occurred. Was his friend lying dead somewhere after all? He flew off again, combing the ground afresh as he went. He went this way and that, and then back again, frantically searching the Reserve yard by yard for the sight he dreaded to see. None of the night creatures watched Tawny Owl's agony. For a long time they had been in refuge. But as the sun came up, Tawny Owl dropped with exhaustion. And there – high, high up in the glittering blue of the winter sky Kestrel soared, and saw him fall.

Later in the day Mole, whose joy in tunnelling had been unindulged while the ground had been at its hardest, now found his freedom restored. Where the snow had melted the ground was very soft once any overnight frost had disappeared. Mole had made a new shaft that ran up to the surface, and was poking his head into the open, his pink snout quivering excitedly. As it happened he was almost squashed by a hoof of the Great Stag who was walking that way.

The giant animal looked down at the tiny velvet-clad body beneath him. 'I beg your pardon,' he said. 'I didn't see you at first. I'm looking for your friend Fox. I understand the humans returned to the Park last night.'

'Yes, Badger told me of it,' replied Mole. 'We all thought we'd seen the last of them.'

'Your leader is very brave and doesn't always think of himself. It appears that he may have piled up some trouble for his efforts the other night. It is now our turn to assist him. Hence the reason for my visit.'

Mole gave the Stag directions to Fox's earth, and went to tell Badger of his encounter.

Fox and Vixen were not in their den. They were out foraging, for it had now become unsafe to leave shelter at night. So the Great Stag, having assured himself of their absence, passed the time by grazing where he could until they should return. Eventually he saw them coming as he chewed a mouthful of moss.

'Greetings,' he said simply. 'I've come to inform you that the entire deer herd is at your disposal if you need us in your *new* dispute with the human killers.'

Fox listened to the Stag's gentle tone of irony. 'I fear there's nothing new about it,' he replied. 'I have always looked upon them as our enemies as well as yours.'

'Have you decided on any course of action should they return again?'

'Oh, they'll be back,' Fox said. 'I hardly think they'll be satisfied with their work so far. Kestrel tells me there are two dead foxes. The men must know there are many more than that still living.'

'My advice would be for us to stay under cover every night until they decide to come no more,' said Vixen, 'but Fox won't listen.'

'Simply because we have no way of knowing their intentions,' he explained. 'How long would it be before they came looking for us in our earths? Then there *would* be no escape.'

'You have a plan then?' the Stag asked.

'Only a poor one, I'm afraid. But it may work.'

'I am all ears.'

'To be honest,' began Fox, 'it isn't really a plan at all. I've merely been thinking along the lines of finding the safest spot in the Park and then going there. It occurred to me that there is one place these poaching humans might perhaps not care to venture to, and that is the grounds of the Warden's own garden, around the Lodge. If we holed up in there we might avoid them.'

'Hm,' the Stag murmured, considering. 'And what of the other foxes in the Reserve?'

'My immediate concern, naturally, is for my mate and my friends,' Fox said. 'But it would, no doubt, be possible to pass the word to them, in case they should feel like joining us.'

'I can foresee problems,' the Stag commented. 'These other foxes haven't the same feelings for your friends as you have. I should imagine they would look upon the presence of your mouse and rabbit friends as a ready-made food supply.'

'There would be no need for the voles and fieldmice to leave their homes,' answered Fox. 'The humans are not interested in small fry like them. But it's true; the question of the rabbits needs some thought.'

'Well, I have an idea that might make yours unnecessary,' the Great Stag told him, 'if you are willing to go along with it. It is perfectly simple. If the humans return, and appear to be bent on killing again, I have orders for the whole of my herd to charge them *en masse*. With that sort of force arraigned against them, I don't think they will need a lot of persuading to leave.'

'What if they use their pistols on the deer?' asked Fox.

'We're quite prepared for the possibility,' answered the Stag. 'But it's a risk we must take. We feel it is time we repaid your good turn to us. In any case, I honestly doubt if these wretched humans will stand still long enough when they see us all thundering towards them. There will be more than a few pairs of lowered antlers for them to negotiate.'

Fox and Vixen could not help but chuckle as they pictured the scene. 'I think it's an admirable and very generous idea,' said Vixen.

'It's certainly that,' agreed Fox. 'The only thing that comes into my mind is, that it could only work once. If

they are still determined to enter the Park after that,
they would make sure of the herd's whereabouts first.
You can't cover every corner.'

'Then we must make sure our charge is so terrifying
that they are dissuaded for good from coming back,' the
Stag said. 'Are you willing to give it a try?'

'Assuredly, yes.'

'Then I'll go to make preparations.'

'I will arrange for sentries along the perimeter as
before,' Fox said. He turned to Vixen. 'I wonder what
happened to Tawny Owl?'

Kestrel knew. He had found the exhausted owl on the
open ground, without even the strength to fly up into a
tree.

'I'm glad you've come back,' said the hawk, 'but sorry
to see you in this state.'

Tawny Owl slowly shook his head, too weak to reply.

'I have an apology to make,' Kestrel went on. 'At
Fox's insistence. I'm afraid I'm to blame for not telling
you to stop flying to the dump. It was a rotten trick and
I very much regret it.'

Tawny Owl blinked once or twice and nodded. 'All
– for – gotten,' he gasped.

'You need something to eat to restore your strength,'
said Kestrel. 'I'll see if I can – '

'No,' said Tawny Owl. 'Just rest.'

'But you can't stay on the ground – too vulnerable,'
insisted the hawk.

'Can't – fly. Too – weak,' came the reply.

'I see. Well, I'll keep a look-out until you've recovered
a bit.'

From the sky, where he floated effortlessly on air currents or hovered in his inimitable way, Kestrel could see

Mole, the Great Stag, Fox and Vixen. He wondered what was afoot. After checking once or twice on Tawny Owl's progress, he swooped down to speak to Fox.

'I've found Owl,' he said. 'Goodness knows where he's been. He's completely exhausted.'

'Where is he?' Fox asked. 'I need him tonight.'

'Don't know if he's much use at the moment,' said Kestrel. 'What's astir?'

Fox explained the Great Stag's idea.

'I understand,' said the hawk. 'I'll take you to Tawny Owl.'

The sight of Fox approaching him across the parkland was the best medicine for Tawny Owl that could have been produced. Now, at last, he knew his friend was safe. He tottered to his feet and stood, a little unsteadily.

'My dear Owl,' Fox said in great distress. 'Whatever has happened? You look dreadful.'

'It's all right – now,' said Tawny Owl. 'Thank heaven you're still alive. And Vixen too?'

'Yes. She's well.'

'I'm so glad. I saw the men last night – with guns. I meant to tell you, but – well, you know how I react when my pride takes a blow. I'm sure Badger has told you he saw me carrying the – er – well, you know,' he finished lamely.

'I understand perfectly,' said Fox. 'I won't question you any further. None of us will. But you must rest all you can. I shall need you as a look-out again tonight. Will you be able?'

'By then I shall have recovered,' Tawny Owl assured him. 'I think I can fly a little now. I'll go home and sleep properly. Where will you need me?'

'The same place as before. Our friends the deer are preparing a little reception committee.'

Tawny Owl nodded and, still bleary-eyed, took his leave.

'Kestrel,' said Fox. 'I'm relying on you to get the others to their places by the fence. They must be there by dusk.'

'Your wish,' answered Kestrel, 'is my command.'

'Very well,' said Fox. 'And tonight I, for once, shall stay firmly in the background.'

Sure enough, Fox's belief in the poachers' persistence in revenge was proved well-founded. This time they were spotted early on in the evening and the message was passed back along the lines to the Great Stag who quickly mustered his herd. It was then necessary for Fox, Vixen, Badger and Weasel to make themselves scarce before the advance of the men. Along with Hare and the birds, they decided to watch events from the Hollow from where, if necessary, they could make a quick escape to their homes.

The poachers seemed to be in a very ugly mood. Any sign of movement anywhere was enough to set them shooting and, at each report, the watching Farthing Wood animals shuddered at what might have been the fate of some unsuspecting night creature.

Foot by foot, the men entered further into the Park. Foot by foot they decreased the distance between themselves and the White Deer. The deer waited in some agitation. They disliked standing still as danger approached. Some cropped the grass nervously, while others tossed their heads and flicked their short tails. Only the Great Stag, at their head, stood impassive.

They saw the men getting closer from behind the line of trees that helped to screen them. The Great Stag's eyes narrowed as he waited for the right moment. The men remained ignorant. Then he threw his head back and roared like a stag in rut. The deer herd bounded

through the trees and raced towards the poachers. The
men looked up, startled, at the white mass that galloped
towards them, their hooves thundering as in a stampede;
a forest of antlers lowered in line. With shouts the men
turned and began to run hell for leather back across the
grassland. Neither paused a second to take aim. They
could only run and run, as fast as they could, away from
the white animal tide that threatened to engulf them.
Fear lent wings to their feet, for otherwise they must
have been caught.

As they neared the Park fence, the deer slackened
their pace and swept round in a circle, back towards the
open land where they usually stayed, the Great Stag still
leading them. The men had gone.

From the Hollow came excited voices.

'Did it work? Have they gone?' asked Hare.

Tawny Owl flew to see. 'Yes, they've gone,' he
reported.

'And this time for good,' said Badger.

'How are you so sure?' Weasel wanted to know. 'We
all believed that last time.'

'Twice they've been defeated by animals,' said
Badger. 'Are they prepared to risk a third tussle?'

'Only if,' said Tawny Owl slowly, 'they are sure they
can win.'

Fox looked at him. 'Well,' he said, 'we still have my
idea in reserve.'

—18—

Two Friends Return

All was quiet again in White Deer Park for some days.
But in the last invasion by the poachers another of the
Farthing Wood rabbits had lost its life – this time by
the gun, for the men had shot indiscriminately. Fox felt
this loss more deeply than any, for he knew that it was
he that had, indirectly, caused the death of one of his
friends. Rabbit had come to inform him of the death.

'Another one of our does gone,' he had said after
explaining how he had found the body. 'And this Park
was to be a haven for us! What sort of a haven is it when
we rabbits have been thinned out to a mere remnant of
those that lived in Farthing Wood?'

'I know, I know,' Fox answered miserably. 'I've had
the same from Vole and Fieldmouse. It's very distress-

ing. We couldn't have expected such a terrible winter
– nor this other threat to our survival. The idea of a
Nature Reserve is that it should be a sanctuary for all
wildlife within. These murderous humans seem to have
no respect even for their own laws.'

'Well, let's hope the winter has sent its worst,' rejoined
Rabbit. 'But what can we expect from the humans?'

'Who knows?' Fox answered frankly. 'They may be
back again. They may not. Shall we try and be optimistic
about it?'

'I suppose it's all we *can* do,' agreed Rabbit.

'At any rate,' Fox said brightly, 'you rabbits will soon
be back at your usual numbers, I'll warrant. Your powers of recovery, you know . . . .'

'Why is it the only thing we seem to be renowned for
is how fast we breed?' Rabbit wanted to know. 'I bet
we're no more prolific than the mice. But, you see, Fox,
any danger that's around inhibits our desire to breed.
You know how timid we are.'

'I do indeed,' Fox said. 'Never ever will I forget the
river crossing.' He referred to an incident during the
animals' long journey to the Park when the rabbits had
panicked badly and caused a disaster.

'All right, all right,' nodded Rabbit. 'Neither am I
ever likely to, even if allowed.'

'No hurt intended, I assure you,' said Fox quickly.

'Don't mention it,' was the reply. Then Rabbit smiled.
'Where else in the Wild would a fox talk so politely to
a rabbit?'

Fox smiled back, and Rabbit turned to go.

The afternoon brought an excited Kestrel to Fox's
earth. His piercing cries brought Fox and Vixen hurriedly to the surface.

'What is it, Kestrel? You *do* seem in a state,' Fox said.

'I've just spotted that ginger cat walking in the Warden's garden,' he shrieked.

Fox misunderstood the motive for the hawk's excitement. 'Calm down, calm down,' he said. 'You just make sure you don't go in too close, and he won't attack you again. Your scars healed perfectly, didn't they?'

'No, no, it's not that,' Kestrel said hurriedly. 'I hadn't even thought of it. You don't seem to have grasped the significance of the cat's reappearance. The Warden must be back!' He looked triumphantly at the pair of foxes, as if he had brought the man and his cat back personally.

'Of course!' said Fox. 'The cat disappeared at the same time, didn't he? Oh but, Kestrel, can we be sure?'

'I would have hovered around a little longer to *make* sure,' said Kestrel, 'but I wanted to bring you the news.'

'It's marvellous news,' said Vixen. 'It means we can all breathe again. The poachers won't dare come back now.'

'I'll fly straight back and see if I can spot our protector,' Kestrel offered. 'Then we can spread the word.'

'Oh, this calls for a celebration,' said Fox happily. 'If the Warden is indeed back with us our worries are over.'

The Warden *had* returned and, to prove it, was seen on his rounds later in the day by many of the animals. Badger and Fox stood together by Badger's set talking.

'What changes will he see since he went away?' Badger mused. 'If only we could tell him of those who have been killed.'

'If he counts the head of white deer he will see their numbers have dropped,' said Fox. 'But he may not be suspicious of it.'

'How I wish those slaughterers could be brought before him,' growled Badger. 'Why should they escape their punishment?'

'Well, we're helpless in the matter,' said Fox. 'But, at

least, no more creatures will meet their fate in the Park
at *their* hands.'

Little did Fox imagine then that Badger's wish was to
be fulfilled, and that the animals of Farthing Wood were
to be the instruments of bringing the offenders to justice.
For the poachers, ignorant of the Warden's return, were
about to make one trip too many to the Nature Reserve.

Fox's own cunning, which perhaps led him to antici-
pate better than other creatures the way humans might
behave, was to be proved right again in his doubts
expressed to the Great Stag. The poachers, it seemed,
were still determined to wreak revenge where they could,
although they now knew they must avoid the deer herd.
That very evening they entered the Park at a different
point, intent on redressing the balance in their favour
by the work of their pistols.

Relieved, as they thought, of the need to stay under
cover at night, a lot of the animals, as well as Tawny
Owl, were abroad at the time on their various errands.
But, separated as they were, they all stopped in their
tracks at the same instant as they heard once more the
report of a gun.

Fox and Vixen were, as usual, together. 'I don't believe it,' Vixen whispered. 'They can't have come back
again.'

'The noise came from that direction,' Fox indicated.
'We haven't heard it from there before.' He scowled.
'The murdering scoundrels,' he said thickly. 'Come on,
Vixen, we'd better get back.'

But Vixen did not move.

'What's the matter?' Fox asked. 'We can't stay here.'

'Perhaps it would be better *not* to go back,' Vixen said
cryptically.

Fox looked at her in astonishment.

'Do you recall your latest plan?' she reminded him.

'The Warden's garden?' he asked. 'But it's not necessary, now he's back. These men are *his* quarrel now.'

'Exactly,' replied his mate. 'And we can lead him to them – or rather *them* to him.'

'Phew!' gasped Fox. 'That's a little ambitious – even for us.'

'Yes, it is,' she acknowledged. 'But don't we all want these men caught? Well, we *could* make that more likely.'

Fox, as so often, looked at her in sheer admiration. 'You are a wonder,' he said. 'I'm sure we *could* do it. But we must be very, very careful.'

At the sound of the gun Tawny Owl had automatically played his part. He flew straight to where the shot had been fired to locate the danger. He saw the men and, this time, no victim. The shot had gone astray. Back in the direction of the home area he winged his way and, spying Fox and Vixen from the air, told them what he had found. Fox sent him to warn Badger, Weasel and any of the others around to exercise the utmost caution, and to tell them of Vixen's suggestion. Silently Tawny Owl flew off.

'I want to handle this myself,' Fox said to her. 'I don't want you at risk too.'

'I'll stay well clear,' she replied. 'But I'll be right behind you.'

Fox slunk off through the shadows to offer himself as bait to the poachers, while Vixen crept in his wake, twenty yards distant. The men were easily spotted, stirring up the dead undergrowth with sticks for any hapless creature cowering beneath. But Fox, safe behind a broad oak tree, yapped as he had yapped before in their hearing. The men looked up and saw a shadowy figure under the trees. At once they gave chase, both firing haphazardly. Fox, his body close to the ground, sped away through the copse towards the Warden's Lodge. Behind the men ran Vixen, nervous, frightened, but with every nerve tingling.

Tawny Owl had rounded up Badger, Hare, Weasel and Rabbit. Then he went on to inform the Great Stag and the deer herd. Together all these animals began to converge from different directions on the focal point. No-one wanted to be left out of the adventure, and Rabbit had a particular wish to see himself avenged. The lights were on in the cottage, for the Warden also had heard the gunfire and was preparing to investigate. Badger even spotted Ginger Cat roaming outside the door. All seemed to be set for the finale.

Fox ran swiftly on a looping course for the cottage lights, making himself moderate his speed to keep the men within distance of him. As he neared his goal, he saw the Warden framed in the doorway and, to the left of the Lodge, the deer herd milling about in spectral array. Too late the poachers saw where they were running and stopped. As they tried to swing away to run from their fate, the deer herd rushed towards them, surrounding them, and buffeted them off their feet. The Warden raced over and shouted back towards his open door. While Fox and Vixen delightedly mingled with their watching friends a second man, whom Badger recognized as the animal doctor, ran out of the house. The poachers were collared and marched indoors. For a moment, in the doorway, the Warden turned back. He looked at the array of wild creatures strangely gathered together before his home. Each one of them looked towards him, and an expression came over his face of a wonderful compassion and affection that lit an answering flame in their own hearts. The moment passed, but there was a timelessness about it that was never to be forgotten. When he had gone, the most complete and utter silence reigned.

Finally the Great Stag spoke, rather stumblingly and inadequately. He was greatly moved. 'My friends, today we have formed a new bond of companionship,' he said. 'Today we are at one with Nature – er – and humanity.'

No-one else spoke or moved. The air above, the ground beneath were shot with magic; a strange echo of an Ancient World that none of them could comprehend had sounded in White Deer Park.

—19—

Thaw

The spell was broken by the movement of Ginger Cat who walked nonchalantly over to Badger. He seemed quite undeterred by the memory of their fight.

'We meet again,' he purred enigmatically.

Badger nodded. 'I hope in happier circumstances?' he ventured.

'Certainly,' came the reply. 'I'm quite aware I owe my life to your forbearance. Er – how is your friend the hawk?'

'Perfectly well,' answered Badger. 'And yourself?'

'Oh, couldn't be better,' the cat said. 'But I must say I'm relieved to be back here. I was taken to a spot miles away and shut up with a lot of other cats in cages while my mast – ah, I mean the man, was treated for his illness.'

Badger smiled at the cat's slip of the tongue, and Ginger Cat smiled back. He and Badger knew each other pretty well.

Fox and Vixen came over for a word, and the Great Stag led the deer herd away.

'Well, you all look a lot happier since I saw you last,' said Ginger Cat. 'And I'm glad to see, Fox, you've put on a little weight.'

'Oh yes,' said Fox. 'We've had some hard times, but we've come through all right.'

Badger recalled Toad's last words before hibernation when he had wished they would all 'come through' the winter. How long ago that seemed. And now, with the temperature steadily rising, they could all look forward to their friend's re-appearance. But, of course, they had not all 'come through'. What changes Toad would see in their numbers.

'You seem very pensive, Badger,' remarked Ginger Cat. 'What is it?'

'Oh, nothing really,' he said. 'Just thinking of old friends.'

Weasel, Tawny Owl, Hare and Rabbit joined them.

'Three times we've overcome those humans,' Rabbit said proudly. 'They must think the Park is jinxed.'

'The ones we've just seen caught?' Ginger Cat enquired. 'What happened before? You must tell me your news.'

'I will,' Badger offered. 'But another time, my feline friend. It's been quite a night.'

Hare felt inclined to mention to his cousin Rabbit that he had not seen *him* much in evidence on the two previous occasions, but decided against it. It was not a time for needless criticism.

The animals and Tawny Owl bid Ginger Cat farewell and, together, wandered slowly away from the cottage.

'I think we're entitled to have that celebration now,' Vixen said to her mate.

'Yes, I think so too. Now, truly, our troubles are over.'

'But our party is incomplete,' said Badger. 'It would be churlish to ignore the hedgehogs and, most of all, Toad.'

'Pooh, there's no knowing when *they'll* be back with us,' said Rabbit. 'And in any case they've played no part in our adventures.'

Now Hare felt he must intervene. 'I think some of us here present could hardly be said to have played much more of a part than they have,' he said pointedly. The remark was not lost on any of the others, Rabbit included. He looked a little foolish.

'Well, well, that's as may be,' said Badger, smoothing things over. 'But I don't think any of us need to have particular qualifications to enjoy ourselves together.'

'Why don't we make it a double celebration?' suggested Vixen. 'To mark our survival through our first winter and also to rejoice at seeing our hibernating friends again.'

'I think that's an excellent idea, Vixen,' said Badger. 'Don't you, Fox?'

'I do. Incidentally, does anyone realize we've none of us thought of Adder?'

'Certainly a case of out of sight, out of mind,' Tawny Owl remarked. 'But then, he's never the most genial of characters.'

'Nevertheless, it would be unthinkable not to have him with us,' Badger declared. 'In his own way, he's been a loyal enough friend.'

'As I have cause to remember,' murmured Vixen.

'Then it's postponed until the spring?' Weasel summarized.

'Perhaps not quite that long,' said Fox. 'The first

really mild spell will bring the hedgehogs out. And probably Toad, too. I'm not exactly sure how long snakes need to sleep.'

As February progressed to its conclusion, the final traces of snow and ice disappeared completely from the Park. The long, hard winter, which had begun so early, released its grip at last. Everything pointed to the fact that a warm spring was approaching, perhaps sooner than usual. Mild breezes blew and, underfoot, the ground was soft and spongy with water where the snow had melted. Most days were blessed with sunshine, however, which prevented the Reserve from becoming too waterlogged.

Already the earliest buds were swelling when the hedgehogs climbed out of their beds of thick leaves and twigs. Their first thought was food, and insects, slugs and spiders were in such abundance because of the mild weather, that they could never have guessed that for months previously their friends had battled against starvation. The hedgehogs' elected leader, having feasted grandly, went to look for signs of his old travelling companions.

As always, Kestrel was the first to spot this new movement on the ground. He dived downwards to intercept his recently emerged friend. 'Hallo, Hedgehog! Hallo!' he called as he hurtled down.

'Kestrel! It's good to see you!' said Hedgehog enthusiastically. 'How have you been?'

'Better than most,' Kestrel informed him. 'How did you sleep?'

Hedgehog laughed. 'Like a log – as always,' he replied. 'And the others? Have they fared well?'

'Not all of them, I'm afraid. You have been well out of the troubles we've experienced since we last saw you.'

'Dear, dear,' said Hedgehog. 'Has it been a bad winter, then?'

'The worst any of us can remember,' answered Kestrel. 'And that includes Badger.'

'But tell me,' Hedgehog said, looking concerned, 'have any lost their lives?'

'Many,' said the hawk simply. 'The voles are reduced to a single pair – Vole himself and his mate – and the fieldmice only one better. The rabbits have suffered badly, too. And the squirrels have had their losses.'

'This is shocking,' responded Hedgehog. 'I never expected anything like this. But Fox, Badger, Vixen . . .?'

'The larger animals have all survived – but only just. I tell you, Hedgehog, you can't conceive how near to death we all were. I think this winter has left its mark on everyone.'

'Is little Mole then – ?'

'No, no. He's all right. I think he suffered less than anyone. It appears his beloved worms are easier to find in cold weather – it restricts their movements.'

Hedgehog nodded. 'And the other birds?'

'Yes, Owl and Whistler have made it, too. But the winter hasn't been the only thing we've had to contend with.'

'Good gracious! What else?'

'Well, come along. Come and see the others and you'll hear all about it. I'll meet you at Badger's set.'

So Hedgehog made his way along and soon was surrounded by a number of the other animals. Together they told him of the harrowing events during the preceding months. At the end of it, he felt glad and relieved that *some* of his friends were there to greet him.

'And I've slept through it all in blissful ignorance,' he said wonderingly.

'Best thing to have done,' Hare told him. 'You've had a happy release.'

With the re-appearance of the hedgehogs, the animals knew that their party, although reduced, would soon be together again. One particularly warm morning in early March they all decided to make the trip to the Pond, as Badger was quite convinced that Toad and Adder would be tempted by its pleasantness from their burrow.

As they approached the water, the scene of such a dramatic occurrence during the winter, there were already signs of activity. The Edible Frogs had woken and were splashing about furiously, or sitting by the water's edge, croaking. And nearby, on a sunny slope, basking delightedly in the warm rays of the sun, who should they find but Adder?

'Mmmm,' he murmured dreamily as he spied the company, 'don't talk to me. I'm not really awake yet.'

The animals laughed but ignored his request.

'Certainly not alert,' Fox corrected him, referring to his proximity to the frogs, 'but definitely awake.'

'Where's Toad?' Badger asked. 'Did you leave him behind?'

'Oh no,' drawled Adder. 'When I awoke the hole was quite empty. He must have decided to greet the sun before me.'

'I wonder where he is,' said Badger. 'We couldn't have missed him.'

'I've no idea,' said the snake. 'But please – leave me. Let me doze.'

'Unsociable old so-and-so,' muttered Tawny Owl. 'We'll get no sense out of him for the moment.'

Fox was looking for the patriarch of the Pond, the large frog that knew Toad best. Perhaps he could throw some light on Toad's absence. He found him, newly glistening, surveying the scene from a piece of flat rock.

'Oh yes, I saw him,' he answered in reply to Fox's question. 'Two days ago. He was making off towards the Park boundary.'

'*What*!?'

'Yes – there, in that direction.'

The animals were stunned. What could he be up to?

'Perhaps he's lost his memory,' piped up Mole. 'During his long sleep, I mean,' he added, thinking he may have sounded silly.

'You all seem to have lost yours,' rejoined Adder in his lazy lisp. 'It's obvious what's happened. It's Spring. Toad's returning to his birthplace.' His red eyes glinted in the sun as he looked at their astonished faces contemptuously. 'He's on his way back to Farthing Wood.'

—20—
Whistled Off

The rest of the animals and the birds were dumbfounded. They looked at each other with blank faces. It was too incredible. Yet it had happened before. They all owed their knowledge of the Park's existence to Toad, who had discovered it and travelled across country for the best part of a year to bring news of it to the beleaguered Farthing Wood. On that occasion, however, he had been returning to his old home – Farthing Pond – only to find it had disappeared; destroyed by humans.

'But *this* is Toad's home now,' said Squirrel. 'He led us here. His old home no longer exists. How can he have forgotten all that?'

'I think he can't help himself,' observed Kestrel. 'It's his homing instinct. In the Spring it's like an irresistible

urge that draws Toad and creatures like him back to
their birthplace to spawn and reproduce themselves.
And Toad's birthplace was Farthing Pond.'

'It's quite true,' agreed Tawny Owl. 'None of us can
forget when, on our journey here, Toad started doubling
back because the pull of his old home was still so strong.'

'Well, he can't have gone far,' said Fox. 'Not in two
days. We must find him and reason with him.'

'No time like the present,' said Badger. 'He may not
even have left the Reserve yet.'

'I'll see if I can spot him,' Kestrel offered. 'But his
camouflage is so good it might be difficult.'

'There's no need for us all to go,' said Fox. 'That
would only delay things. Badger and I will go with
Vixen and, Whistler, perhaps you can assist Kestrel in
the search?'

'I shall be delighted to do anything in my power,' said
the heron, flapping his wings and making his familiar
whistling noise.

'We'll visit you again, Adder,' Fox told the still motionless snake. 'I hope by then our party will be
complete.'

'You can visit if you wish,' replied Adder. 'But I can't
guarantee to be in the same spot. I have other things to
do apart from lying around here waiting for your return.'

'Ungracious as ever,' said Tawny Owl loudly, but
Adder was quite used to such remarks and only flicked
his forked tongue in and out in a derogatory manner.

While the other animals dispersed, the two foxes and
Badger trotted off in the direction of the Hollow. It was
here they had all spent their first night on arriving in
White Deer Park, and it was close to the hole in the
fence through which they had first entered. Fox was
quite sure Toad would be travelling on the same route
if he had, indeed, intended to leave the Reserve.

Fox and Vixen skirted the Hollow while Badger entered it to make quite certain Toad was not safely there, all the time waiting for his friends at the traditional meeting-point. But he was not, and when they arrived at the boundary on this side of the Park they found Kestrel waiting for them.

'No sign as yet,' he announced. 'I think he must be outside.'

'What a nuisance he is,' said Badger. 'Now we'll all be exposing ourselves to risk on his behalf.'

'It's obvious we can't stay together outside the Park,' said Fox. 'We shall be far too conspicuous. But he can't possibly be far away, travelling at his pace. Kestrel, can you scout around in the immediate area for a bit? He may only be a matter of a few paces away.'

But when Kestrel alighted again the answer was the same. Whistler, too, had had no luck. 'There seems to be a distinct dearth of toads in the area,' he informed them in his droll way.

'There's nothing for it, then,' said Fox, 'but that we'll have to go through the fence. We'll split up and try a separate patch each.'

'Wouldn't it be wiser for you to leave it until nightfall?' suggested Kestrel.

'Safer, yes,' admitted Fox. 'But more difficult. Toad is a small animal and would be even harder to locate in the dark.'

'We'll keep our eyes open for you all, then,' said Kestrel. 'And we can warn you if necessary.'

'Thanks,' said Fox. 'Well, Vixen, Badger, shall we go?'

The three animals passed singly through the broken fence and Fox allotted them each their areas. 'If you find him,' he said to them, 'make the birds understand and they can round up the other two of us.'

So they each went their different ways, using sight and scent in their search.

It was Vixen in the end who found their lost friend. Perhaps half a mile from where she left the Park a narrow and normally shallow little brook ran bubbling across country. On its banks sat two small boys watching the water – now swollen by the thaw – run gurgling past them. Occasionally they would dip their nets into the stream, for they were collecting sticklebacks and water-bugs and anything else that came along. By their side on the bank were some big jars full of water into which they were emptying their nets whenever they caught a new specimen. All this Vixen saw as she approached as close as she could before having to hide herself among some gorse scrub. From this vantage point she could watch securely and see everything. What she saw in one of the jars made her heart skip a beat. For it was a toad, and she knew that, as likely as not, it was her toad. But then she was not so sure, for another of the jars also contained a toad, and this one was considerably larger than the other.

The two poor entombed creatures were jumping up and down in the water inside the jars, banging their blunt noses against the glass in frenzied and utterly useless attempts to escape. Their exit was firmly sealed by metal lids. Now Vixen was in a dilemma. For there was nothing she could do to free the toads. Yet she knew she must prevent the boys taking the jars away with them before she knew if her friend was one of the captives. She certainly needed Fox's advice and as quickly as possible, because the boys might choose to leave at any time.

From the safety of the gorse-bushes she barked, hoping one of the birds might be close. She saw the boys look up at the noise, and peer all about them. But they could see nothing, and soon turned their attention to the stream again.

Neither Kestrel nor Whistler heard Vixen's call, but Whistler had seen the stream and the boys while on the wing and now came looking for the three animals to warn them of the presence of humans. Luckily, as Vixen was closest, he found her first.

'I've seen them,' she nodded as he landed awkwardly beside her. 'And I think I've seen Toad.'

'Perfect!' cried the heron. 'Then we can collect him and make a hasty retreat.'

'It's not as simple as that, I'm afraid, Whistler,' she answered, and explained what was in the glass jars.

'How awful! Whatever can we do?' he boomed.

'I don't know. But you must bring Fox. He'll think of something. And tell Badger, too.'

'At once,' said the heron and flapped noisily into flight again. Vixen shuddered as she saw his huge form rise above her, immediately catching the attention of the two fascinated little humans who began to point and chatter excitedly. Fortunately, however, they did not move from the stream bank.

Fox and Badger came quietly and cautiously to join Vixen behind her prickly screen. They listened to her news.

'Of course it may not be Toad,' said Fox, 'but, naturally, we can't take the chance.'

'Oh dear, oh dear,' said Badger anxiously. 'Poor creatures. This is just the same way he was captured in Farthing Pond and brought all this way from his home.'

'A blessing in disguise, as it turned out,' Fox reminded him. 'Otherwise there would have been no White Deer Park for *us*.'

'I know, I know,' Badger nodded. 'But it is no blessing this time.'

'Well, there's only one thing to do,' declared Fox resolutely. 'We must rescue both these toads.'

'Of course. But how?'

'We'll take the captors by surprise. They're young. They may scare easily. If we all rush on them together, barking and snarling, they may run. To take them by surprise is our only hope. Hallo, here's Kestrel!'

Whistler had also informed Kestrel of developments. No sooner had he heard than the hawk had flown close to the brook, hovering as he examined the jars' contents with his phenomenal eye power. He came swooping up to the three animals. 'One of them is Toad all right,' he screeched. 'The smaller one.'

'Get Whistler back here,' Fox ordered peremptorily. 'I have need of his great bill.'

The heron came wheeling low to listen to the plan.

'As we make our charge you must sail in and snatch the jar up in your bill. Make sure it's the one with the smaller of the two toads inside,' Fox told him. 'Right, all ready? Together then!'

Across the grass hurtled Fox, Badger and Vixen making the utmost racket possible. The two boys jumped up, uncertain what to do. As they hesitated Whistler soared over and plummeted downward like a dive bomber. Barely giving himself time to land, he snatched at a jar and lumbered away, surprised at the object's weight. The boys seized the other jars, including the one containing the second toad, and made off along the bank, leaving their nets behind as the fierce animals approached them. Then Fox, Badger and Vixen heard Kestrel screaming at Whistler in the air. 'It's the wrong jar! You've got the wrong one!'

Partly in alarm and partly because his bill was already aching dreadfully at the unaccustomed weight, Whistler let go of the jar, which crashed to the ground and instantly shattered. Out jumped the strange toad, none the worse for the experience, having been buoyed up by the water. 'Thank you! Thank you!' it called in its croaky voice and began to hop away as fast as its legs could carry it.

Now Whistler felt he must atone for his error. He came sailing back after the frightened boys and stabbed at them with his pointed beak, with the idea of making them drop Toad. So vicious were his attacks that this ploy met with quick success. All the jars were dropped by the shrieking boys, the one carrying Toad rolling down the bank and landing with a plop in the stream. There it was buffeted and swept along by the current, the jar pivoting end to end as it spun away.

Inside the jar Toad was stunned, dazed, stupefied. One minute the jar had been standing on end on the bank, then it had been grabbed up in the air and he had bobbed up and down while the boy ran with it; then it had fallen with a thud to the ground, rolled over and over and now was racing along on the water, the reeds and rushes shooting past on either side of his clear glass prison. He did not know that any of his friends were involved in the events, for all had happened too quickly. The next thing he knew the jar came to rest against a submerged barrier in the water. He looked out of the glass and saw two stilt-like legs pressed against the side. Then down came a huge beak and Toad, jar and all, was hoisted up, higher and higher and higher still into the sky.

'Don't drop him!' shouted Fox. 'Carry him to the Park!'

'And back to the Park with us!' cried Badger. 'The party is complete!'

—21—
Home or Away?

Once safely inside the Park fence again, the five friends made for the Hollow. Whistler carefully deposited the jar on the ground and they all stood looking at it. By now Toad had recognized the faces and was leaping about desperately.

'Now what do we do?' Kestrel queried. Whistler was resting his aching beak and was unable to speak. The three animals stared at Toad and frowned. Toad settled down and stared back.

Eventually Whistler said, 'The other toad came to no harm when I dropped it. May I suggest a repeat performance?'

Fox shook his head. 'No. We can't risk it. The other

toad was lucky not to have been cut by the glass. But it may not be such a lucky drop again.'

'Well, I'm afraid if that lid doesn't come off soon, Toad might suffocate,' Badger said worriedly. 'We don't know how long he's been in there.'

'What if we found a large stone and dropped it on the jar?' Kestrel suggested.

'Who could carry such a stone?' Fox asked. 'And it would be even more dangerous for Toad inside.'

'I think there's only one way he'll get out of there,' Vixen said.

'Well, Vixen, what is it?' Fox asked quickly.

'The Warden,' she replied.

'Bravo!' cried Badger. 'We'll take the jar to him. He can open it.'

'Well, Counsellor, you've done it again,' Fox smiled at her. 'Whistler, are you up to portering a little further?'

'The heart is always willing, my dear Fox. But my poor bill does the carrying,' he answered. 'However, if it's a case of life and death. . . . '

'I'm afraid it is,' said Fox. 'We'll meet you at the cottage.'

So once again the baffled and desperate Toad was hoisted into the air, and once again the ground rushed away from beneath him. The next time he was set down he was terrified to see a cat's face come and peer at him, and he became more frantic than ever. Whistler stood by the side of the jar enigmatically. His large size made him quite fearless of the Warden's pet. He knew Fox, Badger and Vixen would be a long time arriving for, even without snow on the ground, the journey was a considerable one. Kestrel discreetly stayed well out of the way.

'Whatever have you got here?' Ginger Cat whispered, prowling all round the container.

'An old friend of mine,' answered Whistler, 'who's got himself into a spot of bother.'

'He has, hasn't he? He won't get out of there very easily.'

'Not on his own, no. Is your master within?'

'I have no – ' Ginger Cat began, then shrugged. 'I believe so,' he finished. 'I see now. You want his assistance. Bring that object outside the door, and I'll try to attract his attention.'

Whistler complied, and Ginger Cat commenced an almighty howling outside the cottage door. There was no response. 'I'll have to fetch him,' he said, and squeezed through the cat flap. Whistler heard more miaowing and wailing going on inside and then, at last, the door opened. Ginger Cat stepped daintily out, followed by a puzzled Warden.

The man looked down and saw a sedentary heron guarding a large glass jar with something inside it. He did not know what to make of such a sight. Whistler decided to give him a clue. 'Kraaank,' he cried raucously, and pushed the jar towards the man's feet. The man bent and picked up the jar and saw the toad inside. Whistler snapped his bill excitedly, producing a sound like a castanet. The man looked at him and looked back at the jar. He knew herons ate creatures like frogs and could only surmise it had discovered this titbit and could not get at it. He unscrewed the lid and gently tipped Toad out, intending to save him from the two predators at hand. But before he could pick up the small creature, Toad leapt away as fast as he could, making for cover.

Ginger Cat saw the movement and made as if to pounce. But Whistler forestalled him. 'Leave it all to me, Toad, my friend,' he said and carefully lowered his beak. The Warden watched enthralled as the heron, instead of gobbling the morsel straight down its gullet as he had expected, gently took it up and flew away into the centre of the Park.

Fox, Badger and Vixen saw Whistler coming, carrying Toad, and ceased to run. Then they made a circle round Toad as he put his feet hesitantly on the ground, and gave him encouraging licks.

'Dear old Toad,' said Badger, almost overcome. 'What an adventure you've had! Oh, it's good to have you safe with us.'

'Thank you, Badger, thank you,' said Toad. 'And, Whistler, thank you most of all. I never thought I would see any of you again.'

'Why did you do it? Why did you leave the Park?' Fox asked. 'We came looking for you this morning at the Pond and Adder said you had gone.'

'I just can't stop myself, Fox,' Toad answered. 'I know it's silly, but in the spring I feel I have to go home. I seem to lose all control over myself. It's like being taken over by some kind of Power, much greater and stronger than I am.'

'But this is your home now,' said Badger. 'There *is* no other home for you. Your birthplace no longer exists.'

'I know. I know it. But I *have* to go.'

'Well, you see what happens when you stray outside the safety of the Reserve,' Fox admonished him. 'You're lucky to be back here.'

'Oh, don't you think I know it? You're all so sensible. Everything you say is true. You'll have to restrain me.'

'Perhaps we should have kept you in the jar until you can see sense,' Badger said and laughed.

'If only Adder had been awake when I woke,' Toad said, 'he might have dissuaded me. Oh, it's wonderful to see you all. Where are the others? Are they all right?'

'Not all of them,' Vixen said quietly. 'It was a cruel

winter, Toad. Some of your friends are no longer around to welcome you back.'

'But – but – surely – ' he stammered, 'there are – more – than just – you four?'

'Oh *yes*,' Fox said reassuringly. 'You've already seen Kestrel. And there's Mole and Hare and his family – well, less one actually – and *most* of the rabbits and squirrels and Weasel, of course. And Tawny Owl – he's indestructible.'

'And all the mice?'

'Er – no, not all. Well, not many, really. They took it the hardest.'

'The hedgehogs?'

'Yes, yes, the hedgehogs are all right. They slept through it all, just like you and Adder.'

'And then, Toad, off you were going to go without even coming to see if we were still alive?' Badger said pointedly.

'Oh, Badger! I feel so guilty,' said the wretched animal. 'How could I? Never to know what you've all suffered!'

His friends fell silent as they watched Toad's anguish.

Badger, compassionate as always, spoke first. 'What can we do to help?' he asked.

'I don't know,' croaked Toad miserably. 'Except not to let me out of your sight – at least until the mating season's over.'

'Well, well, perhaps we can keep shifts,' Badger said jokingly.

'We've a lot more to tell you about our months without you,' said Fox. 'And Adder hasn't heard the tale yet. You'll both want to meet up with all the others again, won't you? I think we should all meet in the Hollow just like we used to. We haven't all been together since last autumn.'

'An excellent idea,' agreed Badger. 'We must pass the word. Er – Toad, I want you to stay with me for the time being. For safety's sake, you know. Would you care to climb on my back?'

While his friends had been thus occupied, Kestrel had continued in his usual pastime of skimming over the Reserve on effortless wings, soaring and diving again. But he saw something that made him drop earthwards in curiosity. Through the gap in the fence where Fox, Badger and Vixen had recently passed in and out of the Park now came a solitary, plump toad – the very one Whistler had rescued and then dropped. Kestrel landed and spoke to the stranger.

'Are you seeking sanctuary here now?' he asked. 'You'd be wise to do so.'

'In a way,' replied the toad. 'This is my home. I was born here in the pond. It's spring and I've been travelling towards it since I came out of hibernation. During the summer I wander quite a way and last winter I hibernated outside the Park.'

Kestrel was struck by the irony of the opposing directions Toad and the stranger had taken to return to their respective birthplaces, meeting in the middle, as it were, by the brook-side. 'How strange,' he murmured. The toad gave him a quizzical look which prompted him to explain.

'Yes, that is the way of things,' said the toad. 'We didn't speak. I was already in a jar when the young humans caught your friend. I believe he'd been swimming in the stream.'

'So you are returning to mate?' Kestrel asked.

'Yes. I'm full of spawn at this time of year,' replied the toad, revealing that she was a female. 'When I'm paired the eggs will be released in the water and fertilized by my mate.'

Kestrel glared at the toad. An idea had struck him. 'I beg your pardon,' he said. 'I'm not an expert on amphibia. I hadn't realized you are a lady toad. What are you called?'

'Paddock,' she replied.

'I'm delighted to have had this talk,' said Kestrel. 'And I think our friend will be interested to hear about it.'

'May I say how grateful I am for my rescue,' said Paddock. 'Now my babies will be born in safety.'

'I hope we may meet again,' the hawk said courteously. 'But now I'll leave you to continue your journey.' He spread his wings again.

In the air he floated blissfully on warm currents, thinking hard. Unexpectedly, he had perhaps discovered the one thing that might keep Toad in White Deer Park. The pull of Farthing Pond could perhaps be surmounted by Toad's desire for a mate.

——22——
Life Goes On

No sooner had Kestrel come to this conclusion than he went in search of Fox, who told him that Toad had been restored to them. The hawk described his discussion with Paddock and asked Fox's opinion of his idea.

'Kestrel, I really think you've hit upon something,' he replied. 'After all, the sole reason for these journeys of toads and frogs to their home ponds is to breed. We'll introduce a dash of romance into our friend's life.'

'Where *is* Toad?' asked Kestrel. 'Perhaps we should intercept Paddock's journey to the pond before any other male shows interest.'

'A good point,' acknowledged Fox. 'Come on. He's with Badger.'

'By the set they found Toad talking to an excited

Mole. Badger was doing the rounds of the Farthing Wood animals, now back in their individual homes, to tell them of the meeting in the Hollow.

'Isn't it grand to have Toad back?' Mole chattered. 'It's just like old times.'

'Did Badger get tired of carrying you?' Fox asked Toad with a grin.

'He made me get down,' Toad said ruefully. 'He said I was tugging at his coat so. It's my grasping pads, you see.' He held up his horny front feet, one at a time, to demonstrate. 'They become very developed at this time of year. That's so that we males can hang on tight to our mates and not get separated.'

'Well, I think we can find something else for you to grasp on to,' said Fox, delighted that Toad had unwittingly introduced the subject himself. 'But first, you must hang on to me.'

'Now it really is like old times,' chuckled Toad. 'Remember how you used to carry me on our journey here, Fox?'

'Of course I do,' said Fox. 'Now, up you get. Ouch!' He winced. 'I see what Badger means. Ow! Well really, Toad, you didn't grip as hard as this even when I rescued you from the fire.'

'I'm sorry,' said Toad. 'I'll try not to tug too much. Where are we going?'

'Wait and see,' was the mysterious reply. 'Now, Kestrel, which way please?'

The lady toad had not progressed very far into the Park. She had paused to refresh herself with some insects and seemed to have settled down to digest them.

Toad dismounted of his own accord by leaping from Fox's back. 'My, what a beauty!' he exclaimed as he saw Paddock. He looked at Fox with a wry grin that seemed to express better than words what he thought of

his friend. Fox grinned back and only stayed long enough
to see Toad grasp the unprotesting Paddock firmly round
her middle. He was amused to see how much larger than
Toad she was as she waddled off with her affectionate
burden on her way to the Pond.

'Well I never,' Fox laughed to himself. 'And not a
word exchanged! I wonder how Vixen would like me to
be so matter of fact?'

Kestrel also had been watching from the air. 'I
thought so,' he muttered. 'Easy as pie.'

Some days later Adder was seen sunning himself in the
Hollow.

'Hallo, stranger!' cried Weasel. 'We've all been waiting for you to put in an appearance. We're having a
get-together.'

'Very nice, I'm sure,' remarked Adder. 'But you are
mistaken if you believe I came to this spot out of any
gregarious tendency. The fact is I could no longer witness the shameless scenes in that Pond with equanimity.'

'What *are* you talking about, Adder?'

'The length and breadth of the water is alive with
courting couples,' he replied, 'whether they be frogs,
toads or newts.'

'Well, naturally – it's Spring,' said Weasel. 'Or hadn't
you realized?'

'I'm quite aware of that,' Adder snapped. 'But they
seem to have no regard at all for others in the area with
the way they're carrying on. Even Toad has been affected by it,' he added primly.

'This sounds to me like a touch of jealousy,' Weasel
remarked pointedly.

'Rubbish,' returned Adder. 'It's not a touch of anything except perhaps good breeding.'

'More like a lack of breeding, in your case,' Weasel rejoined wickedly.

'If you'll excuse me, I don't care to converse in this manner,' Adder told him, and began to slither away.

'Don't go!' cried Weasel, who now regretted his unkind remark. 'I didn't mean what I said. I'm sorry. Please stay. We hardly ever see you.'

Adder, never very susceptible to overtures of friendship, flickered his tongue in an uncertain manner. He hated to give signs of weakness. In the end he compromised. 'I'm going on a hunting trip,' he told Weasel. 'I haven't eaten for five months. But when I've managed to put a little plumpness behind my scales I'll be back.'

Weasel had to be content with this vague promise, and went to convey it to the rest of the community.

'Well, at least he doesn't intend to shun us completely,' said Fox.

'Best thing for him to do is to hunt himself up a nice female adder,' Tawny Owl observed crustily. 'She would take some of the starchiness out of him.'

'Isn't he a character, though?' Vixen laughed. 'He really is quite unique.'

'Thank goodness for that,' said Hare. 'Just imagine two like him around.'

'So it seems as if our celebration is to be delayed once more?' said Badger. 'I wonder when Toad will leave the Pond?'

'Not till the mating season's over,' answered Fox, glancing a little coyly at Vixen. 'And we know how long that goes on.'

Back in White Deer Pond, Toad and Paddock were still united as she dived underwater to lay her eggs. Other toads had already done so, for strings of eggs could be seen wound round weed and plant-stem. But the offspring of Toad and Paddock were destined to start

their tadpole life in a different setting. For these eggs, as
they descended in the water, attached themselves to
some very different objects sticking up from the mud:
the rusting remains of two quite harmless shotguns.

At last the day dawned when all the animals were ready
to hold their celebration. Fox and Vixen made their way
to the Hollow where many of their friends had already
gathered. They could see Badger and Weasel chatting
lightheartedly with Kestrel, while Hare and Rabbit exchanged views from the midst of their families. Toad,
Adder and Tawny Owl had assembled on the lip of the
Hollow and looked towards the pair of foxes as if awaiting their arrival.

'Dear, dear friends,' murmured Fox. 'How glad I am
to see them together again. I think we should count our
blessings that so many of us are still here to take pleasure
in each other's company.'

'Yes, indeed,' said Vixen. 'It's due to our ties of friendship more than anything else that we were able to survive
our troubles. Alone, it could have been another story.'

Fox nodded. Now they could see the smaller animals
bunching together in a corner of their meeting-place.
Mole was there with the mice, the squirrels and the
hedgehogs. In the air a familiar whistle heralded the
arrival of their friend the heron.

'A fond greeting to you all,' said Whistler joyfully as
he landed amongst the sprouting bracken. 'This is a
wonderful day!'

'Then let's make it one we shall always remember,'
said Fox. 'So that, whatever may happen in the future,
whatever fate may befall us, we shall remember that this
day, together, we rejoiced to say that WE ARE ALIVE.'

Fox's Feud

Colin Dann

Fox's Feud

Illustrated by Terry Riley

Contents

For Deborah

—1—

News

One day during the first spring in White Deer Park, Badger was visited by an excited Mole.

'Badger! Badger!' he called, as he dug his way into the darkness of his old friend's set. 'Have you heard the news?'

'News? News? No, no, *I* haven't heard any news,' replied Badger a little peevishly. He sometimes felt he was a little neglected in his underground home.

'It's Vixen!' declared Mole, beaming. 'She's had four cubs. Fox is so proud! Oh, you should see them . . .'

'When was this?' Badger interrupted. 'Why hasn't Fox been to see me?'

'They were only born last night,' Mole explained. 'Tawny Owl told me all about it. I went to visit them at once. Oh! Badger, you must come. Why don't we go together now?'

'Certainly, if you're sure it would be convenient,' replied Badger. 'Nothing I'd like more.'

'Of course it is,' said Mole. 'Fox instructed me to come and give you the news straight away.'

It was Badger's turn to beam then, and the two animals hastened out of the set, chatting cheerfully.

It was a crisp, sunny spring morning in the Park. A plentiful dew had soaked the ground and each blade of grass and clump of moss glistened refreshingly. Badger sniffed the air briskly. 'It's going to be a wonderful day,' he pronounced.

He and Mole left the little beech copse where Badger had constructed his new set, and directed their steps to another group of trees, in the midst of which lay Fox's earth. In no time Mole's velvet coat was soaked by the dew.

'What a state to arrive in, as a visitor,' he complained. 'Badger, you go on. I must make myself more presentable.'

Badger chuckled and trotted ahead. At the entrance to the earth he paused to listen. There were voices inside. 'Er – hallo,' he called down hesitantly. 'Fox! It's me – Badger. Can I come in?'

The voices ceased for a moment, and then Fox's head appeared at the entrance. 'Badger! How nice to see you. Mole told you the news? We're so thrilled. Come along, old friend.'

Badger followed him down with an expectant smile. He found Vixen curled up on a bed of soft hair, with four tiny, fluffy creatures huddled around her. A warm, truly motherly expression lit up her face. Badger's kind old heart melted at the sight. He was at a loss for words. 'This is a happy day indeed,' he murmured. 'May they have a more peaceful life than we have known.' He looked at Fox.

'Thank you, Badger,' said Vixen quietly. 'I hope so too.'

'Er – will they be foxes or vixens?' Badger enquired a little awkwardly.

'Two male, two female,' Fox replied promptly. 'They'll keep us busy, the four of them, once their eyes have opened.'

'Yes, they certainly look a healthy bunch,' Badger remarked. 'And it's good to see *you* looking so well, Vixen.' He paused. 'Well, I won't intrude too long,' he resumed. 'I expect you want to be on your own.'

Fox made some polite remarks, but Badger was determined not to outstay his welcome.

'I'll come back again, if I may, in a few days,' he promised. Fox accompanied him to the exit.

On his way back to his set, Badger came across Mole basking on top of a hillock in an effort to dry his fur. 'The cubs were all you said they were,' he said to his friend. 'I must admit, on seeing that cosy little group in Fox's earth, I felt a few regrets for a family life.'

'Well, Badger, it's never too late,' Mole said comfortingly. 'You must get lonely in your set, all by yourself.'

'I am at times,' Badger agreed. 'But – no, I'm too old and stubborn in my ways to share my home with any female. I do sometimes feel homesick for my old set in Farthing Wood. Of course, I had my memories there – my family lived there for generations. Here it's different . . .'

Mole cut in quickly before Badger could wax maudlin. 'It's like a new beginning,' he observed. 'The cubs will have their father's characteristics – or some of them. The spirit of Farthing Wood will be renewed – here.'

'Don't get carried away, Mole,' Badger cautioned. 'Farthing Wood will be only a name to them, and life in Farthing Wood as it was for us and Fox and the rest of the band, will be only a story for them to listen to. Here in the Park they'll never know the difficulties and the dangers that were always part of our life there.'

'That's so,' Mole agreed. 'But that's no bad thing, is it, Badger?'

'No – except that, in the face of any danger, they may not be so well equipped for survival.'

Mole pondered this idea for some time, recalling the viciousness of the past winter in the Park. At length he said: 'I'm sure Fox will ensure they will be able to look after themselves.'

Badger smiled. 'What about you, my friend?' he teased. 'You're young. Are you ready yet for a more serious role in life?'

Mole blinked in the unaccustomed brightness of the sunlight. 'I don't often think about it,' he answered. 'But I should like to be settled and happy one day.'

Badger was true to his word and revisited the fox cubs a week or so later. Their eyes were now open and they seemed to be taking a lively interest in everything that went on inside their comfortable earth, which was still the only world they knew. The arrival of Badger was an occasion for the greatest excitement until their father returned with a selection of choice titbits from his evening hunting foray for Vixen. Although the cubs were still suckling, they watched inquisitively as Vixen daintily accepted the food from Fox's jaws.

Badger was amused to see one of them, already slightly larger than his fellows, totter forward to nose at his parents. 'He'll be their leader,' remarked the wise old animal. 'That's plain to see.'

Vixen nodded. 'He'll follow in his father's footsteps.' she remarked. 'The other male cub is not so sure of himself.'

'But the little vixens are charming,' Fox interrupted. 'Just like their mother.'

A noise outside the den attracted their attention. Weasel came towards them out of the early morning daylight.

'There's a strange fox snooping about up there,' he said. 'A big male with a long scar down his muzzle. He seems to be very curious about what might be happening in your den.'

'I've seen him around several times,' Fox said. 'I don't like the look of him, and I've asked Tawny Owl to keep an eye on the den when I'm out hunting.'

'What does he want?' Badger asked with a serious expression.

'I don't know,' replied Fox. 'We may find out one day. He's lived in the Reserve a good number of years – that I do know – and he and his mate have produced many a litter of cubs to populate White Deer Park. I think Vixen and I may be looked upon rather as intruders on his preserve.' All this was said out of earshot of Vixen.

'I asked what his business was here,' Weasel informed his two friends, 'and he replied that the whole of White Deer Park was his business, and who was I to question him?'

'Dear, dear, Weasel, do be careful,' advised Badger, cautious as ever. 'We don't want any misunderstandings with the Park's older residents. Most of them were probably born here, you know.'

'Don't worry about me,' Weasel answered quickly. 'I

keep myself to myself. But I have noticed, since the winter was over, that the acclaim Fox attracted from the residents for his defeat of the poachers seems to have soured slightly.'

'Are we resented, do you think?' Badger asked with a concerned look.

'Not exactly,' replied Weasel. 'But I think there are those here among the Park's original community who feel we ought to recognize our position here as newcomers more clearly than we do. And one of them is our friend Scarface out there.'

'In other words, it's more their home than ours?' Badger summarized.

'Exactly.'

'Well, they accepted us readily enough to begin with,' Fox remarked. 'I don't think there's any real ill feeling. But, I suggest, Badger, we should get everyone together in the Hollow one night soon and talk about the situation. Perhaps it would be as well for us to tread extra warily for a while.'

Badger and Weasel wholeheartedly agreed with Fox's advice and, accordingly, took their leave of Vixen. The scarfaced fox was no longer around when they left Fox's earth and they went their own ways quietly.

Two days elapsed and then all the creatures of Farthing Wood met at dusk in their habitual meeting place in the Hollow.

—2—
Developments

It was the first meeting of all the creatures from Farthing Wood since the winter, and so it was clear to all of them that it was to be of some importance.

'It seems,' began Fox, 'that one or two of you have noticed an undercurrent of – er – unfriendliness running through some of White Deer Park's inhabitants. Now we don't want to find ourselves looked upon as intruders, and I wanted to caution you all to be particularly careful in your behaviour towards the native animals in the future – until things seem quieter again.'

'The Park animals seem to think we have encroached rather on their territory, I believe,' Rabbit remarked.

'That could be true in the case of you rabbits,' suggested Weasel wryly. 'There are so many more of you now than there were when we arrived at the Reserve last summer, despite your losses during the winter.'

Some of the animals laughed but Rabbit was not amused. 'We're not the only ones to have increased our numbers,' he said indignantly. 'What about the hedgehogs? And Toad left his mark in the pond. Even Fox and Vixen now have a family.'

'No offence meant, Rabbit,' Weasel assured him. 'But I think you might have been right about the question of territory. There *are* certain rights respecting that, after all.'

'Humph! Lot of nonsense!' snorted Tawny Owl. 'Plenty of space for everyone. There aren't that many of us.'

'Have you encountered any difficulties, Toad?' Fox asked him.

'No, no,' Toad shook his head. 'Of course, the frogs have known me a long time,' he said, referring to his first visit to the Park. 'They accept me in their pond with the utmost friendliness but, you see, I don't see many of the other creatures. My small legs don't carry me so far as some of you larger fellows.'

The animals chortled at this remark of Toad's, recalling the epic journey he had made alone from White Deer Park across miles of country to return to his home pond in Farthing Wood.

He smiled at their mirth. 'Well, my travelling days are done now, anyhow,' he said. 'I shouldn't relish the prospect of our moving to a third home.'

'No question of it,' Fox assured him hurriedly. 'White Deer Park is our home now. It's a Nature Reserve and we've as much right to be protected as those that were born here.'

'Well said, Fox,' murmured the sardonic Adder, 'and

may I say, from one carnivore to another, I find the irony delicious.'

Fox looked somewhat embarrassed at this unexpected comment, but Badger came to his rescue.

'It's the Law of Nature, Adder,' he reminded him, 'and that is unalterable. We can't all be grass-eaters.'

'Of course not,' drawled Adder, 'especially when there are so much choicer items available.' He leered at the mice, who ignored him totally. They knew perfectly well their common Farthing Wood background meant they were quite safe from the snake's intentions, and that he seemed to feel that such remarks were expected of him.

Hare said: 'My surviving youngster has grown up here. Leveret barely remembers Farthing Wood, so he's far more familiar with the Park's surroundings. The native hares seem to look upon him almost as if he, too, had been born here. He certainly mixes quite freely.'

'I wonder if there are any grounds for apprehension at all,' Kestrel remarked airily.

'Not in your case, certainly,' Vole rasped. 'You spend more time patrolling the countryside outside the Park than you do within its confines.'

'Have you ever thought there might be a reason for that?' Kestrel chided him gently. 'If I always hunted inside the Park, there is a very great danger that some time I might kill the wrong vole or fieldmouse. Small creatures like you look very alike when I'm hovering high up in the sky.'

'That had certainly occurred to *me*,' Fieldmouse assented. 'But, well, you know Vole doesn't always see things so clearly.'

'I must apologize, Kestrel,' Vole said contritely. 'I should have realized you had our interests at heart.'

'Well, well, no harm done,' said Badger the peacemaker.

'Er – is there any more to be said, Fox? This wind is beginning to get very chilly.'

'No more for the present, I think,' said Fox. 'We must all be on our guard for a bit, that's all. I think we should all remain in our corner of the Park for the time being also. That way, if anyone needs to raise the alarm at any time we are in a position to act together quickly.'

At this point Whistler the heron flexed his great wings, producing the familiar shrill sound as the air rushed through the bullet-hole in his damaged one. 'Perhaps a few more of you should have done as I,' he announced in his lugubrious tones, 'and mated with a member of the indigenous population. There can be no swifter way of achieving acceptance amongst a foreign community.'

About three weeks after the meeting in the Hollow, the fox cubs could be seen playing with their parents in the spring sunshine outside their earth. One day Tawny Owl was watching them, sleepily, from a nearby willow tree. He noticed that, although none of them strayed far from a convenient bolt-hole to the den, one cub was slightly more adventurous in his wanderings. His small, chocolate brown body was cobby and healthy looking, as indeed were those of his brother and sisters, but his infant frame seemed to be just a little stouter.

'He's going to be a bold young fellow,' Tawny Owl mused to himself. 'Never still for a moment. Now the others are quite happy to sit at times, and just enjoy the warmth of the sun on their bodies.' He chuckled at their antics. 'Yes, one in particular seems very fond of that.'

Vixen spotted the bird half-dozing on the branch. 'Won't you join us, Owl?' she invited. 'Or are you too sleepy?'.

'Nothing of the kind, nothing of the kind,' Tawny Owl

replied huffily and promptly flew to the ground.

Fox greeted him cheerfully. 'Glad to see you, Owl,' he said. 'Well, it looks as if our fears were groundless. Old Scarface has not been near recently.'

'No. I expect he's occupied in much the same way as you at present,' Tawny Owl observed knowingly.

'Oh? Is he a father again?' Fox asked quickly.

'Oh yes. His mate produced three cubs about the same time as Vixen.'

'Have you seen them?' Vixen wanted to know.

'Not yet,' replied the bird. 'I don't venture over to that section of the Park since our agreement in the Hollow. However,' he added archly, 'I'm sure they couldn't be as delightful as yours, dear Vixen.'

'Oh, flatterer!' she laughed. 'This one we call Charmer actually.' She indicated one of the female cubs. 'She has very winning ways. Her sister is Dreamer.'

'Very appropriate,' agreed Tawny Owl, noticing the cub thus named was the one he had singled out from his perch. 'And the others?'

'The big male cub is Bold,' Fox told him with more than a hint of pride in his voice. 'But we haven't as yet found anything quite applicable to describe his brother.'

'I daresay it'll suggest itself before long,' said Tawny Owl.

'Oh yes,' Vixen agreed. 'They all have their own personalities.'

At that moment the cub in question chose to investigate the family's visitor and approached the owl, wagging his little tail.

'Already as big as me,' Tawny Owl said with amusement. The little cub sat down directly next to him and commenced to sniff him all over. Finally he lay down over Tawny Owl's talons and sighed deeply.

'I think this one's just named himself,' the owl

remarked. 'At any rate, I shall call him Friendly.'

'An excellent name,' Fox assented. 'Don't you think so, dear?'

Vixen nodded happily. There seemed to be nothing that could disturb the peace of such a perfect day. For a while longer Tawny Owl watched the cubs playing and then, finding it increasingly difficult to stifle his yawns, he made an excuse and flew back to his tree for a long nap before dark.

At dusk he awoke with a start to see a familiar shape skulking in the shadows. The scarfaced fox had evidently decided to resume his reconnaisance.

'What on earth is he up to?' Tawny Owl muttered to himself, as he watched the animal pause at one of the entrances to Fox's earth. 'He's listening for something, I'll be bound.'

The beast stood motionless, head cocked at an angle, for some moments. Then he sniffed carefully all round the entrance and listened again. Finally he moved slowly off into the darkness.

Tawny Owl was puzzled. 'Very curious,' he commented.

He was still cogitating when Fox emerged from the earth and paused while he, too, sniffed the air. Then he looked up towards the willow. 'Are you there, Owl?' he called.

'Yes.' Tawny Owl alighted on the ground beside him.

'Have you seen anything?' Fox asked him.

'Scarface has been back.' Tawny Owl described his movements.

'I knew it. I smelt him.'

'He must have detected *your* scent,' Tawny Owl surmised, 'and then decided to go back.'

'Exactly. Had I been out hunting . . .' The friends exchanged glances.

'You can rely on me,' declared Tawny Owl. 'I'll see no harm's done.'

'But, with all due respect, would you be a match for such a tough customer?' Fox queried hesitantly.

'Vixen and I together could deal with him, if necessary,' the bird assured him. 'And, in any case, it may not come to anything. Perhaps it's just harmless curiosity?'

'Perhaps,' said Fox. 'But I don't like it. His secretiveness . . .'

'Are you hunting tonight?' Tawny Owl asked him.

'No. I'll stay put this time. But tomorrow I must. And then . . .?'

'Maybe we'll learn a little more about our interested visitor,' said Tawny Owl coolly. 'As for now, I think I'll pay a call on Badger. We don't want him to feel he's being left out of anything.'

—3—
A Warning

The next night was clear and crisp, with a bright half moon. Tawny Owl was in position on the willow branch well before dark, and Badger joined him at the foot of the tree, concealed in a clump of bracken.

When it was quite dark, Fox quitted his earth to go hunting. He gave no sign of any kind that he was aware of his friends' presence. They saw him trot nonchalantly away in the moonlight.

For some time all was quiet. Badger shivered once or twice in the chill evening air and wished he could move about a bit. Neither he nor Tawny Owl spoke. A breeze began to whisper through the leaves of the willow, and with it another faint sound – a regular pattering sound.

Footsteps! Badger tensed under the bracken. The noise came nearer . . . pitter patter, pitter patter . . . and then a long, dog-like shadow was visible on the ground. The pattering ceased. Out into the moonlight came the scarfaced fox, treading very slowly and carefully towards the main entrance to the cubs' den.

By the opening he stopped again and looked all round warily, snuffling the air. For a moment he looked towards the spot where Badger was hidden. The moon shone full on his face, scarred and hideous from a score of battles. Despite himself, Badger's stout old heart missed a beat. Then the animal turned again and lowered himself to creep stealthily into the hole.

At once, Tawny Owl glided noiselessly down from his perch, and Badger rushed forward. Scarface sprang back.

'You've no reason to go in there,' said Tawny Owl. 'What exactly is your game?'

'I'm not accountable to you,' snarled the fox, angry at being detected unawares.

'But you're accountable to the inhabitants of the den who, to my knowledge, have not invited your presence.'

'A social call from one fox to another is no concern of a bird's,' Scarface sneered.

'It is in this instance,' Tawny Owl informed him calmly, 'as I was specifically requested to keep watch for intruders.'

'Intruders?' snapped Scarface. 'Intruders? How dare you talk to me of intruders. I've lived in this Park all my life – *and* my kind with me. I've more right to enter this earth than those who are already in it – cubs or no cubs.'

'Just because you were born here doesn't mean you own the Park, you know.' Badger spoke for the first time. 'There's more than enough room for everyone to live comfortably without any interference being called for. *We* all lost our original homes thanks to human intervention, and we came here for the very reason that it was safe from human hands.'

'Yes, yes, we've all heard about your heroic journey from Farthing Wood,' the fox said sarcastically. 'I was at the reception party when you arrived, just like everyone else. The Park could absorb *your* numbers rightly enough. But now you've started breeding . . .'

'Some of us have,' Badger corrected him. 'I myself have no mate. Neither does Tawny Owl here. But you've nothing to fear from our party. We like to keep ourselves to ourselves.'

'You have to eat, don't you? I'm sure you don't leave the Park every time you go hunting.'

'Of course not,' replied Tawny Owl imperturbably. 'Do you?'

Scarface bristled with anger again. 'The whole of this Reserve is my hunting territory,' he seethed. 'From time immemorial my ancestors lived and hunted here, long before it was fenced off by humans, or even had a name. When it was still wild and unchecked countryside, they roamed here freely. And it will always be that way. My cubs will hunt here after me, and their cubs after them . . .'

'And so on ad infinitum,' Tawny Owl remarked drolly.

Scarface looked at him dangerously, baring his fangs. Badger quailed slightly, though Tawny Owl stood his ground. In slow, menacing tones Scarface said: 'No other family of foxes will be allowed the freedom of the Park. Tell your gallant leader to stay in his own quarter if he values the safety of his mate and her cubs. My family is large: I have many dependents. Don't let him think he can outwit me. I've lived many years and I've yet to be bested.' With a final snarl, he loped off into the shadows.

'Well, well, well,' Badger whispered, 'what an alarming character.'

'Pooh, nonsense,' blustered Tawny Owl, who was secretly shaken by their confrontation, 'nothing but idle threats. We thwarted his little game all right. I believe he was about to do some mischief to Vixen's cubs.'

'I'm sure of it,' agreed Badger. 'But I'm not convinced we've seen the last of him. I have an unpleasant feeling you and I have made an enemy for ourselves tonight, Owl.'

Tawny Owl stretched his wings and shook his feathers in an effort to hide a distinctly disconcerted expression. 'Oh, I don't know . . .' he began.

'Sssh, here's Fox back,' Badger interrupted him. He quickly acquainted Fox with the recent events. Fox invited them down into his earth while he took food in to Vixen. They all sat silent for a while.

'I shall do exactly as he asks,' Fox announced finally.

'What!' exclaimed Tawny Owl.

'Yes, Owl. Vixen and the cubs must be my first consideration. I won't do anything to put their lives at risk.'

'Quite right, my dear fellow,' Badger concurred. 'I should do exactly the same. That creature has a very vicious look about him.'

'And when the cubs are fully grown?' Tawny Owl prompted.

'Well . . . then it might be time to think again,' Fox said cautiously.

'You know you can always count on our support in any way,' said Tawny Owl.

'I know, and I thank you for it, just as I thank you for dealing with that villain just now. But this is my quarrel. I don't want to involve others.'

'Any quarrel of yours is our quarrel too, you know, Fox,' Badger reminded him. 'Remember the Oath we all took before we left Farthing Wood.'

'Of course I remember,' replied Fox. 'But that Oath was sworn to ensure the mutual protection of all our party while we were on our journey. We've made new lives for ourselves here – all of us. I don't want to endanger my friends for any selfish reason.'

'Well, I think in the event of any trouble,' Badger opined, 'you will find that everyone will get involved, whether you request it or not. Our ties are more lasting than simply for the duration of a journey.'

'That is indeed a comforting thought, Badger, my dear friend,' said Fox who was evidently quite moved. 'And Owl – what a true friend you've been.'

'Oh, don't mention it,' Tawny Owl said self-consciously. 'Glad to be of assistance, I'm sure.'

Just then Vixen, who had finished eating, came forward. 'Fox told me the gist of what occurred tonight,' she said, 'and I want to thank you both for standing guard as you did. If you look at the cubs, you can see how successful you were.'

They could see them blissfully asleep in a huddle, completely unaware of the interest provoked by their existence.

'They'll soon be big enough for me to take them hunting,' she added. 'They're coming along fast.'

'Yes, yes, they grow so quickly,' said Badger fondly. 'It's a shame in a way. But they need to be able to stand on their own feet as soon as possible.'

'Never more so than in the present case,' Tawny Owl remarked, but Fox gestured him to silence.

'Well, it's been an eventful evening,' he summarized. 'Owl, Badger, I'm sure you both feel the need to eat. We'll keep in touch.'

Badger took this as a hint that Fox wanted to be alone with his family and began to amble towards the exit, but the somewhat insensitive Owl lingered.

'No hurry, no hurry,' he said. 'My stomach takes second place to the pleasure of your company.'

'Now, we mustn't outstay our welcome,' Badger said pointedly. 'Fox has other claims on his time.'

Tawny Owl noticed his gaffe but endeavoured to appear unconcerned. 'Of course,' he said, 'I just wanted to make it quite clear I was not in any discomfort.'

Badger had already made his farewells and left the earth.

'I'll be on watch again tomorrow evening,' Tawny Owl assured Fox awkwardly. 'Never fear.'

Fox smiled. 'All right, Owl. Thank you.'

Tawny Owl cleared his throat. 'Well – goodbye,' he finished lamely, and finally left them alone.

——4——

First Blood

The time came when the four cubs were ready to go on their first hunting trip. Many of Fox's and Vixen's friends came to witness this important outing, among them Badger, Mole, Weasel and, of course, Tawny Owl. It was dusk as they gathered outside the earth, and watched Vixen shepherd Bold, Charmer, Dreamer and Friendly towards the entrance.

The cubs emerged with various degrees of enthusiasm. Bold looked keen and alert; his robust young body was tingling with excitement. Charmer stayed close to her mother, watching her every movement, but Dreamer, as usual, seemed to be in a world of her own – wandering off to sniff at a patch of grass or a twig as if she had all the time in the world. Friendly made a beeline for the onlookers, wagging his tail furiously as he recognized each of them in turn.

Vixen called them together again and had a few last words with Fox, who impressed on her once more not to attempt to hunt outside their own corner of the Park. She took a necessarily quiet farewell of him and of their friends and led the cubs away. Shortly afterwards Fox followed, making sure he was out of sight and keeping far enough behind for his scent to remain undetected. For, although it was Vixen's job to instruct the cubs, he was determined to be within reach should anything untoward occur.

'Keep close to me,' Vixen told the cubs, 'and there's no danger. Do you understand, Dreamer? No wandering off!'

'Don't worry, Mother,' the cub replied. 'I'll stay with you.'

Bold was snuffling the night air keenly as the little group trotted on. A hundred exciting scents were wafted to him on the breeze and his young feet fairly danced along in his exhilaration.

'I want complete quietness now,' Vixen ordered, as she led them into some long grass. Friendly, who had been chatting to his sister cubs, fell silent. They followed their mother in a line, nosing their way through the tall stalks. A variety of insects scattered in their wake – beetles, crickets, spiders and earwigs. Some tumbled into their path, and following their mother's example, they snapped them up. They quickly discerned which were to their liking.

But Vixen was after larger game. They arrived on the banks of a stream rich in water-rats. She showed the cubs how to exercise their patience while nothing seemed to appear; then, when the prey was spotted, to freeze if it approached or, alternatively, to stalk it from behind. She

showed how to pounce and pin it with front paws and
how to render it immobile with the jaws.

The cubs at first were clumsy and too eager, and for a
long time they caught nothing. The water-rats were far
too nimble and knowing for them. But Bold caught a
water-shrew at the stream's edge and this success spurred
him on. Vixen helped the others and, eventually,
Charmer and Friendly were also successful. Only
Dreamer, who had eaten rather too many insects and
earthworms on the way, showed little aptitude.

'You will go hungry tonight,' Vixen told her. 'Then
tomorrow perhaps you will try harder.'

All the time Fox watched them from further downstream.
When he saw they were about to leave he disappeared.
He was satisfied that there was no danger abroad and that
they would soon be safely back in the den again. He had
completely failed to notice a familiar figure, hidden in the
shadows on the opposite bank. Scarface had also been
watching the cubs' lesson, but from a quite different
motive.

At that very moment in another area of the Park his
mate was going through the self-same procedure with her
cubs. Scarface looked with anger and resentment at
Vixen's cubs, comparing his own unfavourably with
them. Vixen's seemed sturdier and more agile. In reality
only Bold was bigger, but he likened the cub's brother
and sisters to him in his mind's eye. He jealously watched
Bold's dawning skills and knew that he could be supreme
among all the foxes one day. 'But that shall not be,' he
muttered darkly to himself. 'No interloper will supercede
me and mine while I live. This young cub must be dealt
with before he grows any more.'

He watched Vixen set off with the cubs following, and
then swam across to the other bank silently. As they re-
entered the long grass, he ran quickly round the outside

to head them off. Vixen emerged first, then Charmer and Dreamer, and finally the two male cubs. Scarface set up a loud yapping and barking to startle them. Vixen halted stock still, but all four cubs leapt into the air in alarm. She saw the hostile fox speeding towards them.

'Quickly!' she cried. 'Run for the earth!'

The cubs set off as swiftly as their legs could carry them, while their mother faced about to encounter their attacker. But Scarface twisted out of her reach and raced after her young ones. In no time his longer legs brought him up to their heels. He knew he would have time only to catch one cub, and he immediately singled out Bold for attack. Running in amongst the cubs, he scattered them and isolated Bold by shielding him with his body. Then he bared his fangs and prepared to lunge.

But Bold was not so named for nothing. Taking Scarface completely by surprise, the plucky little animal snapped at the old fox first, and bit him neatly on the foreleg. Scarface actually fell back a pace or two in utter amazement at the cub's audacity. For a moment he was dumbfounded; then, with a wild snarl, he sprang forward again.

By now Vixen, with her famed swiftness, was catching up with the aggressor. As she ran, she let out a piercing scream as a signal to Fox. The eerie cry cut through the night air like a knife, and was heard not only by Fox but by a number of the other Farthing Wood animals.

Before Scarface could aim again at Bold, Vixen was in between them, snapping viciously at the hideous muzzle while she protected her bravest cub. The other three were now out of danger and well on the way back to their den. While Vixen and Scarface lunged and feinted at each other, growling horribly the whole time, Bold ran round his mother and bit his enemy from behind with his sharp young teeth.

Scarface was in a fury – the attacker became the attacked. As he swung backwards and forwards, he spied in the distance Fox galloping in their direction. He knew it was time to break off the contest. With a final wild snap at Vixen which caught her a glancing blow on the shoulder and made her yelp, Scarface broke free and made off at a good pace back to his own kind.

Fox saw this as he approached and felt inclined to race after him, but Vixen's cry of pain had decided him to attend to his family first. He was quickly assured when it became obvious Vixen had only sustained a scratch. While he comforted his mate, Fox said: 'That creature is beginning to interfere a little too much in our affairs. If he wants to really stir up trouble, I'll give him something he didn't bargain for.'

'He was after Bold,' panted Vixen. 'I don't know why – the other cubs didn't interest him.'

'Where are they?' Fox asked quickly.

'They got away, luckily. They should be back in the den by now.'

Fox sighed with relief and then smiled down at Bold, who was wagging his tail as hard as he could, begging for recognition.

'You're a game one,' his father said to him. 'I saw you helping your mother.'

'He was defending himself before I came on the scene,' Vixen told him. 'He bit that hateful creature before he had a chance to *be* bitten.'

'No, did he though?' Fox murmured. 'What, he attacked old Scarface?' There was pride in his voice. 'My word, that *is* something.'

'I thought he was going to kill me,' said Bold quietly, 'so I had to do *something*.'

'Well, you certainly seem to be able to look after yourself,' Fox praised him. Yet, even as he spoke, in his heart he knew the brave little cub would from now on be the prime target for their enemy – even more so than before. Scarface would never forget his humiliation of this night.

Fox made Vixen tell him in detail exactly what had happened from the time he let her out of his sight. 'So he's not even true to his word,' he muttered afterwards. 'We *have* kept to our own area, and still he has sought us out. Well, now we know where we stand for sure.'

They heard a familiar voice calling them. 'Fox! Vixen!' It was Badger. He ran up to tell them that the other cubs were safely in their earth, in the care of Weasel and Mole. Then he stopped in dismay, looking down at Bold. 'But where's Dreamer?' he asked.

'What?' gasped Vixen. 'Wasn't she with the others?'

'No, only Charmer and Friendly are in the den. We thought she was with you.' Badger looked almost as worried as the parents.

'Then wherever can she . . .?' began Fox.

'She's wandered off somewhere again,' Bold said. 'She's always doing that. I'm sure she'll be all right, Mother,' he added comfortingly.

'We must search for her,' said Fox. 'Badger, will you take Bold back to join the others?'

'Of course, Fox. Anything I can do – you know that.'

Fox and Vixen split up to comb different areas, calling softly to their lost cub. Inside the earth, the three other cubs and their guardians waited anxiously.

It was Fox who found her. Vixen heard his cry – an angry, baffled cry of distress. She found him standing over the body of Dreamer. She was dead, and her young body had been badly savaged.

There was no doubt in their minds who had done the deed. Fox's face was very grim. With menace he said: 'Now indeed he will have a fight to contend with.'

—— 5 ——

Out of Bounds

The savage killing of an innocent cub was a considerable shock to the Farthing Wood community. There were those who thought it should be avenged, while others advised greater caution. Amongst the smaller animals there was widespread alarm. They had thought themselves safe and now it appeared there was a new threat to their lives.

The strongest advocates of taking revenge for the death of Dreamer were the birds – Tawny Owl, Kestrel and Whistler. Fox, however, was wise enough to recognize that, in the event of a prolonged state of conflict, they stood to suffer least. Their wings were their constant passport to safety. For a long time he brooded over what course of action to take. Vixen's grief was an aching wound in his heart, and he itched for battle. But he did not want to further endanger the survival of his other three cubs. So for the time being Scarface's blow remained unanswered.

Over the next few weeks the cubs were never allowed to wander far, and at night both Fox and Vixen accompanied them on their hunting trips. Soon the three were very nearly as big as their parents and Bold, in particular, was wishing to become more independent. It was Vixen who finally said to Fox: 'We can be overprotective, you know. Shouldn't we be encouraging them to rely more on themselves now?'

'I suppose you're right,' Fox acknowledged. 'But do you think they're ready to meet *all* the dangers around?'

'Time will tell,' said Vixen realistically. 'In any case, the dangers you are referring to will always be present. The cubs are aware of them, too.'

Fox relented. 'I'll tell them they're free to go where they choose, but within reason. We don't want to invite trouble.'

The next day Fox and Vixen hunted alone, and the cubs were left to their own devices. Bold was eager to explore further afield and, before he left them, he made Friendly and Charmer promise not to mention this.

With what sense of freedom and adventure he set off in the moonlight! His natural confidence made him feel he was equal to anything and he trotted along quite fearlessly. He went first to the stream of the water-rats and slaked his thirst at its edge. He had never been to the other bank and, without further ado, dog-paddled easily across. Here there were new smells, new sounds to absorb. Bold watched an owl flitting from tree to tree, calling in its metallic voice to its mate. A stoat brushed in front of him, intent on its own business. Bold caught himself a morsel and paused to eat it under a birch tree.

'Hallo,' whispered a voice nearby. 'I don't think I know your face.'

Bold looked around him and detected a movement under a gorse bush. He looked closer. 'Oh – hallo,' he said in reply. 'You must be Adder.'

'That is the case,' said the snake.

'My father has often talked to me about you,' Bold went on.

'Really? What did he say?'

'He said you were a remarkable creature,' Bold said innocently.

Adder chuckled. 'Not so remarkable for a snake,' he said. 'But it seems we legless individuals always appear unusual to those who have them.'

'I don't think he was referring to that aspect at all,' Bold assured him. 'My father and mother have good cause to remember some of your deeds.'

Adder knew the young fox was referring in particular to a certain action on his part during the animals' journey to White Deer Park, when he had virtually saved Vixen's life. But it was not his way to acknowledge it. 'I'm glad to hear it,' was all he said. 'For my part, I have the greatest admiration for your parents. Incidentally, I trust I am not delaying you at all?'

Bold was much too polite to say he had wanted to explore alone, and he thought Adder was a particularly interesting character to whom he might do well to listen. 'I should be glad of your company,' he said, more or less truthfully.

'I heard, of course, of the tragic incident involving your sister,' Adder told him. 'It seems there are certain rivalries in existence in the Park. I must say I have been surprised at the somewhat subdued response from your father. At one time he would have reacted quite differently – but then he hasn't always had the particular responsibilities he has had recently.'

Bold was surprised at the snake's outspoken manner, but he recalled that Fox had told him that Adder had never been one to mince his words.

'I'm sure if that scarfaced animal ever came close to our den again, my father would kill him,' the cub said proudly.

'Ye-e-s,' drawled Adder, 'possibly. The only drawback is that, if he did return, he might not be unaccompanied.'

'Neither is my father unaccompanied,' Bold answered hotly. 'I'm nearly as big as he is, and I would certainly not see him fight alone.'

Adder grinned wryly. 'I don't doubt it for a moment,' he assured the cub. 'You youngsters are bound to be eager to prove yourselves.'

Bold felt the snake was amused at his ardour, but for once Adder had not intended to be sarcastic, and hastened to reassure him.

'I should know that any offspring of Fox and Vixen would be bound to have a stout heart,' he said.

This compliment both to himself and his parents flattered the cub.

'Er – were you spying out the land by any chance?' Adder enquired.

'Not exactly,' replied Bold innocently. 'I just wanted to explore a little further than before.' He did not care to admit that he was out on his own for the first time.

'The only reason I asked,' resumed the snake, 'is that I know Scarface and his brood patrol these parts.'

Bold swallowed hard. Despite his determination to be courageous, he was not yet ready to face the enemy on his own. 'Oh,' he said quietly. 'Er – do they cover a lot of ground?'

Adder saw how the land lay. 'Oh, a great deal,' he replied, a hint of his old maliciousness creeping into his feelings. 'They seem to feel they have the right to roam wherever they choose.'

These words caused Bold to shake off his trepidation. 'And why shouldn't I, too?' he said with resolution.

'No reason at all,' Adder consented, wondering if he was wrong to spur the cub on. 'Feel free to go. I've no wish to hold you back.'

Now Bold felt that he must go on. He turned to Adder. 'I'm grateful to you for your advice,' he said politely. 'Will you be in this vicinity for some time?'

'Oh, hereabouts,' Adder replied non-committally.

'Well then, if I don't return this way tonight, will you seek out my father and tell him?'

Adder loathed to be given commissions of any sort, or to feel himself bound in any way by the wishes of others. He was on the point of delivering a retort, but confined himself to pointing out that he might be moving on anyway.

'I know Fox would appreciate it,' Bold urged him.

Unwittingly, the cub had probably chosen the one motive that struck a chord in Adder's scaly old heart. He owned few allegiances, but Fox commanded one of them.

'You may count on me,' he said simply.

Bold made his farewells and trotted forward carefully, sniffing the air in every direction as he did so. The hairs of his coat seemed to stand up independently as, with every step, he felt he was penetrating deeper into alien territory. Pretty soon, he was sure he detected the smell of a fox. He instantly flattened himself against the ground and waited.

The smell strengthened. He heard the sound of fox paws on the ground. A young fox came into view, pausing every so often and sniffing the air cautiously, just as he had done. He saw the other cub look all around as if trying to pinpoint him.

Bold realized he had nothing to fear. The other cub was just as nervous of their encounter as he was, and also far less robust in his appearance. He got to his feet quietly and waited.

The other cub spotted him and was startled. He even backed a couple of paces instinctively, snarling as he did so.

'I mean no harm,' Bold said clearly. 'I'm merely looking around.'

'Well, you shouldn't be looking around here,' the other cub said sullenly. 'You're no relation of mine, and we don't allow strangers in our domain.'

'But you've no objection, apparently, to venturing into theirs?' Bold answered.

'You're one of the Farthing Wood creatures,' said the cub. '*That's* your domain.'

'On the contrary,' Bold replied coolly. 'I'm as much a White Deer Park fox as you are. I was born here too, you know.'

The other cub was silenced by this remark.

'What do they call you?' Bold asked in a not unfriendly manner.

'Ranger,' came the reply.

'Well, I'm known as Bold,' said Fox's cub, 'and I would like to ask you: is it necessary for you and I to continue the quarrel of our parents? We might be friends elsewhere. Why not here?'

Ranger said nothing. He seemed about to respond to this gesture of good will, when his father suddenly appeared. With his customary vicious snarl, Scarface got between Bold and his own cub.

'You are going to regret straying from the safety of your family,' he said with measured iciness. 'This will be the first and the last time you enter our boundaries.'

Bold stood his ground, wondering what move was going to be made. He tensed his muscles, ready to spring into flight the moment he had to. He kept an unwavering gaze on the old scarred muzzle of his enemy, ensuring that Ranger also was constantly in his circle of vision.

Ranger, in fact, appeared to be very ill at ease. He kept shifting his weight from one paw to another, looking quickly from his father to Bold and back again.

Scarface suddenly growled impatiently at him, comparing his restlessness unfavourably with the coolness of Bold. Ranger slunk back behind his father. Bold and Scarface continued to eye each other.

In a split second before the old fox launched himself forward, Bold read the intention in his eyes. He leapt nimbly aside and Scarface rushed past him a few yards before he could check himself. Bold faced him again and, this time, as he hurtled towards him Scarface signalled to Ranger to attack Bold's rear.

But Bold was far too supple for one old and one inexperienced fox. He had his father's swiftness and agility. He slid away from the attack and began to run back on his old path, back towards Adder.

With a wild bark of fury and frustration Scarface leapt after him. Ranger followed, more out of a sense of obedience than a desire to do so.

Bold ran easily and confidently, knowing he had the better pace. Then he heard a yelping cry behind him – an eerie wail of a cry, repeated over and over again. He quickened his pace, knowing Scarface was calling to his own kind for assistance.

Bold raced on – it was all he could do. Then, some yards ahead, he saw a flurry of movement. At the sight his blood ran cold. About a dozen foxes were running towards him, spreading out in an arc to encircle him.

Behind him Scarface's gasps rasped in his ears. He knew his case was hopeless. The other foxes surrounded him and halted his progress. Silently they awaited the arrival of their sire.

Bold looked fearfully from one pair of eyes to another. They were full of intent. There was no mercy in any of them.

——6——

Some Support

Adder, who had been watching during the remainder of the night for Bold's return, felt the first rays of the summer sun strike his body with their warmth. He knew it was time to report the cub's absence.

Slithering as quickly as he was able through the bracken and leaf litter, he arrived at the stream-bank. Adder was a good swimmer and the stream presented no problems. He forded it easily, and climbed the other bank. But Fox's earth was a good distance away and Adder knew it would be hours before he could reach it. His body was not constructed to travel long distances at speed. It was essential for him to find someone who could pass the message more quickly.

He knew of no Farthing Wood animal who had set up

home in the immediate vicinity. Kestrel would be the perfect messenger, but there was no way in which Adder could pass it to him hundreds of feet up in the air, even should he be flying over the Park. He might encounter one of the other birds, but Tawny Owl was likely to be asleep, while Whistler spent most of his time at the waterside. But the heron was not always to be found along the banks of the stream and Adder could spare no time on what might prove to be a fruitless search. So he struggled on overland.

As luck would have it, as his mosaicked body rippled through the long grass, he came upon Hare resting on his form of flattened stalks.

'*You* don't often pass this way,' Hare said.

'There's a reason for it,' Adder told him, and explained the urgency of the message. 'It's a definite stroke of luck running into you. You've probably got the fastest pair of legs in the whole Reserve.'

Hare did not hesitate. He was up and bounding away through the grass without so much as a farewell. Adder found himself a warm patch of ground and decided to do some basking. He was sure events would catch up with him again later in the day.

Minutes later, Hare's breakneck speed brought him to the entrance to Fox's earth. Inside he found Fox and Vixen, Friendly and Charmer already deeply concerned at Bold's failure to reappear. When they received the news that he had deliberately strayed into Scarface's territory, they conjectured the worst.

Fox looked strained. 'We must go after him at once,' he resolved. 'It may not be too late.'

'I'll go and alert Badger and some of the others,' Hare offered.

'No.' Fox shook his head. 'I've said this before and I'll say it again. This is mine and Vixen's quarrel. We'll deal with it ourselves. I don't want any of our friends getting hurt on our account.'

'Very well,' said Hare. 'But if you need help, it would be absurd not to ask for it from any reason of pride.'

'There are four of us here,' Fox indicated his family. 'Friendly and Charmer are all but fully grown. We will go, as a pack, to search for our missing one.'

'We won't be looking for any trouble,' Vixen added. 'We don't want any fighting. Our only concern is to find Bold and bring him back.'

'I wish you well,' said Hare sincerely.

'Thank you for bringing us word,' said Vixen. 'We may be able to thank Adder ourselves.'

Hare watched the family depart. He had little confidence, either that they would find Bold or, if they did, be able to bring him away, and all of them return unscathed right from under the muzzle of Scarface. In the sunlight again, he sat pondering. He did not care to defy Fox's wishes, yet he knew Badger and Tawny Owl, at least, would never forgive him if he did not warn them of the developments.

'I suppose all I can do is to pass on to them Fox's words,' he said to himself, 'and hope that they'll respect them.' He pondered again. 'Of course Tawny Owl is bound to act impulsively, as usual. Perhaps I'll just tell Badger.'

Having decided this, Hare ran quickly to Badger's set and found him entertaining Mole. He described the situation in a few words.

'I *knew* they were going to have problems with that one,' Badger said afterwards. 'But, after all, he's not really a cub any more. He has a life of his own now. Of course, the maturity isn't there . . .'

'Oh, why won't Fox let us help him?' bewailed Mole.

'I'm sure Scarface would respect the combined forces of all the animals of Farthing Wood.'

'A lot of you are so small as not to influence his thinking in any way, *I'm* sure,' Badger remarked. 'No offence, Mole, you understand. But an old warrior like Scarface is hardly likely to take much account of you or Vole – or Toad, for that matter. He's quite capable of making a tasty morsel of you for his supper.'

Mole looked a little hurt. 'Well, my intentions are noble enough, anyway,' he defended himself. 'But there's a lot to be said for numbers.'

'I think Mole's right, actually,' Hare agreed. 'Most of the creatures in the Park still think there's a certain aura about us. We made that famous journey – against all odds. We are looked upon as being exceptionally resourceful – why should we be intimidated by any danger that confronts us here after all we endured before?'

'That's it exactly!' cried Mole. 'I couldn't have put it better myself.'

'The only thing being,' Badger reminded them, 'that we are required not to get involved.'

'I suppose Fox wouldn't have any objection if we just followed along behind at a safe distance?' Hare queried. 'You know – just to satisfy ourselves everything was all right?'

Badger looked at Mole knowingly. 'What do you think, Mole?' he asked.

'Oh, I shouldn't think there could be any complaint about that,' he surmised.

'Then we'd better leave at once,' Badger said immediately. They had found the excuse they needed.

'We'll collect Weasel on the way,' he said. 'And as many of the others as possible.'

Hare voiced doubts about Tawny Owl.

'Oh no, we can't leave Owl out,' Badger said loyally. 'You leave him to me. He won't do anything rash, I'm sure.'

Mole took up his old travelling position on Badger's back and the three animals set off. Weasel made the party four in number and then the ranks were later swelled by Hedgehog, Rabbit and Squirrel. Tawny Owl was soon located and they all had a welcome surprise when Kestrel came swooping down towards them, having spotted the party from the air.

'I thought something was afoot,' he remarked when Badger had explained all. 'I'll fly on ahead and see if I can find Fox and family.'

The animals felt something of their old spirit of camaraderie returning as they went along, and they recalled their many adventures together on their long journey to the Park. At that time they had been united by a common desire to reach safety in a new home. Now, again, they had joined together in a new crisis. The safety of their old leader, Fox, in the *new* home was threatened and it was their duty to support him.

They arrived at the spot where Adder had encountered Hare, but the snake was no longer to be seen.

'He's probably concealed himself somewhere,' suggested Weasel. 'Adder was never one to admit to a community spirit. He always preferred an individual approach.'

'But he was never one to be found wanting in times of danger,' Badger asserted. 'I shouldn't be surprised if he isn't accompanying Fox and Vixen. They must have passed this way.'

The return of Kestrel brought them further news. 'Fox and Vixen are on the other side of the stream,' he told them, 'with the two other cubs. They've seen and heard nothing and they are proceeding very cautiously indeed.'

'Was Adder with them?' Mole enquired.

'No. No sign of him,' the hawk replied.

'He's probably sleeping somewhere like the sensible creature he is,' Tawny Owl observed and yawned. 'Best thing to do when the sun's up.'

'Adder never *really* sleeps,' said Mole. 'Not like we do. He's got no eyelids.' He giggled.

'We all have our own features, Mole,' Badger pointed out. 'Adder might make a joke of your short-sightedness.'

Mole fell silent. He had been touched on a raw spot.

Tawny Owl was still yawning. 'Dear me,' he remarked. 'I didn't realize I was so tired. Perhaps I should have carried on dozing. I probably won't be of much use.'

'I don't know whether any of us will be of use,' returned Badger. 'Fox doesn't want us to interfere. It's really only a case of giving moral support.'

They moved on to the stream and swam across in a line, Kestrel and Tawny Owl flying overhead. Once on the other bank they fell silent. The feeling that they were entering hostile territory came over them very strongly.

Rabbit whispered: 'Do you think there's a lot of point in our continuing? I mean, this area is patrolled by that hideous scarfaced fox and his family and – well, Hare and I are their natural prey.'

'You mean there's no point in *your* continuing,' Weasel emphasized dryly. 'Well, I suppose support that is given so timidly cannot really be called support anyway.'

'Just a moment, Weasel,' Hare came to his cousin's rescue for once. 'Rabbit has a right to be timid. Hares and rabbits are no match for foxes.'

'We haven't seen any foxes yet,' Weasel reminded him.

'I can smell them,' said Rabbit. 'I feel as if I am walking

right into their waiting jaws.'

'There's a nice thick bank of nettles there,' remarked Tawny Owl. 'Why don't you animals hide yourselves there for a while, and Kestrel and I will do some reconnoitring?'

The animals concurred, and the two birds left them for the time safely concealed.

An eerie stillness pervaded the air – all the animals felt uneasy. Rabbit, most of all, was unable to settle.

'It's like the calm before the storm,' he whispered to Hare nervously.

Squirrel ran up the trunk of the nearest tree on to a lofty branch to 'a point of vantage' as he put it.

Suddenly the sound of running footsteps was heard, approaching quickly. The animals peered out from the undergrowth and were amazed to see none other than Bold racing from the rear of the position they had reached, towards the stream.

Badger hailed him, and the cub halted on the bank. The animals ran towards him in a group.

'I escaped,' he panted. 'I'm too fast for them.' His shoulder was a little bloody. Bold discounted it. 'There was a bit of a scuffle,' he explained. 'Things really looked dangerous for a time. I've run hard – I must have a rest.'

Badger and Weasel led him to the nettle-patch.

'I'll just take a breather,' said the cub, 'and then I'll tell you what happened.'

7

The Result of Thoughtlessness

After a minute or two, Bold was more composed. He explained how he had become surrounded by Scarface and his tribe the previous night, and had fully expected they were going to kill him.

Mole gasped. 'How dreadful! What have you ever done to them?'

'Nothing,' replied Bold, 'except humiliate their leader on one occasion. But he has my sister's death on his conscience. He must have thought I had come for revenge.'

'What, against so many?' Badger asked incredulously.

'No, against himself.'

'I hardly think . . .' began Badger. 'I mean, if your father didn't . . .'

'Oh, my father is *too* cautious,' said Bold.

'In the wild,' Weasel pointed out, 'caution is the essence of survival. In the meantime your father and the whole of your family are out looking for you in the alien territory from which you have just escaped.'

'But we must stop them – get them back,' urged the cub.

'How do you propose we do that? Follow them?' Hedgehog enquired. 'We're too small and too few.'

'But *I* was on my own and *I* outwitted them,' Bold reminded him, a trifle boastfully.

'Well, tell us how,' said Hare. 'We're still waiting to hear.'

'Yes. Well, as I told you, I was surrounded. I was lucky it was night-time, for it was also hunting time, and it seemed that hunting was the foxes' priority. Scarface told his henchmen to escort me to an unoccupied earth, which they did. I was then forced inside, while some of the group stood guard at each of the exits.'

'And then?'

'They stayed behind while the others went after their prey.'

'How long were they gone?' Mole asked. 'You must have been terrified.'

'I don't know how long they were gone, because I knew that if I was still in that earth when they got back I would never get out alive. So their hunting was my breathing space. I started to talk to one of the animals left on guard, and managed to persuade him inside. He was not as big as I, and I made a rush at him, baring my fangs. As he sidestepped, I altered my direction in mid-career and bolted out of the exit. Once outside I skipped past the other guards and then I simply ran and ran and ran, knowing my life depended on it.'

'How does your shoulder come to be injured?' Badger wanted to know.

'There was a tussle on my way back. As I was running quite blindly, as fast as I could, I ran across two foxes busy stalking their quarry. One of them made a half-hearted lunge and grazed my shoulder. I don't think I was even recognized. I was just looked upon as a rival for their food supply.'

'Well, you are a remarkably lucky young fellow,' Badger observed, 'to have reached safety again.'

'I think my cunning and fleetness of foot had something to do with it,' Bold retorted.

Not for the first time Badger detected the note of boastfulness in Bold's remarks.

'Perhaps so, perhaps so,' he conceded. 'But because of your rashness in coming to this area in the first place you have put the lives of your family in danger and, to a lesser extent, ours also.'

'I'm sure my father will see everyone is quite safe,' Bold maintained.

'But he is groping in the dark, so to speak, isn't he?' Badger remarked. 'He doesn't know where you are, and until he does he will continue to search for you.'

Bold's face dropped a little. 'Can't we send word to him?' he suggested.

'But, you see, we don't know where *he* is. Kestrel and Tawny Owl have gone to find him. But when they do, they still won't know about you, will they?'

'Oh dear,' said Bold. 'I do seem to have caused rather a lot of bother.'

'You must learn to think before you act,' Badger continued sternly. 'That is the caution Weasel was talking about earlier.'

'I take your point, Badger, and I apologize. Can I do anything?'

'I don't see that you can, any more than the rest of us until we're more sure of the situation. We shall just have to wait here until the birds return.'

'I bet there were some recriminations when Scarface returned from hunting and found you gone,' said Mole. 'It's surprising they haven't come searching for you.'

'They must have been diverted by the sudden appearance of Bold's family,' Weasel remarked. 'In any case, they'll probably presume that by now he's safe back in his own territory.'

'I feel so guilty now,' Bold said contritely, 'leading you all into trouble like this.'

'Well, well,' said Badger kindly, 'as long as you learn your lesson from it.'

Squirrel came racing back down the tree-trunk. 'Kestrel's coming!' he called to them as his small body leapt jerkily over the ground. He had scarcely rejoined the party when Kestrel landed beside them. He uttered a cry of amazement when he spotted the fox cub. 'Goodness gracious! How are you come here?'

Badger related Bold's story.

Kestrel glared at the cub angrily. 'There's your father confronting your enemy and demanding your return and all the time you're lying here in safety,' he screeched.

'Where *is* my father?' Bold asked the hawk hastily. 'Is he in difficulties?'

'You could put it that way,' Kestrel returned scathingly. 'Why, is he to have the good fortune of being rescued by you?'

The bird's sarcasm was lost on Bold, who was more concerned with his family's whereabouts. 'Please tell me, Kestrel,' he begged, 'where he is – and the others, too.'

Kestrel relented a little as he recognized the real concern in the cub's voice. 'Your mother and sister are quite safe. They're lying low a little way ahead. Apparently your father went ahead on his own to the enemy camp, but your brother followed him.'

'You must get Vixen and Charmer back here with us straight away,' said Badger. 'Tell them Bold is safe. But surely, Scarface will have told Fox his cub is no longer with them?' he added on a thought.

'I don't know what they've told him, but Fox and Friendly are in real peril. They're completely surrounded by hostile animals.'

Bold gulped. 'I *must* help them. I caused the trouble,' he muttered woefully.

'You'll stay here with us,' Badger said sharply. 'When your mother and sister return, you must all go back to your den. Fox will find a way out of his predicament, I know.' But his words belied his true feelings, and he feared for his friend's safety.

Kestrel flew off again and soon Vixen and Charmer could be seen on the path back. Bold greeted them lavishly.

'I told Kestrel to pass on the news to Fox,' said Vixen. She looked at Badger worriedly. 'How will he ever get away?' she whispered.

'By superior cunning,' Mole answered confidently. 'Scarface is not in the same league.'

Vixen smiled thinly at Mole's attempt at cheerfulness. 'I believe he has Owl with him,' she said. 'Perhaps the two of them –' She broke off lamely. A miserable silence followed.

Bold became more and more restless. Then, suddenly, he cried out: 'Here's my brother coming!'

Friendly was indeed coming, but a more woeful, dejected beast would have been hard to find. He crept up to his mother and licked her muzzle forlornly. Then he looked at Bold. 'I'm glad to see you safe and unhurt,' he said. 'But we cubs and our mother are only allowed to be so at the expense of our father.'

All the animals began talking at once. 'What do you mean?' 'What's happened?' 'Is he dead?' 'What have they done to him?' came the cries.

Friendly looked at them all expressionlessly. 'So that I might go free, Fox has offered himself to the enemy to do with him what they will.'

'What *will* they do? Oh, this is too awful,' cried the anguished Vixen in despair. 'Friendly, you should have stayed with your father,' she moaned.

'I wanted to,' muttered her offspring, 'but he insisted – he ordered me away.'

'And Owl? Kestrel? Are they with him?' Vixen wailed.

'Oh yes,' he replied. 'The birds will stay with him. But what can they do amongst a dozen or so hostile foxes?'

'A dozen!' all the animals cried, looking from one to the other in horror, each one hoping another would make some sort of suggestion. Bold looked sicker and sicker with each passing minute. His sturdy form seemed to wilt as he felt the full impact of his recklessness.

Badger, as nominal leader, knew that it must be he who should make a decision. Yet what could he decide? The little band of friends was outnumbered and outmatched to a hopeless degree by a dozen foxes. He pondered miserably. The other animals found themselves, one by one, looking towards him for guidance.

Badger stood up and shook himself, trying to assume an expression of resolve. 'Well, my friends, we seem to be in a pretty pickle,' he said. 'We can't go forward and attack in the hope of freeing Fox, because we'd simply be hastening our own ends. Rabbits and squirrels and moles are not much of a test for an army of foxes. No, we can't risk anything like that. So I don't see any point in our remaining here; it would be far better to return to our homes while we can.'

The other animals looked at him in astonishment. 'We can't just abandon him, Badger,' said Weasel.

'No, no. *I* shall go to them. A supposed show of force would only antagonize. They must know me as a reasonable sort of fellow and I shall go along with the argument that they owe Fox something for his efforts last winter in ridding the Park of poachers.'

'That could be more of a hindrance than a help,' warned Weasel. 'Don't you remember how the poachers shot some foxes in the hope that one of them might be our Fox – because he caused so much annoyance? Scarface might argue that Fox had been responsible for these deaths rather than doing anyone a service.'

But Badger was not to be put off. 'At any rate,' he insisted, 'he *was* responsible for the capture of the poachers in the end by the Warden – and that was certainly a serviceable act for all the Park creatures. And, you see, I'm getting on in years now, and if anything should go wrong it's far better that it fall on my head rather than any of yours. You've got families or are still young and –'

'Oh, Badger!' cried Mole. 'Let me come! Don't go alone. Foxes won't bother with me. I'm of no account. I can't bear to think that anything might happen to you!'

Badger smiled at his adoring friend. 'No, Mole, old fellow, it wouldn't do. I'm very touched, but – well, I should be worrying about you all the time and that would be a bit of a hindrance, really, wouldn't it?'

Mole knew there was no answer to that argument.

'Now, everyone,' Badger went on. 'Please, all of you, go back home. Fox and I *will* come back all right – you'll see. Friendly, you'd better give me directions.'

This done, the brave old creature smiled shyly at them all and shambled away, leaving them to watch his disappearance almost before they had begun to accept it. It was in all their minds that, now both of their accepted leaders had placed themselves at risk, who in future would speak for the animals of Farthing Wood should anything untoward occur?

—8—

A Snake in the Grass

Such was Badger's faith in Fox's abilities that he became more confident as he trotted along, thinking his thoughts. He had no doubts that Fox could outwit his opponent, given the opportunity. He also found it difficult to imagine even the unpleasant Scarface exhorting his clan to tear Fox to shreds in cold blood. His methods were usually of a secretive nature – a surprise attack, catching the victim unawares. He recalled how he himself with Tawny Owl had thwarted Scarface at Fox's earth when the cubs had been much younger, and so had probably been blessed with his enmity ever since. But he was not afraid. Like all the animals of Farthing Wood, Badger was used to being on his guard – a habit induced by the greater dangers that had prevailed in their old home. So he was quite unprepared for the scene he found before him when he arrived at the spot.

Under a solitary Scots Pine, on which perched Tawny Owl and Kestrel, sat a very calm looking Fox. Facing him, and some yard or two away, stood Scarface and his assorted dependents. They were standing quite still. The space in the middle, between the two groups, was occupied by none other than the Great Stag, the leader of the White Deer herd which gave the Park its name. He seemed to be addressing all of them. No one noticed Badger coming along, so he too sat down a little way off, but near enough to hear what the Stag was saying . . .

'In my view all the inhabitants of the Reserve owe something to the animals who came here from Farthing Wood. The humans who came poaching last winter amongst my herd were a danger to all creatures, not just us deer, and it was due to Fox's bravery and resourcefulness, more than anything else, that the Park was finally rid of them.'

'Not without some loss of life to my clan,' Scarface growled.

'We too lost some of our numbers,' the Stag reminded him. 'And the toll could have been a lot higher on all sides had those men not been stopped.'

Scarface was silent. No animal cared to gainsay the inherent authority of the Great White Stag. The other foxes sat pensively, as if digesting the words they had heard. Badger wandered over to his friends by the pine tree.

'Er – I think now would be a good time to leave,' he whispered, and turned to give a greeting to the Stag. Fox nodded, and the two began to walk back along the path without exchanging further words. The two birds waited a little before they followed. The Stag seemed to feel the scene was at a close and made his exit.

Badger turned once as he and Fox proceeded quietly on their way. Scarface had remained motionless, an almost baffled expression on his face. He appeared to be conscious that somehow he had been outwitted, without quite realizing how this had been achieved. His dependents, to the last animal, watched him curiously as if waiting for a reaction. Meanwhile Badger and Fox were putting themselves at a safe distance.

'Well,' said Badger finally, 'the Great Stag's presence certainly saved the day. How did he come to be involved?'

'More by luck than judgement,' replied Fox. 'It was uncanny in a way. Quite suddenly he just materialized on the scene.'

'Did Kestrel fetch him perhaps?'

'No, no. The birds seemed as surprised as everyone else at his arrival.'

'There's more to this than meets the eye,' Badger rejoined, and fell to musing as they went along. No more was spoken on the subject for the time.

Their friends had all moved on from the earlier hiding-place and, as Fox was, naturally, still concerned for his family, Tawny Owl and Kestrel flew on to tell Vixen all were safe. Fox and Badger re-crossed the brook and, once on the other side, began to feel their relief. As they breasted their way through the long grass, a familiar figure reared up in their path. It was Adder.

There was something of a self-satisfied look in his expression that the preoccupied Fox did not at once notice. But Badger recognized it all right. 'Hallo,' he said knowingly. 'Do I detect the missing link in the recent chain of events?'

Fox looked a little puzzled as the snake's favourite leer was directed at Badger.

'How pleasant to see you both,' Adder hissed non-committally. 'This is developing into quite a parade. I've just watched the whole of the Farthing Wood community go past me.'

'Yes, indeed,' said Badger. 'And I know that the deer herd often go up to the stream there to drink. Perhaps you've seen *them* today too?'

'Aha!' cried Fox who had now got the thread of things. 'So you're the culprit, Adder!'

'Oh, I'm quite innocent in all respects,' Adder replied with feigned indifference. 'I often feel we snakes have a quite undeserved reputation for a sort of low cunning.'

'No, my friend, there is nothing low about you,' said Fox, 'apart, of course, from your necessary adaptation to life.'

Badger chuckled at the allusion, while Adder broadened his leer still further.

'Once again, I believe I am indebted to you,' Fox told him. 'But the result of my recent encounter will probably mean we shall all have to be even more cautious in the future.'

'I think one young creature has learnt his lesson today, at any rate,' Badger ventured to say.

'I'm sure he has,' Fox agreed. 'When I see him I shan't feel it necessary to raise the subject any further.'

Adder began to glide away.

'Before you go, Adder,' Fox called, 'where can we find you if we need you again?'

'I shall be within walking distance,' said the snake enigmatically. And Fox knew that that was the most he could get out of him.

'He saw the Stag all right,' Badger said as they continued on their way, 'and sent him in the general direction of the Scarface territory.'

'Yes,' said Fox. 'He'd hate to be counted reliable, but that's exactly what he is.'

From there it was not long before the two animals reached their homes. Badger went to his set, leaving Fox to be re-united with his family. A very humble Bold was the first to welcome him. Fox's only remark to him was: 'A little too much too soon, young fellow.'

—9—
A Wild Sort of Day

The following day the animals' attention was completely
occupied by the weather. An immensely strong wind had
got up and was bellowing through the Park, snapping
saplings and bending grass into great rolling waves of
threshing green. Even great trees were shaken where they
stood; the newly leafed branches tossed and cracked in
anguish, unloosing a furious shower of twigs on to the
ground.

The smaller creatures cowered in their homes,
shivering as they listened to the howls and screeches of
the rushing air. Birds flew wildly from tree to swaying
tree, unable to find a secure foothold. Only Kestrel stayed
aloft, buffeted all round the sky like a ball of paper, and
revelling in the wildness.

Unable to rest, Fox emerged from his den to investigate, leaving Vixen in charge. Every tuft of his fur was instantly assailed by the wind and blown all over the place. He narrowed his eyes against its fury and set off at a trot in no specific direction. In the woods he saw the trees heaving at their roots, like boats straining at anchor in a storm-tossed harbour. A creaking and moaning were audible everywhere. One small hawthorn tree cracked in two and crashed to earth, sending a frightened rabbit skipping away through the undergrowth. Rooks where wheeling over the tree-tops, raucously bemoaning their wrecked nests.

Fox saw a brownish shape spread wings and flit from one tree to another in a restless, disconcerted manner. He recognized Tawny Owl. He ran after him silently, knowing that if he called his words would be dashed to pieces by the strength of the wind. He caught up with Tawny Owl who looked down at him with an expression of alarm. 'This is terrible,' the bird cried. 'There's just no shelter anywhere.'

'You'd be better off on the ground,' Fox shouted back. 'It's firmer footing than any tree.'

Tawny Owl took his advice and then stood in a hunched attitude, looking slightly ridiculous with his feathers blown all awry. 'I hate this weather,' he complained. 'It's most undignified.'

'No good worrying about appearances,' Fox told him. 'You can't escape Nature.'

Tawny Owl snorted. He was not prepared to be consoled. They walked to a clearing in the trees and Owl pointed upwards with a jerk of his head.

'Look at that idiot Kestrel,' he grumbled. 'He's been up there all day.'

'He seems to be enjoying himself,' Fox commented.

'Precious little enjoyment in being blown to bits, I

should have thought,' replied Tawny Owl. 'Trust him to make a spectacle of himself.'

Fox chuckled at his friend's bad temper. 'Never mind,' he said. 'The wind's bound to blow itself out eventually.'

Just then an animal raced past them, out of the wood into the clearing, and dashed about in every conceivable direction in a completely aimless way. Fox and Tawny Owl looked at each other. 'Hare!' they both exclaimed together and laughed.

'He goes quite mad in this sort of weather,' said Tawny Owl. 'It's the same for all his kind.'

They watched Hare racing and leaping about, as if exhilarated by the day. Sometimes he would stop briefly and rear up on his hind legs, but a second later he would dash off again. Once he stood up and seemed to look right at them, but if he did he paid them no more attention than if they had been a couple of the dead leaves that were chasing each other over the ground.

'He wouldn't have noticed us if we had been directly in front of him,' Tawny Owl remarked. 'Every thought goes out of his head on such occasions.'

As Hare raced off again they were startled to see another animal running after him.

'It's a fox,' whispered Owl.

'And I know which one,' Fox answered grimly.

'Well, Hare's in no danger, anyway,' said Tawny Owl. 'There's no catching him.'

'Not if he runs in a straight line,' said Fox. 'But he's veering all over the place. In this mood, as you say, he's quite unaware of anything. He's just as capable of running himself into that creature's jaws as anything else.'

'Well, there's nothing we can do,' said Tawny Owl with a shrug, 'if he won't see or hear us.'

But Fox's fears proved to be groundless, for Hare had

evidently decided to finish capering for the time. He saw the alien fox as he stopped and lay down at a distance. Then he was up and bounding away at his matchless speed to complete safety.

Fox heaved a sigh of relief as Scarface, his enemy, consoled himself by lapping from a puddle in a hollow in the ground. His eyes looked straight ahead as he drank and, presently, he spotted his adversaries. With a muffled growl and a glare he slunk aside, eventually breaking into a slow trot.

'A nasty piece of animal flesh if ever I saw one,' remarked Tawny Owl. 'There'll be no hope of taking our ease as long as he's loose in the Park.'

'H'm. I'm afraid his occupation here is likely to be a lengthy one,' mused Fox. 'As he's told us, he'd been here a long time before we arrived. The Park is his home and must remain so, despite our wishes.'

'He must be of a great age?' wondered Owl.

'Who can say? But a hardier, tougher creature you'd find it difficult to meet. If there were any weakness in him from old age, he couldn't have survived that last terrible winter.'

'Pity!' ejaculated Tawny Owl. 'I know I'm pessimistic, but I've got the feeling that that character won't rest until he's done us some real harm.'

Fox looked at him sadly. 'You seem to forget, Owl,' he said quietly, without a hint of bitterness, 'that Scarface has already done that as far as Vixen and myself are concerned.'

'Oh! No, I . . .' stammered the bird, who *had* momentarily forgotten. 'I – I – didn't mean . . . I'm sorry, Fox,' he finished weakly.

'It's all right,' said his friend. 'Even we try not to think too much about her.'

The wind continued to howl horribly through the tree-tops. Weasel and Badger were the next to brave the elements, unable to rest. They came, complaining, up to the other two.

'I'm surprised you notice anything,' Tawny Owl said to Weasel. 'You're so slight and close to the ground.'

'Obviously, then, it hasn't occurred to you, that the frailer the body, the greater the damage,' Weasel answered sourly.

'Well, there *are* a lot of bad tempers being aired today,' said Fox.

'Wind creates bad temper,' said Weasel. 'A breeze is one thing, but this . . .'

He broke off as, just discernible through the wind's roar, the steady whistling beat of their friend the heron's wing could be detected. Presently his long body and thin trailing legs were seen approaching. He alighted and bowed to them in his old-world manner. 'A wild sort of day,' he commented.

'Very pleasant to see you about,' smiled Fox, as Whistler carefully arranged his one sound and one bullet-scarred wing across his back.

'I am glad to have seen you so soon,' the heron replied. 'I've been looking for you. I've just seen the scarred fox on the prowl and, from the look of him, he's up to no good.'

'He never is,' said Weasel. 'That's nothing new.'

'He was here,' Fox told them. 'Stalking Hare – quite uselessly, as it turned out. But thanks for coming anyway, Whistler.'

'He had an air about him,' said Whistler. 'An air of – er – how should I describe it? I think the word "wickedness" would suit as well as any other.'

'I believe you are right about that,' Tawny Owl agreed. 'That was the same sort of impression I got. It's as if he's determined to stir up trouble somehow.'

'Dear me. What can we do?' asked Badger.

'Nothing at all,' said Fox. 'He's free to roam where he will.'

'I hope the mice and voles are all under cover,' said Badger. 'They're so vulnerable.'

'At least Kestrel can keep a look-out while he's up there,' said Fox in rather a helpless sort of way.

'Humph! Not him!' grunted Tawny Owl disparagingly. 'He's too busy with his acrobatics to do anything useful. Such a show-off!'

'Now, Owl, I'm sure he plays his part as we all do,' Badger said. 'These are dangerous times and everyone is expected to use extra caution.'

'He never has a good word to say for Kestrel,' Weasel remarked bluntly. 'It's perfectly obvious there's a certain degree of jealousy in his attitude.'

'Jealousy! Jealousy?' expostulated Tawny Owl. 'And what is there to be jealous of in his tomfoolery? When Kestrel learns how to hunt in pitch blackness with pinpoint accuracy or to fly in total silence through the length of the Reserve without so much as a bat knowing about it, *then* I might have cause to envy him. But all he can do is to make an exhibition of himself.'

'Of course, you wouldn't concede there is a certain amount of skill or speed in *his* flying?' Weasel said sarcastically.

'That's enough, you two,' Fox said quietly. 'This is getting too ridiculous. If the wind puts you in this frame of mind, the best thing is to keep yourselves to yourselves.'

'Well, well,' intoned Whistler. 'And I've always looked upon you Farthing Wood creatures as inseparable. Perhaps a certain degree of tension in the air accounts for this contretemps?'

'I think there's a lot to be said for that observation,' said

Fox. 'Weasel, Owl, please – don't let's fall out amongst ourselves. There's never been a time when we should stick together more than now.'

'Yes, of course, Fox. I apologize,' said Weasel to Tawny Owl who looked away, ruffling his feathers.

'Owl?'

'Oh, very well. Er – sorry. To *Kestrel* I mean,' he said defiantly, glaring at Weasel.

The others laughed. Tawny Owl shuffled his feet, aware that he had ended up looking absurd again. But his discomfiture was soon forgotten. The unmistakable scream of a hare pierced even the deafening wind's bluster. The animals at once set off in a run towards the sound, while Tawny Owl and Whistler took to the air, the wind's fury forgotten.

Soon they saw Hare and his remaining leveret, now grown as big as himself, hurtling towards them. Their long elastic legs bounded over the ground.

'What is it?' Fox called. 'What's happened?'

Hare collapsed in a heap at his feet, great shuddering moans coming from him. He was unable to speak.

'It's my mother,' panted Leveret. 'Killed by Scarface.'

—10—
A Council of War

The animal's expressions on hearing the news showed a mixture of anguish and rage. But none of them appeared shocked. It was almost as if they had expected something of the kind to happen. Compassion for the two hares was their immediate concern, and they gave all the comfort they could which, for the most part, was unavailing.

Weasel was the first to voice all their thoughts. 'Now it's no longer just a quarrel between foxes,' he said. 'Whether we like it or not, we've all become implicated.'

Through his misery Hare said brokenly: 'This calls for revenge. She – she was slaughtered – just where she lay on her form. There was no warning. No scent, you see – the wind took that away . . .'

'Two deaths now in our community,' said Weasel, 'and the cause of both of them – Scarface.'

'We can't let this pass,' said Tawny Owl. 'We must fight back.'

'Oh dear,' said Badger worriedly. 'We mustn't do anything hastily. We have to be so careful. We're in the minority.'

'We will do nothing rash,' Fox said quietly. 'We shall plan properly. But Hare's mate didn't travel all that great distance from Farthing Wood to be savaged to death in her new home. If we have no security here we have nothing. This bloodthirsty creature doesn't kill for food but from envy and hatred of us.'

'I believe there is an element of fear in his behaviour,' observed Whistler.

'Yes,' agreed Fox. 'And he will have *reason* to fear us, too. I can promise him that.'

'Don't forget, Fox, our little band is weak compared with the forces Scarface can draw on,' warned Badger. 'We don't want to bite off more than we can chew. Wouldn't it, perhaps, be better to invoke the authority of the Great Stag in the affair?'

'Stuff and nonsense, Badger!' snorted Tawny Owl. 'What could he do? Scarface has just given the best possible demonstration of what he thinks of the Great Stag's authority!'

'Quite right, Owl,' said Fox. 'But there will be no pitched battle between the Farthing Wood animals and Scarface's army of foxes. Never fear, Badger,' he added reassuringly. 'It is subtlety that's called for here and that's where we have the advantage.'

No one paid any attention to the indirect compliment Fox paid himself, for they all knew he was the master of cunning. Only Tawny Owl liked to believe his own wits were a match for Fox's and he prepared himself to give the advice that would be needed.

But Fox continued: 'Scarface is our enemy. We have no real quarrel with his subordinates. I'm sure that they would do nothing on their own. That means we must eliminate their leader.'

'Do you mean *kill* him?' Leveret asked.

'Of course he does,' Tawny Owl chipped in. 'It's obvious that must be our first move.'

'Not first move, Owl. *Only* move,' said Fox calmly.

'Oh – um – yes, naturally. Er – would that be sufficient, do you think?' Tawny Owl answered, trying hard to appear full of wisdom.

'I think so,' replied Fox. 'Scarface is the trouble-maker. Without his presence, I am convinced the other foxes wouldn't interfere any further with us. So we have to find a way of removing that presence.'

'If I thought I could achieve that,' said Hare, 'I'd willingly sacrifice myself.'

'No!' said Fox shortly. 'My dear friend, we want no more sacrifices. I don't want another life lost.'

'No, no,' said Tawny Owl importantly. 'No *one* of us is equal to a contest. But together . . .'

'Together, what?' queried Weasel mischievously, who was quite aware of Tawny Owl's high opinion of himself.

'Quite clearly we have to ambush him,' came the peremptory answer.

'What, all of us?'

'Certainly.'

'Including the voles and fieldmice? Yes, I'm sure they would be very useful, Tawny Owl.'

'Er – humph! Well, no, not them specifically. You know I didn't mean *literally* – er – well, the whole – er – of us,' the bird spluttered.

Fox came to his rescue. 'I think I have a better plan,' he announced, 'though ambush does come into it, in a way.'

Tawny Owl completely regained his self-composure at these words and stretched his wings in a haughty way while he directed a look at Weasel which quite plainly said: 'You see!'

'I'm thinking along the lines of a great deal of stealth and surprise being used,' explained Fox. 'That would certainly be necessary. Now, who do you think fits best into that category?'

'Are you perhaps referring to yourself?' queried Badger.

'No, not at all,' answered Fox. 'I'm far too big. As I see it, there is only one candidate. He is capable of lying in Scarface's path, completely hidden. And he has the capacity to kill with one blow.'

'You can only be thinking of Adder?' remarked Whistler.

'Exactly,' said Fox. 'Scarface would be poisoned. Now, the only difficulty I can foresee is Adder himself. Will he cooperate?'

'Well, Fox, you know, he's such a strange creature,' said Badger. 'There's no knowing how he would react to such a suggestion.'

'Surely there *is* only one way to react?' said Hare. 'Is he with us or not?'

'That is never in doubt,' Fox said stoutly. 'But he does hate being told what to do. If we could somehow put it in his mind that he is the key to our safety, there would be no question of his not acting. He would make the decision himself and woe betide us if we should praise him afterwards.'

'That's Adder all over,' admitted Weasel. 'Well then, someone has to have a little talk with him.'

'Who is closest to him?' queried Hare.

'No one's close to Adder,' remarked Tawny Owl.

'Well, who is he most receptive to?'

'How about Toad?' suggested Weasel.

'That might work,' agreed Fox. 'But Toad would have to be found first and I don't know anyone who's seen him recently.'

'Toad's not the one for this job,' said Tawny Owl deprecatingly. 'It calls for someone with the utmost subtlety.'

'That lets you out then,' said Weasel rudely, who saw where Tawny Owl's remark was supposed to lead.

'How dare you!' he snapped. 'We all know *you're* incapable anyway.'

'Now, now,' Fox pleaded. 'Don't start again. D'you know, I think innocence may serve as well as guile with Adder? Then he's less likely to suspect he's being used.

'Now my cub, Bold, is always talking of the snake. I think he really admires him, and Adder probably knows it. He might be just what we're looking for.'

'An excellent idea, Fox,' enthused Badger. 'And Bold will feel he is going some way towards making up for his recent misdemeanour.'

'Then it's settled,' said Fox. 'I shall go and speak to him straight away. He can search out Adder tomorrow and the thing will be done.'

'Will you let us know how things go?' Weasel wanted to know.

'Yes. Let's meet again and Bold himself can tell you,' suggested Fox. 'In the meantime, Hare, you and Leveret must lie low. Farewell to you all for the moment.'

'Is Adder's venom really so powerful?' Leveret asked as Fox trotted away.

'I believe so,' Badger answered him. 'I understand even humans are fearful of snakebite.'

'Then he carries a deadly weapon indeed,' the young hare murmured. 'How I wish he had been close at hand when my mother was attacked.'

—11—
Bold and Cunning

Bold, of course, received his father's suggestion enthusiastically. He was overjoyed to be chosen to undertake the important mission of priming Adder. His brother, Friendly, was also keen to be involved and pestered his father to let him go too, until he eventually relented.

'Very well,' said Fox. 'I suppose there's no harm in it, as long as you leave Bold to do most of the talking.'

This confidence in his ability made Bold positively glow but, far from becoming conceited, he was only too aware of the trust being put in him. Fox explained to him Adder's whereabouts.

'We'll leave early,' said Bold. 'There's no time to be lost where lives are at stake.'

So, just after first light on the next day, he and Friendly

left the den to search for the unsuspecting Adder. Fox turned to Vixen and said: 'If he's successful in this, I think he's entitled to a little more independence. If he shows signs of wanting to leave the earth permanently, we must let him.'

'I never expected to have to chase *him* away from the family home,' remarked Vixen, 'but it's a task that often falls to the mother fox when the cubs are too clinging.'

'Yes, that's certainly one of the less pleasant of a vixen's duties,' remarked her mate. 'In your case, it may be our other two cubs who have to be chivvied a little.'

Vixen said: 'I think Friendly will go wherever his brother goes. It's this one who could be the problem.' She nodded towards Charmer who was still sleeping.

'Unless, of course, she should find herself a mate,' Fox pointed out.

Bold and Friendly went cautiously in the direction of the long grass and bracken that was close to the boundary stream. This was certainly where they expected to find Adder. After the previous day's rumbustiousness, this morning was calm, fresh and full of scents.

'What a wonderful morning to be out adventuring!' Friendly exclaimed to his larger brother cub.

'It's a very serious undertaking we're entrusted with,' said Bold. 'We should feel honoured.'

Friendly looked thoughtful. 'I hope we don't let anyone down,' he said doubtfully. 'Supposing we can't find Adder?'

'If Adder's around, he'll be sure to be keeping an eye open on everyone's comings and goings,' Bold replied confidently.

'Mole says his eyes are always open,' chirped Friendly as they entered the long grass, 'because snakes don't have eyelids.'

'Nonsense,' said Bold. 'How does he sleep then?'

'Perhaps Adder doesn't need to,' answered Friendly. 'He's not very active.'

Bold paused to scratch his flank. 'If you think that, you can certainly never have seen him stalking his prey. When he strikes, he's like lightning.'

'Thanks for the compliment, youngster,' came a drawling voice close at hand. Presently Adder slithered into view. 'It's a rarity to hear anyone saying anything pleasant about me.'

Bold felt he had made a splendid start. 'I know my father and mother have nothing but good to say of you,' he added eagerly.

Adder chuckled drily. 'That's loyalty for you,' he lisped.

Bold was not sure if he was referring to himself or his parents. Adder was looking at him penetratingly. 'Were you searching for me by any chance?' he asked.

'Oh no,' Bold fibbed. 'We were – er – just enjoying an outing.'

'Yes, that's it. Just adventuring,' Friendly chipped in.

Adder held Bold's gaze for a moment longer. 'Well,' he said at length, 'I'm glad to have seen·you.' He seemed to be about to move on.

'Er – won't you stay a little longer, Adder?' Bold asked hurriedly. 'We – we don't see you often.'

Adder's expression remained inscrutable, but a glint came into his red eyes. He was beginning to see how the land lay. 'All right,' he responded. 'Delighted to be in such demand, I'm sure.' The sardonic tone to his voice was now unmistakable. Friendly began to look flustered but Bold struggled to appear cool. He tried to think of an opening to the all-important subject. Adder waited.

'My – er – my parents send their regards,' he said.

'Thank you. Did they expect you to see me then?'

'Well, no. But, you see, they knew we might come this way and, of course, well – you're often about,' Bold floundered, looking round at Friendly for support.

'Ah yes, I did say I would be hereabouts,' Adder said knowingly. 'Are Fox and Vixen well?'

'Oh yes. *They* are,' replied Bold with evident relief at the looked-for opportunity presenting itself.

'You imply that someone is not well?' Adder rejoined.

'Hare's mate was killed,' Friendly announced rather baldly.

'That is bad news,' said Adder. 'How did it happen?'

'She was killed by Scarface,' Bold answered.

Adder's intuition had by now grasped the true purport of the cubs' appearance. Their inexperience was no match for his slyness. He knew they had been sent to look for him for some purpose. He laid a trap for them.

'No doubt Fox wants all the Farthing Wood band to avenge in some way this latest death?'

Friendly fell straight into the trap. 'No, not all. Just one,' he blurted out. Bold glared at him.

'I see, I see,' Adder hissed. 'And where do I fit in?' (He knew perfectly well, of course.)

'My father merely wanted you to know what had occurred,' Bold said, hoping to retrieve the situation, 'so that, if you felt you could help in any way, er – well –'

'I would do so?' leered the snake. 'Yes, yes, you need say no more. I understand perfectly.' He was enjoying himself. 'I'm to be the tool to carry out the job.'

'Why didn't you keep quiet?' Bold snapped angrily at his brother. 'You heard my father. It was to be left to *me*.'

'Oh dear, oh dear,' sighed Adder. 'Do I detect a slight lack of rapport?'

'I should have come alone,' muttered Bold.

Adder was greatly amused by the young foxes'

discomfiture. In his smoothest manner he said: 'You really don't have to find an excuse to visit me, you know I shall always be pleased to see you. I have thoroughly enjoyed our little chat.'

Bold's pride in his selection by his father was now utterly deflated. He had simply not been clever enough for the likes of Adder. His crestfallen appearance, however, stirred a flicker even in the snake's dry old heart.

'You may tell your father that I shall do all in my power to even the score,' he told the cub, 'and,' he added, 'nothing would give me greater pleasure.'

Bold pricked up his ears and looked at Adder in astonishment.

'Next time you come to see me,' said that knowing reptile, 'I hope it will be solely for our mutual pleasure.'

Then he was off, weaving his patterns through the long stalks of grass and producing only the barest rustle of noise.

'I believe even our father could be outwitted by his cunning,' Bold whispered in admiration, and wondered if he heard an answering chuckle through the fern fronds.

'We did it! We did it!' crowed Friendly.

But Bold was too happy to reprimand him again and turned hastily back to tell Fox of the result of their encounter. 'Listen, Friendly,' he said. 'There's no need for us to mention that Adder guessed we had been sent deliberately. After all, our triumph will be marred a little if we admit we were bested.'

'Isn't that being dishonest?' Friendly asked innocently.

'Even if it is, it doesn't matter. We've achieved the required result, haven't we? Scarface will be killed, and that's all that matters.'

Friendly was not happy about hiding the complete

truth, but decided he would say no more as he had already come close to wrecking the whole plan. Yet Bold's lack of honesty was to prove a costly mistake, and one which he was to regret for a very long time.

—12—

Death of a Fox

Fox and Vixen were proud and delighted at the outcome
of their cubs' meeting with Adder, and Fox lost no time
in spreading the good news that the snake was ready and
willing to strike against Scarface. The other animals were
relieved and, some, a little surprised that the immature
Bold had succeeded so easily in implanting the idea in
Adder's subtle brain.

Tawny Owl had said: 'So he fell for it, did he? All credit
to the youngsters, then. It's no easy matter to hoodwink
that rascal.'

Hare was particularly satisfied. 'I'm only impatient for
the thing to take place,' he told Fox. 'It'll bring a measure
of security to creatures like the rabbits and ourselves who
feel specially at risk.'

Badger was the last to hear and, despite sharing all the creatures' relief, was still a little doubtful as to what might follow. 'I only hope you're right about the other foxes' lack of aggression,' he remarked to his friend. 'If they should decide to gang up on us afterwards, there's no knowing how many deaths could occur.'

'Don't worry,' said Fox calmly. 'They will have no leader. With Scarface out of the way they will have no one to motivate them. He brooks no rivals in his neck of the woods, so it's certain that he won't have groomed a successor.'

'When does Adder expect to do it?'

'Who can say, Badger? He must wait for the right opportunity.'

'And then – when it's done – how long before we know?' Badger persisted.

'Only so long as it takes Adder to find one of us,' said Fox. 'Unless, of course, Kestrel spots anything. I know he means to keep a sharp look-out for Scarface's movements.'

'Oh dear, I wish it were all over,' Badger sighed. 'Our lives have been fraught with anxiety recently. It'll be a welcome change to be able to wander about freely again without feeling the need to keep turning one's head.'

But things turned out to be not at all as anyone had expected. Some days passed before they were all to learn the true situation that had arisen. The chain of events that led to the discovery of the truth began with Whistler deciding to fish further upstream than he usually did.

He and his mate had been standing patiently in the shallows of the boundary stream, watching for a likely catch. From the corner of his eye Whistler detected a moving shape on the bank. He looked up. It was a young fox he had not seen before who was tracking the water-rats. Although he had crossed to the 'wrong' side of the stream his pursuit appeared harmless enough (except to

the water-rats) and Whistler went back to peering into the
water. He became thoroughly absorbed again, and he
and his mate were eventually able to make a hearty meal.
When they were quite satisfied, Whistler looked around
again for a sign of the stranger. He spied him a long way
off, still wandering along quite innocently. The heron
was surprised to see the animal jerk suddenly to one side
and utter a sharp yap of alarm. He watched a little longer,
but as nothing further developed, he forgot the incident
and, tucking one leg up comfortably, prepared to join his
mate for a nap.

They awoke as the sun was sinking. A series of piteous
howls, each more protracted than the last, sounded close
by. For a while Whistler had difficulty in locating the
noise, but finally traced it to the same fox he had seen
earlier.

'Is he in pain?' his mate enquired.

'It sounds distinctly like it,' agreed Whistler. 'I think I'll
investigate.'

He found the fox staggering heavily in an uncertain
way in no particular direction. His breath was coming in
gasps and, even as the heron watched, his legs seemed to
give way and he fell on his side. He made efforts to get up
again, but his limbs only trembled spasmodically,
appearing to be all but paralysed. Whistler at once
divined the cause. Adder had bitten the wrong animal.

There was no saving the creature now. His end was
near. For a moment Whistler wondered what to do first
and, even as he hesitated, other foxes loomed out of the
dusk on the other side of the stream, attracted by the
dying animal's cries. They called to him and he replied
weakly. Now Whistler was awake to the danger at hand.

He was not afraid for Adder, who would obviously
have made good his escape long before. But if the fox was
able to identify the particular snake that had attacked

him, the information would soon be passed to his kind. Scarface would not take the action lying down. Whistler knew his duty. He swiftly flew back to his mate.

'Something has gone horribly wrong,' he told her. 'Adder has made a terrible mistake. We must warn our friends that Scarface is still alive, and the wrong fox has been killed. Find all of them you can and pass the word. I will go this way. We must be quick. Goodness knows what may happen now if Scarface suspects the worst.'

As the two herons set off in urgent search of the Farthing Wood creatures, Scarface himself arrived on the scene as the poisoned fox died. The others who had crossed the stream suspected nothing of the significance of the death. Their relative had disturbed a snake and paid the penalty for alarming it. But the hardened veteran of their tribe had a different nature. He sniffed the dead animal carefully for any clue. Then he sat down and stared at his minions.

'An unusual occurrence,' he remarked to them; but none responded. He looked from one to the other. 'You had, each of you, better go more carefully in future. Snakes should be avoided unless you're sure you can handle them. I myself have killed a good number in my time. Yes, and eaten them. Have any of you seen the snake in question?'

They shook their heads.

'There is one snake who is often to be seen in this area,' said the wily Scarface. 'If any of you should happen to see it around, perhaps you will let me know.' Then he turned his back on them and swam back across the stream.

Whistler flew straight to Fox and called him out of his earth. Fox looked grim when he had heard all. 'What on earth is Adder up to?' he demanded. 'This is no time for playing pranks. Now we're all in trouble.'

'Could he have mistaken the other animal for

Scarface?' asked Whistler.

'Not Adder,' Fox replied firmly. 'Scarface is unmistakable. I shall have a few sharp words to say to our friend when he comes to report his deed. In the meantime we shall have to post sentries in case of an attack. You go on, Whistler, and warn the rabbits and the hares to keep well out of sight.'

Fox ran off to round up Badger, Weasel and Tawny Owl. Then he positioned them and himself and Vixen at different look-out points where they remained through the dark hours. At dawn, after a quiet night, they disbanded and Fox lay above ground to await Adder. Kestrel, high up above alien territory guarded all of them.

The morning wore on. Inside Fox's earth Bold dreaded the appearance of Adder. If the snake were accused of inviting new danger he would have no qualms in placing the blame fairly and squarely on the shoulders of the cub. Vixen noticed his nervousness, while Friendly's distress was even more apparent. However, she wisely held her tongue until the cubs revealed themselves.

Early in the afternoon Adder approached Fox's den. He saw Fox drowsing, head on paws in the warm sun, and calmly coiled himself up until Fox should wake. When he did so, Adder was wearing a distinctly smug and self-satisfied expression.

'I don't know what you're looking so pleased about,' Fox growled. 'We've heard of your achievement from Whistler. If I may say so, I think you behaved in the most irresponsible manner.'

Adder's expression froze and, as always, he betrayed not an inkling of his feeling. 'You may say exactly as you please,' he hissed quietly, 'for all the effect it will have on me.'

Fox glared at him. 'Really, Adder, I've always credited

you with more sense. As if the situation hadn't been bad enough already . . .'

'Er – what situation are you referring to?' Adder asked coolly.

'Oh, stop playing games!' spluttered Fox angrily. 'I'm talking of the animosity between us and Scarface's brood.'

'It seems as if I took my life in my hands for no purpose,' Adder observed. 'Having redressed the balance of our most recent loss, I now find I was not expected to do anything of the kind.'

Fox relented a little as he recognized reluctantly that Adder must have put himself at some considerable risk for the enterprise. 'But Adder,' he reasoned, 'why act so rashly? If it had meant waiting a few days more for the correct target to show, what would it have mattered?'

'Target?' queried Adder. 'I don't follow you.'

'Do you mean to tell me that you didn't know the target was Scarface?'

'Ah, I begin to understand your reaction,' said Adder. 'I'm afraid I have to disillusion you. No mention was made of Scarface to me by either of your – er – messengers.'

'WHAT?' exploded Fox so loudly that Bold heard him inside the earth.

'It was merely put to me that I was to avenge the death of Hare's mate – which I have done,' the snake explained. 'I'm afraid the significance of killing Scarface himself didn't occur to me.'

'It was the whole point of the thing,' Fox said wearily. 'We decided that, as he is the only real threat to our safety, he should be put out of the way. I was quite sure in my mind that none of his band would have had the idea of blaming his death on us. But it appears we have all been labouring under a misapprehension.'

'I'm afraid we have,' agreed Adder. 'Perhaps you should have questioned your offspring more closely?'

'I'll question him now,' said Fox meaningfully. 'Bold! Come out here!' he bellowed down.

The cub emerged sheepishly from the earth. 'It's all my fault, Father,' he said in a low voice. 'Adder told us that he would even the score, and I assumed he would attack Scarface.'

'How could you assume such a thing when you never even mentioned Scarface's name?' Fox demanded. 'Now see what has happened. You've succeeded in creating a more dangerous situation than before by your dishonesty. You failed in the task I gave you but reported it as a success.'

Bold hung his head and Adder felt disposed to put in a good word. 'I suppose I'm partly to blame,' he said generously. 'I should have realized where your thinking lay. However, the prospect may not be quite as perilous as you imagine. I'm quite sure I wasn't recognized by my victim, and there are many other adders in the Park.'

'A small grain of comfort, I'm afraid, Adder,' said Fox, shaking his head. 'I know Scarface. He won't rest until he's proved his own suspicions and then – woe betide us all.'

—13—

A Matter of Heart

Fox and Adder parted, each with a certain amount of self-reproach. The snake was privately furious with himself for not recognizing where the main danger to his friends lay, and he decided at once to make good what he should have done before. But this he kept to himself. As for Fox, although he ticked off Friendly for being an accomplice of Bold's dishonesty, he then let the matter drop. He felt a share of guilt himself for placing too much confidence in his inexperienced cubs.

While the animals took turns to keep watch at night for the dreaded coming of Scarface, Adder lay low and pondered how he could get at him now that the beast would be more wary than ever.

Scarface, of course, had his spies and soon discovered

that the Farthing Wood creatures were on guard at night.
This served to confirm his earlier suspicions that the
killing of his dependent had been no accident. He
resolved to first settle the score with Adder, and then
attack the rest of the community in the daytime, catching
Adder's friends unawares.

However, it was no easy matter tracking a snake who
knew he was in danger. Adder, like all his kind, spent
most of his life among the roots of bracken and heather
and was not often encountered in the open. Sometimes
hot sunshine would tempt him out to bask, but Scarface
was not foolish enough to expect Adder to go in for any
sunbathing at present. If any snake *was* seen to be basking
now, it would not be the one he was after. Thus Scarface
and Adder were now committed enemies. So cautious
did they become that they both might have been
rendered invisible. It remained to be seen who should be
the first to break cover.

This situation gave a breathing space to Fox and his
friends. The nights were unusually quiet and uneventful
and Fox considered relaxing the guard duty he had
imposed. But Vixen warned him against it.

'That might be just what Scarface is waiting for,' she
said. 'He's very clever and could be trying to wear us
down.'

'Yes.' Fox sighed. 'You're probably right – as usual.
Your advice is sound and I'll abide by it.'

'There's something uncanny about the quietness at
night,' Vixen remarked. 'It's unnatural.'

'It can stay as quiet as this for ever for my liking,' Fox
replied. 'At least no more lives will be lost.'

Vixen nodded. 'I think you could give the cubs a turn
of guard duty,' she said. 'The training will be useful and
it'll take some of the weight off the rest of us.'

Fox agreed and Bold, Friendly and Charmer were

thrilled to be of use. Bold, in particular, was grateful to be
given another chance after his previous failure.

One night while he was keeping watch, Friendly and
Charmer went their separate ways to hunt. They were
allowed to do this as long as they did not stray too far.
Friendly kept religiously close to home in his wanderings,
but Charmer was rather less careful, and realized
suddenly she was a long way from the den. She had
caught nothing and was loth to return with an empty
stomach. She gave herself a few moments longer before
she must make her way back. As she trotted along,
muzzle to the ground, searching for a scent, she became
aware that she was being watched. She paused, one front
paw raised, to sniff the air. The unmistakable scent of fox
was in the air. Her body went rigid as she looked about
her. She saw a pair of eyes glinting in the bright
moonlight. A figure approached.

'I've seen you before,' it said. Charmer was relieved to
see it was just a cub like herself.

'Yes, I recognize you,' she responded. 'You are one of
Scarface's cubs.'

'I'm Ranger,' he told her. 'Once I met your brother:
the big cub.'

'That's Bold,' she said. 'I am called Charmer.'

'I can well understand why,' Ranger told her gallantly.

Charmer looked taken aback. 'I – I must return home,'
she muttered.

'Not on my account,' said Ranger. 'I bear you no ill
will. This quarrel is none of my doing. It is our parents'
battle.'

'My sister cub was killed by your father,' said Charmer
sullenly. 'We have no love for your tribe.'

'I understand,' answered Ranger. 'But I am not
responsible for my father's actions. He is a jealous animal
and a proud one. I am only a fox cub.'

Charmer looked steadily at him. He was talking sense. 'For my part, I think it's regrettable we can't all live in peace,' she said.

'I'm of the same opinion,' Ranger agreed. 'Perhaps our generation see it differently.'

Charmer sighed. 'Nevertheless our loyalty lies with our family,' she reminded him.

'That is true,' Ranger said flatly.

There was a pause. 'Er – are you hunting?' he asked her.

Charmer smiled. 'Unsuccessfully,' she answered.

'If you're hungry, I can show you good sport,' Ranger offered. 'There's a colony of mice nearby.'

Charmer hesitated. She wondered if any of them were the fieldmice she was forbidden to kill – the old companions of her father.

'Do come,' the young fox urged her softly. 'It's much more fun hunting with another.'

Charmer relented and followed where he led to a patch of scrub. 'There's a regular nest of them in there,' he said. Satisfied that the spot was too far away from the home area for any Farthing Wood mice to be involved, Charmer's mouth began to water in anticipation.

Ranger looked at her and said: 'I'll see if I can drive them out to you.' And he did just that. In no time Charmer had pounced on four plump creatures and had made short work of them. She was appreciative of Ranger's interest.

'You're very skilful in coaxing them into the open,' she smiled.

'Ah. I'm getting quite familiar with the ways of these mice,' he said, smiling back. 'I often spend an odd hour here. Sometimes I just stalk them if I'm not hungry.'

'I'm surprised there are any left,' Charmer laughed. They looked at each other for a long moment and something indefinable passed between them. Charmer looked away shyly. 'Thank you for taking the edge off my appetite,' she said softly. 'But I must be going. My brothers may come looking for me.'

'I'll come some of the way with you,' Ranger said hopefully.

'No.' She answered quickly, thinking of Bold's reaction if he should see them together.

'As you wish,' he said in a regretful tone.

'I'm sorry,' Charmer said quietly. 'I think it's best.'

'Well, I hope we may meet on another occasion,' Ranger said, leaving a question in the air. 'As I said, I often come to this spot. You will know the way now, I think.'

'Yes, but I don't always come as far as this,' she replied non-committally. But, even as she said it, she knew she would return.

'A safe journey back,' Ranger wished her.

'Thank you. The same to you.' Charmer smiled sweetly and set off at a trot for home. Ranger watched her go. His blood was singing in his veins. The thought of his father and of the young she-cub's parent was a long way from his mind.

Charmer saw Friendly ahead as she approached the earth.

'I was out looking for you,' said her brother. 'Were you lucky in your hunting?'

'Yes, very lucky,' Charmer answered rather breathlessly.

Friendly looked at her sharply. She seemed to be glowing with health, and there was something in her tone – he was not quite sure what. He questioned her no further and said nothing as they passed the spot where Bold was lying hidden. But he decided he would stay closer to his sister on their next outing.

*

The next night was Friendly's watch and Bold showed no sign of wanting to keep Charmer company. He preferred to be alone. Charmer went straight to the patch of scrub but Ranger was not there. She was bitterly disappointed. She waited a little, passing the time by pouncing on unsuspecting mice. Of course, it was not likely (she told herself) that he would come to that place every night. But she kept her ears cocked to catch every faint sound. At last, when she had given up all hope, she heard the sound of approaching feet and her every nerve tensed. She knew it was Ranger for she recognized his scent. He came carefully, snuffling the air for any strange smell. Then he saw her. They smiled at each other.

'I'm very glad to see you,' he said, wagging his tail.

'Oh, I – I felt like mousehunting,' she whispered. He caught her expression and they both laughed.

'I've caught some water-rats,' he said. 'Will you share them with me?'

'Where are they?'

'Oh, not far. Up by the stream.'

'Oh, no, I couldn't, I'm afraid,' Charmer said. 'It's too far for me. I'm not supposed to wander that far afield.'

'Oh, I see. Well, perhaps I could bring them a little nearer,' he suggested.

'That would be very kind,' she murmured.

Ranger loped off and soon returned carrying two carcasses. 'You start on those,' he said generously, 'and I'll fetch the rest.'

A few minutes later they were enjoying their meal together.

'It's amazing how famished I get,' said Ranger between mouthfuls. 'Soon I hope to hunt for bigger game.'

Charmer thought of Hare's mate and let the comment pass unanswered.

'You have a good appetite yourself,' Ranger went on approvingly, and Charmer knew what he was leading up to.

'I don't know if it would be possible for us to hunt together,' she told him. 'We might run into my brothers, or, worse still, my father.'

'Would that matter?' Ranger asked innocently. 'We mean no harm.'

'I don't think my family would see it that way,' she replied softly.

The words were hardly out of her mouth when Ranger froze and pricked up his ears. There was an angry growling close by and then Bold raced on to the scene, hackles rising. Charmer had not reckoned with his more venturesome spirit. Luckily she was obscured by a low branch of the shrubs and only Ranger had been seen. She decided the best course of discretion was to make herself scarce. Ranger stood his ground, though nervously.

Bold stopped dead, his fangs bared and his tail swishing incessantly like an aggressive cat's. He had no intention of attacking the smaller cub, but had hoped to frighten it away and achieve a moral victory for himself. But Ranger met his fierce gaze steadily.

'You're a cool customer,' Bold acknowledged, despite himself. 'You seem to have gained a little in stature since we last encountered one another.'

'I have a new source of confidence,' Ranger answered him enigmatically.

'Well, I have no wish to fight you now,' said Bold. 'The Park is as much yours as mine.'

'I'm not looking for any trouble,' said Ranger. 'Why need we assume we're on opposing sides?'

Bold laughed shortly. 'I think your father can be left to explain that to you,' he commented. 'I'm sure that one day he will see to it that you and I join battle.' Then he left the other fox standing where he was. No trace of Charmer was to be seen.

On his way back to the family den, Bold paused for a word with Friendly. 'Have you seen our sister?' he asked. 'There's a strange fox-cub abroad and she should keep out of harm's way.'

'Oh yes, I've seen her,' replied Friendly with the ghost of a smile, at once understanding the situation. 'And I can assure you,' he added pointedly, 'I've never seen her looking better.'

Bold had no reason to read anything into his words, and thought no more of the matter apart from reporting his meeting to his father. As for Friendly – he liked to think the best of everyone, as his name implied, and he certainly was not going to expose any secrets his sister might have. He only stuck to his decision to see for himself, when the occasion should arise, how serious the affair was becoming.

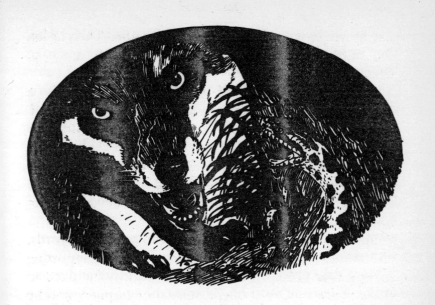

—14—
Adder at Bay

For days Adder remained in hiding, confining himself to a small area of dense vegetation not far from the boundary stream. He was completely concealed but could detect any movement by others close by. In this way he hoped to catch Scarface off guard when the fox decided to begin his wanderings again. Also Adder was deliberately starving himself. He wanted to maintain his store of venom intact – there was none to spare on his usual prey.

Going without food was no problem for Adder. As a reptile a good meal could last him many days, provided he did not move around much and use up too much energy. In his present, rather torpid, state he could fast for a long while. It was not until about the seventh day that the first pangs of hunger struck him, and even then they were mild enough to be ignored. However, Adder was experiencing another sort of problem. He was cold. A spell of very cool, cloudy weather had prevailed for a time and, in his dark place of concealment, no spark of sunlight filtered through to warm his blood. Unlike his mammal friends, the snake could not regulate his body temperature internally – that was why in the cold winter months he was obliged to hibernate. He relied entirely on external warmth to keep himself active, and he knew that if he could not heat his blood sufficiently first, he would be simply too sluggish to move against the enemy with the necessary speed when conditions permitted.

More days passed and Adder became more and more torpid. Then one morning he knew the sun was beaming again. He was desperate for warmth and knew that, come what may, he must venture forth and bask for a spell if his plan was to go forward. With the utmost care, he slid slowly from his screen of vegetation and found a small open space surrounded by bracken where the sun could be enjoyed in seclusion. There had been neither sign nor sound of Scarface and his tribe. But, unfortunately for Adder, he had no idea that Ranger was making nightly trips across the stream to keep tryst with his new friend and that, on this particular morning, he was returning late to his father's territory.

The cub, after his latest meeting with Charmer, had been so full of spirits that he had run the length and breadth of the Reserve in his new mood of confidence. The dawn had begun to break as he had lain, intently watching the activity of a ginger cat inside the perimeter of the Warden's garden. It was an animal he had not come across before, and it was only the eventual disappearance of the cat that had set him in motion again on his homeward trail. As luck would have it, as he approached the banks of the stream again, he had chased a rabbit into the very clump of bracken that fringed the sunbathing Adder. Ranger saw the snake and immediately recalled his father's words. He ran straight off to tell him.

Scarface received the news without enthusiasm. 'A snake is a snake,' he said. 'But I doubt if it is the one *I'm* interested in. He is far too secretive.'

'Well, he's lying not far from the spot where our cousin was killed,' Ranger persisted. 'Shall we investigate?'

'I think not,' Scarface replied sourly. 'You look in need of a rest.'

'Oh no, Father, I feel quite fresh,' Ranger asserted.

'That's for me to decide,' Scarface remarked bluntly, and the cub knew he was dismissed.

The old fox sat alone and contemplated. Although it was unlikely that the basking snake was the one he wanted, he could not afford to ignore even a slender chance. There might be some way of trapping the creature into admitting its guilt. If it appeared unsuspicious of him – well, he could still kill it anyway. One poisonous snake less was no bad thing. But he wanted no companions. This exercise called for all his timeless skill and cunning. He trotted in a half circle from his den and crossed the brook downstream. Then he slunk noiselessly and slowly towards the patch of bracken Ranger had described. His paws made no sound on the ground.

Under and through the stalks of fern went Scarface. His feet trod carefully on the soft ground, but even he was unable to avoid just the barest rustle as he brushed the dry fern fronds of last year. Adder detected nothing until the fox, in a final burst, breasted through the last clump to the clearing.

The snake wriggled quickly to one side as Scarface leapt out at him, his teeth showing. Then a chase began as Adder bolted for thicker cover, while his pursuer jumped this way and that, trying to head him off. Escape was now the only thing in Adder's mind – a counterattack was impossible. The element of surprise, essential when attacking a larger animal, was lost in this instance. Scarface snapped again and again, but amongst the bracken Adder was difficult quarry. The fox snarled with frustration. 'You – can't – get away,' he panted. 'You must pay – the – penalty – for daring – to attack – one of my – tribe.'

Adder was too busy to answer, even had he the inclination. So Scarface still had no idea if he were pursing the right snake. At last, just as Adder appeared to be cornered and the fox made a lunge, the snake found a hole in the ground and shot into it. But he was not quick enough. Scarface's ancient teeth closed on the end of his tail and held him fast. An agonizing tug of war followed. Adder grimly tried to pull himself away while Scarface's grip tightened as he attempted to haul the snake clear of the hole. During the struggle Adder's tail was actually bitten right through and the surprised fox was left holding over an inch of his vanished quarry in his jaws.

Deep in the burrow, Adder nursed his wound. It was a severe one but not fatal. When the pain subsided a little he took stock of his position. He knew Scarface would now wait outside the hole, hoping for his reappearance. How long he would wait Adder could not guess. But he could outlast the fox's appetite; of that he was quite sure. Now he thought of the trouble brought on himself by his attempt to help his friends, and he felt very aggrieved. Why had he involved himself in a dispute between foxes or, at best, between mammals? He would have done better to leave them to their own dirty work. If he survived his injury, his body would remain mutilated for all time. He thought bitter thoughts. After a time he painfully turned himself round in the burrow and was relieved to find that he was, at least, still mobile. He could smell Scarface's scent penetrating the hole and he seethed with anger. He crawled painfully nearer the entrance.

'You can wait there till you drop with hunger,' he gasped. 'I will stay here until I die if necessary.'

'You miserable crawling worm,' Scarface snarled. 'Did you think you could kill me like any other fox?' He was intent on discovering if he had cornered his true enemy.

'A violent end is your just desert,' Adder hissed back. 'You will meet it one day, though I may not be your slayer.'

Scarface listened closely. Still the snake had not committed himself. 'You have slain one,' he suggested cunningly, 'but you will never increase your tally.'

Adder remained silent. He was aware he must not reveal himself as the culprit for, if he did, he might never leave that place. At length he said: 'You have wounded me but I have escaped you. *You* can never claim you killed me, however long you sit outside this hole.' Then Adder said no more and Scarface knew that, eventually, he would have to leave the snake where he was.

Still he waited a while, and as he waited he felt more foolish. He had failed to discover who the snake was and, if the real fox-killer was yet roaming free, he was wasting his time here. The day wore on and, suddenly, as softly as he had come, he went away. Adder was left alone in the burrow.

As he lay wounded, he began to plot again. Despite his bitterness against his friends, who knew nothing of his suffering, a scheme entered his subtle brain. He had a new and more valid reason for revenge on his assailant. He had literally been caught napping by Scarface. But when the time was ripe, he would turn the tables on him and avenge this day's work for ever.

―15―
Caught Off Guard

The nightly meetings of Charmer and Ranger continued. No whisper of the arrangement reached Fox's or Vixen's ears, and only Friendly had been witness to it on one occasion when he had stealthily followed his sister's tracks. He kept to his private pact and remained silent. Charmer had no idea she had been trailed. Then one day Fox asked *her* to take the watch for that night.

He had resisted Vixen's suggestion up until then of including Charmer amongst the cubs required to do their duty. Now, after days of quiet, he decided the risk of an attack was far less likely. He believed Scarface had not yet been able to satisfy himself of the connection between the snake-biting and the Farthing Wood creatures.

Charmer gulped when her father made his request.

She was not averse to keeping watch, but she knew there was no way she could let Ranger know she would not be keeping their appointment.

'Could I perhaps take my turn tomorrow night?' she asked hesitantly.

'It's my turn tomorrow,' Fox told her, 'and your mother and I want to hunt tonight. What difference is there?'

Charmer was unwilling to arouse her father's suspicions by labouring the point, so she was obliged to concede. 'None at all, Father,' she answered meekly.

Friendly heard the conversation and wondered if he should meet Ranger and explain Charmer's absence. But that, of course, would be tantamount to admitting his own participation in the affair and that might well have repercussions. So he decided against it.

So it was that Charmer settled herself for the night at a convenient point while feeling concern for what Ranger might think. Every moment seemed an age in the darkness. Behind her, the family earth was empty. Fox and Vixen had trotted off together and her two brothers roamed free as well. She longed for the morning, or at least someone to talk to. She could see no movement anywhere, and the only sound was of the slow rustle of leaves in the night breeze. The night wore slowly on. Then she saw Tawny Owl flutter to the ground from a nearby tree. She called to him.

'Ah, good evening, Charmer, my dear,' he said in his rather pompous way. 'It seems you are our protector tonight.'

'Yes, for the first time,' she replied. 'But there's nothing around to cause any alarms.'

'It's a tedious job perching to wait for something that never turns up,' the bird remarked. 'I really can't see much purpose in continuing these vigils.'

'My father believes Scarface might be waiting for us to curtail them,' Charmer said.

'But we can't continue like this indefinitely,' Tawny Owl persisted. 'We're losing our independence.'

'I suppose he would say that that would be preferable to losing our lives,' Charmer answered loyally.

'H'm. Yes, yes,' muttered Owl. 'But I think Fox is sometimes just a little too cautious.'

'What would *you* do then?' the cub asked innocently.

'Me? Oh well, *I* would go and have a chat with Friend Scarface and see if we could come to an understanding.'

'Of course, we foxes haven't the safety element of a lofty branch to speak from,' Charmer said cheekily. 'We always have to stand our ground.'

'Er – yes, quite!' Tawny Owl said shortly. 'But I'm always willing, you know. Always willing.' He strolled up and down with his wings folded for a moment or two, rather self-importantly.

'Dear old Owl,' Charmer said to herself. 'Always full of suggestions but never carrying any of them out.' She smiled. 'Shall I mention your idea to my father?' she asked out loud. 'Or you could yourself, if you wanted to wait? He should be back shortly.'

Tawny Owl stopped pacing. 'Er – no, no,' he said hurriedly. 'No need for that. I've got to get on. He knows he can always count on me without asking. Er – good night, m'dear.' He rose into the air and flew away abruptly.

Charmer chuckled to herself. 'I shouldn't tease him really,' she thought. 'He's a good friend.'

The smile died on her lips as she saw a familiar shape in the distance, moving uncertainly in a variety of directions. It was Ranger who had come searching for her. Her heart started to pound as she realized the danger that threatened him if Bold or her parents should return. She must warn him. But she dare not leave her post.

The cub came hesitantly forward, stopping to sniff the air and then lowering his muzzle to the ground. He had, no doubt, picked up her scent. In the end Charmer stood up and Ranger spotted her. He ran quickly up to her.

'Where have you been?' he began at once. 'I waited and waited. Then I started to worry so I –'

'Sssh!' Charmer cut him short. 'You mustn't stay here. You're in danger. My father and brothers are out hunting and may come back at any moment. You've got to leave me.'

Ranger looked at her in bewilderment. 'But why didn't you come? he asked. 'I thought some mishap had overtaken you.'

'I can't explain now,' she said quickly. 'I'll do so tomorrow. But, please – go!'

'I met Bold before,' he protested. 'He's no savage. We understand each other . . .'

'You *don't* understand!' she interrupted him sharply. 'If he sees you, there's no knowing what he might do. You're out of bounds and –' Even as she spoke she saw Bold only a matter of yards away, trotting purposefully back to the den. 'Go! Go!' she wailed.

Ranger looked round, following her gaze. But he was too late. Bold had seen him. He raced up and immediately stationed himself in front of his sister protectively.

'I see I returned just in time,' he growled. 'You've come too far out of your way on this occasion.'

Ranger stepped back a pace but made no further move. 'Don't mistake me. I mean no harm. But I can defend myself.'

'We shall see, we shall see,' Bold whispered menacingly as he began to circle round the strange cub. 'Charmer, go back to the earth.'

'No, no,' she cried. 'Let him go, Bold. He came in friendship.'

Her brother paused. 'Oh, what is this? How do you come to talk of friendship with an enemy? What has been going on here?'

'Nothing has been going on,' Ranger was swift to reply. 'You sound like my father. Why do you feel enmity towards me? I've done none of you any wrong. I came to talk to Charmer in peace.'

Bold swung round on his sister. His eyes blazed. 'So you invite the enemy right into our camp?' he snapped. 'This is how you guard your friends!'

'There was no invitation, Bold,' said Ranger evenly. 'Your sister had no knowledge of my approach.'

'Were you asleep, then,' Bold demanded of his sister, 'that a strange fox could come almost up to our earth unawares?'

'No, I was wide awake,' she retorted. 'I saw him come.'

'You *saw* him and gave no alarm?' Bold barked. 'You are a fine sentry, sister!'

'I know Ranger to be no threat,' she explained calmly.

'Oh, and so you would have thought the same if his father had been behind him with a dozen other foxes?' Bold was furious. 'You were put in a position of trust,' he growled. 'Now, how do you justify yourself?'

Friendly now joined the scene and saw how things were. 'Come away a second,' he whispered to his brother. 'There's something you should know.' But what he told Bold only made the cub more angry. He rushed back and leapt at Ranger.

'You'll leave my sister alone!' he snarled, and snapped at the smaller cub viciously.

Charmer ran between them despairingly. 'Don't fight! Not over me,' she pleaded.

It was at this juncture that Fox and Vixen appeared. 'Bold! Charmer! Stand away!' Fox commanded. 'What is happening here?'

'Your daughter is a traitor,' Bold panted. 'She defends our enemy against her own brother!'

'It's not so, Father,' Charmer almost wept. 'I want no one to fight over me.'

Fox and Vixen exchanged glances. Friendly decided to act as mediator. 'Charmer and this strange cub, Ranger, are friends,' he said simply. 'Bold feels they shouldn't be. I believe Ranger to be quite harmless.'

Fox looked at each cub carefully. Then he spoke to Ranger. 'I know you to be one of Scarface's cubs,' he said. 'Is this true what I hear?'

'Yes,' said Ranger. 'I make no secret of it. Charmer and I met by chance and we have become friends.'

'I see,' said Fox coolly. Then he turned to the vixen cub. 'I left you on guard. Is this how you break my trust?'

'But I didn't,' sobbed Charmer. 'I have been at my post all night. Tawny Owl will vouch for me. Ranger was foolish enough to come in search of me, even into such a dangerous situation.'

Vixen smiled at her daughter. 'There's no real harm done,' she said soothingly to Fox. 'I think we'd better hear this story from the beginning. Ranger, you return to your own family for the present. We have some talking to do in our own den.'

'I'll go at once,' he said politely.

'Is he to go free?' Bold cried. 'To go back and inform his father we keep watch for him every night?'

'I want no battles,' Ranger said hotly. 'I shall tell him nothing.'

Fox pondered for a moment. 'Very well,' he said. 'I

shall hold you to your word. You are on your honour. But if ever I find out you have tricked us, it will be the worse for you.'

Ranger cast one sad glance at Charmer and turned on his heel. They watched him go. Then Fox led his family into their earth.

Some time later, when Charmer had explained everything, Vixen nuzzled the frowning Fox. 'These things happen, my love,' she said kindly. 'We never prepared ourselves for such a turn of events.'

—16—

The Attack

Ranger's father, meanwhile had been brooding over his course of action. The episode with Adder had put him in a very black humour. It seemed to Scarface that every encounter with his enemies ended in frustration. He had not managed to kill the snake and he longed to give vent to his pent-up fury in some way. In his own mind Fox and his friends were to blame for everything that went wrong for him, and he seethed with anger and jealousy. His mate, his cubs and his other dependents kept well clear of him in his latest mood. They expected an eruption and went about uneasily, scarcely conversing, and wished the storm would break.

On the night of Ranger's altercation with Charmer's family, the cub returned to find Scarface's tribe gathered to listen to their scion's intentions. He slunk to the back of the group when his father was looking aside.

'I can wait no longer,' Scarface was saying. 'These creatures are a threat to us all as long as they live. I intend to dispose of every one of them. We will attack them in the daylight hours when they are unguarded. It will be a swift attack, in full force, and those that are hidden will be searched out. I want complete destruction of every one of them, their homes and even their memory. I hope I am understood?'

No voice disputed.

'It is arranged, then,' pronounced Scarface with satisfaction. 'In two days we will assemble here as the light breaks. Now go and strengthen yourselves for the struggle.'

As the group broke up, Ranger wandered off alone to think. His heart told him he should warn Charmer so that, if she felt as he did, at least the two of them could escape the battle, even if it should mean leaving the Reserve. Why *should* they suffer for their parents' enmity? Only *their* lives mattered now. Ranger cared not a jot for Charmer's brothers, nor for her father and mother, and he had no conception of their bonds with the other animals who had come with them to the Park. That was his first reaction. Yet he knew Charmer would never agree to desert her family. She would be less selfish for the future of the pair of them, even if she wished to be his mate. Then, what of his own family? He owed them some loyalty. Could he really be coward enough to run away as they fought for their existence? The more he thought, the more he returned to the same conclusion. Somehow he must prevent this battle.

It would be useless to try and change his father's mind, even for the sake of unity in the Reserve. Scarface was blinded by his hatred for Fox and his desire to be the undisputed authority over the Park's inhabitants with the sole exception of the Great Stag. But what if he gave warning to Charmer to move her family to a place of safety? Yet, after recent events, would she still come to their meeting place or would she be forbidden? If she were not there the next night it would be too late to avoid the collision.

Daylight came and Ranger was still undecided. He felt that many lives might depend on his action, and the full weight of the realization bore down on him. At length he resolved to go that night to the meeting-place and, should Charmer not appear, he must once again go in search of her. Then, worn out with anxiety, he lay down and fell into an uneasy sleep.

It was dark when he awoke and Ranger at once set off in the hope of seeing Charmer. He was quite astonishingly hungry and any likely morsel that crossed his path was immediately snapped up. He was unaware that he had slept a very long time. When he reached the meeting-place and found Charmer was not there, he had no way of knowing that she had got tired of waiting for him and left.

Now Ranger waited, more and more anxiously as time passed. Bitterly disappointed, he knew he would have to pluck up his courage and go deep into Charmer's home area again. But he did not get so far on this occasion. A fox came out of the hawthorn thicket right in front of him, barring his way. It was his father.

'Aha!' said Scarface with a look of cunning. 'Another one testing the lie of the land!'

Ranger was too taken aback to reply.

'Good lad, good lad,' his father went on, not unkindly. 'I never knew you had it in you, Ranger. Up to your father's old tricks, eh? Well, you shall be in the forefront with me tomorrow. We'll teach them all a lesson, you and I. Come on, my boy. Kill me something – I'm starving. I've seen all I want to see for tonight.'

So Ranger was trapped into accompanying his parent back through the area he had just crossed. Even when he was lucky to flush out a partridge Scarface insisted he stay and share it with him. There was no escape. As a final resort, he tried to persuade his father to abandon the attack.

'Must we continue to look upon ourselves as their enemies?' he asked. 'There will be pain and death on both sides.'

'We can't expect to emerge unscathed from a battle,' came the reply. 'My old face bears witness to that. But they *are* our enemies. Yes, a few will fall. But we shall prevail in the end.'

'Why can't we all live in harmony?' Ranger tried again. 'There is plenty of room in the Park for all. We need never come into contact with them.'

'There *was* harmony until the Farthing Wood fox arrived with his conceited cronies,' Scarface snapped. 'But we were here first. The right is on our side.'

'Surely we shall appear to be the aggressors if we attack them? Please, Father, is there no other way?' Ranger begged.

'No other way? Oh yes, we could surrender, I suppose,' sneered Scarface. 'I was wrong about you after all, I see. You're the same cowardly milksop I took you for. Would that you were *his* offspring and his mine!'

Ranger's spirits sank completely. It was hopeless. In despair, he thought of the morrow. Nothing could save those creatures now. But while there was blood still in his

body, he vowed that Charmer should come to no harm –
even if it should mean fighting Scarface himself.

There was one factor in favour of the newcomers to White
Deer Park, quite overlooked by Scarface, and that was
Kestrel. Ever since the slaughter of Hare's mate he had
maintained his observation of the Park by day. High in
the summer sky his piercing gaze detected movement
around Scarface's territory. He dropped height and
found the foxes massing behind their leader. He waited
no longer.

Swift as an arrow he sped to warn his friends. The first
he saw was Rabbit who was nibbling clover with some of
his kin. 'Get down to your warren!' screeched Kestrel.
'There's trouble coming!'

'Is it Scarface?' Rabbit called as his relatives bolted for
their burrows.

'Yes – no time to lose. Is Hare about?'

'Haven't seen him,' Rabbit shouted over his shoulder
as he scuttled for cover.

Kestrel flew on to Fox's earth. Luckily he was lying in
the sun near its entrance. 'This is it!' Kestrel warned him.
'He's coming in force.'

Fox leapt up. 'Right, warn all you see to hide
themselves. Come back to me later.' Kestrel sped on,
scanning the ground. Fox called to his family: 'Quickly,
all of you, off to Badger's set. Tell him the reason and go
deep down. I'll follow.'

With Vixen leading the cubs to Badger's safer home,
Fox loped off to Weasel's nest. In no time Weasel was
following Fox's family to the set. Leaving Kestrel to
search for Hare and Leveret, Fox now thought of the
voles and fieldmice. The little creatures might be safe
enough in their holes but some could be wandering

abroad and, in any case, Fox did not want to risk their being dug out of their tunnels by the vindictive Scarface. He found Vole and broke the news.

'Where are we to go?' Vole shrieked in alarm.

'Badger's set,' said Fox. 'Waste no time. The enemy is on the move.'

'But it's a long way for tiny legs like ours,' Vole squeaked.

'Then start at once!' Fox snapped impatiently. 'You'll be safer there, believe you me.' He ran on to warn the fieldmice, who, fortunately, were a little closer to Badger's home. On the way he shouted to a squirrel: 'Get aloft, all of you, and don't come down till I tell you!'

In the next few minutes, a small stream of mice were scurrying as fast as they could go in the wake of their larger friends. Fox paused, panting for breath. As he did so, he saw Whistler approaching. The heron had seen Scarface's troop crossing the brook and had come at once.

'Thanks, my friend,' said Fox. 'Find Tawny Owl and wake him up. We may need him. But stay well out of harm's reach.' Then he ran off to alért the hedgehogs.

Kestrel found him almost driving his spiny little friends before him in his anxiety to get them underground. Fox and the hawk compared notes. Hare and Leveret had been located and Kestrel had sent them to join their cousins in the rabbit warren.

'I should have preferred us all to be under one roof,' said Fox, 'but there's no time for that now. Have you seen anything of Toad or Adder?'

Kestrel shook his head.

'Well, they'll have to fend for themselves,' Fox said hurriedly. 'I dare say they'll be safe enough.' He stopped and cast about, as if mentally ticking off the animals one by one. 'H'm. All accounted for that can be, I think,' he murmured. 'Kestrel, you've probably saved the day. Owl and Whistler will be waiting for you. Now I must run.'

The last of the mice were entering Badger's set as Fox came racing up. The hedgehogs had overtaken them and, in Badger's deepest chamber, plunged in total darkness, Fox was greeted by his worried friends and family.

'There's one missing,' Badger told him.

'Who's that?'

'Mole.'

'Oh well, he's one we needn't concern ourselves about,' Fox replied. 'He's not likely to surface when he hears all those footsteps up above.'

The animals fell silent as they strained to catch a sound of the approaching marauders. Outside the set, Whistler and Tawny Owl were perched well out of sight in a lofty oak tree. But Kestrel had returned to his natural element – the sky – to watch the enemy.

Scarface, with Ranger and his other cubs alongside him, came cautiously into sight with the other foxes close behind. Everything was perfectly still and silent around them. The fox leader looked puzzled. He had intended to catch his rivals unawares; yet there was no sign of any movement of any sort. Surely some creatures would be about? Then he happened to look up and see Kestrel wheeling free across the blue expanse above them, and he understood.

A crafty grin stole over his fearsome features. He turned round to his followers. 'My friends,' he said softly, 'it looks as though we have some digging to do.'

Ranger looked at his sire in alarm as he saw him directing his band to Fox's earth. Now he must defend Charmer against whatever threat might face her. He ran ahead of the other foxes and reached the entrance first.

He heard Scarface's dry chuckle behind him: 'Oh, are you going to make up for your previous timidity by your eagerness now?'

He entered Fox's den and at once picked out Charmer's scent amongst the others that pervaded the place. He quickly emerged again. 'It's quite empty,' he announced.

Scarface frowned. 'Is it indeed?' he hissed. 'Now where can our Farthing Wood friends be lurking?' He started to look around him and then sniffed the ground thereabouts. 'Oh yes, there's a trail here to be followed,' he muttered. 'Ranger, come here. Your nose is sharper. Lead me to them!'

The reluctant cub bent his muzzle to the ground as directed. A confusing variety of scents assailed his nostrils. Amongst them was one he knew he would recognize anywhere. He thought quickly. Here was a chance for him to lead the wretched band astray.

'Well?' boomed his father. 'Don't just stand there. Track them!'

Ranger followed Charmer's scent for a while to give himself some idea of which direction she had travelled. Then he veered off after a hundred yards or so, losing her completely. For a time Scarface and the others followed in silence. But eventually the old fox became impatient.

'Where are you taking us? We're no nearer discovering them!' he cried testily.

Ranger stopped. 'It – it seems to peter out here,' he said hesitantly.

'Can't you even follow a trail?' snapped his father, bending his scarred head to the path. 'Oh, I can't smell anything! You, come here!'

Another cub's nose was put to the test to no avail.

'Ha! So you've lost it?' Scarface snarled at Ranger

angrily. 'Get to the back of the pack. You're worse than useless.'

Ranger slunk away, wondering what the outcome of his misdemeanour would be. Scarface was furious. 'I'll not be frustrated again!' he swore. 'I'll take some spoils!'

Even as he was cursing, a sort of miniature earthquake seemed to take place right in front of his eyes. A blunt snout and then a furry head, besprinkled with mould, peered out of a hole. Poor Mole, who had heard the running feet above one of his tunnels, had come to see what he had thought was his friends gathering.

'Hal – lo,' said Scarface menacingly. 'You look as if you might be of help.'

Mole jumped. 'Oh! Help? Help to whom?' he cried nervously.

'You're one of the Farthing Wood fox's friends, aren't you?' wheedled Scarface.

'What if I am?' said Mole stoutly. 'Why do *you* ask?'

'Well, you could leave this message for me,' answered Scarface, accompanying his words with a vicious snap at the little creature. His jaws raked the delicate fur of Mole's body and tore through the skin. But Mole turned tail and frantically began to dig himself back into his tunnel.

'Dig him out! Dig him out!' Scarface commanded. 'We'll have one victim!'

But Mole had no rivals as a tunneller and he was soon yards away on the route to Badger's home before his attackers had barely disturbed the soil.

Scarface now rounded on his companions. 'So even a mole is too much for you, it seems? You can't track, you can't dig! Perhaps it's just as well we've done no fighting. You might have had to tackle a hedgehog or a squirrel and then how would you have managed?'

His tribe skulked away from him, looking cowed and resentful. Scarface sneered at them. 'I think you all need a bit of training,' he said. 'Our fierce friends can't stay hidden all day. You'll have to face them eventually. And if any of you have other ideas I'll have you fighting each other!'

Leaving them behind, he went and lay down by himself to wait. 'I've got all the time in the world,' he said to himself. 'I'll make them come out or they'll starve to death.'

—17—
Underground

When Mole stumbled into Badger's set he was amazed to find most of his other friends already there. But he quickly realized the reason for it. He described his tussle with Scarface and Badger jumped up to examine the little animal's wounds. Because of the darkness he had to do this by scent. Mole told him that the damage was only slight.

'How many of the enemy are there?' Fox wanted to know.

'I didn't have time to count,' Mole answered. 'But there certainly seemed to be quite a horde of them.'

Fox looked exceptionally grim but, thankfully, his expression could not be seen in the blackness.

'We'll stay put for the present,' he told them all, 'until

I'm more sure of developments. Does Scarface know of your set, Badger?'

'Probably. He seems to know most things,' answered Badger. 'We're very vulnerable in here, you know, Fox,' he added. 'We have no food – any of us – and there's nothing to stop Scarface coming down here just as you did.'

'We have *one* advantage,' Fox pointed out. 'Our enemies can only come down your tunnel one at a time. So we can dispose of them in the same sequence.'

'But Badger has more than one entrance to his set,' Weasel remarked. 'What of that, Fox?'

'Then we must block all but one,' replied Fox.

'No!' Badger said sharply. 'If we leave ourselves only one exit we could be trapped here.'

Fox thought for a moment. 'I think you had better give me a short tour,' he said to Badger. 'Then I shall know how we're fixed.'

Badger nodded and led Fox out of the chamber. Once away from the others Fox asked: 'What do you think our chances are of defending this place?'

'Slight,' Badger said bluntly. 'All you can do is to post the strongest animals at each entrance.'

'How many entrances do you have?'

'Four.'

Fox mused. 'It's all but hopeless,' he said wearily. 'As a fighting force we are effectively six strong: Vixen and myself, Bold, Friendly and Charmer and yourself. Weasel's too small to be of much help. As for the others, all that can be said is that their hearts are in the right place.'

'I wonder why Scarface chose to come during the daytime?' remarked Badger.

'Obviously he knew about our watch system at night,' Fox said. 'I think I know where that piece of treachery stems from.' He was thinking of Ranger.

Badger looked at him blankly. 'Surely we don't harbour a traitor amongst us?' he whispered.

'Not exactly,' Fox answered. 'But the workings of the heart can blind us to our duty.' Of course, he had then to explain the development of Charmer's friendship with one of Scarface's cubs.

'Goodness gracious!' exclaimed Badger. 'This is one development I never looked for.'

'That's pretty much what Vixen said,' Fox told him. 'Naturally, Charmer trusted her new friend implicitly.' He made a sour face. 'As if I hadn't enough problems already.'

'There's just a chance she might have been right to do so,' Badger observed. 'I think we may be in danger of making Scarfaces of all the other foxes.'

'I suppose there's something in what you say,' Fox allowed him. 'Perhaps I am maligning him. But I feel this raid is too much of a coincidence.'

'You're probably right,' agreed Badger. 'The cub's loyalty is bound to lie with his father.'

'Unlike *my* cub, I suppose?' Fox suggested bitterly.

'Not at all,' Badger declared. 'That's a bit strong, my friend.'

They were silent for a moment or two. Then Fox said: 'I wish I knew what was going on outside.'

'Why don't you ask Mole to go back the way he came and have a look?' Badger asked.

'No, bless him, I wouldn't expose him to that savage's mercy again,' Fox answered. 'In any case, his eyesight's so poor he wouldn't be able to discover much.'

'*I'll* go then,' Badger volunteered. 'I'll be very careful, and I shall know by their scent how close they are. I needn't go outside at all.'

'Thanks, my dear fellow,' said Fox. 'Meanwhile I'll post

someone at each of the other exits.'

Badger shuffled off down the tunnel and paused near his main entrance hole. Exercising his powerful sense of smell he turned his striped head in all directions, sniffing for the tell-tale odour of the group of foxes. Then he went back to the chamber.

'There's only a faint smell,' he announced, 'so they can't be very close.'

'Good,' responded Fox. 'But I wonder what he's up to?'

'We shall know soon enough, I'll be bound,' said Weasel.

'I'm worried about Hare and the rabbits,' Fox confessed. 'They won't know what's going on, and we know how jittery the rabbits are. If Hare can't keep them calm, they might start to panic down in their burrows and then they'll be coming out and running all over the place. Scarface and his tribe would have a field day.'

'Surely one of the birds will come and tell us of any further movement?' Vole asked querulously. '*They're* all out of danger. Aren't they thinking of us?'

Fox nodded. 'I'm sure Kestrel will come,' he said soothingly, 'and, don't forget, you have him to thank for giving us all the breathing space at the beginning.'

The day dragged on and, just as Fox was wondering if his faith in the hawk was misplaced, Kestrel could be heard calling outside. Vixen, who was now guarding the main entrance answered him.

'Scarface is coming nearer,' Kestrel told her. 'I think he must have guessed now where you're all hiding. You'd better tell Fox.'

But Fox was already coming up the tunnel. 'Kestrel,' he called. 'Please go and see how the rabbits are doing. They must stay out of sight.'

The hawk flew off and Fox and Vixen peered together

out of the entrance. They could see Scarface now, leading his band towards the set. Amongst them they recognized Ranger.

'So he *is* involved,' muttered Fox to himself. 'Come on, my love, back to the chamber,' he said aloud. 'I'll get the cubs back from the other entrances. Guards are of no use against such an army. Our only hope is to stay completely quiet. We may fool them yet.'

Back in Badger's deepest chamber, the animals hardly dared to breathe. They felt that the artful Scarface would be listening for the slightest sound. The smaller creatures' nerves were stretched to breaking point but, for the sake of all, they tried to hold on.

After what seemed an eternity a scuffling noise was heard, and they knew that one of the enemy had entered the set. The noise came nearer. Fox tensed himself, ready to spring on the animal.

'Is anyone there?' whispered a voice in the darkness.

No one replied.

'Charmer? Are you there?' came the voice again.

'Father, it's Ranger,' whispered Charmer. 'Perhaps he's come to help.'

'Help?' hissed Fox. 'He's the arch-villain in this raid. Help? Yes, he helped his father all right, telling him to strike in the daylight. But if he comes any closer I'll make sure he's no help to anyone again!'

'No, Father, please,' moaned Charmer. 'Let me talk to him. He'll listen to me.'

Before Fox could stop her, she had run out of the chamber towards Ranger. 'Here I am,' she said. 'It's me – Charmer.'

Fox rushed after her. 'Get outside before I kill you,' he threatened Ranger.

'You don't understand,' came the reply. 'I offered to be the first to look round here.'

'Of course you did,' said Fox. 'You'll want all the credit for finding us.'

'No! No!' said Ranger vehemently. 'You've got me all wrong. I'll tell my father the set's unoccupied.'

But before Fox could register his surprise at these words, a sneering voice cried down the tunnel: 'The game's up, my friend. You and your cronies are trapped. The set is completely encircled. Ranger, come out! I want no clashes down there. We'll fight them in the open when we've starved them out!'

Ranger turned this way and that, torn between obedience to his father and his feelings for Charmer.

'I believe I've wronged you, my young friend,' Fox said to him. 'Go back outside now. I won't have your father's wrath turned against you.'

Ranger turned unwillingly to leave the set. He felt he was leaving his heart behind him. 'Whatever happens, you have one opponent less,' he told them, 'for *I'll* do no fighting.'

Fox and Charmer went back to the chamber.

'I'm afraid we're surrounded,' Fox said simply.

'We'll die here! We'll die here!' wailed one of the female fieldmice.

'Not if I can help it,' Fox answered her quietly. 'I propose to see just what that scarfaced killer is made of. It's me he really wants dead. Well, he can try his strength against me, but in a fair fight. I shall challenge him to single combat.'

—18—
A Battle

There was an excited buzz of conversation in the set as Fox crept into the tunnel and vigorously shook himself in preparation. Vixen followed him worriedly.

'Must you do this, dearest?' she asked him.

'It's our only hope,' answered her mate. 'If we stay here we shall all be slaughtered or starved to death.'

'But Scarface is treachery itself,' Vixen urged. 'You can't trust him. Even if he should accept your challenge, he might set the others on you if you showed signs of winning.'

Fox smiled gently at her. 'I know you are concerned for me and, were it just you and me, things might be different. But I must take this risk for the others' sake.'

'Oh, why must they always depend on *you*?' she

whispered fiercely. But she knew Fox would not be budged.

He answered: 'It was my quarrel in the first place. I'm doing no more than my duty.'

Then she watched him go out into the sunlight.

At Fox's appearance Scarface yapped in triumph. But there was no movement towards him as yet. Only Tawny Owl and Whistler flew to a closer perch, while Kestrel hovered low in the air, ready to swoop down if necessary.

Fox looked at Scarface steadily and then his glance turned to the other assembled throng, who were fidgeting nervously. He noticed Ranger had placed himself well back in the rear.

'You have come in strength, I see,' said Fox coolly. 'Do you need all these to overcome me?'

'You have your followers also,' Scarface growled.

'No.' Fox shook his head. 'No followers – only friends.'

'Oh yes – your precious friends. Well, today they are going to regret they ever were your friends.'

'You have no dispute with them,' Fox said. 'It is me you fear.'

Scarface's eyes blazed. 'Fear?' he barked. 'You talk to me of fear? I didn't acquire these scars by being afraid. I fear nothing!'

'An idle boast,' Fox answered provokingly. 'I say you fear me; and I believe your fear has governed all your actions since I first came to the Park.'

Scarface tensed himself and seemed about to spring on the taunting Fox, who watched him through narrowing eyes. But then his body relaxed again. 'You are clever,' he said. 'I see what game you're playing.'

'Game?' Fox queried. 'I haven't come to play, but to fight.'

The tribe of foxes began to mill about, murmuring to

each other. It was clear their confidence did not match
their leader's.

'You are an arrogant creature,' Scarface replied with a
cynical grin. 'You would set yourself against the whole
pack?'

'Not I,' said Fox. 'Why would I wish to fight them?
Only *you* have made yourself my enemy.'

'Oh, so you wish to fight *me*?' Scarface chuckled.

'To settle this issue once and for all – yes.'

'You're a cool customer, I'll give you that. But, you see,
the odds are against you.'

'I believe we have an even chance,' Fox replied, 'in a
fair fight.'

Scarface fell silent. He seemed to have fallen into a
trap. If he should refuse the fight, he would be taken for a
coward. He looked up with a grim smile. 'Why do you
offer yourself as a sacrifice?' he asked with a grudging
respect.

'Because I fight on one condition,' answered Fox. 'If I
prove victorious, my friends are to go unharmed.'

Scarface broke into a harsh laugh. 'And all this for a
collection of mice and hedgehogs,' he rasped. His face
became as hard as stone. 'All right, you have your wish,'
he growled. 'And when I've killed you, I'll fight your
cubs, one by one, and destroy them all.'

Fox was quite aware of the seriousness of his situation.
He had laid his challenge at the feet of an animal more
hardened and experienced in battle than any in the
whole Reserve. The only advantage on his side was his
comparative youth, for he had no illusions about the
other's strength and cunning.

The two animals faced each other as if assessing the
opponent's qualities. Fox decided to take a defensive
stance and so, at Scarface's first rush, he had ample time

to swing aside. Then Scarface again rushed headlong at him but Fox dropped flat on his belly, and Scarface's jaws snapped at the air. But the old warrior turned quickly and bit savagely at Fox's scruff. Fox broke free, leaving Scarface with a good mouthful of his fur. The other foxes watched in silence as their leader paused before his next move, while his adversary backed steadily away.

Scarface raced forward again and, with a leap, crashed right on top of Fox, bowling him over and driving all the breath from his body. As Fox lay, gasping painfully, Scarface barked in triumph and, teeth bared, lunged for his throat. But Fox scrambled clear in the nick of time and stood with heaving sides, his lungs labouring with difficulty. From the corner of his eye, he saw the heads of Vixen, Badger and Bold at the entrance to the set, watching in dismay. With a supreme effort he gulped down more air and held himself ready again. Now Scarface came in close, snapping left and right with his awful jaws, while Fox stepped further and further back at his advance. He felt his enemy's teeth and knew that Scarface had tasted blood. They reached a patch of uneven ground and Fox stumbled, his back legs stepping into a dip of the land. Scarface got a grip on his muzzle and held on, biting deep. But Fox kicked out fiercely with his front legs, knocking him back on to his haunches, and then followed up with a lightning thrust at his front legs.

Scarface yelped with pain as Fox's teeth sank into his lower leg and he tried desperately to shake him off. But Fox held fast, pinioning him to the ground and, as Scarface fell on his back trying to wrestle free, Fox transferred his grip to the other animal's throat. To kill was not in Fox's mind but he resolved to weaken Scarface so much so that he would be in no mood for fighting for long days to come. Even as Scarface struggled at his mercy, Kestrel zoomed down with a message: 'The Warden is coming this way.'

Fox maintained his advantage for a few moments longer and then loosened his grip. Scarface lay still, his breath whistling agonizingly through his open jaws. Fox saw the approaching human figure and then ran for Badger's set. Ranger and the rest of the band had already dispersed. The Warden came up to the injured Scarface and bent to help him. As he did so, the animal made a feeble snap at his extended hand, rolled over on to his feet and limped away, his brush hanging in a dejected manner between his legs.

In the set Fox was greeted as a hero again. Most of the animals thought Scarface was dead.

'I didn't kill him,' Fox said as he sat heavily down by Badger while Vixen carefully and soothingly licked his wounds.

'Why not? Why not?' cried Vole. 'Let us finish him off now!'

'The Warden came,' Vixen explained quietly, pausing for a moment in her work. 'But Scarface is defeated. He won't be back.'

'If he recovers he'll be back,' said Hedgehog pessimistically. 'He's as vindictive as a household cat!'

'If he comes again, he'll come alone,' said Fox wearily. 'His tribe's heart is not in this business.' He turned to Charmer. 'Ranger has seen to that, I think,' he added with a kind smile.

'He won't dare to come alone again,' Badger said. 'He met his match today.'

'He has a few more scars to add to his collection as well,' Bold said proudly. 'Father, you were magnificent.'

'Once again, Fox, your bravery has saved us all,' said Weasel. 'But it's to be regretted you weren't able to complete the job.'

'Fox hasn't the killer instinct,' said Vole sourly, 'yet he was quite content for Adder to do the work.'

'It might be as well for us small creatures that he hasn't,' Fieldmouse admonished him, 'else *we* wouldn't be sitting here so comfortably in his presence now.'

Vole scowled at him but accepted his point.

'Let's get back to our normal lives,' Fox said to them all. 'We've been living a false existence. To my mind the threat of Scarface is over. We've skulked in his shadow long enough.'

'Hear, hear,' responded Mole politely. 'He wounded me but *I'm* not afraid of him.'

All the animals laughed at this piece of absurdity and a new, more light-hearted mood prevailed.

'Now will someone please go and release those poor rabbits,' said Fox, 'else they may never come out again.'

— 19 —

By the Stream

It was some days before Adder recovered sufficiently from his pains to go far from the hole that had saved his life. He was ignorant, of course, of Scarface's attack on the Farthing Wood creatures and of his battle with Fox. So the snake maintained his seclusion in case Scarface might come again for him. He was not going to be caught napping a second time!

He managed to sunbathe in complete secrecy, and the warmth of the sun and what titbits of food he was able to catch were the best possible medicine for him. His shortened tail was soon completely healed. This restored most of his old self-confidence and he gradually ventured further afield.

It was about a week after Scarface's raid that Adder

came into contact again with one of his old travelling companions. He was lying concealed by vegetation on the stream bank when he noticed Toad splashing about in the water. Now Adder would never have admitted to anyone that he had recently felt lonely and forgotten, but the sight of his old friend gladdened his scaly heart so much that he actually called out to Toad.

'Hallo? Is that you, Adder?' Toad answered, kicking his way to the bank. 'Where are you?'

'I'm over here,' came the reply, and Adder showed just enough of himself for Toad to locate him.

'Well, well, I haven't seen you in an age!' cried his friend.

'No. You don't come up this way much, I believe?' said Adder.

'Oh, I get around quite a lot in the course of my wanderings during the summer,' Toad told him. 'I saw Fox a day or so ago. It seems there was some sort of fight.'

'Really?' Adder replied non-committally, but he was, in fact, greatly interested.

'Yes, between Fox and that scarfaced villain. Fox came off best, I'm glad to say, but not without his share of suffering.'

'Is the – er – scarfaced fox dead?' Adder enquired.

'No, unfortunately.'

'Ah, I'm glad of that,' Adder hissed.

'Glad?' cried Toad. 'How can you say that?'

'Oh, I have an old score to settle,' replied Adder nonchalantly, drawing the rest of his body into the open as he spoke.

'Goodness me, Adder!' Toad exclaimed. 'Whatever's happened to you?'

'Quite a tale really,' Adder punned sarcastically. 'Scarface and I had – er – a difference of opinion.'

'That menace has left his mark on too many of us for

my liking,' said Toad angrily. 'I understand Fox nearly killed him, but the Warden arrived on the scene just at that moment. Apparently Scarface made a raid with his subordinates with the idea of killing all the Farthing Wood animals.'

'Fox was the hero once again, then,' Adder surmised.

'Yes. At any rate, he did enough damage to prevent Scarface from contemplating a second attack. But, Adder, tell me how you got mixed up with him?'

So Adder explained about the cubs' mission to him and how he had bitten the wrong fox, so that Scarface had sought to avenge his death.

'It sounds to me as if you were selected as a sort of weapon,' observed Toad. 'I'm surprised at Fox.'

'It was my fault, to be honest,' Adder admitted. 'I was supposed to strike at Scarface himself.'

'Well, you've certainly paid the price for it.'

'I have. And no one has been to inquire if I am still alive,' Adder said bitterly.

'Then they don't know about your scrap?'

'Oh no. I'm just left to myself, you know.'

'Well, Adder, you always liked to live like that before,' Toad reminded him.

But Adder ignored the remark. 'They *will* hear of me when I've done what I mean to do,' he said enigmatically.

'Er – you won't do anything you'll regret later, will you?' Toad asked apprehensively, wondering if Adder contemplated some sort of punishment for his friends' negligence.

'Oh no. I shan't regret it,' answered Adder with a secret smile. 'I shan't regret it at all.'

Toad looked a little uncomfortable. 'I suppose you – um – don't feel disposed to enlarge a little on your plan?' he asked warily.

'As a matter of fact, my dear Toad,' said Adder

smoothly, 'it's a plan that will be realized in your own natural element – water.'

'Water? Are you going to swim somewhere, Adder?'

'I can reveal no more at this stage,' the snake answered. 'But, rest assured, you will hear it all eventually.'

Toad knew Adder would be questioned no further, so he returned to the subject of the snake's tail. 'I really am most upset to see you in this state,' he said kindly. 'Is the wound very painful?'

'Not any more, thank you for asking,' said Adder, 'apart from the occasional throb when I move. I'm only glad that, like you, I haven't the nervous system of a mammal. I'm told they feel things so much more *deeply*.'

Toad nodded. 'Well, if there's anything I can do . . .' he began.

'No, no,' Adder interrupted. 'Please don't trouble yourself about me. But – er – if you are ever inclined to bring yourself to this vicinity of the Park again, I shall be – er – naturally – er – well, delighted.'

'I shall certainly do so,' Toad said warmly, feeling highly honoured by the snake's uncharacteristic approach to friendliness. 'Goodbye for now, Adder, and – take care!' With a couple of kicks from his back legs he launched himself into the stream's current. Soon he was lost to sight as he let himself be carried downstream.

Adder went back into hiding to review his plan for the hundredth time.

Further downstream Whistler and his mate were dozing on their stiltlike legs in the shallows. It was the arrival of Toad in the form of a soft bump against his leg that caused the heron to wake up.

'Why, Toad!' exclaimed Whistler. 'I might have eaten you!'

But Toad was not fooled. He knew that only frogs,

rather than toads, were palatable to the heron when he could not get fish.

'How pleasant to see you and your charming companion,' Toad said politely. 'You both look in the pink of health.'

'Yes, we certainly cannot complain,' Whistler replied. 'We eat well and we keep out of danger.'

'I wish the same could be said of our friend I've just left,' remarked Toad.

'Who might that be?'

'Adder. He's in a very sorry state.'

Whistler looked puzzled. 'I'm surprised to hear that,' he said. 'But do explain, Toad.'

So, just as Toad had related the details of Fox's fight with Scarface to the snake, he now described Adder's unfortunate encounter.

Whistler listened with a look of concern. 'I deeply regret the fact that no one's been near him,' he said afterwards. 'I, for one, would certainly have done so had I known he was close at hand – and hurt into the bargain.'

'Well,' said Toad, 'I never expected to say this of Adder, but I think his feelings have been more hurt by Scarface than his body.'

'I shall go and see Fox and the others and get them all to atone for their neglect,' said the heron.

Toad thought for a moment. 'No, I wouldn't do that,' he advised. 'Adder won't take kindly to a mass demonstration of sympathy. It would only embarrass him.'

'Yes, I see,' said Whistler. 'But he wouldn't object, I hope, if I paid him a visit?'

'I'm sure he wouldn't,' said Toad. 'But it may not be easy to find him. He's got some important idea he's mulling over and he is keeping himself to himself.'

After a pause Whistler observed: 'You know that Scarface has been more of a threat to us all than the rest of the animals in the Park put together. He's killed or wounded quite a number of our community. While he remains alive he remains a threat.'

'If only Fox had been able to remove that threat,' Toad said feelingly.

'Yes, I fear we haven't seen the last of him,' Whistler replied in his lugubrious tones. 'Oh, I'm sure if more of you had done what I have, we shouldn't have experienced all this trouble!'

'What do you mean – paired ourselves off?' enquired Toad.

'Exactly. If more of us could have mated with those already in the Park – why, there would have been no need for these imaginary barriers and boundaries that seem to exist. But I beg your pardon, Toad, I'm forgetting – you *did* find a partner, didn't you?'

'Yes – Paddock,' Toad answered, smiling a little self-consciously.

'But where is she now? Have you deserted her?'

'Oh, we amphibians only come together in the spring,' Toad explained. 'Once the females have left their spawn in the water we go our separate ways. But that's not to say we won't meet again next year,' he added mischievously.

Whistler laughed. 'Well, I think I prefer a more long-lasting relationship,' he said. 'But – each of us to our own, I suppose, Toad.'

'Yes, indeed,' he replied. 'But there's a lot in what you say and, while we're on the subject of romance, I hear from Fox that Charmer has attracted some interest from a cub in the enemy camp.'

'Is that so?' Whistler shook his head as he pondered Toad's words. 'Well,' he said, 'if that develops it might, perhaps, hold some hope for us all in the future.'

— 20 —

The Next Generation

The 'romance' that Toad had referred to was certainly
developing and now Fox and Vixen encouraged it. After
Ranger's sensitivity at his father's attack on the Farthing
Wood creatures, Fox had learnt more from Charmer of
how he had tried to forestall Scarface's aggressive
intentions.

The two cubs now hunted together nightly and in this
way news from each camp was exchanged and spread
around. Ranger reported on his father's recovery and the
opinions current amongst his other relatives, while
Charmer told him of the feelings of her own friends. It
seemed that neither side wanted a renewal of hostilities,
but the one unknown factor was Scarface himself.

'What mood is your father in?' Charmer asked one

night when Ranger had told her he was moving about again.

'He's very quiet,' he answered. 'Almost subdued. My mother has had to catch him his food and I think he feels degraded. He must have hated being so helpless.'

'He ought to be grateful to her,' Charmer retorted.

Ranger smiled thinly. 'Gratitude is not in my father's line of behaviour,' he answered. 'It's more than likely he feels resentment.'

'Does anyone dare to tell *him* how they feel?' she asked.

'Not as yet,' Ranger admitted a little shamefacedly. 'But I know he would never be able to organize an attack again.'

'That's good news anyway,'

'But I'm afraid you can't rule out his doing something on his own when he's out and about again.'

Charmer smiled to herself. 'What a difference between your father and mine,' she murmured. 'Scarface would never have spared my father if he had had the advantage in that fight.'

Ranger shook his head sadly. 'I can't deny it,' he said. 'Oh, I'm so tired of all this!' he cried suddenly. 'Why can't we just live our own life?'

'But we can,' said Charmer sweetly. 'What's to stop us?'

'Oh, he'd cause trouble for us,' Ranger said angrily. 'Can you see him allowing me to choose for my mate a cub of his enemy's?'

'I don't see how he could stop you,' Charmer answered. 'The Reserve is large and we could make our home well away from any other creature.'

'Wherever it was, it wouldn't be far enough away,' Ranger said bitterly. 'We'd have to go right outside the Park boundaries.'

'If it should prove necessary, then so be it,' said Charmer.

Ranger looked at her in astonishment. 'Do you mean that?' he asked her.

'Of course. My future lies with you.'

'Then when shall we go?' he cried.

'We don't yet know if it will be necessary,' she said smoothly. 'Let's be patient.'

They walked together through the woodland, a cool night breeze caressing their fur and murmuring softly to itself in the tree-tops. The Park seemed so peaceful to them then.

'It would be a shame to leave the place we were both born in,' Charmer said presently. 'Perhaps we're getting too pessimistic.'

'I'd like to think so,' answered her admirer. 'It would be nice to bring a third generation into the world here.'

They passed out of the wood into the open grassland. The White Deer herd roamed, ghostlike, through the foreground. The Great Stag stood alone on a slight rise, his graceful neck stretched upward as he browsed from a willow tree. He turned his head slowly as he detected the two fox cubs, now very nearly fully grown, moving towards him. He spoke to them.

'You make a heartening sight after the conflicts this Park has seen recently,' he said. 'Let your generation not recall the ill feeling of their predecessors.'

Ranger and Charmer exchanged affectionate glances. 'We see no reason to carry on the quarrel,' said the male cub.

'Very sensible,' nodded the Stag. 'This Park was reserved as a quiet haven by humans for wild creatures. It would be a pity to destroy their ideals.'

'Your words would carry more weight if delivered to my father,' Ranger said with remarkable honesty. 'For months he's been possessed by a consuming jealousy that has caught up many other creatures against their will, and I'm afraid it's blinding him to any other consideration.'

'I shall see if I can speak to him,' the Great Stag offered. 'In the meantime I wish you both well.'

The two foxes ran on, joyful in each other's company. For the present, anyway, they were able to enjoy the freedom of the Park. They raced together across the open expanse, exulting in the looseness of their young limbs. Then they chased each other in and out of the bracken, calling to each other excitedly.

Some distance away, Bold watched their antics. Despite Fox's change of heart, the cub did not approve of Ranger's friendship with his sister and he scowled. To him Ranger was merely Scarface's cub and should be treated as such. He was privately furious with his father for allowing their enemy to live and longed for the day when he could fight Scarface and become the new hero. Ranger and Charmer ran towards him and he greeted them half-heartedly.

'You're spending a lot of time together,' he remarked sourly.

'There's no one I'd rather spend my time with than your sister,' Ranger told him gallantly.

'So I see,' Bold answered. 'She seems to think more of you than her own family.'

'Oh, Bold, don't be silly,' said Charmer. 'I can't stay with my family for ever. Ranger is my future. You and Friendly ought to find yourselves some nice young vixen cubs and make your own lives.'

'There's such a thing as a family sticking together in times of trouble,' Bold said roughly.

'Maybe one way of avoiding trouble would be if you started to mix a little with my family,' Ranger suggested, in a way echoing Whistler's words.

'I could never have anything in common with any

relative of Scarface,' Bold retorted.

'Don't be so pompous, Bold,' Charmer told him.

'Can't you forget my father?' asked Ranger. 'We're not all like him, you know.'

'But I remember how you all ganged up on me at his bidding,' Bold answered angrily, 'how you trapped me and stood guard over me. I was lucky to get away.'

Ranger sighed. 'There's such a thing as forgiving and forgetting,' he said. 'Things are different now.'

'*Are* they?' sneered Bold. 'For how long? I wonder. Until your father feels he is fit enough to attack us all again?'

'But, Bold, none of us would go with him next time. He couldn't do much on his own.'

'A fox can do quite a lot against hares and rabbits or – or – moles,' spluttered Bold.

'The Great Stag has promised to pay him a visit,' Charmer said quietly, 'in the interests of all.'

'I'm sure he'll listen!' snapped Bold sarcastically, turning his back. He began to walk away. 'He really paid him heed last time!' he called over his shoulder.

'Oh dear,' said Ranger. 'We shall never get on while this animosity continues.'

'Pay no attention to him,' Charmer said soothingly. 'He won't do anything.'

'He sounds as bitter as my father sometimes,' Ranger muttered. 'I don't understand him.'

'I think he's a bit envious of us,' said his companion.

'Well then, he should take my advice. I've got some lovely sisters!'

Charmer laughed, and Ranger followed suit. 'Oh, let's forget them all!' he cried. 'While we're together we only have to think of each other.' He bounded off. 'Catch me!' he called back.

— 21 —

Retribution

The Great Stag did not at once carry out his intended visit, and the delay proved Bold's words to be prophetic. It transpired that Scarface had only been biding his time while something like his old strength returned to him. Then, in an excess of spite, unaccompanied and unexpected, he hunted the more defenceless Farthing Wood creatures. Fieldmouse was killed, along with several of his near relatives, and his cousin Vole, while having a narrow escape himself, saw his mate and all but one of his small family slaughtered. The only other survivor was, unluckily, also a male.

Before the news of the night's killings had been broken, Scarface had added to his toll, in the early morning, four rabbits, three of which were inexperienced kits, and a young squirrel. With a sort of fiendish appetite, the killer had eaten all the dead mice and voles and one of the rabbits, and those he was unable to consume he carried away, one by one, and hid in a gorse patch. Only the body of the dead squirrel was left as a sign, as Scarface returned home.

Since Fox's triumph over him, the nightly watch had been lifted and so, when the dreadful tidings spread to his den he fell into an agony of self-blame.

Rabbit, Vole and Squirrel arrived at the earth in the utmost distress which had an underlying current of anger. Anger at Scarface but, in Vole's case in particular, anger at Fox as well.

'You should have killed him, Fox!' Vole almost screamed at him. 'I *knew* it was wrong to spare him! Now see how I've suffered. My poor family . . .' He broke off, inconsolable.

'You were right. He came alone,' said Bold. 'But the cowardice, the vindictiveness of such a creature doesn't entitle him to live!'

'My life is over,' wailed Vole. 'There are no female voles left. I must now eke out my days alone. And you had it in your power to secure our safety for good!'

'Fox was interrupted by the Warden,' Vixen said defensively.

'No . . . no . . . he's right,' Fox said brokenly. 'I *could* have done it. I could have done it,' he ended in a whisper.

Outside the earth the rest of the community was gathering as the events became common knowledge. Badger came into the den. 'Now he has to die,' he said in a hard voice. 'Let us go and finish the job, Fox.'

'Oh, where was the Stag?' cried Charmer. 'He was to have stopped all this!'

'Scarface listens to nothing but his own evil heart,' Bold answered her. 'I told you how it would be.'

'Yes, yes,' moaned Fox. 'I've become too soft. *I* killed my friends as much as he did.' He hung his head in despair.

'You weren't to know, you weren't to know,' Vixen kept repeating to him, sharing his agony in every degree.

'But I *should* have known,' he muttered. 'It was my duty. Oh, that wicked, wicked creature!' He stumbled out into the open air, followed by the others. All the rest of the animals were there, save for Adder. Even Toad was among them.

'Weren't *you* anywhere around, Owl?' Rabbit demanded. 'Couldn't you have done something?'

Tawny Owl resettled his wings and looked away uncomfortably. 'Er – no,' he said. 'I'm afraid I was in another quarter.'

'What protection have we, then?' shrilled Vole. 'We're sitting targets, it seems!'

'Well, you see, Vole,' Tawny Owl muttered apologetically, 'I – er – naturally don't hunt on my own home front, so to speak. Accidents might occur and – well, the sentry duty seemed to have been lifted –'

'Accidents!' broke in Squirrel. 'How would you describe these killings then?'

'They certainly weren't accidents, Squirrel,' said Hedgehog. 'This was planned vindictiveness. I knew this might happen . . .'

'Who cares what you know?' snapped Vole. 'All the warnings in the world have had no effect.'

'I suppose anything I do is too late now,' whispered Fox. 'I can't bring those poor dead creatures back. But will you let me try to make atonement?' He looked beseechingly at the three bereaved animals. 'I'd like to go alone,' he said, and everyone knew what he was referring to. 'No danger must attach to any of you again – not now . . .'

There was a stirring of sympathy for Fox at these words and Mole, typically, started to sob.

'We've *all* suffered for the loss of any one of us,' said Hare. 'The blame can't be put on any one animal's shoulders.'

'Quite right,' said Weasel. 'Why should Fox put himself in this position? We are in danger of forgetting that he and Vixen were the first to be deprived of a member of their family.'

'In my opinion,' said Whistler slowly, 'this whole sorry saga might never have taken place if we hadn't isolated ourselves in the first place. We came to live in the Reserve. We should have mingled more with those already here of our own kind.'

'Wise words, Whistler,' Badger conceded. 'We've made the error of trying to build ourselves a new Farthing Wood inside the Park.'

'Wise words they may be,' said Weasel, 'but wise after the event.'

Whistler shook his head in his solemn way. 'I did recommend you all to follow my example long ago,' he said, 'but, so far, only Toad has done so.'

'After my own fashion, yes,' Toad said quickly.

'Perhaps, then, this is the signal for the future?' suggested Hare. 'I myself must choose another mate from among the White Deer Park does, if I wish to be paired again.'

'There's a lot of sense in the idea,' said Vixen, looking at Charmer. 'We must try and become now, like those who were already here, the Animals of White Deer Park.'

Fox looked at her in admiration. 'Of all now present, I alone found my partner on our journey here,' he said. 'I couldn't have hoped to find a better one in this Park. But my family can be party to this excellent plan and one of them – I think most of you know who – is already carrying it out.'

'Ranger!' said Bold scathingly. 'A cub produced by our mutual enemy!'

Charmer looked at him with pain in her eyes. 'If you think he wouldn't deplore these killings as much as we all do, you don't know him!' she said bravely.

The other animals murmured together. There seemed to be mixed feelings about this proposed alliance. Kestrel seemed to sum up the situation when he asked: 'In the light of Charmer's relationship with this Ranger, who may well have a good heart, how can we stand here plotting to kill his father?'

Fox looked at the hawk pensively. 'It's a valid point,' he said. 'That may have been at the back of my mind when I spared him before.'

'And so *we* have lost our loved ones for the sake of a strange cub!' said Vole bitterly.

Whistler came to Fox's rescue. 'Scarface and his tribe have always hunted here,' he pointed out sedately. 'Lives could have been lost anyway by the usual law of the wild.'

'Yes,' said Hare. 'We rodents must always run the gauntlet of death whenever there are carnivorous animals around. One of my leverets was killed last winter by a creature from the Reserve.'

'A stoat,' said Badger. 'One that I once had words with myself. Yes. One can't go against nature.'

'Then what of Scarface now?' demanded Rabbit. 'Is he still to be allowed to live on?'

There was a long silence. No one wanted to be the first to speak. At last Fox said: 'I'll be advised by the Great Stag. Are you content to be so?'

None of the animals seemed prepared to argue, not even Vole.

'Then it's settled. I'll go now and tell him of the night's

events. He is the acknowledged overlord of the Park. It must rest with him.'

'And how can we defend ourselves in the meantime?' Squirrel wanted to know.

'It's easy for tree climbers like you,' said Rabbit. 'But for Vole and myself . . .'

'Stay together here, all of you,' said Fox, 'while I pay my call. I'll be back just as swiftly as I can. You'll be quite safe in a bunch.'

He loped off, leaving Badger and Vixen in nominal charge. He was not long gone, and when the animals had debated at length what the Stag had agreed to do, they were astonished by the arrival of an exhausted Adder who brought them information none of them had expected.

—22—

A Snake Under Water

After his talk with Toad, Adder had decided it was time to put his plan into effect. In a way he was thankful for his solitude, for it would enable him to act without the threat of interference. But before he could do anything he needed to see that Scarface was up and about again. Keeping close to the stream, he coiled himself amongst the willow-herb and watched the comings and goings along the banks. One day he caught a water-shrew but, apart from that, he ate nothing. Then came the night of Scarface's solo raid.

Adder saw him limp up to the stream's side and gingerly lower himself down the bank into the water. Then, not without difficulty, the fox swam across. Adder watched him limp away with satisfaction. Now he had only to wait for Scarface to return. He noticed the spot on the bank where the animal had chosen to descend, which was less steep than most, and expected that Scarface would try to recross at that point. He slithered down the opposite bank and entered the water.

Adder was a good, but not enthusiastic swimmer. Usually he only swam at all when it was essential to do so. Now he was entering the water voluntarily. At first the current of the stream carried him along a distance, but Adder exerted his strength and, keeping close to the shore, undulated his way back to the crossing point. Then he found a strongly rooted patch of weed in midstream and wrapped his body securely round it, leaving only his head above the surface. In this way he passed the night.

He was very glad when dawn broke, for the water was cold. With daylight it began to warm up. Adder kept his unblinking eyes trained on the home bank, confident that he was all but invisible from the shore. At last, in the early morning light, he saw the awaited figure approaching.

There was a quite distinguishable expression of slyness and cruelty on the animal's face as he looked this way and that around him. He sat down on the top of the bank and yawned, watching the water. For some minutes he sat quite still, his ears pricked for any slight sound. Then he looked across the stream, directly at Adder.

The snake shrank back into the obscuring ripples until only his nostrils were above water. Another few minutes passed. Nothing happened. Adder peeped above the surface again. Scarface was still sitting on the bank, but had his head turned, looking behind him. Adder knew then he had not been detected.

Scarface looked round again and stood up. Slowly, very slowly, he clambered down the bank. Adder tensed

himself. The fox waded into the stream and began to
paddle stiffly towards midstream. Adder waited, immobile.
At the last moment he loosened his grip on the weed
stem and, as Scarface came level, gathered his remaining
strength and struck upwards. His fangs sank into the fox's
soft hind parts under his flank, releasing their full store of
venom. Scarface yelped with pain and alarm, but Adder
merely dropped back into the water and allowed himself
to be taken downstream at the pace of the water. Scarface
regained sufficient composure to struggle to the other
bank and haul himself clear. By this time Adder was out
of sight.

Already weakened by his recent fierce battle with Fox,
Scarface lay shuddering on the shore, frightened and
angry. The creatures from Farthing Wood had struck
back at him again. Were they to be the undoing of him
after all? It was some time before he could bring himself
to give Adder due acknowledgement for his plan of
revenge. It had been masterly and he admitted final
defeat. He decided not to attempt to get back to his den.
Soon he would die like the younger fox had done. He
realized that he had been the real target of his enemies all
along. 'Well, at least I've taken some of them with me,' he
muttered to himself, chuckling in his throat. 'They won't
forget *me*!'

Meanwhile Adder had pulled himself out of the water
and was sluggishly making his way back to the scene of
his triumph. He felt empty and weak – but victorious. By
the time he came within range of Scarface, the poison
had begun to take effect, eliminating him from any
danger.

Scarface at once recognized the snake's blunt tail. 'So it
was you,' he whispered. 'The Farthing Wood Adder?'

'The same,' Adder acknowledged wryly.

'Well, you've achieved more than your brave leader could do,' Scarface told him. 'Perhaps you should change places?' He gasped as the first tremors began to shake his body.

Adder watched him without emotion. 'You've got no more than you deserved,' was all he said.

'Maybe,' Scarface answered hoarsely. 'That's the way of things.' He trembled more violently. 'You've – killed – me,' he panted, 'but – remember . . .' He drew a deep, racking breath. 'I'm not – the end of – my line . . .' His words were expelled painfully and harshly from his lips. They were his last.

Adder stayed no longer. The threat implied by Scarface went unheeded by the snake. He was quite satisfied with the end of Scarface. He swam back across the stream and at once set off on the long journey towards his old friends, to bring them the news. It proved to be as well that he did so.

On his way back through the Reserve he nearly wriggled directly under the massive hooves of the Great Stag.

'Take care, my friend,' cautioned the leader of the White Deer.

'Some of us have our eyes rather closer to the ground,' Adder answered irritably. 'We can't look up at the sky like you do.'

'Quite so, quite so,' said the Stag good humouredly. 'You seem to be in something of a hurry?'

'Perhaps I am,' said Adder warily.

'Well, I'm not prying,' the Stag went on. 'You have your own business to attend to.'

Adder could not resist a dry laugh. 'I've just attended to it,' he hissed sinisterly.

The Great Stag looked at him circumspectly, noticing

his mutilated tail. 'You've been in the wars, it seems,' he
remarked presently.

'I have,' said Adder. 'But I survived.'

The barest emphasis in the way he answered was
noticed by the deer immediately, who already had his
suspicions. 'Am I to surmise, then, that your adversary
did not?' he asked penetratingly.

Adder's reply was merely a sardonic grin.

'It comes into my mind that you may have saved me a
journey,' the Stag observed.

'As I don't know where your journey lies I'm afraid I
can't enlighten you,' answered Adder.

'Shall we stop hedging, my friend?' suggested the Stag.
'I was on my way to visit the scarfaced fox.'

'Were you indeed?' drawled the snake. 'Then I can tell
you that you will find him quite close by.'

The Great Stag sighed. 'Your caution does you credit,'
he said, 'but I beg you to answer a civil question. Is there
any point in my continuing on my journey?'

'Er – no,' said Adder.

'Thank you. Now I understand the situation. But you
may be concerned to hear that some of your travelling
companions were killed last night by the – er – animal
under discussion.'

'That news serves only to increase my gratification at
what I have just done,' said Adder. 'But who of my
friends were killed?'

The Stag told him.

'I see,' said the snake, relieved, despite his recent
accusations, that Fox was not among them.

'I hope the Park will now return to its former state of
quietude,' said the Great Stag.

'Likewise,' answered Adder. 'And now, if you'll excuse
me, I have some news to convey.'

'Of course.' The Stag stood aside and watched Adder

continue on his way. He shrugged to himself. 'Well,' he mused, 'it seems that actions speak louder than words.' He stood for some time looking into the distance. Then he turned and started to walk majestically back in the direction of his herd.

—23—

Loss and Gain

It was not until quite late in the day that the stiff, prone body of Scarface was discovered. His mate, who had wisely never interfered in his schemes, at last decided his absence from the earth was unusually long. She looked for him in every likely spot and, finally, accompanied by Ranger and one of her adult offspring, went to the stream.

It was Ranger who recognized the cause of Scarface's death. After consoling his mother as best he could, he spoke to his elder brother. 'This is the work of snakebite, Blaze,' he said to him. 'The appearance of our father is very similar to that of our cousin who was also killed in this way. It's almost certainly by the same snake.'

'You're very probably right,' agreed Blaze. 'Our father might have been hunting him.'

'I'm sure he was,' said Ranger. 'Some time ago I saw a snake in this area and I told Father where to find him. I thought he had been exterminated.'

'You should have killed the creature yourself,' said Blaze.

Ranger nodded. 'Now I wish I had,' he answered. He had no idea Adder was in any way connected with Charmer's parents or their friends. 'But Scarface was a jealous parent,' he went on. 'He would only have reproached me for doing his job.'

'That's how he was,' Blaze agreed. 'But what now? Any of us might meet the same fate!'

'Then we must eliminate the chance of it,' Ranger asserted. 'I'll comb this area for the culprit, if you go back and round up as many of the others you can. Then together, we must uncover him.'

Blaze led his mother back to her den. She was too stunned to participate in any hunt. Then he returned to the scene of the killing with eight more of his tribe.

'Not a trace of him so far,' Ranger announced. 'We must work quickly before darkness falls.'

But, though they searched high and low, there was no sign of Adder for, of course, he had left the area hours ago. As dusk began to steal over the Park, Ranger and Blaze called the search off. 'We can continue tomorrow,' said Ranger, who was already thinking of his meeting with Charmer. 'We'll have the whole day ahead of us, and we're sure to catch him in the end.'

The foxes disbanded and Ranger made his way to the usual meeting place. He felt no sorrow for his father's death, for there had been no particular bond between them. But for his bereaved mother's sake, he was determined to avenge his killing.

Charmer arrived at the spot, uncertain how to conduct herself. To her parents and all the Farthing Wood

creatures, Adder was a hero. Even more so as he had
narrowly escaped death himself from the very jaws of
their mutual enemy. But she was well aware that the dead
fox had sired Ranger and had, therefore, a claim on his
feelings.

Ranger greeted her in his normal manner, noticing,
however, her reticence. 'I suppose you have heard of my
father's death?' he surmised.

Charmer nodded silently.

'Well, I realize you have no reason to grieve,' he said.
'I've no illusions about your sentiments on the matter –
or of your friends. Scarface made himself your enemy.'

'I'm only regretful on your behalf,' she said to him. 'As
for us – well, there's a general feeling of relief that what
had been an abiding threat has now disappeared.'

'You're very honest,' Ranger answered, 'and I'm glad
you are so. My only concern is that my father died the
way he did.'

Charmer looked down uncomfortably.

'I shall, of course, put that right,' Ranger remarked.

Charmer looked at him sharply. 'What do you mean?'
she faltered.

'We have to rid ourselves of that snake,' he explained.
'We can't allow him to pick us off one by one.'

'But the first death was an accident!' she protested.

Ranger glanced at her curiously. 'How would you
know that?' he inquired.

'Adder killed the wrong fox,' she answered. 'It should
have been –' She broke off, aware of her indiscretion.

'My father!' exclaimed Ranger. 'Now I comprehend.
So this was all arranged. You know this snake!'

'Of course!' she replied hopelessly. 'He travelled with
my father from Farthing Wood.'

'And now he's disposed of two of my family,' Ranger
said in a cold voice.

'Just as Scarface disposed of one of mine,' she reminded him. 'And several of our friends.'

'Several?' he queried.

Charmer told him of the recent killings of the fieldmice, the voles and the rabbits.

Ranger fell silent. Then he said quietly: 'That, of course, I didn't know. There's fault on both sides.'

'You mustn't feel vindictive towards Adder,' said Charmer. '*He* was fortunate not to have been killed by Scarface earlier. As it is, your father has marked him for ever.'

'An adder is a strange creature to make a friend of,' Ranger observed.

'There are reasons,' replied Charmer. 'My parents owe him a great deal. He once saved Vixen's life.'

Ranger nodded. 'Then I understand the bond,' he admitted. 'And I am aware that your father could have killed mine had he chosen to do so.'

For a long time the two cubs looked at each other. They seemed to have reached a point of crisis in their relationship. Then Charmer broke away, sobbing. 'If only none of these awful things had happened,' she moaned. 'I suppose it's too much to hope that we should remain unaffected by it!'

Ranger moved to comfort her, nuzzling her repeatedly and licking her fur. 'Wounds do heal,' he said bravely. 'In time all will be forgotten. We should think of the future.'

Charmer looked at him hopefully. 'Are you prepared to forgive?' she whispered.

'Of course,' he replied. Then he recalled the snake hunt arranged for the next day. 'Where is this Adder now?' he asked.

Charmer hesitated. 'I'm not sure,' she answered defensively.

Ranger looked at her piercingly. 'You needn't worry,'

he assured her. 'I won't try to search him out. I'll tell the others I got rid of him myself. They don't know one snake from another.'

She smiled with relief. 'He's somewhere in the company of Toad,' she said confidingly.

'Well, let's forget him,' said Ranger. 'And all the others. Let's make our own plans.'

'Yes,' said Charmer. 'We're of an age to act independently. Bold and Friendly have already left the family home. Once they heard – you know . . .'

Ranger nodded. 'Will they look for mates now?' he asked playfully.

'I suppose so,' she answered. 'At least, I think Friendly will. As for Bold . . . I can't say.'

'Do you wish us to stay in the Park?' Ranger asked presently.

'I would prefer to,' said Charmer. 'I don't know the world outside.'

'No,' said Ranger. 'Nor I.'

'From my father's stories it sounds a hazardous place,' she went on. 'You really do have to live by your wits there. Survival is everything.'

'I imagine the only thing to be said in compensation is that there are no boundaries to your freedom,' he said.

'Except human ones,' Charmer said pointedly.

'Exactly. Well, home is where the heart is. And as long as you are in White Deer Park,' he said gallantly, 'that's where my heart will be.'

'Oh – oh!' she chuckled. 'Now who's the charmer?'

Ranger grinned. 'You make me so,' he told her. 'Now, where do you think we should have our den?'

—24—

A Singular Discussion

The animals' reaction to Adder's news overwhelmed
him. Already exhausted by his aquatic exercise and then
his long crawl across the Park, the snake lapsed into
speechlessness at his friends' wild congratulations. For a
long time he was unable even to explain the reason for
his blunt tail. When he was eventually able to do so, their
excitement was only heightened and, despite their recent
losses, Rabbit and Squirrel joined in the mutual fervour.
Vole alone was unmoved.

When the exhilaration had subsided somewhat he
said: 'This news has come too late for my relief. If
Scarface had been killed a day earlier I should have been
the first to rejoice. However, I'm glad for others' sakes.'

'You must find yourself a *new* mate, Vole,' Hare told

him. 'It's the surest way to ease one's grief.'

'Perhaps,' said Vole, 'and from your words, I guess you are already making moves in that direction. But for poor Fieldmouse even that consolation is denied.'

There was no comment that could be made on this statement and all of the creatures present felt the poignancy of it.

'Let's be thankful, anyway,' said Vixen quietly, 'that so many of us *have* survived. Now we can look forward to more peaceful times.'

'This will mean more independence for us all as well,' said Fox. 'The whole of the Reserve is ours again, to roam in at our leisure. We shall all be as free as the birds of the air.'

Kestrel and Whistler laughed, while Tawny Owl pretended to ignore the remark. For him, it smacked of a certain sarcasm.

'Don't look so straightfaced, Owl,' Kestrel teased him. 'We don't mind a little joke at our expense, do we? Fox knows we've all pulled our weight in this recent sinister business.'

'Humph!' mumbled Tawny Owl. 'I long ago told that Scarface what I thought of him.'

'Of course you did, of course you did, and we appreciate it,' said Weasel with mock solemnity.

Mole tittered while Tawny Owl struggled to retain his dignity. Vixen quickly changed the subject. 'Well, who is going to act on my earlier suggestion?' she challenged. 'The need to integrate ourselves with the natives of the place is now our prime task.' She looked round at the assembled group. 'I'm sure you're all very eligible,' she laughed. 'Who'll be the first?'

'It appears that Hare is likely to be,' remarked Whistler. 'But what of all you youngsters: Bold, Friendly and – you, Mole.'

'Me?' cried Mole nervously. 'Oh dear, I hadn't really thought about it – mating, I mean . . .' He lapsed into a tongue-tied embarrassment.

'High time you did, then,' Whistler admonished him with jocular gravity. 'But, let me see – Vixen, we seemed to be surrounded by bachelors!'

'A bachelor I am, and a bachelor I shall always be, I fear,' sighed Badger. 'Who'd want an old fogey like me? My mating days passed in solitude in Farthing Wood. I was the remnant of the badger population there and –'

'Yes, yes,' cut in Fox, before he started rambling on. 'Don't let's talk of the past. And, anyway, Toad found himself a mate in the delightful form of that plump young Paddock, and *he's* no juvenile.'

'Toad might have a new mate every year – it'd make no difference to him,' observed Weasel. '*We* have to look more carefully.'

'Well now, Weasel, don't be too sure about me,' Toad answered. 'I was rather taken with Paddock, you know. I may just look out for her next spring. But I had no idea *you* had any designs along these lines?'

Weasel gave a little cough. 'Well – er – there comes a time, Toad, for all of us, I suppose . . .'

'Splendid, Weasel!' boomed Whistler. 'Are there any more of you sly dogs around?'

'We rabbits take it all in our stride,' said Rabbit, almost contemptuously. 'We have to keep our warrens well populated, you know.'

'Why?' Adder's lisp was suddenly heard again. 'Does that give you more of a choice for your mating pursuits?'

The others laughed. The rabbits, of course, were notorious for their breeding record. But Rabbit turned the tables. 'What of yourself, Adder?' he asked coolly.

'Yes, my friend,' Whistler joined in. 'When will you allow yourself to become entwined in the knot of love?'

Adder despised this sort of talk and scowled at the heron. 'There are some of us,' he hissed, 'who may not have come to the Park with the sole object of pairing off with the first female of the species he happened to come across.' This was intended as a gibe at Whistler who had named the need for a mate as a purpose for joining in the animals' journey. But he brushed it aside.

'I make no excuses,' he said. 'A solitary life is not for me. But each to his own, I'm sure.'

'We haven't heard from the other birds,' said Hare mischievously. 'Tawny Owl may be a crusty old bachelor, but what plans do you have, Kestrel?'

The hawk looked piercingly into the distance, as if raking the horizon with his powerful glare. 'It would probably surprise you to learn, Hare,' said he, 'that I have had no time to devote to such activities, as long as I felt myself to be the guardian of the safety of you all during the daylight hours.'

'No offence intended, I assure you,' Hare said quickly.

'None taken, I assure *you*,' Kestrel replied, shifting his rather unnerving gaze to his questioner. 'And, may I say, now that my services can, it seems, be dispensed with, that I shall enjoy the extra freedom it will bring me.'

'Very delicately put,' said Weasel. 'But I believe you might have been a bit premature, Hare, in your assessment of Owl. He should be allowed to speak for himself.'

'Well, you know – er – everybody,' Tawny Owl began uncomfortably, 'I must say that I have regarded myself as the – er – nocturnal counterpart of Kestrel – despite what happened last night,' he added hurriedly. 'I'm not very well versed in courtship procedures, you know,' he went on with rather more than his usual openness, 'but Vixen's idea is – er – a good one, I feel and – er – if the opportunity ever should arise when I – ahem! – well, when I might feel so inclined – I – I should grasp it!' he ended abruptly.

The other creatures hid their amusement at his discomfiture, but Adder could not resist one of his leers. 'And I'd always thought,' he drawled, 'that the inclination was necessary on both sides.'

Now there was laughter, but of a good-natured sort, and Tawny Owl was obliged to grin sheepishly.

'I think what I've heard is most encouraging,' Vixen remarked. 'Bold and Friendly, the part you play in my plan will have a great deal of significance. Your sister has set an example.'

'Well, Mother, the family den is too small for us all now,' said Bold. 'Friendly and I must take our chance as it comes. There are wider horizons to explore.'

Fox and Vixen exchanged a glance. It seemed to both of them there was a veiled implication in these words. But they wisely made no comment.

The gathering began to break up, and the two male cubs dispersed with the other animals. Charmer watched them go without a pang. She had thoughts only for Ranger now.

'I hope they follow your lead,' said Vixen quietly, following her eyes.

'Things aren't so settled for me as you think,' Charmer murmured. 'We can't forget that it's Ranger's father's death we've been celebrating.'

'We haven't forgotten,' said Fox. 'But Ranger won't mourn for long, I believe. Scarface was not the best of parents, and I think I'm right in my assumption that Ranger cares more for you.'

'I hope so,' said Charmer. 'Oh, I do hope so.'

'What is equally important,' went on Fox, 'is that there will be no successor to Scarface. He was a natural leader – the others of his tribe are just followers. Such a situation as we've found ourselves in can't arise again.'

'That's true,' Vixen agreed. 'But I have to confess that I sometimes wonder if we haven't ourselves bred a cub with a similarly strong character.'

Fox nodded. He had felt the same himself. 'It's fortunate for us, then,' he murmured, 'that he should include some of our more sensible characteristics in his make-up.'

—25—

Cubs Apart

For Bold and Friendly there soon came the parting of the ways. Vixen's words were very much in Friendly's mind. He had begun to see his quest for a mate as a sort of duty. But Bold had other ideas.

'Shall we take a look around Scarface's old territory?' Friendly suggested.

Bold recognized the reason for the suggestion. He smiled at his brother cub. 'There's plenty of time for everything, you know,' he said. 'The young vixens over there aren't likely to get paired off all at once. I want to see a bit more of the world first.'

'The Reserve, you mean?' Friendly asked. 'Oh yes, it's true there's a good deal of it we haven't been able to explore.'

'Not just the Reserve,' Bold answered impatiently. 'There's a whole world *outside* White Deer Park. Why confine ourselves within the Park's boundaries?'

Friendly looked at him in amazement and in some trepidation. 'You'd go outside the Park?' he whispered.

'Why not?'

'What of all the dangers? It's hostile country out there. Why did our parents leave it to settle here?'

'Hostile!' Bold gave a short laugh. 'It hasn't been exactly amicable inside here recently! And, in any case, if you can go out of the Park you can always come back in again.'

'If you're still alive to do so,' Friendly said pessimistically.

'Oh, don't exaggerate,' Bold said. 'I can't imagine that you're risking your life as soon as you step through the fence.'

The two cubs looked at each other intently. They both knew they had to separate. 'Well . . .' Bold began.

'We will see you again, won't we?' Friendly asked, almost timidly.

'Of course you will, you chump,' Bold answered him. 'I shan't suddenly just disappear.'

Friendly nodded. 'Look after yourself,' he murmured.

'You too.'

They stood a moment longer and then parted without a further word. Friendly went half-heartedly in the direction of the stream. But Bold's steps were eager and vigorous. He sniffed the air and then broke into an easy trot. His eyes searched ahead of him for the Park boundary.

Friendly was overtaken by dusk before he had gone far and decided to catch himself some supper. Bold had been right in one respect. There was plenty of time for this mating business.

After he had eaten, he found himself a spot to sleep. He felt listless and rather lonely. There would be no returning to his parents' earth any more. Even Charmer would be no longer there. She and Ranger would be searching for a new home. He yawned once or twice and then curled himself up head to tail, listening to the night noises. In a few minutes he was asleep.

Bold ran on, exhilarated by his independence. He crossed the Park, running silently through the grazing White Deer herd, to the fence which bordered open country. Then he stalked along its length, looking for an exit. He found a hole and squeezed through it. He paused, snuffling the air, on the threshold of a new world. His ears were pricked to catch any new sound. But he detected no strange scents, no strange noises. He ran on through the night.

Early the next morning, Friendly awoke to see Charmer and Ranger standing over him. He rose to his feet, wagging his tail in greeting, and giving his coat a vigorous shake.

'Ranger and I have been seeking a spot for our den,' Charmer explained. 'We're on the way to look over the area on the other side of the stream. Will you come too?'

'You never know what you might find there,' Ranger added, with a chuckle.

'I'll come gladly,' Friendly said. 'It's new territory to me.'

'Have you seen Bold?' Charmer asked.

'Yes. He was with me for a while,' answered Friendly. 'Then he went off to explore further afield.' For some reason – perhaps a sort of loyalty – he did not mention Bold's intention of going outside the Reserve.

Charmer nodded. 'He's a law unto himself,' she said.

The three cubs arrived at the banks of the stream.
Already Scarface's mate and many of Ranger's relatives
had gathered and were continuing the search for Adder
under the direction of Blaze. Ranger looked a little
awkwardly at Charmer who had obviously guessed their
purpose.

'I'll tell them what I said,' he whispered to her. Then he
called to Blaze. 'You're searching for nothing!' he cried.
'The snake is dead!'

The foxes stopped and looked at him.

'Dead? What do you mean?' Blaze wanted to know.

'*I* killed him,' Ranger lied unblinkingly. 'Last night – I
found him.'

'But how do you know if it was the culprit?' questioned
Blaze.

Ranger thought quickly. 'We had – er – a little talk,' he
replied. 'I made sure before I despatched him.'

For a long while Blaze stared at him. Then, at last, he
said: 'Well, it seems we're wasting our time.' He paused.
'Our mother wants us to dispose of Father's carcase,' he
went on.

'Then do as we did before,' Ranger suggested, 'when
our cousin was killed. Push him out into the water.'

Friendly was watching the other foxes with the utmost
interest. He had marked out one vixen cub as particularly
appealing. He glanced at his companions. 'Why don't we
cross over?' he asked.

They swam across and Ranger assisted Blaze in
pushing the remains of Scarface into the stream. The
current caught the body, twisting it round in a spiral as it
slowly transported it downstream. The dead leader's
mate stood on the brink to watch it go.

'I shall bear no more cubs,' she said, almost to herself.
'I am old in spirit if not in body.' She turned and gave an
appraising look at Charmer and Friendly. 'Well, it's your

life now that matters,' she said to Ranger. 'Times change. For all his faults, we shan't see his like again.'

'No,' agreed Ranger. 'We can be quite sure of that. But come, Mother, won't you return home now? You look tired.'

'What does it matter where I go?' she muttered dispiritedly. 'My life is as good as over. I want no other mate.'

Ranger said no more but led Charmer away from the stream into the area that had recently been the exclusive domain of Scarface. Friendly let them go and began to mingle with the other foxes, edging as close as he could to the vixen cub that had caught his eye.

She seemed to be aware of his presence for she started to look everywhere but at Friendly, in a confused sort of way.

Scarface's mate turned slowly back, following in the wake of Ranger and Charmer. Blaze and the others followed behind her. Then, at intervals, the other foxes broke off from the main party to go about their separate lives. In the end only Ranger's mother, Blaze, Friendly and the vixen cub were left.

'My mother naturally feels aggrieved,' Blaze said, turning to Friendly. 'But my father's death means an end to the fighting and the – the rivalry.'

'I'm glad you see it in the same way,' Friendly replied happily, aware that the vixen cub was watching him. 'My parents named me Friendly and it's in that manner I like to live. The Park should produce no enmities. You were born here. So was I. It's our home and that's all that matters.'

'It is indeed,' affirmed Blaze.

Friendly wished he would go on ahead with his mother. Presently Blaze seemed to sense this. 'Well, we shall probably see each other around from time to time,' he said. 'I don't know where you're making for. But I must leave you now.'

He moved away deliberately, and Friendly felt very grateful.

'My cousin is very diplomatic,' said the vixen cub shyly. 'I'm glad to talk to you.'

'I wanted to make your acquaintance ever since I saw you by the stream,' declared Friendly. 'What should I call you?'

'My name is Russet,' she replied.

By break of day, Bold had travelled a long way from the Park. He felt brave and powerful and equal to anything. In the early morning light the skylarks rose from their grassy roosts high into the sky, pouring out their burbling song. The country seemed empty, wide and challenging.

Bold slaked his thirst from a puddle of moisture and felt a bracing breeze unsettle his fur. This was the place to live. No narrow limiting boundaries for him! He travelled on tirelessly, and it was several hours before he saw the first human. Even then it was only a solitary walker with a small dog – smaller than Bold. The stout cub laughed at the sight and raced fearlessly past the figures with his yapping bark. Why had his parents deserted such a world? Here you could be your own master. He galloped on: on towards the horizon.

—26—
The Animals of White Deer Park

Over the next few weeks the new peace and security of the
Park did turn many of the animals' thoughts to other
things. They did not seek out each other as they had in
the old times and, alone in his set, Badger began to regret
his solitary ways. He missed the visits of Mole and
wondered where his little friend had got to.

In his dark subterranean labyrinth, Mole was living a
new life. He still collected and stored his beloved worms
for his appetite was as voracious as ever, but something
had occurred one day that had turned his world of
tunnels and meals upside down. During one of his
periodic feasts, he had heard a scratching noise – a noise

of small feet coming, not from above, but from alongside his tunnel. He had frozen into stillness, a half-eaten worm hanging limp from his sharp little teeth. The noise came nearer. Suddenly a hole appeared through the tunnel wall, and another mole's pink snout pushed its way in.

The intruder pulled its body through the hole and spoke breathlessly. 'Sorry to interrupt,' said the creature. 'It seems that my tunnel has sort of led me into – er – your tunnel.'

The voice was a female one, and Mole got quite flustered. 'Qu – quite all right,' he stuttered, nearly choking on the worm he had not finished eating. 'I'm just having a meal. Er – would you like to eat a worm or two?'

'Nothing I'd enjoy more,' said the female, following Mole to his store. 'Well,' she said when she saw it. 'I must compliment you on your choice. I've never seen such plump ones.'

Mole was delighted but tried not to appear so. 'I am known as something of a connoisseur,' he admitted nonchalantly. Soon they were eating together. 'I haven't seen you before,' Mole said.

'No,' replied his visitor. 'It's probably just coincidence. I was born very near here last summer. My parents were killed soon after. I've never strayed far from the area.'

'Well, well,' said Mole. 'How strange. Er – do have another worm.'

'These really are delicious,' she enthused again. 'Do you have a name?' she asked suddenly.

'My friends just call me Mole,' he answered. 'That's because none of them *are* moles.' He tittered.

'None of them moles?' she asked in astonishment. 'What do you call friends then?'

'Oh – foxes, badgers, owls, that sort of thing,' he exaggerated.

'Oh – now you're teasing me,' she protested.

'Not at all,' he answered. 'I'll take you to see Badger now, if you don't believe me. He's my closest friend,' he added a little boastfully.

'How extraordinary!' she exclaimed. 'Don't they try to eat you?'

'Certainly not,' Mole replied. 'You see, my friends are rather special creatures.'

'I see,' she said. 'Well, won't you tell me more?' She was all agog.

'Of course, if you wish it,' he said. 'But you haven't told me *your* name?'

'You can call me Mateless,' she said archly.

Mole gulped as she moved closer to him to listen. 'Very well,' he said nervously. 'Er – well, about my friends.'

Then he told her all about the animals' beginnings way, way away in Farthing Wood, of the wood's destruction and how they had banded together to help each other on their long journey to safety. He might have made his part in the event a little more courageous than it actually had been, but that was only natural. Mateless was enthralled, and Mole was so captivated by her admiration of him that he completely forgot his nervousness, and grew tremendously in confidence.

The upshot was that Mateless never did return to her own tunnel and that was how Badger came to be feeling lonely.

Eventually, of course, Mole could wait no longer to introduce his delightful new friend to Badger, and decided one day that they must pay him a visit. So he led Mateless (who by now was feeling she should have a new name) down the connecting tunnel into Badger's set.

They heard Badger snoring peacefully in his sleeping chamber and Mole went along to prepare his friend.

'Oh! Hello, Mole!' cried Badger, rousing himself, and

very pleased indeed to see the little creature. 'Wherever have you been lately? You've quite neglected me.'

'I must apologize,' said Mole, 'but I've had other business to attend to.'

'Really? What sort of business?'

Mole giggled excitedly and told Badger to wait a moment. Then he went away and returned, bringing a very coy young female mole with him.

'Goodness me! What have we here?' exclaimed Badger, before he could stop himself.

'My new acquaintance,' Mole announced proudly.

'Well, well, well,' Badger rejoined. 'Well I never! Er – enchanted to meet you,' he added politely.

'She's called Mateless,' Mole whispered.

'How extraordinary,' remarked Badger. 'And is that what you call her, Mole?'

'Well, actually, yes, I do,' he admitted, recognizing the absurdity of the name.

'It seems to me, then, that it's time it was changed,' Badger said pointedly.

'What do you suggest? Badger, will you chose me one?' Mateless whispered flatteringly.

'Me? Er – well – er – yes, I suppose so,' he answered. 'I don't know if I'm much good at that sort of thing. Well, let's see. Hmmm.' He pondered, muttering words to himself. Mole waited, anxious that Mateless should approve the choice. Badger continued mumbling. The longer he went on, the more uncomfortable Mole felt, while Mateless began to titter. When he heard her laugh, Badger stopped. He looked round, grinning craftily. 'How about Mirthful?' he asked.

Mole did not know what to answer. But Mateless appeared to be delighted. 'Yes, a lovely name! A lovely name!' she squeaked.

Badger smiled broadly. 'It's more becoming than Mateless, anyhow,' he declared.

'Thank you, Badger,' said Mole. 'You're quite right.'

They stood grinning at each other for a moment.

'Er – have you heard news of the others?' Mole asked suddenly.

'I haven't seen much of any of them,' Badger replied. 'As far as I can judge, they're all busying themselves with plans similar to yours. They haven't time really for an old loner like myself.'

Mirthful looked concerned. '*Must* you live alone?' she queried. 'There are other badgers in the Park, I'm certain.'

Mole tried to shake his head at her surreptitiously, but Badger noticed. 'It's all right, Mole,' he said. 'You don't have to spare my feelings. I know your charming young friend is trying to be helpful, but it's too late in the day for me to make adjustments to my life style. I'm afraid I wouldn't take kindly now to another badger's ways – neither would they to mine.'

'We can still come and see you, at any rate,' Mole said loyally.

'Of course you can, and you'll always be welcome,' said Badger. 'But you'll find less and less time for visits as time goes on, I'm sure.' He smiled at his little friend. 'Dear Mole,' he said. 'You have other loyalties now.'

A little later, when the two had returned to their tunnel, Badger left his set to go and talk to Fox. He sensed that evening was falling and he wanted to catch him before he went off hunting.

Fox and Vixen were overjoyed at the news about Mole. 'My suggestion really did take root,' Vixen enthused. 'Weasel and Kestrel have both found mates for themselves, and so, too, has Hare.'

'And Leveret,' Fox reminded her. 'We forget about the younger generation.'

I don't,' declared Vixen. 'Not when I can watch our own family's progress.'

Fox looked solemn. 'You know, Badger, I feel quite a different animal these days,' he said. 'Things are changing so quickly. I don't feel like a leader any more. That whole episode with Scarface changed my life.'

'How do you mean?' Badger enquired.

'It's made me look at myself in a different way. I know that if I had had that fight with him while we were on our journey here, I'd never have spared him. I would have thought of the safety of the party – the Oath we took. I couldn't have let him live. But here, I was always conscious that he had been here before us. The Park, if anything, was more his than ours. So I held back. Of course, I regretted it deeply. I could have saved a lot of lives by finishing him off.'

'Well, Fox,' said Badger, 'it's something that can't be altered. The rabbits and voles – and poor Fieldmouse – can't be brought back.'

'I know I have to live with it,' said Fox. 'But I've lost my self-respect to some degree. I know I'm to blame.'

'You have to stop feeling responsible for everything,' Vixen said. 'You brought the animals here with Toad's directions. You can't live their lives for them now.'

'No,' said Fox. 'But what Adder did – *I* should have done.'

Badger thought he detected a hint of envy in Fox's voice. He was no longer the supreme hero. By way of comfort he said: 'As far as I'm concerned, my life goes on as before. I don't ask for anything except a little company at times.'

'There will always be that available,' Fox answered affectionately.

The three animals watched Tawny Owl flitting from tree to tree in his secret noiseless way. Fox laughed. 'There's another who'll never change,' he said, 'no matter where he might live.' Then Fox lowered his head and looked into the distance. For a long time he stared into the darkness beyond, as if he were watching something far, far away.

Outside the Park, where the evening breezes blew here and there across the open countryside, a sturdy young fox loped over the downland into the enveloping night.

The Fox Cub Bold

Colin Dann

The Fox Cub
Bold

Illustrated by Terry Riley

Contents

For Cathryn, Matthew and Tara

—1—
The Real World

The summer sun shone, wide and warm, on the countryside. The fox cub Bold saw the broad horizon lit by its
golden rays and narrowed his eyes against the glare. He
felt he stood in the midst of a new world. The rolling
downland and its scattered coverings of woodland and
bracken were spread before him and around him.

'This is the real world,' he whispered to himself. 'The
wide, wild natural world.' In all the expanse the only
movement to be detected was the restless flight of a bird
here and there or the lazy waving of greenery caused by
the slightest of breezes. The cub repeated his phrase to
himself in a delighted murmur – 'the real world, the real
world. . . .' The spirit of adventure that had filled him as
he had stepped outside the limits of the Nature Reserve

where his family lived sharpened to a new pitch. He leapt forward and raced across the turf, glorying in his own health and vigour. His eyes sparkled, the blood sang in his veins – he felt as free as the air.

From a tree-top a solitary magpie was watching. 'Here's a topsy-turvy creature,' it muttered. 'A fox out parading in the daytime for all to see, and a young one too. His parents didn't teach *him* stealth. Humph!' he rasped. 'He'll learn the hard way, I suppose.'

Bold was not fooled by the temporarily empty landscape. His father had told him enough about life outside the haven of the Park for him to appreciate its dangers. And who knew more of such things than his father, the fox from Farthing Wood? For he had travelled across this country, leading his assorted band of animals and birds from the destruction of their old woodland home to a new future in the protected Reserve. On the journey all the creatures, strong and weak alike, had been bound by a sworn oath – a pledge to help and defend each other. This had continued after their arrival in the Reserve and had been maintained by them all ever since. But Bold relished his feeling of complete independence. He had confidence in the strength of his body and, as for his character, well, his parents had not chosen his name for nothing. The narrow limits of White Deer Park were not for him. He had decided to live the True Wild Life – accepting its thrills and its perils alike.

A bank vole started in his path and went scurrying away through the grass stems. Bold checked his headlong career. But it was some moments before he reminded himself that any game, big or small, was now prey to his hunting skill. He owed no loyalties, no allegiances here. No animals in the real world were bound by the oath. By the time he set off again the little beast had disappeared from sight. Bold made no attempt to hunt for it, deciding it was probably already cowering inside its bolt-hole. He went on now at a slower pace, sniffing the pungent air and carefully scanning the terrain for any sign of life.

The magpie continued to view his progress, noting the vole's escape. 'Not a great hunter, it seems,' it had said to itself. 'Well, he'll have to do better than that or *he* won't survive long.' It flew away to another tree, chack-chacking loudly as it went.

Bold looked up at the sound. The startling black and white of the bird's wings flashed like a signal against the sky's hazy blue. It landed on a branch, its long tail dipping and rising to maintain its balance. As Bold trotted on, the bird flew off again to investigate something that interested it on the ground. The cub saw it begin to peck at the object of interest, tugging with its bill this way and that in its efforts to free a morsel.

Bold recalled his own empty stomach. He had not eaten since leaving White Deer Park, and now here, perhaps, was a mouthful or two for the taking. He was more than a match for any bird. He had only to run forward. . . .

As he dashed up, the magpie rose awkwardly into the air, uttering a scolding, irritated cry. Bold discovered the mutilated remains of a long-dead wood pigeon. As he was by no means averse to a meal of carrion, whatever its rankness, he snapped at the skin and bone eagerly.

The angry magpie eyed him from a nearby vantage point, wondering if he would leave anything. In the end it could not contain its frustration. 'Is this your idea of hunting?' it screeched down at him. 'The foxes in this area prefer to rely on their skill in stalking *live* quarry. They roam at night when we birds have long since tucked our heads under our wings. Any real fox would turn up its nose at a poor scrap like that.'

Bold looked up in astonishment. The reference to a

'real fox' certainly jarred on him. 'Where I come from I was taught not to ignore any source of food that might mean the difference between eating and going hungry,' he returned. 'But I can assure you I know all about night foraging.'

'Really?' said the magpie sarcastically. 'But I suppose it's easier for you to snatch a meal from a being weaker than yourself?'

'I'm not in the habit of doing such a thing,' Bold replied, 'though I'm certain most creatures would accept it as one of the laws of nature – unfair as it seems to you.'

'Unfair and greedy,' remarked the magpie.

'Well, you've made your point,' said Bold. 'As it happens, there's really nothing but feathers left on this carcass anyway. So I'll gladly relinquish the morsel.'

The magpie, somewhat mollified, said: 'Is it your habit to be abroad in the daytime?'

'Habit? No. I'm no different from other foxes in enjoying the greater security of the dark. I've been exploring my new domain.'

'*Domain?*' echoed the magpie. 'If you see this area as your domain you're in for a few surprises, my youngster.'

'I doubt it,' said Bold confidently. 'I have as much right to roam here as any other creature. I accept their rights so they should accept mine.'

'Oh, they should, should they?' said the magpie, letting out a cynical chuckle. 'Well, we shall see. I wasn't only referring to other beasts, I might tell you.'

'Of course, you mean humans,' Bold answered, quite unperturbed. 'Well, they're not exactly unfamiliar to me, either.'

The magpie shook its head. 'I don't know where you have travelled from, 'it said, 'but your over-confidence makes me think it must be somewhere a lot less fraught with danger than this quarter. If I'm right in my view, you'd do well not to stay around here too long.'

Bold laughed. 'My very motive for coming here was a quest for adventure,' he said naively. 'I want to be a part of the real world.'

The magpie was scornful. 'Then you might get more than you bargain for,' he retorted. 'You obviously know nothing of what you speak about.' And he flew away, impatient with the cub's presumption.

Bold was amused. 'Well, I must have upset him,' he murmured. 'Perhaps we'll meet again some time when he might have changed his tune. I'm a creature of *quite* a different stamp from the one he takes me for.' He ran on, dauntless as ever. He looked back once, and was quick to notice that the bird had returned to the disputed remains of the pigeon.

—2—

The Bold Young Fox

That night, after a short nap, Bold did indeed go hunting.
The air was warm and still as he entered a small wood. He
came to a spot where there was a thick covering of
ground-ivy. Amongst this vegetation the rustlings and
scurryings of small animals could clearly be heard. Bold
set himself to catch his supper.

Half in sport and half in earnest, he spent a good part
of the night tracking and pouncing on the less lucky of
those shrews and mice who were engaged on their own
urgent quests for food. His hunger finally satisfied, the
cub curled himself up under a holly bush, his head on his
paws, and fell gratefully asleep.

Although he was well concealed from human scrutiny,
Bold's presence in the wood was well noted by the wild

night creatures, large and small, as they ambled amongst the trees or flew overhead on their particular errands. To some, he represented a competitor, to others, an additional danger to heed. Certainly, by daybreak the existence of a strange young fox in the neighbourhood was common knowledge to the wood's population. Bold, of course, remained blissfully unaware of the interest he had attracted.

He awoke late in the day. He got up and stretched elaborately. A pool of water on a patch of ground dotted with sedges attracted his attention. Bold quenched his thirst, lapping the water slowly while his eyes took in his surroundings. Already his old home was forgotten. There was so much to explore, so many new sensations awaiting him. Eagerly he trotted off towards the boundaries of the wood, feeling strong and refreshed.

Another bright, sunny August day greeted him as he emerged into the open downland. On the threshold of this gloriously wide expanse he paused briefly to look about him. Again, empty countryside met his gaze. Joyfully, confidently, he went loping along. The warnings of the magpie on the previous day seemed meaningless in such a landscape.

Later a sole human figure appeared on the horizon, accompanied by a dog no bigger than Bold himself. The fox did not even change his direction. His easy, even lope brought him within fifty metres of the two. The man watched him pass. The dog, intent on a particularly rich mix of scents on the ground, ignored him completely. Bold was exhilarated. He felt invincible; equal to any challenge.

He encountered no more human figures but, as he ran through some long grass, he flushed a skylark from its vulnerable nest on the open ground. The mother bird soared high into the air, uttering its cry of alarm. Bold had not yet tasted eggs so, fortunately for the lark, he did not know that they were good to eat. He ran on with an excited yap and the speckled, white eggs were soon once more covered by the warm breast feathers of their parent.

Everywhere he ran, birds would fly up out of his path. Rabbits, browsing close to their burrows, would bolt instantly at his approach. Bold came to feel the stature of being the most powerful member of the indigenous wildlife, feared and respected by all others. Only another fox or, perhaps, a badger could rival his position of supremacy. Small wonder that his self-confidence was unbounded. Should he see that magpie again he would laugh in its face!

By dusk he had travelled a considerable distance. He looked forward to the night's hunt and hoped for more exciting prey than before to test his skills. But first he must rest. There was a tiny stream running across country at this point – just a ribbon of water over which he could easily leap. An ancient, solitary hawthorn stood on one bank, its lower boughs almost dipping themselves into the rivulet. Bold made straight for this tree and settled himself comfortably under its umbrella of foliage.

He did not sleep at once but remained watchful. The evening song of birds preparing to go to roost pierced the still air. The metallic cough of a pheasant rang out periodically. No thought of his friends, his brother and sister cubs, nor even of his redoubtable father, entered Bold's thoughts. Only the vaguest picture of Vixen, his mother, flitted across his mind's eye. He remembered the way she had taught him to stalk his quarry in the Nature Reserve as he remembered her lithe, supple motion.

He was startled from his drowsy state (though hoped he hadn't shown it) by the sound of what was obviously a large bird making its landing in the crown of the hawthorn. Bold barked warningly but, to his surprise, the bird stayed where it was. It let out an answering 'caw', safe in the knowledge that it was well out of reach, and peered through the interlocking branches.

'Oh-ho!' it cried. 'So here's the bold young fox. I've seen you off and on today.'

Bold looked up, but the darkness of the bird's body was almost totally obscured by the gathering night. He realized his companion was a Carrion Crow, as black as soot from its beak-tip to its feet.

'You flatter me by your interest,' replied Bold bluntly.

'A large creature like you could hardly be missed in the daylight,' returned the crow, 'and I must express my gratitude to you.'

'Gratitude? Whatever for?'

'Finding a meal for me. The lark's eggs you spurned soon filled *my* stomach.'

'Each to his own habits,' said Bold and yawned.

'And *your* habits seem to be unique among foxes,' remarked the crow.

Bold sighed. 'You mean my daytime activity?' he asked patiently.

'Exactly.'

'What's so unusual about it?' protested the fox cub. 'It's not unknown for foxes to be about in the daylight.'

'Round here it is,' said the crow succinctly.

'Well, it isn't where *I* come from,' Bold persisted, 'and I can see no reason why I shouldn't continue to explore my surroundings whenever I feel like it. You birds are a nervous lot – always on the move, never still for more than a moment. You seem to read danger into every-thing.'

The crow ignored Bold's last remarks. 'Where *do* you come from?' it inquired.

Bold hesitated. If he mentioned the Nature Reserve, he

would only be inviting a sarcastic comment from the bird. 'Oh – er – a good distance away,' he said vaguely.

'Things may be different there,' said the crow. 'There *are* places, I believe, where human beings are not allowed to intrude on the freedom of wild creatures. But I've never been in any.'

Bold did not know if the crow was making a clever guess at his origins. In any case he disregarded it. 'Well, I've seen nothing to fear in these parts in the way of human presence,' he boasted.

'Then you've been very fortunate,' the crow observed. 'But I warn you – there are some days when the whole countryside is full of them.'

'I'm grateful for your warning,' said Bold. 'But I'm quite able to look after myself. And now, if you have no objection, I'll compose myself to sleep.'

'Don't mind me,' said the crow. 'I'm about to settle down as well.'

The next few days seemed to support Bold's assertion that there was nothing to fear. As before, human appearances on the downland were restricted to infrequent sightings by the cub. Single figures, a couple or, at the most, three together. He kept well clear of those and on these times did not range so far. He had found a good hunting territory to which he returned again and again. The fine weather continued.

Then one day, while the cub was actually lying among some bracken sunning himself, his safe empty world suddenly took on a new character. He was at the top of a small rise of ground, and up this rise, coming straight towards him, was a large party of people, about thirty in number. They were a party of ramblers and they advanced quickly. Bold had no time to hide himself, and anyway the ferns thereabouts were neither thick enough nor tall enough to have served as a screen. For the first time the young fox knew himself to be frightened. He had never before in his life seen such a large number of people together.

As he jumped up to run, the first among the group spotted him and immediately pointed him out to all the rest, with enthusiastic cries and gestures. Of course they meant him no harm. He was merely an object of interest. The sound of their raised voices alarmed Bold even more and he dashed blindly hither and thither in panic, getting amongst their feet and almost succeeding in tripping some of them up. At last he saw a clear space ahead and raced towards it, expecting every moment that the terrifying mass of people would give chase. In his ignorance of humans he had absolutely no idea that he could easily outrun any of them.

He turned his head fearfully as he ran and was amazed to see his discoverers standing stock still, calmly watching his escape. The next time he turned they had gone on their way. Bold stopped running.

When he had recovered from the danger of his first encounter with man, he took stock of his situation. It seemed to him that, once again, the threat of danger had turned out to be groundless. His relief was tremendous. His self-confidence took another boost but this, for Bold, was to prove to be his real danger.

— 3 —

The Game Wood

Over the next few weeks Bold ranged wide and far. He entered an area of human habitation – of farmland and scattered hamlets. He had attained his full size and was a splendid specimen of a male fox. He was well-built, muscular, with a beautifully healthy coat and brush; he was also clean-limbed and able to run quite tirelessly at a considerable speed. Though he had the sense not to stray too close to the man-made buildings and dwellings, he had developed a fearlessness of his only real enemy which amounted to arrogance. His innate cunning and cleverness were more than a match for Man's.

Food was plentiful and his diet was a varied one. On one occasion he killed a cock partridge as it rose from the ground in front of him. From that moment on he acquired a taste for game. In his nightly hunting forays his continual searchings took him to every corner of the district, but he was not often successful. Then one evening he came to a place where the scent of game seemed to hang in the air. It was a wooded area entirely fenced off from the surrounding countryside, but the fence was old, warped and damaged and no obstacle to a determined young fox.

Inside the boundary there was evidence of the scent of Man. Where the ground was soft and damp the unmistakable marks of his trail were plain to see, but Bold had no concern for it. He was on the track of something of far more interest. His mouth watered freely in anticipation of the delicious meal that awaited him. Cautiously, noiselessly, he stole through the undergrowth. He knew his quarry was not far away.

Under a thick cover of bramble a hen pheasant was disturbed from her rest. Bold pounced and, with a quick snap of his powerful young jaws, all was over. That night he feasted handsomely.

There was a large beech tree standing on a hump of ground, the roots of which were partially exposed. Underneath the roots an invitingly secluded hole attracted Bold's notice. He sniffed carefully all around and inside it. The smell of badger was very strong, but no sound could be heard and Bold decided the occupants were away from home. He had no fear of badger. An old male animal – a close companion of his father's – had figured largely in his early life in the Reserve. Bold went inside the hole and along the tunnel for a few paces before curling up to sleep.

Towards morning he awoke instantly at the approach of the owner of the set. Bold prepared to leave his makeshift den – it had served his purpose well. At the entrance to the tunnel a sow badger was standing uncertainly, sniffing the air around her home with caution. An encounter with a fox was not one to be undertaken without hesitation.

But Bold was disposed to be friendly. 'Please don't be alarmed,' he said. 'I certainly mean no harm.'

'Are you alone?' the badger asked nervously.

'Quite alone,' Bold replied.

'Foxes and badgers tend to keep apart in this wood,' she went on. 'That must be why I've never seen you before.'

'No. I'm a stranger hereabouts,' Bold told her. 'I only found the spot by chance.'

'Then I can guess your reason for coming here.'

'I was led here by my nose.' Bold explained jocularly.

'Yes, a lot of foxes come for the same reason,' remarked the badger. 'Most of them don't stay long, however.'

'Competition?' asked the cub.

'You could say that,' she answered, 'though it's not the sort of competition you're thinking of.'

'What then?'

'Haven't you seen the footprints?'

'Oh, yes. But I paid no attention to them,' he bragged.

'You'd be foolish not to,' she said. 'They're your real competition.'

'Humans?'

'Of course. Why do you think the wood is so rich in game birds?'

'It didn't occur to me.'

'Well, I'll tell you,' said the badger. 'They're released here by men for *their* use.'

'Use? I don't understand,' said Bold. 'Do *they* eat them?'

'I believe so. At any rate, they hunt them.'

'Hm.' Bold pondered. 'No wonder foxes don't often choose to stay. But you – you've made your home here!'

'*I'm* comparatively safe,' she said. 'I'm not so inclined to drool over pheasant and they – the humans I mean – seem to know that.'

'I see. But there don't seem to be any men about at present, so perhaps I'll risk staying on.'

'They haven't started hunting yet. But, let me warn you, you *would* be running a risk. There is one human who is always around here keeping an eye open for anything that might be after his precious birds.'

'Oh – one! I'm sure I'm capable of dealing with him,' Bold said easily.

'Yes, well – maybe. But summer's on the wane and *that's* a sign that they'll soon be coming in force. They flush the birds out of these coverts and shoot them in the open. And when *that* happens, woe betide any other creature who may be around. We're *all* game then.'

'I'll worry about that when it happens,' Bold said lightly. 'Thank you for your advice – and your warm den.'

The badger brushed past him. 'Very well,' she said. 'But just remember – it *is* my set.'

'As you say,' he acknowledged, and went on his way.

Bold paid some heed to the she-badger's warning by leaving the enclosure during the daylight hours to continue his explorations. But when night fell again, he returned. Ears cocked for the faintest sound of human tread, the cub set out to track down his second victim.

Now that the scent of fox – a new fox – had spread through the wood, the nervous game birds were not so easily caught napping. But there was one creature who had been injured previously by a stoat and was unable to fly. Bold made short work of him. And, in the succeeding nights, Bold's desire to test his hunting skills was more than satisfied.

As time went on he became expert in the pursuit of pheasant and, although he was not always successful in catching his favourite prey, his appetite was only increased by failure. So a pattern was established in his life which, for a week or two, did not change.

Each evening he left the wider area of farmland and entered the enclosed wood. He never came face to face with the gamekeeper, but both were very much aware of the other's existence. When danger threatened, Bold always managed to elude his enemy.

From time to time the young fox came across the sow badger or one of her family. They showed surprise that he continued to thrive in their wood but he swept their astonishment aside contemptuously. He became prouder than ever of his skill and began to believe he really did have exceptional abilities.

One night, when his usual luck deserted him, Bold decided to investigate a fresh corner of the wood. In this quarter, in addition to the mouth-watering smell of pheasant, Bold detected a new, ranker odour. He soon discovered it source. Hanging from a line attached to the enclosing fence an assortment of rotting carcasses swayed slightly in the night air. The grisly collection was comprised mostly of birds such as crows and rooks, but the decomposing bodies of a weasel and a stoat were also included. Bold realized at once he was looking at the handiwork of his enemy the gamekeeper.

He stood, horrified but fascinated by the sight. To his keen nose, the smell was overpowering. The bodies had obviously been hanging there a long time to warn off would-be attackers of the precious game birds. No fox, or the remains of a fox, was among the grotesque collection. Bold was exultant. The man held no sway over his kind. These were small fry – weaker creatures unable to look out for themselves. But a fox such as he was a different matter. No human was capable of meddling in his affairs.

Shortly afterwards he caught his prey. He did not carry it under cover to devour in safety. He took it to the gamekeeper's 'gibbet' and slowly, brazenly, he consumed it, underneath those quivering trophies. Only a handful of feathers and bones were left behind as evidence of his defiance.

—4—

The True Wild Life

The next night Bold entered the wood with extreme caution. For, unimpressed by the gibbet, he was still realistic enough to expect the gamekeeper to react in some way to his gesture of contempt. As he crept along, not far from the badgers' home, a sharp cry of pain rent the air, followed by grunts and snorts of a most distressing kind. Bold hastened towards the sound and, along one of his regular paths, he found the sow badger caught fast in a horrible metal trap. The more she struggled, the more its vice-like grip seemed to increase. A strong, noose-like wire bore down upon her back, making her gasp for breath and almost threatening to cripple her.

Bold sniffed gingerly at the snare, preparing to leap

away on the instant if it threatened him too The poor she-badger, panting painfully, looked at him with dull, hopeless eyes. The cub was convinced this trap had been sprung for him, and that the luckless badger had blundered into it instead. Quite unknowingly, she had saved him from almost certain death. He stood heavily in her debt. He looked more closely at the man-made device.

'I'm going to try to help you,' he told the badger coolly. 'Keep quite still.'

The trapped animal had already ceased to struggle. The pain was too severe. She heard Bold's words in amazement. What could he mean? Why didn't he run away while he was still safe? The strongest of all instincts for any wild creature on its own was self-preservation. *She* had been caught, not he. She continued to cower where she was, unable to answer him.

Bold had discovered that the strong wire that was pinning her body so cruelly to the ground was the only obstacle to her freedom. Once inside, it was impossible for the ensnared beast to free itself, for the wire could not be reached over its own back. But, from outside the trap, the wire could be sprung or snapped. Bold's only tool was the strength of his jaws.

'I'll bite this wire,' he muttered to the badger, but half to himself. He tried to get a grip on it, but it pressed too deep into her flesh and it was impossible for him to get his teeth round it without wounding her. A harsh gasp of pain escaped her lips at his first attempt. He tried again at another point. Again she winced in agony, closing her eyes. Frustrated, Bold withdrew temporarily.

He sniffed the air, while his ears constantly strained for a sound of the trap-setter. All seemed quiet. He moved forward again with increased determination. Now he noticed that at one end of the wire there was a short piece that did not pass over the sow badger's back. He fastened his side teeth on it and bit hard. Absolutely nothing happened.

'This may take a long time,' he said. 'But we have the entire night ahead of us.'

The sow badger lay fatalistically at the gamekeeper's mercy. She listened, in a quite uncomprehending manner, to the rasping of Bold's fangs on the wire. What was he doing it for, when in all probability the result would only be injury to himself as well? The night hours slowly crept by.

As Bold made one of his several pauses to rest his aching jaws, he thought he heard a steady tramp . . . tramp in the distance. He froze, his every nerve and muscle quivering with tension. Yes, there was no doubt of it. Something was approaching, and that regular tread could only be the sound of human footsteps. The gamekeeper was coming to assess his handiwork!

Bold attacked the wire with renewed ferocity and desperation, knowing that at any moment he would have to flee. Then, quite suddenly, the weakened wire snapped with a fierce backward lash that nearly blinded him. Almost at the same moment, the badger pulled herself clear and, instinctively, ran straight for her set. Bold raced after her.

In the deeper darkness of the lair they lay panting side by side. Bold's eye streamed with water and, in one corner, a thin trickle of blood ran where the point of the severed wire had pierced. The badger's back, too, had been cut and throbbed insistently.

'Why? Why?' she kept muttering.

Bold did not answer, but rubbed his bad eye with the back of one paw as if it would heal it.

Overcome by their experiences, they fell into an uneasy sleep.

The sow badger awoke first. Her back still smarted, but the realization that she was still alive flooded over her joyously. It was as though she had cheated death. But – no! *She* hadn't cheated it. She remembered her companion. She smelt the blood on his face and began to lick at his fur, gently and with gratitude. Bold awoke and shook his head in an attempt to free himself of the pain.

'*Why* did you do it?' she asked him.

He looked at her for a moment. 'That trap was laid for me,' he replied.

The badger still couldn't fathom his meaning. 'Surely, then,' she faltered, 'that was your escape?'

'Yes,' he said. 'I escaped death – because of you.'

'Then why should I live?' she persisted in bewilderment.

Now it was Bold's turn to have no understanding. 'But why should you *die*,' he emphasized, 'because of my good fortune?'

'That's Life,' she answered in a matter-of-fact way.

'No. That's Death,' he corrected her. 'And too great a sacrifice.'

'My carelessness led me into the trap,' said the badger. 'I had only myself to blame.'

'I owed it to you to help *you* to escape as long as I ran free,' Bold tried to explain. But he could see that she still didn't understand. Was this, then, the True Wild Life after all? This natural indifference to another's suffering, even to another's fate, when the cause of it had been oneself? In *his* upbringing, the law instilled by his father and enshrined in the oath, had been to help one's friends in trouble, and to expect the same from them. But even there, in the Nature Reserve, he seemed to remember that the law only applied to a particular group of creatures – those animals and birds who had banded together long ago to travel across country to the safety of the Park.

The badger interrupted his thoughts. 'I shall be forever grateful to you,' she was saying, 'and I'm now very much in *your* debt.' She paused. 'If I follow your example – and it seems I must – I offer you my help, and that of my clan, if ever you need it.'

'I am glad I freed you,' said Bold simply. 'And I –

'And you've wounded yourself in doing so, I fear to say,' she broke in.

'It will heal,' he said.

'Does my licking help?' she asked him.

'It does soothe,' he answered.

She resumed her task.

'Tomorrow I move on,' the cub said decisively. 'This episode has taught me I shouldn't linger here.'

'You are wise,' she answered.

'But first,' said Bold with bravado, 'I shall have one more meal of pheasant.'

'And I,' responded the badger, 'shall help you catch it.'

—5—
Humans Can Be Dangerous

Bold's last taste of game in the wood passed off without further interruption by the keeper. He and the sow badger made their farewells and the cub parted from her, urging her to be more cautious than before.

His eye still pained him and it tended to water, so that his vision was a little impaired. But, in spite of the injury, he had escaped the clutches of Man – indeed had bested him – and continued to lead what seemed to him to be a charmed life. However, Bold was to discover that he had tarried a little too long in the area.

He found a thicket of gorse which was ideal to lie up in during the day. It was within the farmland, but in open country, and it became his regular refuge. He marked it carefully in several places to proclaim his ownership. One morning, soon afterwards, he woke to the sound of gunfire.

He jumped up and, keeping under cover, looked out across the terrain. A line of men, all with firearms, stood at intervals of some metres along the crest of a slight ridge. Birds were wheeling in the sky, flying in panic from the death that stalked them below. Reports of gunfire were repeated regularly and a good number of the birds suddenly crumpled up in flight and crashed headlong to the ground. Fresh stocks of partridge, beaten from the open country, and pheasants, roused from the nearby copses where they had been released when young, came flying overhead in wave after wave. The men, raising their weapons, dealt destruction on all sides. The shooting season was in full swing.

Bold remembered the sow badger's remarks about no living thing being safe when guns were around. The awful crack! crack! of the hideous machines terrified the young fox. Should he run or stay under cover? Suddenly a pheasant plummeted to earth with a muffled thump right under his nose and then he saw a large dog coming for it. His mind was made up.

Avoiding the path of the retriever, he dashed away from the gorse patch at full stretch and away, as he thought, from the gunfire. As he ran his bad eye watered abominably and it was this that caused him to make a fatal mistake. He seemed to be running in a mist and he was almost on the second line of guns before he saw them. One of the sportsmen, who was in the act of reloading, gave a shout to his companions as Bold came up. A fox was fair game when their minds were on slaughter and, as Bold veered sharply in mortal fear, he saw one man raise his weapon and take aim at him. The fox increased his speed, heard a sharp crack! behind and, the next instant, felt a fierce sear of pain in his right thigh. Bold fell.

The sportsman cried out triumphantly. Before anything more could happen, a new covey of partridges came overhead and, mercifully, engaged the men's attention. Bold pulled himself up. He could put no weight on his wounded leg which felt quite numb until he tried to stand. Then a fresh surge of pain shot through him. Instinctively, he resorted to his three good legs and so, half dragging the injured one along the ground because he couldn't lift it, he limped slowly and wonkily across the field. Every moment he expected the impact of the second gunshot which would finish him off. But it didn't come. Luckily for him, the game in the air was better sport.

It seemed an age – an eternity – before he had dragged himself to a sort of safety, collapsing into a drainage ditch. His leg bled freely and was throbbing unmercifully. A trickle of water in the ditch bottom cooled him a little and he drank some of it. Though he didn't know it, the lead shot from the gun had passed right through his thigh which was very fortunate but, in doing so, had ripped the muscle drastically. He dared not stay still for long and so he began to limp along the ditch where at least he was out of sight.

The ditch ran right through one of the spinneys, but Bold pulled himself out of it when he reached the comparative obscurity of the overhanging trees. Now he had to find proper cover – and quickly. He made straight for a thick clump of bramble, hauling himself through the tearing briars to its very heart. He felt weak and dizzy and had scarcely enough strength left to lick the blood from his fur.

The noise of gunfire, though quieter in here, continued

unabated. Bold's greatest fear now was of the dogs. Would they come tracking him? He guessed that a trail of blood led right up to his hideout. No dog could fail to unearth him if once put on his scent. There was nothing he could do but wait. He had no means of defending himself. If the dogs came it would be the end of him, he knew, and the best that could be hoped for then would be a quick death. Bold tried to remain alert but his weak state induced an uncontrollable drowsiness and he drifted into unconsciousness.

When he awoke it was dark. He had no idea how long he had slept but all was peaceful again. No guns, no dogs. The blood around his wound had dried and his fur was caked with it. He tried to raise himself, eager to test the leg, but it had stiffened so much that he could not even bend it. He sank back again, wondering what on earth to do. He was not hungry but his feverishness had caused a raging thirst. He lay a little longer, feeling unutterably dejected and lonely. It was at such a time, he reflected, that one hankered for companionship – of any sort. Now he wished that his brother cub, Friendly, were with him. *He* would have tried to lift his spirits.

Then he scolded himself for his regrets. Was this the correct attitude at the first setback for a brave young fox who had chosen an independent path – who had *yearned* for complete freedom? Of course not. But then, this was more than a setback. He hadn't reckoned on becoming crippled in his fine new life. But perhaps he wasn't crippled – it was too early to be sure of that. And anyway, he should count himself lucky to be still alive. But . . . but . . . what was the good of being alive if one was crippled? For a young fox that would be a living death. Yet . . . this was the first true test of his character. He *mustn't* fail himself. He must be resolute; determined to overcome his

difficulties . . . . His thoughts ran round and round in his
mind until he dozed again.

The next time his eyes opened, it was still dark. Bold's
thirst was now so pressing that he knew that somehow he
must move himself from that place to find water. He
dragged himself from the midst of the bramble bush,
trailing his bad leg. Once in the open part of the wood, he
tried again to stand on all four paws. Again the wounded
leg collapsed under him. The pain was too great to bear.
Bold gritted his teeth and hobbled forward on three legs.
He found a puddle in a dip in the ground and lapped at it
greedily. For a long time he drank until his tremendous
thirst was assuaged. Then he sat down awkwardly, taking
care that his weight rested on his good side.

Well, here was a fine situation! An animal who relied
on speed and stealth to catch his prey and who now
wouldn't be able to pounce even if he could get close
enough to it! There could be no more hunting trips for a
bit. Insects, worms and fruit were the best he could hope
for. However, at least his eye no longer hurt him, though
it did still run.

Oh, he *was* hungry. He cast around a bit, saw nothing,
and then he remembered the bramble clump. He eased
himself upright and limped back to his hideaway. The
bush was loaded with ripe blackberries. Here, at any rate,
was some sort of a meal.

Bold was busy garnering the fruit which really required
very little effort when he saw a movement among the
thorny stems. A dormouse was engaged on the same
errand, sitting on its haunches while it delicately nibbled
a berry in its front paws. Oblivious of the large animal's
presence, it systematically turned the fruit round with its
little claws to get at the best bits, then discarded the
remains to search for a fresh one. Bold held himself still.

The creature presented a welcome addition to his meal if only he could catch it. He watched the mouse come closer and closer. At last it was within range. Bold lunged forward, snapping his jaws. They closed on thin air. The dormouse jumped in fright onto the ground in front of him, and then scuttled away. Bold limped hopelessly after it. Of course it was too fast for him and ran up the trunk of an elder shrub. Once safely out of reach it sat, quivering, on a stem and looked down at him with its black, bead-like eyes.

'You're lucky I'm injured,' the fox said grudgingly, 'otherwise you wouldn't be sitting up there, I can tell you.'

'If you can't catch a mouse, you'll soon starve to death,' replied the escaped animal.

'Don't you be too sure,' said Bold. 'I'll search you out in the daytime when you're asleep.'

'You'd never find me,' chirped the dormouse. 'I'll be way out of your reach.'

'Just you wait till my leg's mended. Then you won't be so cocky!'

'Oh yes, I'll sit around here until that happens, shall I?' the dormouse said derisively.

Bold scowled. 'You'll be my first mouthful when I'm fit again, I promise you that,' he snarled. He was furious at being on the defensive before this tiny creature.

But the dormouse continued to look steadfastly at him as if he were of no more account than a piece of dead wood. Bold turned away and had the mortification of having to display his awful limp in all its detail as he went. He had to content himself with settling down again to his meagre meal of blackberries.

A shower of rain in the early morning brought out the worms and snails and Bold was really quite glad of the chance to gobble up a number of them. The cool dampness of the day refreshed him and seemed to soothe the constant nagging pain in his right leg. But with the onset of daylight he crept back to his lair amongst the thorns to nurse his hurts, his misery and his pride.

—6—
Friend or Foe?

For at least a week, Bold confined himself to the same small area in the wood. His activities consisted of sleeping, limping a few yards to grub up some insects or slugs, and burying himself under cover at the slightest sounds of human voices or dogs. The weather was cooling rapidly and there was a distinct nip of frost in the air at night. Bold's leg hurt him less but he knew now that the muscles were damaged irrevocably. He would never again stretch or bend his leg as before. The best he could manage was an accentuated lurch as he moved along while he tried to put as little weight on it as possible. The young fox was beginning to feel very sorry for himself.

The worst of it, to his mind, was the attitude of the

other denizens of the wood. Despite the fact that Bold was now its largest inhabitant, the smaller animals had soon realized he posed no threat at all. So he was exposed to the total disregard of even the weakest of them as they hopped or scurried around his feet. Indeed, they snatched up from before his nose the very insects that he had been reduced to collecting.

Soon, even the insects and snails were hard to find as the temperatures steadily dropped. Bold eagerly ate any berries, bulbs or nuts he could find but, for a large animal, they simply were not a sufficient diet. From time to time he discovered scraps of carrion, but these were few and far between and could not be relied upon. He knew that eventually he must leave the wood to search elsewhere.

Autumn had settled in with a succession of bitterly cold nights, when the young fox was forced at last to make a move. By this time, he had developed his habitual lurching limp into a regular method of locomotion which he adopted automatically as he moved around. Although he no longer thought about it, it made pitiful a comparison with his previous vigorous, supple and tireless lope. He never thought now about live prey and the idea of ever tasting game again was long forgotten. His aspirations rose only to discovering enough invertebrate or vegetable life to sustain himself, while the bonus of a fresh piece of carrion was a treat indeed. This was the existence to which he had been reduced; the robust, confident young cub who had wanted to live in 'the real world'.

But, in spite of it all, Bold never once thought of returning to the protection of the Nature Reserve and the help of his old friends. He had made his choice on leaving the Park. Now there was no going back. He left the wood in the middle of November and at once established a routine of hiding during the day and scavenging for whatever was edible at night. On some occasions, when absolutely nothing could be found, he swallowed mouthfuls of grass, but they usually made him retch.

The scarcity of nourishing food made his already weakened body weaker still. It was as much as he could do to drag himself around and, with little hope of things ever improving for him, Bold began to wonder if it was worth bothering at all. He could never again look forward to the savour of meat, or the thrill of a hunting foray in the crisp, nocturnal air. The effort of lugging his useless leg over a large area in an attempt to find sufficient scraps of food to last until the next night seemed increasingly pointless. So, one night, he just remained in the ditch he used for cover and never stirred at all. Two days and nights passed in the same way. He lay unmoving and uncaring, heedless of the sounds around him. He was quite simply waiting for his end.

On the third day, a warm, sunny, autumn morning revived his flagging spirits and he staggered to his feet. He suddenly thought of the sow badger he had rescued in the coverts and who had pledged to return his good deed. Perhaps she could help him if only he could get to her? He pulled himself out of the ditch, but by now he was so weak that he collapsed in exhaustion with the effort. He cursed himself for not trying to reach her set before when he might have had sufficient strength to do so. He lay panting on the ground until he had recovered a little. Then he tried again. He lurched forward a few metres and collapsed again, his breath coming in hoarse gasps. His poor, wasted body shuddered in the extremity of a final fatigue. He knew he could never make it.

In the air a black bird circled nearby, watching his futile movements. It wheeled to and fro, waiting patiently for the young fox to expire. Finally the fox seemed to lie quite still. The bird coasted down and landed a little distance away. It walked slowly forward.

Bold watched it approach with his one good eye, aware of its intentions. 'You'll . . . have to wait . . . a little longer,' he croaked.

The bird came up to him and examined him critically. Then it uttered a harsh 'caw' of surprise. 'This can't be the bold young fox lying in the dust!' it crowed.

Bold opened his weak eye and blinked as he tried to focus properly. 'So it's you,' he muttered. 'The Carrion Crow of the hawthorn tree.'

'The same. And what's happened to you?'

'I've an injured . . . leg. Can't walk.'

'So you're starving to death?'

'I certainly shall . . . die soon unless . . . help can be brought.'

'Help? For a fox? Who would bring help?' the crow said scornfully.

'One that *I* helped . . . not so long ago.'

'*You* helped? Whom have *you* helped?'

'A sow badger . . . caught in a trap.'

The crow rustled its coal-black wings. 'Well, she doesn't seem in a hurry to remember,' it remarked sarcastically.

'She doesn't know I need her,' Bold wailed miserably. 'If only I . . . could reach her.'

'Too late for that,' said the crow. 'She won't even know of your death.'

Bold tried to raise himself, but sank back again helplessly. A thought passed through his mind. 'I need . . . a messenger,' he gasped.

The crow stared at him in amazement. 'Preposterous!' it exclaimed. 'You haven't the audacity to think that I –'

'I *was* thinking that,' Bold admitted.

'Well! You have some strange notions in your head! Carry a message for a fox indeed! You must have come from a strange place with ideas like that. I never heard of such a thing. And from you – who boasted to me you could look after yourself!'

'So I did ... until I got shot.'

'Aha!' the crow cawed triumphantly. 'So the humans caught up with you, did they? I warned you about them, but you paid me no heed. You knew better!'

'I was unlucky. I made a mistake,' the young fox groaned.

'Yes, well, you can't afford mistakes where they're concerned,' answered the bird. 'The way you went around, puffed up with your own cleverness – I'm surprised you weren't accounted for long ago.'

'I don't need a lecture,' Bold muttered. 'I've learnt ... my lesson. Will you help me or not?'

'Why on earth should I?'

'You were grateful ... to me once. Remember the lark's eggs?'

'Absurd animal! You didn't even see them. ...'

'I haven't got time to argue,' Bold said. 'If you won't help me ... I shall die. That's all. *You* can *fly* – how long would it take you?'

The crow shuffled its feet. 'Where does this badger hang out?' it asked ungraciously.

'Not far ... in the pheasant wood ... the coverts.'

'What?! I'm to fly in there under the nose of a gamekeeper? Oh yes, and then present myself as a target for his butcher's collection, I suppose? I'm to risk all that for *you*? You're mad, my young friend. I thought as much before.'

'Then you won't do it?'

'Never! What are you to me?'

'Nothing, I admit. But . . . my death . . . will be on your conscience.'

'*I'll* have no conscience!' the bird exclaimed angrily. 'Your pride has brought you to this, nothing else. *I* say you deserve it.'

'Very well,' said Bold. 'Then the cub of the Farthing Wood Fox will die through lack . . . of a friend.' He had fallen back on his last resort. The name and adventures of his father were a legend among the wild creatures for miles around.

The crow looked at him sharply. '*You* his offspring? But wait – it *does* make sense. Your ideals . . . the brotherhood of the Farthing Wood animals . . . . Of course! Now I see it! You come from the Nature Reserve, White Deer Park. So you thought yourself wiser than your parent!'

'Well, I've been . . . proved wrong,' Bold said. 'Now, will you help?'

'I must try,' said the crow in a new tone. 'If it were discovered that I might be responsible for your death in any way, and you related to the one who founded the oath . . . well, it . . . it . . . doesn't bear thinking about.'

'Thank goodness,' said Bold. 'Then go – *please* – hurry!' As the bird leapt into the air and soared aloft, Bold murmured: 'So, Father, even here you still seem to control me.'

It was by now high noon, and the fox knew he could not expect to see the sow badger or any of her tribe until dusk fell. He decided he must make one more attempt to rise and get back to the shelter of the ditch. A fresh danger might threaten his exposed position at any moment. Somehow, with the knowledge that help was at last at hand to buoy him up, Bold managed to stagger to his feet. There he stood for a while, swaying, his wounded leg just brushing the ground. The ditch was only a matter

of a few tottering steps and then he plunged headlong
into it, utterly spent.

He was startled by the sudden reappearance of the
Carrion Crow.

'It's no use searching in the daylight for badgers,' the
bird told him. 'They never appear until the sun
sinks.'

'But that's hours away,' Bold moaned. 'I might not last
that long.'

'Don't worry,' said the crow. 'There is a solution. *I'll*
feed you. I've discovered something really good. We can
share it.'

'What is it?' Bold asked warily, unsure of the bird's pre-
dilections in the nature of food.

'A rabbit carcass.'

'Can you carry it?'

'No, but I can tear pieces off and ferry them
back.'

The crow was being very amenable. Bold was grateful.
'You're very kind,' he said.

'I'll eat some first, shall I, and then bring some for
you?' suggested the bird.

Bold agreed. He was in no position to dispute. The
crow flew away again and was gone a long time. Bold was
beginning to think he had been deserted after all, when
the crow alighted on the edge of the ditch, its bill loaded
with a large piece of dark flesh. This was tossed in Bold's
direction and at once the crow flew off again.

The meat smelled rank, but Bold was desperate and
chewed it with relish. A second piece was soon dropped
to the ditch bottom. The crow returned four more times,
the last time with the biggest chunk of all which it stayed
to see him eat

'That's the last of it,' the bird announced afterwards.

'I'm very obliged to you,' said Bold.

The sun had at last begun to drop behind the horizon. It was time for the crow to renew its search. Bold gave him directions to the quarter of the game wood where lay the badger's set. The bird disappeared.

The food had certainly put new heart into the young fox. He lay, watching the evening shadows fall, with renewed confidence in his own fate. But he hoped his friend the she-badger would be out foraging early or the crow might not find her, for he could not see well enough in complete darkness.

As it was, night had very nearly enveloped the countryside when Bold's messenger returned once more. 'I've located your four-legged friends,' he told the fox. 'They're rushing about collecting what they can for you now. But I'm afraid I can't be of any more assistance to you. I'm a day creature.'

'Of course, I appreciate that,' said Bold. 'I feel a little stronger already, thanks to you. But how will the badgers find me?'

'I really don't know. By scent, I should think. But that's their problem – and yours too.'

'Did you give them *any* indication of my whereabouts?' Bold asked.

'Yes, vaguely.' The crow paused, aware of the fox's misgivings. 'I'll do one more thing for you,' it said. 'I'll come and find you at dawn, and if they haven't shown up I'll lead them to you. I can't do more.'

'I don't expect it,' replied Bold. 'And I shan't forget this.'

'Very well, then. Till daybreak,' said the bird. Then he was gone, an even blacker shape against the blackness of the night sky.

——7——

A Shadow of Himself

It was a long journey for the badgers to make across open terrain and with their catches in their jaws. There were four of them – the sow badger and three of her progeny, now grown up. Daybreak found them still some distance from their goal, though they *had* been travelling in the right direction. The Carrion Crow spotted them easily and led them towards Bold.

The fox had lain awake most of the night, uttering occasional muffled barks to give a hint of his position. Now he dozed in the ditch, having refreshed himself by licking at the cold dew trapped in the overhanging grass stems.

The crow cawed harshly to waken him, and then, his business done, vanished in pursuit of his own breakfast.

Soon the badgers came clambering into the ditch with their burdens of food. One of them had clawed up some tubers, two of them brought mice, and the sow badger had caught a great rat that had been scavenging by the gibbet. All of the offerings were welcome to the fox, and none of the animals made any noise as he devoured his food piece by piece.

Then the sow badger spoke. 'I scarcely recognize you,' she said.

Bold looked at her, licking his chops. 'My fortunes have dwindled rather since last I saw you,' he replied.

'Perhaps you should have stayed in our wood after all,' she observed.

'Either way I should have fallen foul of the human enemy,' said Bold. 'That gamekeeper was out to get me, and he would have tried another trick.'

'Well, I've seen no traps around since you left,' said the she-badger, 'and I've been very wary, so he must be content with your disappearance.'

'That's why we think that *now* your safest plan is to come back with us,' said one of her offspring, and added: 'You see, the man won't be expecting your return.'

'That's good thinking,' agreed Bold. 'But there's a grave difficulty. I can't travel.'

'Can't you move at all?' asked the sow badger.

'Scarcely. Up till now I haven't eaten for some days, you see. Maybe it might be different now – anyway, I can try.'

'You can take it in stages. We'll bring more food,' she promised. 'Then you can shelter in the set until you've built your strength up.'

'I'm afraid *you're* stranded now, though,' said Bold uncomfortably. 'You can't travel back all that way in broad daylight.'

'We'll find cover and hide up until dusk,' she assured him. 'Then we can all start together.'

Bold told them of the nearby wood where he had hidden himself until recently. 'I'll stay here,' he went on. 'I'll be quite safe – I've been here for days and nothing has been around to disturb me.'

The badgers made themselves scarce. Bold drowsed with a new feeling of hope in his heart. But his faith was ill-founded. He was awakened from his slumbers by a large and muscular dog – a Labrador – who was being exercised in the wood. It smelt the strong odour of fox in the air and gave tongue excitedly. In no time it had galloped up and discovered the luckless Bold cowering in his unprotected lair. Its frenzied barks brought its owner quickly toward the scene. Bold was cornered and completely helpless. His only hope was to feign death for, although this would not fool the dog, the man might be misled. So he lay stiffly on his side in a stark attitude with his tongue lolling from his open mouth, as if he had perished from cold and hunger. The man arrived, quietened the dog, and stood gazing at the animal in the ditch. Bold's heart beat fast. The man prodded him a couple of times with his cane, but each time the fox cleverly rolled back to the self-same position, keeping himself quite rigid. Then the man muttered something to himself and called the Labrador away.

Not until Bold was sure they must be far enough away did he allow himself to stir a muscle. Now it was imperative that he find a safer retreat. He got up and peered cautiously over the top of the ditch. The coast was clear, so out he climbed. He took a few tentative steps. The food had done him some good, for he certainly felt less shaky. He looked around for a place of concealment. There was nothing close enough to hand. Then he remembered that the ditch ran right into the wood to which the badgers had retired. He wondered if he could get that far. Well, at least he would be out of sight as he dragged himself along. There was really no other choice.

The afternoon wore on as Bold limped his way through the mud and dead leaves of the ditch bottom. Of course, he was taking himself further away from his ultimate destination, but that could not be helped. By the time the first trees of the wood closed around him he knew he could go no further and so he sank down where he was. In an hour or two the badgers would be up and around and expecting him to begin another journey. But there was no possibility of that for the present. He must try and keep awake, though; otherwise, they could miss each other.

Through bleary eyes that ached for sleep he at last saw four ghostly-grey shapes moving along under the trees with the badgers' familiar lumbering gait. He yapped to warn them of his presence.

'Why, you've come quite the wrong way!' cried the sow badger. 'Now you've a long trek indeed ahead of you.'

'Had to move – dogs,' muttered Bold. 'Afraid I can't go . . . any further tonight.'

'He's exhausted,' said one of the young badgers unnecessarily.

'*Now* what do we do?' demanded one of the others of its mother.

'I don't know for sure,' she answered. 'This is very awkward.'

'I'm sorry,' groaned Bold. 'But I was lucky to escape.'

'Yes, yes,' she said. 'I understand.' She thought for a moment. 'Well, if you can't be moved, you can't,' she pronounced. 'So I'll have to stay here with you. However, there's no need for all of us to remain behind. You three must go back – now. Four badgers in a wood without a set are too conspicuous. Off with you – and don't stop till you're home.'

'I could try again tomorrow,' Bold offered weakly.

'Yes, well – we'll have to,' said the sow badger. 'Now I must go foraging again.'

The strange wood provided less easy titbits than her familiar one. She brought him a shrew, some bitter bulbs, and a dead toad that had not been quick enough to bury itself away from the first frosts.

'You must eat, too,' Bold remonstrated as she watched over him.

'I managed to dig up a few roots for myself,' she answered unconcernedly. She followed his progress through the meal. 'The crow told me your history,' she informed him.

'My history?' Bold asked. 'Ugh, this toad has an evil taste!'

'Your origins.'

'Oh – the Reserve.'

'I'd never heard of White Deer Park. Of course, the birds know a far wider area of country. But your father –'

'Yes,' sighed the young fox. 'He does seem to be rather well known . . . .'

'Were you perhaps trying to escape from that?' the badger asked him subtly.

'Yes, in a way. But my main idea was to live beyond the confines of the Park. It promised a more exciting existence.'

'Well, you've certainly made up for any lack of excitement in your earlier life,' she remarked. 'But at what cost!'

Bold said, 'For better or worse, it's my life now.'

The following evening the two animals prepared to begin the journey back to the game wood. They had eaten a meal together in companionable silence. Bold had chosen a name for his friend. He called her Shadow because of her constant watch over him. She was amused at the name and seemed rather pleased. They went back through the ditch this time in the opposite direction.

Bold's stamina was still at a low ebb, but he thought he might have sufficient strength to get as far as the gorse patch where he had been lying when the shooting had begun. Their progress was painfully slow.

'I'm relieved that your poor eye has healed,' Shadow had said, 'because you took that knock on my account.' Bold did not tell her that he now realized that his sight had been permanently damaged.

They left the ditch and started across country, Bold hobbling along laboriously. He was very conscious of the fact that his companion was exposing herself to danger because of his slowness. There was almost no real cover until they were amongst the gorse thickets. If daylight should come before they reached them, he must make her run on ahead.

However, they reached shelter without mishap while the darkness held out. For some time during the last stretch of ground Bold had stumbled along blindly, willing his protesting body forward in a sort of haze of exhaustion. When they got amongst the gorse he crashed to the ground like a stone, certain that he could never rise again.

'Bold fox, brave fox,' Shadow murmured compassionately. But he didn't hear her.

They both slept the clock round until the welcome dusk once again folded them in its soft blanket of concealment. Shadow set off as usual in her quest for food. She had not travelled far when she saw, to her astonishment,

her three youngsters in the distance apparently on a
search. They greeted her delightedly and immediately
wanted to know all about Bold.

'It's going to be a longer job than I'd hoped,' she
told them.

'We've hidden some food for you a short way back,'
said one of the males. 'Where do we bring it to?'

Shadow explained and they trotted off to fetch the supplies. On their return they found their parent running
towards them in consternation. 'He's gone!' she cried.
'Bold has disappeared!'

—8—

Alone Again

Bold had watched Shadow set off on her foraging with misgiving. He hated his position of reliance on another. The very thing he had revelled in before – his complete independence – had been completely destroyed. And now, because of his uselessness, he was subjecting another creature to risks he had no right to expect her to share. She – and the crow – had saved him from death. The debt was paid. So, soon after her back was turned, he hauled himself carefully to his feet. His long sleep had re- freshed him and he was able to limp out of sight, round the other side of the thickets.

Bold was not sure what to do next. All that he knew was that he would no longer expose Shadow to the danger of being in his company. If possible, he would make his own slow way to the pheasant coverts and the refuge of her set, and if not . . . so be it! His only concern was that she might come looking for him, but he hoped that she would eventually have the sense to make ground to her own home before dawn threatened. He set his immediate sights on reaching the nearest farmed field. This lay on the other side of a hedgerow which formed the border between farmland and the open country. He knew Shadow would never search for him in such a place.

The darkness, at least, obscured his intentions from her as he staggered into the gloom. It was a cold, starlit night without a breath of air and the frosty grass made a crisp whispering noise as he trod it underfoot. The spectral form of a Barn Owl glided over his head on its silent wings. He saw it hover over the hedgerow, then swoop down, pounce, and rise again almost in one uninterrupted movement. So there was food there too! Perhaps he would be lucky enough to kill something *himself* for a change, if he did not set himself too distant a target.

Bold's damaged leg had loosened up slightly during his recent bouts of enforced exercise and he was surprised – and pleased – at the way he managed to keep going. His exhaustion the previous night had largely been due, he decided, to clambering in and out of the ditch. Now he began to hope that he might be over the worst.

As the first faintly perceptible lightening of the sky heralded the end of the night, Bold lurched into the hedgerow. It was made up of a thick band of closely-knit vegetation that was a perfect resting-place, and here he was to have his first piece of good luck for days. He discovered another fox's abandoned earth, and inside it were the remains of numerous catches. Stale and smelly though they were, the famished Bold made a hearty meal. Used to poor fare for so long, it was the closest thing to a feast for him since the last pheasant. So, replete and well content, he gratefully fell into a much-needed sleep.

The next day he awoke before the light had faded and immediately finished off the last few scraps. He left the earth and looked out across a field sown with swede. Here was another food source that he could use in necessity, for the young vegetables were just beginning to thrust themselves out of the soil. Bold's spirits rose considerably. He felt stronger, more hopeful than he had been for a long time. Now, if he could only prove to himself he could still catch his prey – no matter how insignificant – then he really would feel he was on the road to recovery. There would be no need then for Shadow's set or her ministrations.

Bold set himself to explore the hedgerow and its occupants. Songbirds returning to their roosts fluted and warbled amongst the remaining November greenery. There were inviting rustlings amongst the twigs and dead leaves underfoot. A squirrel raced along the top of the shrubbery like a furry goblin, intent on finding a safe perch to enjoy a hazel nut. Bold slunk along with his uneven gait, ears cocked, nose working overtime to identify every new scent. He stopped dead as he spied a vole squatting on a low twig, balancing on its hind legs while it examined some bryony berries. It was at eye level and well within reach. The fox crept forward another couple of centimetres, holding his bad leg out of the way. The vole remained unaware of his presence. Another centimetre. And another. Snap! Bold's jaws caught on the little beast's tail as it leapt for safety. His grip was not good enough and his lunge forward from three legs tilted him off balance. He went sprawling at the hedge bottom and the vole escaped with no more than a painful nip and a fright. Bold rose and shook himself, ashamed of his indignity. Once again, as in the incident with the dormouse, his ability to catch even small prey had been found lacking. The resulting loss of confidence made him unwilling to test his technique again. To be bested by such tiny creatures! It was mortifying to him. He stared across at the field of young swedes. That was to be the limit of his expectations now. For, with a bitterness born of his incapacity, Bold knew he could never again hunt live prey.

He limped out of the hedgerow towards the root crop sown by Man. It was simple to scratch up the ripening tubers and then to fill his belly with the sweetest of them. The added satisfaction that arose from raiding a food supply of the humans made them taste the sweeter. It was Man that had brought him to this low point and he would avenge himself where he could. Suddenly Bold stopped munching and stood motionless. Yes! That was his future now! The humans would be made to pay for his injury. Wherever they stored food or left edibles lying around he, the fox cub Bold, would capitalize upon it. Men would provide him with the food they had deprived him of catching himself.

Sustained by this promising and daring idea, Bold finished his supper and retired to the earth in the hedgerow to mull it over. It was an excellent plan that would require a mixture of caution and courage, he decided. He was no longer in a position to challenge Man by daylight for he had no turn of speed. His movements must therefore be strictly during the dark hours. So when night fell on his meditations, he issued forth for a second raid on the vegetable field.

As he went about his task, feeling more light-hearted now in the new role he had assumed for himself, he became aware of a ghostly shape moving about on the far side of the field. He hobbled hopefully towards it. To his delight he found Shadow the she-badger enjoying the same tasty roots. As he approached she looked up in alarm and prepared for flight.

'Wait!' he called to her. 'It's Bold! Your friend!'

Shadow paused and waited for the fox to come up. 'Alas,' she said, 'we badgers don't have your keen sight, otherwise .... But I'm glad to see you!' she finished enthusiastically. 'We'd given you up for lost.'

Bold explained the reason for his disappearance.

'I understand you,' she said quietly. 'But you're too particular. We really wanted to help.'

'I know,' Bold answered. 'But, for me, it's better this way.'

'Then I can't persuade you to come back with me to the set now?'

'No. But thank you. I have another plan.'

Shadow regarded him with interest. 'Do enlighten me,' she urged.

'I'm going to live off the humans,' Bold answered simply.

Shadow's jaws dropped open. 'You mean –'

'I mean whenever and however I can,' he finished for her.

'Well!' Her eyes held admiration. 'So you still intend to live up to your name?'

Bold was pleased with that remark. 'I shall try,' he replied. 'But I shan't take stupid risks.'

'Won't that restrict you?'

'Of course it will,' he said. 'But what does that matter? A beast in my condition can't afford risks except minor ones. From what my father told me of human behaviour, wherever they are in evidence food is there for the picking.'

'But a different sort of food from your preference?' queried Shadow.

'I'm already getting used to that,' he assured her. 'I may

have to adapt further still . . .'

'What about your den?' she asked next.

'I already have one base,' said Bold, looking over his shoulder. 'Over there – in the hedgerow.'

'Underground?'

'Exactly. A very lucky find.'

'You certainly seem well set up,' said Shadow, 'and if you can adapt your diet as you say . . . .'

'If I have to, I will,' Bold said with conviction.

'I respect your determination,' she told him.

Bold enjoyed her flattery. It made it seem he did have a purpose, after all, rather than it being just a question of eking out an existence. 'Well,' he said, 'I suppose I might see you from time to time?'

'Very likely,' she said. 'Or one of my family.'

'Till then, Shadow, my friend,' Bold said brightly.

'Good luck,' she whispered, and they parted.

Bold limped back to the earth, greatly heartened. He felt a keen anticipation for the beginning of his campaign on the morrow.

——9——
A Good Catch

Bold could not sleep for a long time. He was excited by what he felt was a new beginning in his life. The unmistakable sound of human voices pierced his consciousness a couple of times during the day, serving as a pertinent reminder of the challenge he had set himself.

At dusk he awoke from a rather uneasy sleep. He lay a little longer in his den, conserving his strength until the full darkness had spread over the area. Then he emerged into a rainy night. The hedgerow dripped with moisture and the air was filled with a sort of misty dampness. Bold was intoxicated by the myriad scents wafted to him by the quivering leaves and plants. There was an aroma of warm little bodies heightened by the smell of wet fur. But his direction lay elsewhere.

He crossed the vegetable field carefully and without hurry, this time ignoring its offer of food. He was after new tastes. He picked up the smell of human spoor and followed it along a well-worn path. As he had expected, it led towards a dwelling-place of Man. This was, in fact, a farmhouse, surrounded by a collection of outhouses. There was a scent of dog in one quarter which Bold studiously avoided. He slunk around the wall of a yard, licking up moisture from a runnel of rainwater as he crept forwards. On the other side of the cottage, a pungent odour greeted his eager nostrils. Literally following his nose, he went to investigate. A gap in the wall led into an area of mixed plants. Bold was able to tell by their smell which ones were intended to be used as food. In one corner there was a sort of mound comprised of all sorts of odds and ends and it was from there that the most interesting scents came. There were scraps of vegetable peelings and one or two rather bald-looking bones among the debris. Bold licked at the bones and swallowed some of the tastier smelling parings. But there was nothing very much here. He stole along the side of the wall for he heard movements under a bushy plant closer to the house.

A pair of bantams had been allowed to make their nest in the open and they had been making nervous noises as Bold betrayed his presence. They scurried away as he approached and the young fox watched them without giving chase. He knew they could have run around all night from one spot to another and *he* would never have a chance of catching one. But what did interest him were the three eggs which the hen bird revealed to his view as she abandoned guard. Bold remembered the Carrion Crow. Now it was time to sample something which he had rejected before. First, he sniffed at the strange-looking objects with great care. They smelt inviting enough, for the scent of the hen's breast feathers was still attached to them. He took one in his jaws and bit into it. Out poured the contents on to the ground while Bold held a mouthful of unpalatable shell. He licked at the liquid, found it delicious, and made short work of the other two eggs. But his exploration of the cottage garden had to end sooner than he wished. A breeze got up and blew his scent downwind to the farm dog. A frenzy of barking broke out and Bold made as fast an exit as he could, leaving the bantams to return ruefully to the robbed nest. Bold saw no other chance of food nearby so he limped back towards the swede field. His hunger was not entirely satisfied, but the vegetables did not tempt him. Safely back in his earth, he felt reasonably content with the results of his first expedition. But he could not get the thought of those two bantams out of his mind. He knew he had no speed to catch them in a chase, but why couldn't his other innate skill – stealth – serve his purpose, especially as he had found the nesting-place? The more he thought, the more the idea appealed to him and his mouth began to water in anticipation. .

Bold decided to pay another visit to the farmhouse garden – but not on the next night. He intended the little pair of fowls to be lulled into a false sense of security. So the next night he hobbled away in another direction to see what he could find. It was a long way to the next human habitation; another farm. By the time he reached its boundaries he was too tired to do much exploring. He was lucky to find another dump of waste, and he contented himself with what edible scraps he could dig out. Now he was in difficulties, for he was too weary to get home. There was no hedgerow here – no cover of any sort, except a few, isolated, large trees which would not hide a fox.

What could he do? He could not be found near the

farm buildings when daylight arrived. But who would
look for him *in* one of the buildings, or even think of finding a fox in such a place? There was an open barn well
stocked with hay that smelt sweet and warm and inviting.
He would be well concealed in the depths of that and,
tomorrow night, he would undertake his return journey.
Bold was delighted with his own impudence and off he
went to the dark barn to bury himself amongst the
bales.

During the day there was plenty of activity in and
around the farm complex. Cows were milked, animals
fed, men went to work and came back. But Bold slept on.
The farm cat stood on the threshold of the hay barn and
sniffed gingerly at the alien scent, fearing to go further.
The sleeping fox was undisturbed. Only the sparrows
who flitted to and fro among the rafters knew of his presence and even they deserted the scene when evening
came.

Bold roused himself from his fragrant couch. It was
time to stir. Two mice killed by the cat still lay at the side
of the barn. The well-fed cat had toyed with them but had
not deigned to eat them. Bold did. It was the first fresh
meat he had tasted since he had left the care of Shadow.
He visited the rubbish patch again and found some fat
worms wriggling amongst the rotting base of the pile.
These and a discarded apple core made Bold's hasty meal
before he began his homeward journey.

All the way he thought of nothing but the prospect of
the following night. The weather was mild and muggy –
the year's last fling of warmth before freezing December
was ushered in. Bold crept gratefully into his earth and
covered his nose with his brush.

Twenty-four hours later he emerged, feeling brisk and
alert for his venture. He reached the nearby farm and
began to slink quietly towards the garden. Because of his

uneven pace, he had to make particularly strenuous efforts to ensure his silence. All the time he tested the air for sound or smell of the guard dog. His progress was painstaking but uninterrupted. Like a shadow he slid into the garden and slowly neared his target. The heavy cloud layer which made the night so warm added a welcome additional layer of darkness to his endeavours.

Bold froze abruptly as he heard soft, stirring noises about a metre away amongst the shrubbery. Had the birds sensed his approach? Seconds ticked by. Nothing happened. He took another couple of steps. Again the sound of rustling feathers – then quiet. Now Bold trod on the soft soil by the plants, front paws first. He had almost ceased to breathe. His rear leg – the good one – followed. He held himself stiff as he prepared to drag round the damaged leg. Only that could betray him now. Slowly, slowly, he brought it level. It brushed a plant, hardly stirring the foliage. But it was enough. Out rushed the bantams, the hen one way, the cock straight into his waiting jaws and crunch! it was done. Bold stayed no longer than it took for him to immobilize his victim. While the hen bird dashed everywhere in panic, the victorious fox limped his way out of the garden. Now he went more quickly but still he listened for sounds of the dog, his heart beating rapidly. He could hardly believe his luck.

As he neared the field of swede he dropped to his belly suddenly as he saw a badger again rooting amongst the plants. He watched the animal, lying doggo. Yes, it was Shadow. He knew her movements. Jealous of his prize, Bold cursed her appearance on the scene. For if she spotted him, he would have to offer to share his meal. She had worked hard to feed him not so long ago. She seemed in no hurry to move on. Tubers and roots were amongst her favourite provender and, as he knew, the ones in this field were especially succulent. At last, while the cock's warm body grew cold, the sow badger seemed to have garnered all she wanted. Her slow enjoyment of her meal irritated Bold beyond measure. His mouth ran dry with his waiting and all the while she munched the roots with every appearance of relish.

Then, when Bold thought he could stand it no longer, Shadow stopped eating and came straight towards him. Bold dropped the bird and sighed. His frustrating wait seemed to have been for nothing.

'Bold!' she cried gladly. 'I didn't see you before.'

He was on his feet now. 'I – er – I've just come this way,' he replied awkwardly.

Her glance picked out the dead fowl. 'I see you've been busy,' she said, comprehending his predicament at once. 'You needn't worry. I'm quite content. You enjoy your catch.'

'No, no,' Bold protested half-heartedly. 'Share and share alike.'

'Wouldn't dream of it,' she answered. 'You must have worked hard for that.'

Bold relaxed. 'Well, yes, I did, it's true,' he admitted.

'I'm sorry, Shadow. It's just that –'

'No explanation required,' she assured him. 'I understand perfectly. You need all you can get for yourself with your handicap. But you've done well!'

'Thank you,' he said. 'I *was* feeling rather pleased with myself.'

Shadow said: 'I won't delay you any longer. I bet you've been drooling!'

She made her departure and Bold made haste to his den. He took a long time over his meal, anxious to savour each juicy mouthful to the full. It might be many days before he was so successful again. Afterwards he dreamed of the game wood, with himself, perfectly sound of limb, picking off the plumpest pheasants to eat without the least effort. So vivid were these exploits that Bold had some difficulty adjusting to reality when he awoke. So much so, that he was consumed with one ambition: to catch the other bird – the cock bantam's mate.

Evening found him approaching the farm again, with the same caution and silence as before. The cottage loomed ahead of him, slumbering in the soft air. Nothing seemed to stir. Gradually he pulled himself towards the garden, hesitating a little as his senses told him that there had been a change made here – as yet he knew not what. Then, in the gloom, he saw a strange shape where the bantams' nest had been, under the shrubbery. The hen bantam had been securely shut away in a pen for the night – the humans had seen the need for her protection. Bold paused, wondering if it were worth his while to investigate the contraption. He limped a little closer.

Suddenly he was frightened out of his wits. The farm dog had been moved from its usual kennel and tethered as an extra sentry under the back wall of the farmhouse. A great black shape leapt out of the shadows, straining like a panther on a rope, and barking fit to bring the house down. Its gleaming fangs and furious eyes were like a vision in a nightmare. Bold turned tail and fled, his damaged leg bumping over the ground in pursuit of the others. Every moment he expected a crushing body to fall on him, bearing him down and pinning him, helpless, to the ground. But the barks became more distant and he started to breathe freely again.

He did not stop until the sanctuary of his earth was reclaimed. He had had a narrow escape and he vowed never to go near that place again. It was as well he had eaten his fill the previous night, for he got nothing this time. But it seemed the humans were not satisfied with giving Bold a scare. They knew a fox had taken the cock, and that he was ranging the area. While he did so he remained a menace. So they set about eliminating that menace.

The farm dog was put on his track the next morning and, as the track was fresh, it was not difficult to follow. Across the vegetable field came the dog, with young men behind carrying spades, and a terrier. Bold heard them as they breasted the hedgerow. The dog barked triumphantly at his entrance hole. Flight was an impossibility. The large animal was pulled back and Bold heard a scrabbling sound. The terrier had been pushed into his earth. Soon afterwards the hole was stopped, blocking out all light.

Bold stood at bay, ready to snap at the little cur who was growling at him in the darkness, his hackles on end, stiff as a hairbrush. There was another hole leading out of the den and slowly Bold backed towards it, watching the plucky little dog in case of a sudden rush. But his back felt a wall of earth. He was holed up with no escape route and the terrier holding him at bay.

Then he heard men's urgent voices and the sound of their spades striking the surface. The soft moist earth began to drop in on him and the edge of a spade scoured his back fur like a scythe. Daylight filtered into the den while the heavy tools beat away the protective ceiling of mould. In a terrifying upheaval of soil, the cowering body of Bold was exposed to the open air like a defenceless grub in its tunnel. The large farm dog, its fury unabated, cracked the peace of the countryside with its deafening roar. The terrier was hauled out of the pit and Bold cringed, waiting for the cruel thud of a spade across his body that would spell his doom. His bad leg collapsed under him and he sprawled on his stomach. His adventures were over.

—10—
Not Guilty

The two young men looked down at the puny, maimed beast quailing at bay. They glanced at each other with raised eyebrows. Was this poor specimen the fox that had killed the bantam cock?

'*He* can't be the culprit,' one observed to the other.

'Must have a mate who did the job,' muttered his companion. 'You can see the feathers clear enough.'

'Quiet, Punch! Stop that row!' yelled the first man to the large dog. It ceased to bark and began to whine and growl exasperatedly in a frustrated manner. The terrier went on yapping shrilly.

'We'd better leave this poor brute,' said the second

man. '*He's* no threat to us. Doubt if he'll see the winter through.'

'Not him, with that injury. And his mate won't stay in these parts now she's got no cover.'

'She might have another earth, though?'

'I don't know of one,' said the man who was holding the terrier. 'But we'd best keep our eyes peeled.'

Bold, awaiting the awful final moment, saw through glazed but astonished eyes, the men turn on their heels and stump away across the field, taking their tools and dogs with them. He scrambled out of the wreckage of his den and pushed his way through the hedgerow to the other side and on into open country as fast as his poor gait allowed. Every second he expected to be pursued. But he limped on, each laboured step taking him further away from danger. No sound came from behind. At last he realized he was not going to be followed and paused to give himself a vigorous shake, freeing his coat from its shower of mould. The ways of men were indeed incomprehensible.

Bold's only thought now was to get as far away from the area as he could before disaster should overtake him again. Fear lent him a new strength and, by late afternoon, he felt he had come a long way. He was in country he had not seen before and now he knew he must rest. His whole body trembled as a result of his exertions, while his legs ached abominably. He staggered into a stand of young holly on the edge of a spinney and fell, rather than lay down, on the carpet of dead leaves underneath, quite oblivious of their spines.

Unknown to Bold, a familiar, black shape was coasting on air currents in the winter sky, occasionally flapping its wings as it lost height. Satisfied that the exhausted fox would be unable to stir for some hours, it flew away over the tree-tops uttering its harsh cries in a sleepy manner as the daylight failed.

Bold was roused at sun-up by a chill wind ruffling his fur. The ground all around the spinney was stiff with frost. Even the edges of the holly leaves had a coating of white. Bold shivered and peered out at a world made silent by thick eddies of mist. Then he blinked in disbelief as he saw a large black bird stepping out of the fog, its bill stuffed with pieces of dark meat.

The Carrion Crow dropped his burden by the fox and croaked a welcome. 'On the move again, I see?' he added, 'then you'll be needing this.'

Bold saw the pieces of stale, raw meat more closely. 'Timely indeed,' he remarked. 'I haven't eaten for two days, and so I appreciate it more than you know.' He took a gulp. 'This *is* good,' he said. 'But where did you find it?'

'Oh-ho! There's plenty more of that if you know where to look,' chortled the crow.

'And where would that be?' Bold asked eagerly.

'In the town.'

'Town?' Bold ate another piece of meat.

'Yes – not far from here. Full of humans and their buildings – *and* their food!'

Bold's ears pricked up. 'What sort of cover is there?' he wanted to know.

'Oh, plenty round about. You'd have to stay on the fringe, of course, and make raids at night.'

'That's rather what I had in mind,' Bold said wryly.

'Sorry. Don't need to teach you your craft, I'm sure,' the crow answered quickly.

'How long would it take me to get there?' Bold asked next.

The crow said: 'I don't know. I can only judge distances as a bird flies. It may be a whole night's travelling time on four legs.'

'Or, in my case, three,' Bold reminded him sardonically. 'Then I'd better start at nightfall.' He finished the meat the crow had brought him. 'What direction must I take?'

'Watch me,' said the crow and took to the air. Bold followed his flight until he became a mere dot in the sky. The bird did not return but Bold knew all he wanted to know. He got up and stretched his three sound limbs. He felt stiff, sore and chilled to the marrow. He needed to get some warmth back into his body, and the only way to do that was to keep on the move. The freezing mist set his weak eye watering, but its enveloping coils were also his friend. No prying observer could see the hobbling fox's feeble attempts to run, and for that Bold was very glad.

A thin sun touched the shrouded countryside but failed to penetrate. Only the wind succeeded in tossing the swirling vapour about like patches of damp fleece. The young fox's blood ran more quickly through his veins as he pattered here and there, whiling away the time to when the sun should finally surrender its fight.

Darkness came early and Bold set his course for his new objective, following the bearing of the crow's flight. He travelled warily and at an easy pace. The wind had dropped and the air was very still. Scarcely a murmur reached Bold's ears from the creatures of the night. After some time he became aware of a faint gleam which seemed to lie on the distant horizon. It grew steadily more bright as he drew nearer. Though he did not know it, it was the lights of the town.

Eventually Bold began to look for shelter. He did not

know how far he had come but, as usual, his legs told him
it was time to rest. He hid himself away in the nearest
piece of woodland, content with his progress for that
night. The next evening he was off again in the direction
of that illumined piece of sky. The mist had disappeared
and presently he heard quite plainly the muffled sounds
of the town. They were, as yet, too distant to be alarming.
He had no experience of the terrifying noises that
humans can make in their daily lives. Motor traffic and
the blare of machinery were beyond his knowledge. The
crow had not warned him what to expect and, at the end
of his second night's travelling, he rested quite
unprepared for the shock that was to come with the
morning.

He had arrived on the edges of some playing fields
where a litter basket had provided him with some mis-
cellaneous pickings. It had been easy to overturn it to get
at the contents and, after he had eaten, Bold laid himself
down at the bottom of a privet hedge. When dawn broke,
the first noises of a wakening town were carried to the
sleeping fox, dispelling his slumbers. Wrapped in his
thick, winter brush he lay without moving, but now wide
awake. The early morning din was as nothing to what
would happen when the town's pulse really began to
beat. Bold was uneasy. He moved from the hedge to find
thicker cover. There wasn't any. He began to panic. The
noise was growing steadily louder. He couldn't keep still.
Every fresh roar made him turn in fright, but he was
limping around in circles. Suddenly he saw what looked
like a dark hole and made straight for it. It was a small
hut, containing some tools belonging to the groundsman
of the playing fields. The door had been left ajar and Bold
blundered in, upsetting the stacked implements and
sending them crashing to the wooden floor. Now quite
terrified, he tottered out again, casting about wildly for

anything that might shelter him. He saw some people walking nearby with their dogs and slunk back to the privet hedge. But the din seemed to fill the air, blotting out his ability to employ even his most basic instincts. At last he heard a muttered croak close at hand.

'Come with me. I'll show you where.' The Carrion Crow was waiting for him, perched very conspicuously in a rowan tree. He took off and flew low, directly across the playing fields. Bold stumbled after him mindlessly. On the other side the bird waited for him to catch up and then flew straight to a patch of waste ground, which was choked with bramble, elm-scrub and thick banks of rusty-leaved weeds. Bold needed no bidding to dive into this mass of vegetation until he was quite invisible. The crow sat on the top of a sycamore sapling and spied out the land.

'You're quite safe now,' he said.

Bold refrained from answering. The last half hour, particularly the crossing of the playing fields in full view, had quite unnerved him.

'You took longer to get here than I was expecting,' the crow went on.

Now Bold said: 'I wish I hadn't come. That dreadful noise! I've never heard anything like it before. I'd have been better off staying where I was.'

'Nonsense!' scoffed the crow. 'No good being safe and secure elsewhere if you can't find anything to eat.'

'I was doing all right,' Bold muttered from the undergrowth.

'You'll do better here,' the crow told him, 'when you've adjusted yourself.'

'That I shall never do.'

'You know, noise itself can't harm you. It is town noise made by humans, and no danger whatsoever to you or any other creature. You simply have to get used to it. It's the same every day. At night, when you'll be around, it's quieter. All you've got to watch out for are the *makers* of the noise.'

Bold had calmed down a little by now. The din had not increased and there was no sign of it approaching nearer to him. It *would* be worth waiting until nightfall to see if the crow's words were correct.

'You'll soon change your mind about things once you start foraging,' the bird reassured him. 'There are rich pickings if you know where to look for them.'

'Very well,' said Bold. 'I shall give it a try. And, by the way, I forgot to thank you for your rescue operation.'

'I have to confess to some self-interest in this,' said the bird honestly. 'You'll be able to tap sources of food I can't reach. So I'm hoping that my diet might be enriched too. . . .'

'I understand you,' said Bold. 'And I certainly owe you a lot. You shall share anything I find – as long as there's sufficient for me.'

'Naturally. And I will do the same for you – for I shall be about in the daytime. So, between us, we can work this patch for all it's worth. No better place in the winter than close to Man's nesting sites.'

Bold was amused at the other's tone. It seemed his own idea of exploiting the humans was now shared by this bird.

'In fact,' the crow declared, 'it's time I rustled up something now. You stay put,' he added as he left, an unnecessary remark as far as Bold was concerned, who immediately fell asleep.

He was still asleep when his partner returned. The crow searched for a sign of him with his beady eyes but to no avail, so good was the fox's camouflage. Presently he cawed irritably.

'You're back,' Bold mumbled drowsily. Only a slight

rustling of the undergrowth betrayed his whereabouts.

The crow waited patiently but Bold didn't stir. 'Aren't you going to see what I've brought?' he croaked. 'It's all yours. I've eaten my fill.'

Bold crept out from his screen and sniffed at the strange-looking object that awaited him – a packet of sandwiches. He sniffed all round it and gave it a tentative lick. 'What's this?' he asked, looking puzzled.

'Man food,' answered the crow. 'I found it on the ground. It's quite palatable.'

'It smells tasty enough but –' Bold broke off to have another look at it. Then he clawed at the paper wrapping. *That* didn't appear to be palatable.

'You have to accept what comes,' the crow explained. 'Can't afford to overlook *anything*. You'll be surprised what you can eat when you get into the habit.'

Bold had never seen bread before, but there was meat inside it and he found himself eating the whole concoction and enjoying it.

'Was this your meal too?' he asked afterwards.

'No,' said the crow. 'I found some food left out for a cat or dog and ate all that.'

'Some poor creature will go hungry then,' Bold opined. 'I think I shall call you "Robber".'

'Don't waste any sympathy on them,' the crow retorted. 'Those that Man feeds never go hungry. So you and I have every right to take what we can.'

'Yes, Robber,' said Bold drily.

'Yes, Bold,' replied Robber.

—11—
The Urban Fox

When night fell, it was Bold's turn to make a foray. Robber had gone to roost in a secluded place at the top of a tall tree, leaving the young fox to gather his courage together. For a long time the noise from the town continued unabated. But as the nocturnal hours marched by, a comparative peace descended, only occasionally interrupted by a sudden, strident sound. Then Bold was ready to move.

He went limping across the fields, now bathed by a fitful moonlight, and made for the black shapes of the human's dwellings. He paused often to test the air as he went. His powerful sense of smell detected a host of strange scents, none of which was familiar to him. But he pressed on, prepared to take cover only if the smell of dog or that of Man himself was recognizable. The first group of buildings he came to lay in complete darkness. Walls or fences bounded them and their plots of land, and Bold skulked along these barriers like a shadow, searching for an opening. For, unlike other animals of his kind, he could not jump. He soon realized he was indeed handicapped for he was thus effectively debarred from entering most of the gardens. Of course he was able to contort himself wonderfully to slink through the slightest gap; he could flatten himself to scramble underneath an obstacle; he could even dig; but any sort of leap was absolutely beyond his scope.

On that first exploratory roam around Bold succeeded in visiting a number of yards and gardens and this was when he discovered what was to be the mainstay of his food supply for weeks to come – the dustbin. Once he had got used to the clang that some of them made what a remarkable collection of unwanted scraps he found in these receptacles! There was always something, it seemed, of which use could be made. It was almost as if the improvident humans had attempted to encourage him to feast upon these puzzling little dumps of food. Bold accepted each and every thing gratefully as he came to realize that his survival appeared to be ensured. Winter would not claim him as a victim after all.

His inquisitiveness kept him so busy that he forgot how far he was from his new hideaway. Dawn was stealing across the sky as he hastily set off on the return journey. He did not remember his duty to Robber, for he went empty-jawed. Back along the human paths he hobbled until he reached the playing fields. The noise had started up again as he made haste across the wide open space. Only when he reached the waste plot did he realize he had not kept to his bargain.

Robber arrived at the spot, intending to leave Bold to

snooze peacefully. He waddled along the ground, jerkily turning his head this way and that as he searched for the delicacy he was sure the fox would have brought him. Of course, there was none. Robber wondered if Bold had not returned. He flew up to a branch and spied out the land. No sign of any animal. Then he 'cawed' three or four times loudly and harshly with annoyance.

'I'm here,' Bold owned up.

'Ah, now I see you,' said the crow. 'Were you unsuccessful?'

'Er – no, not exactly,' Bold replied awkwardly.

There was a pause. 'Oh! So our bargain is to be a one-sided sort, is it?' remarked the crow.

'Not at all,' Bold hastened to explain. 'I – I was caught rather far from home when dawn broke.'

'I see. Well, as you are still in my debt I shall not be expected to find *you* anything now?'

'Of course not,' said Bold in a small voice.

Robber flew away immediately, without another word. Bold did feel a little shamed and decided he would make up for his failure on his next trip.

The next evening came round wonderfully quickly. December arrived with a stinging squall of sleet that drove across the open fields in a spray of ice-needles. The fox's eyes smarted as he battled against the blast, cursing the handicap of his limp. But there was shelter amongst Man's buildings and Bold again began to enjoy his exploring. In one yard he found two bowls, one containing milk; the other fish. He greatly appreciated the thoughtfulness of the humans who had supplied them. There didn't seem to be any other animals nearby to claim the bowls' contents.

He went on cautiously, snapping up pieces of bread missed by birds in one garden, knocking over bins in another to raid the pungent-smelling collections that spilled from them. He had learnt to retire quickly behind a plant or other screen as the bin crashed down; then, if nothing happened after a few minutes, he slunk back to select his pickings. Sometimes the clattering he caused did bring a human into the open. On those occasions, Bold was out of the garden and well away from the scene before he could be noticed.

On this evening he was to find that there were competitors for his food. He was looking into a large fenced area of lawn and flower beds behind an imposing house. The sleet fell slantwise across the grass in a sort of mist. Out of the shadows around the building there trotted a brisk, confident-looking fox that seemed to know exactly what it was about. Bold's muscles tautened as he watched. The animal stepped lightly across the grass with a fluid grace that was a perfect illustration of health and vitality. It made straight for a stone bird-table, the flat top of which was nearly two metres from the ground. With the most enviable agility the fox leapt in one flowing movement up to the top. There it stood, fearlessly surveying its surroundings, before snatching up the remnants of the birds' leavings. Bold was entranced. He knew it to be a female, and he was as full of admiration for her strength as for her grace and elegance. He thought of his own poor frame; his hobbling walk; his inability to jump, and he shrank back timidly to avoid being detected.

As luck would have it, after making a brief circuit of the garden, the vixen came straight towards Bold. Instinctively he flattened himself against the ground. She leapt the fence effortlessly and landed about three metres from him. Some slight involuntary movement on Bold's part betrayed his presence. She turned and looked at him calmly. No trace of surprise or curiosity was shown by her. For a few moments they stared into each others' eyes, then she swung round and trotted coolly away as if he had been of no more interest than a piece of wood.

Bold felt humiliated by her disregard. Although there was no reason for her to pay him any attention, her nonchalance only made him all the more conscious of his poor appearance. He felt that her reaction might have been quite different had she seen him as he had once been in those first glorious weeks after he had left the Nature Reserve. Now he was indeed quite another animal. His physical deficiencies assumed a new proportion in his mind and his confidence fell to a low ebb. What a cringing, struggling scrap of a creature he had become! He crawled away from the fence, his brush hanging lifelessly between his legs. Why continue the fight? He would be better off out of it all.

But life had to go on and Bold had to go on. He pulled a meaty-looking bone from the next container he upset and began his slow, sad, homeward journey. At least Robber would have no cause for complaint this time.

The crow was delighted with Bold's offering and spent a long time pulling and pecking at the fragments of meat that still clung around the bone. Bold slept deeply, utterly dispirited and tired out by his feelings. Robber came back during the day and dropped a share of his kill for the fox to enjoy, for he did not live entirely off carrion. But Bold made no attempt to fetch it. Flying overhead later Robber noticed the untasted morsel and down he came to reclaim it.

'Shame to waste it if it's not to your taste,' he remarked.

'Have it by all means,' said Bold disinterestedly.

Something in his tone made the bird pause. 'Is there anything wrong?' he inquired.

'Of course – everything's wrong,' Bold growled bitterly.

'Everything?'

'Everything with *me*.'

'Aha!' said Robber. 'So that's it. Feeling sorry for yourself. Doesn't do any good, you know.'

Bold held his tongue.

'You're still alive, Bold, my friend,' the bird went on. 'You would have died out there if you hadn't followed my advice.'

'Might have been the best thing,' Bold muttered. 'After all, what am I doing? Just prolonging the agony!'

'Your leg may not always be so bad,' said Robber encouragingly.

'Yes, it will,' said Bold. 'I shall never run or jump again as I used to do. If anything, it's worse than before.'

'You're not very easy to comfort,' said Robber shortly. 'I don't know why I'm bothering.'

'I'm sorry,' said Bold. 'I ought to be grateful for a comrade, I know. But I think I'm beginning to miss my own kind.'

'That's easily solved,' Robber told him. 'There are plenty more foxes around here.'

'I know, I saw one,' said Bold morosely.

Robber looked at him, his head on one side. 'Couldn't have been a vixen, I suppose?' he chuckled.

'Yes, yes – a vixen,' Bold answered.

'Well, that's hopeful, then?'

'Quite the reverse,' the fox said. 'I'm not the most impressive of beasts, Robber.'

'Oh dear. Now, now,' Robber said awkwardly. 'Humph! Well, you'll soon put some meat back on your bones, *I'm* sure.' He eyed the morsel of food with an air of irresolution, for he badly wanted to eat it. Then he seemed to make a decision. He stepped away from it and turned his back. 'Of course, you won't if you let good food go begging,' he said. 'If you don't hurry and eat what I brought you while my back's turned *I* shall eat it.'

Bold saw the sense in the remark and knew the bird was making a real sacrifice, something almost unknown in the crow family except at nesting time. He came out of hiding and gulped down the food, before Robber could change his mind.

'That's better,' said the crow, as he turned back, but Bold thought he detected a note of disappointment in the familiar croak.

'Thank you, Robber,' he said humbly. 'I'm glad you're my friend.'

The crow rustled his wings and started to preen himself as a diversion. He was just a little embarrassed. 'Well,' he said eventually, 'I wish you good hunting tonight.'

Bold wasn't thinking of his hunting. His thoughts were of a certain lithe young vixen and his one hope was that he might encounter her again.

—12—

Whisper

For the next week Bold visited the same large garden where he had seen the vixen. He couldn't get inside it since he was unable to jump the fence. So, each night, he gazed through the palings in a forlorn way, longing for a glimpse of her. Yet she was never there – at any rate, not at the time he was. Bold became more and more disconsolate. He never mentioned her again to Robber, but the wily crow knew how the wind blew in that quarter. Of course he refrained from saying anything.

Then one evening Bold thought he spotted her. There was certainly an animal moving around at the far end of the garden, shadow-like in the gloom. Bold stared into the darkness until his weak eye ached. He sniffed the air for a clue, but the creature was downwind and he could

not catch the scent. If only he could jump! Bold actually
snarled in his aggravation. Then he remembered he
could still dig.

He began to scrape at the soil in which the fence was
sunk. It was quite soft and so he dug in earnest. Every
now and again he paused to see if the animal had come
any closer. Deeper and deeper went Bold's tunnel, but
still he could not seem to reach the bottom of the palings.
Then he stopped digging, for the animal in the garden
had come out into the open. It was the vixen, and she was
approaching the bird-table to repeat her former trick.
Bold resumed his digging.

So determined was he to get under the fence that he
would have failed to notice the vixen leaping over it, if he
had not aroused her curiosity.

'Can you not jump?'

Bold started and looked up. The vixen was poised on
the other side of the palings, ready to spring. Bold saw the
tightened muscles in her powerful limbs. He felt
ashamed of his damaged leg and tried to hide it by tucking it under his body. The vixen leapt the fence.

'Er – no,' Bold muttered. 'No, I can't jump.'

'Are you hurt?'

Bold looked down, unable to meet her penetrating
glance. 'I – I was injured – er – a long time ago,' he said,
scarcely audibly.

'Unfortunate,' she commented. 'I should save yourself
the trouble, anyway. There's very little worth foraging
for, in there. Why are you so desperate to get in?'

Bold was taken aback. 'I– er – well, I wanted to – er – I
was really trying to dig,' he spluttered.

'Yes, I can see that,' said the vixen, looking at him
curiously. 'But what's so important about *that* garden?'

'Nothing, now,' Bold said in a not-at-all bold
voice.

The vixen sat down. 'I think you were trying to get to *me*,' she said quietly.

Bold remained silent.

'I haven't seen you before,' she went on. 'Are you new in the area?'

Bold didn't remind her that she *had* seen him before. 'Yes,' he said. 'I moved in from the country when food became scarce.'

'Very wise,' she replied. 'I come around here quite often in the winter to supplement what would otherwise be a rather frugal diet. But for you, things must be doubly difficult.'

'What do you mean?' Bold asked defensively.

'Why, if you can't jump – you can't run, I suppose?' said the vixen.

'No, I can't,' he snapped. 'And nor could you, if you'd been shot in the leg.'

'My, my, aren't you touchy?' she said. 'Accidents will happen. Why are you so sensitive about it?'

Bold said nothing.

'If I were you, I'd be glad I'd survived,' the vixen went on. 'How did it happen?'

Bold explained the circumstances. The vixen listened with evident sympathy. 'Bad luck indeed,' she said seriously. 'Maybe those humans were avenging themselves on you for stealing the pheasants *they* wanted to kill.'

Bold thought this a shrewd observation. He thought for a moment.'I've escaped death twice at their hands,' he said. 'Now it would be ironic indeed if I survived to an old age by living on their leavings.'

'But a sort of justice,' commented the vixen.

Bold pulled himself out of the hole and shook his coat energetically. It wasn't until he took a few steps that the vixen realized just how serious his injury was. Something moved within her. 'If you'd accept help, I'd be glad to give it,' she told him. '*I* could be your legs.'

Bold winced internally. His pride took another blow. 'I'm not quite helpless yet,' he replied testily. 'But I thank you for your offer,' he added in a more gracious manner.

The vixen realized she had touched him on a raw spot. She thought she had better leave him to his own devices. 'Farewell, then,' she said quickly. 'And good luck.'

Bold almost called her back. But again pride got in the way. He watched her supple young body slip away into the darkness and sighed. How he wished she could have seen him when he had been better favoured!

Quite mechanically he set about finding his supper, his thoughts still full of the meeting he had sought for days. He ate without appetite and took more care over choosing a titbit for Robber than he did for his own meal. He returned home early, full of a sense of regret.

Bold never saw the vixen in the garden again. But the two of them were destined to meet again in different surroundings. About a month after their last encounter, in the middle of winter, Bold was crossing the playing fields now covered by the first fall of snow. An intake of kitchen leavings combined with the exclusion of any fresh meat from his diet, had wrought its change in the fox's appearance. He was thinner than ever and his coat mirrored the lack of really nutritious food. The severe cold heightened the stiffness of his old wound and in every way he looked like an animal who was struggling to hold the threads of its life together. Unknown to Bold, his faltering steps through the snow were witnessed by the vixen, who herself was finding the going more tough. But she had no thought for her own problems as she watched his progress.

The vixen's heart melted at the sight of him and she

was filled with compassion. A few seconds longer she watched; then she hastened after him and, with a few bounds, drew alongside.

Bold turned an astonished glance on her. 'Well,' he said, 'how goes it with you?'

'Rather better than with you, I would think,' she said softly. 'I – I – want to help – or – I want to *hunt* with you,' she corrected herself.

Bold noticed the slip but he felt he couldn't refuse her offer again – nor, indeed, did he want to. It seemed that, since his injury, he was fated to be helped by other creatures. His dreams of independence had turned sour. Yet, despite that, the prospect of the company of this young vixen caused a flicker of excitement inside him.

'I should be glad of your company,' he said diplomatically. 'We might bring each other luck.'

They reached the cover of the first buildings and the vixen stopped. 'Let's not go sniffing for scraps,' she suggested. 'I've discovered a place by the side of some water where there's a colony of rats. But we have to go farther into the town. What do you think?'

Bold began to drool at the idea of eating fresh meat again. 'Lead the way,' he said with bravado.

The vixen looked at him for a moment as if to make certain of his true feelings. Bold licked his lips. 'Very well then,' she said and led off.

Only now did Bold appreciate to the full her skill in hunting. She was so light-footed as to be noiseless; she followed unerringly the path of the thickest shadows, and when it was necessary to cross an open space she skimmed across it on her silken feet like a zephyr. Bold lumbered after her, feeling himself to be like a chain around her dainty legs, impeding her swiftness. She paused regularly to allow him to catch up. Neither spoke a word, but Bold's eyes told her all. Eventually the gleam of water could be seen ahead, where it bathed itself in moonlight. The vixen seemed to melt into the darkness as she crept cautiously forward. Bold limped behind as quietly as he could, maintaining a discreet distance.

'There!' she hissed to him. 'But wait – the water is higher now.' She scanned its edge. 'Yes, the colony is still there, but the water surrounds them now. They've become an island.'

Bold peered over her flank. He was looking at a canal and its still, night-black water. Close to the bank a mound of debris, mud and vegetation was situated, and the beasts who favoured this site as their home were scuttling around it, some squeaking aggressively at others – perhaps at rivals.

'The water level has risen,' said the vixen. 'That makes it easier, because their retreat is cut off.'

'But you'll have to swim?' Bold asked.

'Of course. But that's simple enough, if you don't mind the cold.'

'*I* can't swim,' said Bold hurriedly, 'with only three useful legs.'

'I didn't expect you to,' replied his companion. 'I'll bring enough for both.' She moved to the edge of the bank and let her body sink into the icy water. Only her head showed above the surface as she paddled towards her victims, the ripples streaming back from her shoulders. Now the rats heard her and pandemonium ensued on their little island. The squeaks became shrieks and they dashed about, colliding with each other, and running this way and that in their terrified indecision. The next moment the female fox pulled herself from the canal and crashed amongst them, snapping to left and right as the rats scattered. Some of them leapt into the water to escape the slaughter and began to strike out for the bank.

Bold lay doggo, his muzzle protruding just an inch or two over the grassy edge. None of the escaping animals could suspect that there was another fox awaiting their arrival on land. As they tried to scramble clear of the canal, Bold felled the first two before those behind saw what fate awaited them. But some of the others hastily paddled further downstream and evaded their certain death.

The vixen started to carry her prey back to land. Soon she and Bold were contemplating the results of their night's work.

'You're a wily hunter,' Bold commented with satisfaction.

'You played your part too,' she answered hastily. 'We've more than enough here.'

'Light as a whisper,' he murmured to himself. 'And so I shall call you.'

'Whisper? Then I must have a name for you.'

'I am called Bold,' he said, 'and bold I was. I wish you had known me then.'

'I too,' said Whisper. 'Well, Bold – let's eat.'

They took as much as they wanted and ate in a dark, concealed spot without fear of interruption.

'Tomorrow we can come back for the rest,' said Bold. 'We must hide our catch away.'

This they did, and covered it with earth and twigs. But Bold kept one of the rats back.

'Haven't you had enough then?' Whisper asked him with surprise.

'It's not for me,' he explained.

'Then for whom?'

'Robber – the crow.'

'*Crow?*' she echoed. 'How absurd.'

'No, not absurd,' Bold said patiently. 'We have a

bargain between us. He brings me food – and I him. He kept me alive on more than one occasion.'

'Well, this is strange,' said Whisper uncomprehendingly. 'But I didn't go rat-catching for the sake of a bird.'

'Then it is one *I* caught,' said Bold pointedly.

'Indeed.' She stared at him. 'But your unusual arrangement can end now. You have no need of such an ally any longer.'

Bold held his tongue. He was not prepared to dispute the case. Robber was his friend and he had no intention of deserting him. It seemed that Whisper might be a little jealous.

There came the point on their return journey when their ways lay in different directions.

'Where do you sleep?' Whisper wanted to know.

Bold explained. 'It's perfectly safe,' he added. 'And you?'

'I have an earth,' she answered. 'You would be safer still there.'

'I'm most grateful, Whisper,' he said. 'But tonight I must return to my usual place. Robber will be looking for his titbit at daybreak.'

'Please yourself,' she said shortly. 'I'll be at the waterside tomorrow night.'

'And so will I,' said Bold.

—13—
The Changes of a Season

Robber was delighted and amazed with Bold's present and croaked a harsh little song to himself in his pleasure. 'Things are looking up, Bold, my young friend,' he said afterwards. 'You're a hunter again!'

Bold had to deny his prowess. 'I had help,' he said.

'Oh-ho. It isn't a certain young – er – '

'Yes, yes,' Bold cut in good-humouredly. 'A young female. After today you won't see me here, Robber. She has her own den – with room for me.'

'Well, well, that *is* good news,' remarked Robber. 'Er – I suppose you'll still be hereabouts, will you? I shall stay on till the spring.'

'Oh, yes. Hereabouts,' Bold assented. 'From now on I'll leave you your share of the catch under the privet hedge.'

'Oh, no!' said the crow. 'Forget about me. No need to worry. *I* can manage. You'll have other things to do now.'

'Well, if you want to see me, or need me for anything,' said Bold, 'leave a message under the hedge. Do you follow me?'

'I do indeed, my friend. And you will do likewise?'

'I most certainly will.'

'Good. Then that's settled,' said Robber, 'and very amicably too. And now for that rat.'

The next night Bold and Whisper unearthed their cache of food by the canal and enjoyed their second meal together. This time Bold did not reserve a portion for the crow, and the pair of foxes demolished the remainder of their catch. Whisper was quick to notice this point and the significance of it was not lost upon her.

'You'll be returning with me to my den?' she asked her companion.

'Yes, I shall,' Bold answered diffidently.

'You'll find it a deal more comfortable than sleeping above ground – and warmer too,' she remarked.

They went together to the canal bank to lap at the inky water. There was no sign of activity on the rats' island. It seemed those that had escaped the foxes' hungry jaws had deserted the site. Whisper led Bold away from the canal and along different paths towards the other side of the town. They came to a large churchyard enclosed by an old stone wall. Now they were suddenly faced with a problem, since Whisper's earth lay within this boundary and she had been accustomed to jump the wall at a low point to reach it.

'There must be another way in?' Bold asked her hopefully.

'I don't think so. I completely forgot about your difficulty in jumping. Oh, Bold, what a stupid creature I am! But we're not beaten yet.'

'Of course we're not. You know I can dig.'

'It may be the only way; but let me do a bit of reconnoitring.'

She left him lying, rather too conspicuously for his liking, against the wall where a growth of ivy provided only a scant cover. After making a quick circuit, she came back.

'I think I've found the answer,' said Whisper. 'Follow me.'

She took Bold to a spot where the stones of the ancient wall had started to crumble. She began to scratch at the falling blocks with a backward, kicking motion, and succeeded in making a small hole in the stonework.

'Only big enough for a weasel to get through,' Bold muttered unhelpfully.

'Be patient,' said Whisper and recommenced scratching at the surrounding stones with her front paws. The wall continued to crumble and the hole grew gradually in size. Whisper paused, panting with the effort.

'My turn now,' said Bold and scrabbled vigorously with his claws until the hole was large enough to push his head through. 'Only a little more, I think,' he said, and soon he could slip his body through so that the hairs of his coat just brushed the sides. Whisper followed him. She trotted through the tombstones, this way and that, until, under the lee of the wall on the far side of the churchyard, she reached the entrance to her earth.

Bold looked at it. 'It's well concealed,' he observed. There was thick ground-ivy, and piles of dead leaves that had fallen from an overhanging horse-chestnut lay all around. 'How did you find it?' He followed her inside.

'Oh, in the course of my travels,' she told him.

It was a few degrees warmer inside the earth than the outside air. To a fox that meant everything. Bold stretched himself luxuriously. The smell of the vixen was strong, along with the usual musty dampness of an underground home.

'Are you tired?' Whisper asked.

'Yes,' Bold replied. 'And content.'

'I'm glad about that,' she said. 'I think you've found life very hard recently?'

'I have,' Bold admitted. 'I didn't expect to find Death staring me in the face quite so soon.'

Whisper pondered awhile. 'You must have seen several winters, I suppose?' she murmured drowsily.

Bold, already half-asleep, thought he had misheard. 'What did you say?'

'Oh, I was only wondering about your life before you got hurt,' she said. 'Did you range far over the seasons?'

Now Bold sat up. 'You mistake me,' he said. 'I've yet to survive my first winter.' He was most indignant.

Whisper's mouth dropped open. She was stunned. 'But – but,' she stammered. 'Can this be true? I am –'

'It's certainly true,' Bold snapped. 'I opened my eyes for the first time last spring.'

'You must forgive me,' Whisper answered. 'I had no idea. You seem so . . . . But you're not much more than a cub then? I myself am a season older!'

'This is your *second* winter?' Bold asked. Now he was surprised, though he didn't really know why.

'Indeed it is. You see, I thought . . . . Of course, your injury . . . .' she broke off in embarrassment.

'I hadn't realized I'd aged quite so much,' Bold remarked sourly. He was quite taken aback by the revelation. What *had* happened to his appearance?

'Then you were born nearby, perhaps?' Whisper ventured to ask.

'No, no – a long way away. I roamed wide and far in the early days. It was my idea to be part of the real world . . . .' The words were out before Bold could stop them.

'The *real* world?' she queried. 'What do you mean?'

Bold took a deep breath. 'I was born in a Nature Reserve: a place called White Deer Park.'

'A strange choice – to leave a Reserve for the world outside,' Whisper commented. 'What could be better than such protection; such a safe haven?'

'You are right, Whisper,' Bold acknowledged. 'I left my family behind – my brother and sister cubs – and other friendly creatures. I left the Park of my own free will, alone, in a spirit of adventure. I wanted to discover the things that lay outside the Reserve. But all I succeeded in doing was to become a challenge to Man and – and – suffered for my arrogance. Oh, I admit it! And now it's too late to change course. I shall never again be the strong, healthy animal my father himself was proud to have sired.'

'Alas! Poor Bold,' she murmured sympathetically. 'But tell me about your father.'

Bold grunted. 'What is there to tell about him that's not known already? It seems everyone knows his history.'

'Is he so famous then?' Whisper asked incredulously.

'Yes, he is famous – the Fox from Farthing Wood.'

Whisper drew a sharp breath. '*He* is your father? Oh, Bold . . . .' What more was there to say? The epic journey that his father had undertaken had made him a legend among the animals. Now his son had thrown that all away. *He* had only clamoured for the dangers, the excitement that his father had sought to escape.

'I can never return there,' Bold said. 'You must see that.'

'I see you have been very foolish,' Whisper said honestly, 'and yet, what a brave fox you must have been . . .' Her voice trailed off and she gazed at him with glistening eyes. It was at that very moment that an idea came into her mind that soon became a very firm resolve. Of course, Bold knew none of it. Whisper meant to keep silent until that idea should become a reality. She composed herself to sleep.

Bold stayed wakeful, despite his weariness. Their talk had re-opened old wounds, old regrets and old sorrows for him. He thought of Vixen, his mother – more graceful, more lithe, more skilful even than Whisper. Did she ever think of him? Yes, of course – she must do. But of one thing he felt quite certain. She would never see her bold, brave young cub again . . . .

—14—
Tracked

Whisper's mistaken idea of his own age made Bold determined to examine himself more closely. So, a few days later, when the opportunity arose, he left the young vixen sleeping in her earth, and emerged slowly and carefully into the daylight. Nothing moved in the churchyard. The ground was hard and rimed with frost, but the air was clear and it was brilliantly sunny. Bold made his way to the hole in the stone wall and slipped through; then he set his course for the canal.

He moved along the familiar paths with extreme caution. There was no sense of bravado in this daylight jaunt. The last jot of that had been dissipated long before. He reached the waterside without any trouble and, with some trepidation, peered over the bank. The water was as smooth as silk and a perfect reflection of himself appeared, undisturbed by a single ripple. Bold gazed at it for a long moment, keeping quite still. Certainly, this image was of no youngster, but of a mature fox – an animal who had had to struggle hard to maintain a grip on its existence. The visage was long and lean. A scar over one eye ran into its corner, making it appear as if it were only half open. The fur on the head and body was not a bright red but a darker, duller hue. There was no healthy shine to be seen anywhere on the coat. The damaged leg appeared shrunken and wasted against the three healthier ones and the brush, thin and tufted, hung limply behind as if ashamed of itself. But it was the eyes of the beast that told Bold's story most vividly. There was a dullness about them and a sort of bewilderment in their expression, mixed with a sense of defeat and an overall sadness.

Bold sat down slowly and thought. What a poor specimen indeed had he become. He had been aware of the change in himself and yet, only now, did he recognize its full extent. Why did Whisper bother with a creature like him? There were other male foxes around, surely, to interest her more? Was it pity? A sort of maternal instinct? He could not be sure. Only by asking the question of Whisper herself could he understand, and it would not be easy for him to do that. For, of course, he was not sure he really wanted the answer.

He stayed no longer by that all-too-revealing stretch of water, but limped home as fast as he could. When still some distance from the earth, Bold had to take cover rather suddenly. A huge, brown dog was padding briskly in his direction with no sign of any human companion to restrain it. Bold stood amongst some almost leafless undergrowth with bated breath and a hammering heart, trusting to his camouflage. The dog came close but passed him by, seemingly bent on an errand of its own. When he was sure it was far enough on, Bold crept out and made all haste for the churchyard.

As he neared the wall two tremendous barks – terrifyingly deep and more like bellows than barks – resounded in the thin, winter air. Bold half turned, though he knew full well whence the awful noise came. The great brown dog had picked up his trail somewhere in its wanderings and was following it with an alarming rapidity. Bold stumbled to the hole in the stones and scrambled through. He did not stop to turn again. The bellows told him all he wanted to know about the close-ness of his pursuer. In and out of the headstones he weaved and along the grassy ways until he was safe at the entrance to Whisper's den. Then he turned to see the dog leaping the wall and, for all its size, taking it with the ease of a gazelle.

Whisper, who was of course awake, cried out as Bold almost tumbled on top of her. 'What is it? What is it?'

'A dog,' Bold panted. 'Must have followed me. A huge brute the size of a donkey!'

Whisper cowered against him, making Bold feel twice the animal he really was. 'Don't worry,' he urged. 'It could never get in here.'

The dog could be heard moving outside. Even its hot breathing could be heard as it sniffed and slavered at the hole. Then it gave vent to a series of terrific barks, airing its frustration at the escape of its quarry. The earth rever-berated to each cry.

'Oh, what can we do?' Whisper wailed. 'Why does it stay there, making those awful noises? Is there no man to call it off?'

'I saw none,' Bold answered grimly. 'But perhaps one is out looking for it now. Keep calm – it can't stay there for ever.'

The barks eventually ceased and were replaced by an

angry sort of whine. Whisper's rigid body relaxed a little. Bold ventured a comforting lick. At last the sounds abated altogether.

'Will it go now?' she whispered.

'I expect so – to vent its spleen on some other poor creature,' Bold muttered.

'Well, let's hope it won't be back,' she said. 'And, Bold, thank you – for comforting me.'

Bold glowed. Perhaps there *was* more than just sympathy in her feelings.

'Where did you go?' Whisper asked suddenly. 'You left me sleeping.'

'To tell you the truth, I went to look at myself,' he confided.

'Whatever do you mean?'

'In the canal – I wanted to see my reflection.'

'Ah. Now I understand. And I think I know why.'

'Do you, Whisper?'

'Is it because of what I said about your – er – age?'

'Yes.'

'I wish I'd said nothing. I'm so sorry to think I upset you. I just didn't realize . . . .'

'I know. But don't fret over it,' said Bold. 'It's all forgotten now.'

'I wouldn't want to do anything to hurt you,' Whisper said softly.

'Nor I you,' Bold murmured.

They fell silent, full of their own thoughts. Whisper spoke first. 'We must build you up,' she said with resolution, betraying what her thoughts had been about. 'Whatever we catch in future, you must have the greater share.'

'No, I –' he began.

'I've already decided,' she said with finality. 'You've had no start in life. At any rate, what start you did have was soon lost. You've suffered more than enough for one so young and I – I shall make it my task to help you back to health.'

'But, Whisper, I can never be really healthy again. My leg won't mend.'

'No matter. You'll have flesh on your bones, at any rate.'

Bold marvelled at her determination. 'I'm so glad I met you,' he said.

'Mine was the luck,' she countered. But she didn't reveal why and Bold was left in blissful ignorance, at least for the time being.

Whisper proved to be true to her word. Whatever they managed to find to eat, she ensured that Bold had the best of it, even if the pickings were poor. Once or twice Bold went to the privet hedge to see if Robber had been by, but there was no evidence of it.

One day in Whisper's den the pair of foxes were woken from sleep by the same dreadful bellows from the great dog who had troubled them earlier.

'He still has our scent, it seems,' Bold remarked grimly. 'We must take more care when we are out of the den.'

'Is he always going to be around then?' Whisper asked with alarm. 'I don't know what he's after.'

'Our smell has a certain effect on most dogs,' Bold said. 'A foxy odour usually makes them very excitable.' He avoided answering her question.

As before, when the dog had had enough of sniffing at the entrance to the earth, it made off. That night Bold and Whisper used a great deal more circumspection on their travels. There were no misfortunes. In fact, they struck lucky. In one garden they came across the best part of a cooked chicken tossed into a bin untasted. The rancid flavour of the meat which had been the reason for its rejection by more delicate palates, only added zest to the foxes' meal. After they had demolished the carcass and were sitting back licking their chops, Whisper said: 'You know, Bold, my idea is beginning to work. You're definitely a little plumper.'

'Am I?' he asked with surprise. 'I don't feel any different.'

'Don't you feel – just a little bit stronger?' she said. 'You do look it!'

Bold was rather flattered. 'Well, I . . .' he began. 'Yes,' he went on, 'it's not so much strength as – er – well, some of my old confidence is coming back. And that must be due to you, Whisper.'

'Perhaps I've helped,' she said. 'And if so, I'm very glad. For, after all, that was what I intended.'

And, indeed, as the days passed Bold did gain weight and stature. Even his damaged leg troubled him less. His appetite had improved, his step was less laboured but, most important, he felt differently about his future. He no longer lived from day to day. He looked forward to the end of the winter when food would be easier to find and he and Whisper (he always thought of them together now) could leave the environs of the town and return to the open country. Once again, there seemed to be some purpose in his life. In this new hopeful mood he decided to look for his friend Robber to see how he was making out.

Soon after dawn the next day Bold was on the move, first making quite certain it was safe to be so. In the pallid winter light no other living thing seemed to be wakeful. No bird sang, no small animal rustled a twig or dead leaf. Bold alone shivered in the freezing temperature. He limped around all Robber's usual haunts and finished up at the privet hedge without receiving sight or sound of him.

There he left a message in the shape of a morsel of food so that his friend the crow should know he had been around.

On the way back to Whisper's side, Bold found a stale loaf of bread thrown out for birds to peck at. Never one to miss an opportunity for some extra mouthfuls, particularly in times of scarcity, he ate the bread. Hard and indigestible, it lay heavy on his stomach and it was with a slower pace that he went towards the churchyard. He thought he heard some muffled barks in the distance but as he was close to home he thought no more of it. Mechanically Bold lurched towards the hole in the churchyard wall he and Whisper had made. For a moment he seemed to lose his direction. Then he turned and went along the wall, looking for the loose stones underneath the hole. He paused and looked around in bewilderment. There were none to be seen. A feeling of alarm gripped him. It was now well on into the morning and, while he had been on his wanderings, the wall had been hastily repaired, obviously by human hand.

As Bold stood looking at the wall with the horrible thought in his head that there was now no way in which he was capable of passing beyond it, the barks he had heard earlier were again audible, only much closer. The fox knew instinctively what creature was uttering them. In a feverish haste he continued along the wall and round the corner, vainly searching for some weakness where he might perhaps be able to force an entry. Not a chink of light showed through the stones.

The huge dog came bounding onward, eagerly sniffing at the familiar odour. Bold heard its approach and began scrabbling frantically at the wall, hoping to dislodge it. Miraculously two large stones loosened and fell inwards to the churchyard, leaving a hole through which Bold could pass his head. Now he kicked and hacked in fury with his three good legs. The hole grew fractionally in size as the seconds tripped away. But it was all too slow. With only his head and neck properly through the new hole, Bold heard the dog arrive on the scene, roaring triumphantly. He tried to back, but now the cruel, unyielding stones held him fast. With his back and hindquarters exposed to attack from the rear while he faced into the churchyard, Bold could see the den entrance only metres away. But it might just as well have been kilometres. He could not budge and any second he expected to feel the vicious fangs of his pursuer fastened at last into his helpless body.

—15—
Rollo the Mastiff

Robber the Carrion Crow had spent a lazy morning. He had enjoyed wheeling in the icy air, alighting occasionally to march in characteristic fashion over the steely ground in search of a hardy worm. He made no special effort to hunt for food as he wasn't very hungry. Carrion was plentiful in the hard weeks of winter if you knew where to look for it. It was only by chance that he visited the privet hedge. He had not thought of Bold for some days, convinced that their paths would no longer cross now that the young fox had found a mate (for Robber took this to be the case, unquestioningly). But for some reason a picture of Bold limping painfully across a field came into his mind's eye. It was then that the bird flew to the hedge bottom. Sure enough, there he found the titbit left by Bold earlier that morning. It was only a piece of skin and bone – hardly an edible morsel at all. But Robber knew that the fox had not left it there as a delicacy. He must now find his friend.

He had a rough idea of the whereabouts of the vixen's den. He flapped into flight, coasting and flapping alternately as he steered a course through the air. He heard the dog's barks quite plainly and for some reason (he knew not what) he associated these noises with Bold's message. So he flew towards the noise, saw the huge beast bounding over the ground, and followed it straight to the churchyard.

When he saw Bold's predicament, the crow's heart sank. It seemed as if his young friend had set a trap for himself. What could *he* do to avert disaster? The dog could swallow *him* at a gulp. But perhaps he *could* delay things. He dropped downwards. The dog was balancing itself, preparing to leap the wall, and so Robber assumed it was going to attack Bold's head. As the dog jumped, Bold began snarling in a futile way from his stony prison. The dog made no attempt to snap at the fox, but simply gambolled around while it continued to bark deafeningly. Robber flew at the massive beast, lunging with his beak in a brave attempt to discourage it. Of course, it paid him no more attention than if he had been a gnat.

The din, meanwhile, had awakened Whisper who at once found her companion was missing. Fearing he was in danger, she crept timidly to the entrance hole and looked out, where she saw the scene being enacted.

Bold saw her emerge. 'Keep away, Whisper!' he cried urgently. 'Go back! Go back!'

But Whisper came on. She could not stand idly by while Bold was helpless.

'Robber, make her go back,' Bold pleaded. 'She's quite safe in her den.'

Suddenly the dog stopped its racket and stood quite still, as Robber flew towards the vixen. In a voice as deep as a cave it said: 'What's all the fuss about? You're not afraid of me, I hope?'

Bold's mouth dropped open. He couldn't speak.

'I only want your company,' the dog went on. 'I tried to catch you before but I was too slow, and you wouldn't come out of your den. My life is very lonely. I have no companions at all. Not like you – you must have friends galore.'

Bold couldn't believe what he was hearing. It was too absurd. This huge, powerful beast – stronger than a man – had come to him in friendship. But, even then, what did he expect of him?

'I don't understand,' he muttered. 'How can I help you?' He saw that Robber had succeeded in persuading Whisper to approach no further and that the bird was, even now, preparing to launch another dive-bombing attack on the supposed enemy.

The dog began: 'Can't I just come and converse with you? It would mean –'

It broke off as Robber came sailing valiantly in and raised one massive paw to dispose of the interfering non-entity. Bold was too late to stop it. The dog gave Robber what was intended to be a warning cuff, but the blow of such a powerful beast fell like a sledge-hammer on the poor crow who immediately crumpled into a heap on the ground.

'Robber! Robber!' cried Bold agonizingly. 'Look what you've done, you brute!' he snarled at the unwitting dog. 'You've killed him!'

Whisper now came running up. The dog looked at the foxes aghast. 'I can't have done,' he moaned. 'It was only meant as a tap.'

'You don't know your own strength!' snapped Bold. 'And he was only trying to help me!'

The dog looked stupidly from one animal to the other, and then at the little black body, insensible on the hard ground. Bold thought he had the measure of this great beast who seemed to be a bit dull-witted.

'Do something useful, at any rate,' he barked. 'Get me out of this!'

While Whisper bent over the fallen bird, sniffing gently at the coal-black feathers, the dog began to batter its huge feet against the stones of the wall. In a trice the hole was large enough for Bold to free himself. He made straight for Robber. After some tense moments he looked up at Whisper gladly. 'Why, he's only stunned!' he cried. 'He's beginning to stir.'

The dog lolloped over but Bold said: 'You'd better keep back. We don't want any more accidents.'

Whisper was amused at the meek way the animal at once sat down, looking towards Bold as if waiting for the next directions from a creature only a quarter of its size. But, above all, she was proud of Bold who seemed to be entering a new phase of living up to his name.

'Is . . . is it – er – *he* all right?' the dog asked tremulously. 'I really didn't mean to do it, you know.'

'I think he will be, but he's suffered a nasty shock,' replied Bold. 'Whisper, can we do anything for him?'

'Nothing at all,' she said. 'It's just a question of time. But we might be able to aid his revival.'

'How?'

'Like this . . . .' Whisper demonstrated, breathing her warm breath over the bird.

'I see – warmth,' said Bold, and added his services. Then he turned and looked for a moment at the dog. 'You can help here, my friend, I think,' he said.

The dog was delighted and came forward eagerly, breathing out clouds of steam in the crisp air with his stentorian gasps.

Robber opened his jet-black eyes and saw the three mammals puffing and blowing together quite amicably. He tried to stand.

'Take it carefully,' Bold said. 'How do you feel?'

'Rather at a loss,' answered the bird. 'What's going on?'

'We've been mistaken,' said Bold. 'This great fellow wants to be our friend.'

'No friend of mine,' muttered Robber, ruffling his feathers. 'And I hope he has no enemies!'

'He's very contrite about it,' Bold whispered to him. 'Try to be forgiving.'

Robber struggled to his feet and tested his wings to see if their delicate bones were intact. 'I found your message and came straight away,' he explained.

Bold had to stop and think a minute. 'Oh yes,' he said. 'I see. Actually, I just wanted to see how you were making out.'

'Perfectly,' said Robber. 'At least I *was* . . . .' He directed a piercing glance at the newcomer.

'I'm Rollo,' said the dog naively. 'Rollo the mastiff.'

'Are you indeed?' Robber said grudgingly. 'Well, your master should take better care of you.'

'Yes, he should,' Rollo said warmly. 'He leaves me out in the yard in all weathers and nothing to amuse myself with. He doesn't know I get out, though. I can jump the fence!' He seemed quite proud of this announcement.

Whisper and Bold exchanged wry glances. The mastiff was obviously quite an artless sort of beast.

'Perhaps you'd better be getting back?' Bold suggested. 'Or he *will* discover you can escape?'

A look of consternation passed over the dog's great

wrinkled face. 'Oh – yes,' he said blankly. But he made no attempt to move off.

'We'll still be around,' Bold said reassuringly. 'We live here, Whisper and I. There's always another day.'

'Yes, thank you, yes,' Rollo said, greatly pleased. 'I'll certainly come again.' He started to walk away, but kept looking back at his new friends.

'Until the next time,' Whisper called.

Rollo barked joyfully and bounded away, leaping the wall elaborately as if giving them a demonstration of how he managed to jump his own fence.

'Stupid creature,' muttered Robber. 'He could have killed me.'

'But he didn't, mercifully,' said Bold. 'And we must cultivate his friendship. An animal that size could prove to be a very useful ally, one day.'

—16—

The Ties of Blood

Whisper and Bold were visited frequently by the mastiff in the ensuing weeks. Since he was only about during the day, it meant that the pair of foxes were usually roused from their sleep by one or two of his great barks, summoning them to join him. They tried to be friendly, but Rollo's visits were not always welcome, particularly if they had exhausted themselves hunting for food the previous night.

The turn of the year came and went. The winter weather had not been too cruel. Food was available – not plentiful – but, working in concert, Bold and Whisper usually found enough to eat. Towards the end of January the mating season for foxes arrived. The pair had already established a firm bond in the period they had been together and so this extension to their relationship was quite natural. Bold still wondered from time to time about Whisper's choice of mate, but dismissed his thoughts almost as soon as they took shape.

When Whisper knew she was carrying Bold's cubs she decided it was time to put the next part of her plan into operation. The winter was entering its final phase and there was no time to be lost. She and Bold were lying comfortably in their earth. Whisper said: 'Very soon we must leave here.'

Bold raised his head and looked at her quizzically in the gloom. 'Soon?' he asked. 'Before the end of winter?' He thought she was referring to their eventual return to the country.

'Certainly before the end of the winter,' Whisper answered. 'We have a long journey to make before spring arrives.'

'Journey?' Bold sounded puzzled. 'A journey to where?'

'To a safe place for our cubs to be born,' said Whisper.

'Isn't it safe here?' he asked. 'We haven't been troubled –'

'Not safe enough,' she interrupted. 'I want the cubs to be born in the Nature Reserve like you were.'

Bold caught his breath. 'White Deer Park?' he whispered.

'Of course,' she said. 'You have to take us there.'

Bold saw the sense in his mate's words but was sick at heart. For long moments he said nothing. Then he murmured, almost as if to himself: 'I never thought of returning there.'

'Not on your own – I know you didn't,' said Whisper. 'But we have to think of our offspring.'

'Yes, yes, I see the sense in it,' said Bold lamely. A

thought struck him like a flash of light. Was this the reason for her selecting him? 'Tell me, Whisper,' he said quietly, 'is this why you chose me?'

'For your knowledge of the Nature Reserve? Yes, in part,' she admitted. 'But it was your ancestry that impressed me mostly.'

Bold let his head drop on to his paws. He felt as if a heavy weight bore down on him – the weight of his father's name. 'Then it was not for myself you wished to mate with me?' he said agonizingly.

Whisper tried to reassure him. 'Of course it was for yourself,' she said. 'You have the blood of the Farthing Wood Fox in your veins. I'm proud of you. Now my cubs will make me proud too.'

She couldn't have said a more distressing thing. Bold was crushed. His mission had failed. 'Well,' he said softly, 'it seems my struggles are over.'

'Your struggles?' she echoed.

'Yes,' he said. 'Dear Whisper, had you not realized that I've been trying to forge my own destiny? All my short life I have tried to escape that long shadow cast by my father's fame. I left the Park to live life my own way – to create my own identity. Now I see I shall always live within that shadow – I can't shrug off my origins. It is my fate.'

Whisper was stunned. She couldn't speak.

'I know now,' Bold went on sardonically, 'why you preferred a crippled, haggard specimen, old before his time, to any one of a dozen, healthy young dogs. Hah! *My* only claim to fame is my genealogy!'

'Stop! Stop!' she cried. 'I can't bear any more! Why are you so bitter? You *have* created your own destiny. You've lived a braver, more resourceful life in your one year than is even contemplated by most creatures. What you did took a great deal of courage!'

'And now I go creeping back from the world I chose, with my tail between my legs!'

'You talk as if your life is over!' Whisper exclaimed hotly. 'You are to be a father in a couple of months. Your destiny now is to pass on to your cubs the knowledge and the craft gleaned from your experiences. To teach them, with me, just as your parents instructed you!'

'Yes, yes, I know the role expected of me,' Bold said wearily. 'I'll lead you to your haven of peace and tranquillity; you need have no fears.'

'We have a bright future ahead of us, Bold,' Whisper encouraged him.

Bold could not share her enthusiasm. It seemed to him as if his life consisted only of a past. Eventually he said: 'When do you want to begin?'

'As soon as you – *we*,' she hastily corrected herself, 'feel fit enough.'

The error was not lost on her mate. 'We must try and fatten ourselves up a little for the journey,' he said. 'I think I know how we might be able to do that.'

'How then?'

'Oh – don't worry. You can leave it all to me,' Bold said enigmatically. He spoke no more. Whisper assumed he wanted to sleep and settled herself down. But Bold had never felt farther from rest. So, when the sounds of Rollo's tremendous greetings echoed in the earth, he was glad of an excuse to depart.

'You needn't stir,' he told Whisper who, of course, had also been wakened. 'I'll go and see him.'

Rollo's great tail threshed the air as he saw his small friend emerge from his hole. 'It's a glorious day for scents and explorations,' he told the fox. 'I wish you'd come with me.' This was his invariable invitation.

'All right,' said Bold.

Rollo was overjoyed and spun round in a frenzy, bellowing excitedly. He was unable to believe his luck. 'Will you – will you really?' he cried.

'Yes, but I don't want to follow scents,' Bold informed him. 'Show me your den.'

'Gladly!' The dog set off at a spanking pace among the tombstones and paused by the churchyard wall. Bold went through his usual gap and Rollo landed on the other side with a thud.

'You'll have to go more slowly,' Bold remarked. 'My leg, you know.'

'I know, I know – doesn't matter,' said the delighted Rollo. 'Any pace you like.' They proceeded on their way.

'I saw your friend the crow,' said the mastiff. 'He seemed all right, for he croaked at me loudly enough.'

'Are you sure it was Robber?' Bold asked.

'Oh, yes. It was obvious he recognized me.'

'Yes. I imagine he would,' Bold said with a touch of irony, but it was lost on this simple-hearted monster.

'I want you to help me, if you will,' he said next.

'Help you? Of course I will,' Rollo boomed. 'You're my friend. What am I to do?'

'Not much really,' said Bold. 'Just feed me – and my mate.'

'Feed you? What with?'

'What do you eat?'

'Meat, biscuits – er – well, lots of meat . . . .'

'That will do,' Bold said humorously.

'You want my food?'

'No, no. Only what you don't want. Our appetites are small by comparison. But we need to build ourselves up. We're going on a journey.'

Rollo looked blank. 'Are you planning to leave here, then?' he asked.

'Yes. Whisper wants to find a safer home for the birth of our cubs,' said Bold.

'But you don't have to leave,' protested Rollo who didn't want to lose his friends as soon as he had gained them. 'Your cubs would be quite safe as long as I'm around. I'd make sure of that.'

'I'm very grateful for your interest,' Bold said carefully, 'but I hope I'd prove sufficient to the task of defending my own young ones. However, you won't be required to help, as Whisper's mind is made up.'

'I see. But how long will it take you to find the right sort of place?'

'Oh, as long as it takes us to get there. You see, she's already decided on our destination.'

'She seems to be very determined.'

'She is, I assure you.'

'I suppose, then, I won't be seeing much more of you?'

'I'm sorry to say that it does appear that way.'

Rollo's great wrinkled face wore a look of gloom. 'Could I – perhaps – come part of the way with you?' he asked with a sort of shyness that could have been absurd in such a large beast if it had not been so genuine.

'I really can't see that it would be possible, Rollo,' Bold replied gently. 'We shall be moving by night and – well, stealth will be all-important.'

The mastiff lapsed into silence until they reached his yard. It was a large open pen of bare earth surrounded by a low wire fence. There was a big wooden kennel in front of which stood an empty food bowl and another containing water. There was access to the yard from a door at the back of the adjoining house. Rollo leapt easily over the fence and went into his kennel. He re-emerged carrying two bone-shaped biscuits, which he dropped by the fence.

'That's my 'den' as you call it,' he said. 'There's no meat at the moment, I'm afraid. I ate it all.' He nudged the biscuits through a hole in the links with his muzzle. 'Try those,' he suggested.

Bold lay down and, holding a biscuit between his front paws in the same way as a dog, took a bite with his side teeth. 'Very appetising,' he pronounced after crunching it up. 'I'll take the other back for Whisper. But when will you be given meat again?'

'Tonight,' answered Rollo.

'Good,' rejoined Bold. 'Shall we come when it's dark, then?'

'Yes, do. I'll look forward to it.'

Bold turned and began his slow return to the churchyard. Although he had not mentioned it to Whisper, since the occasion when he had found the wall repaired and had tried to kick out a new hole, his damaged leg had started to hurt badly again. The pain was severe enough to make him wince at times if he brought that leg down too heavily, and so the prospect of a long journey, perhaps lasting some weeks owing to his lameness, was an ordeal he dreaded. But he was resolved that Whisper should remain ignorant.

He reached Rollo's hole in the wall and went through, still carrying the biscuit. Whisper slept so he dropped it by her and stretched himself out gratefully. At dusk the vixen awoke and found Bold by her side again. She let him sleep on while she devoured her titbit.

Bold woke eventually and told his companion about the arrangement he had made with the mastiff. Whisper congratulated him. 'A very sound idea,' she said. 'When does he expect us?'

'Tonight,' said Bold.

They left the earth together and Bold led the way back to Rollo's yard. The two foxes smelt the strong odour of fresh meat from some metres away as Rollo had nosed his meat dish painstakingly across the ground to the fence. He had refrained from tasting the food himself. So it was that Bold and Whisper heard their friend before they saw him, for the huge dog's belly, as empty as a pit, was reverberating with the most ominous rumblings.

'Rollo!' cried Bold. 'You're there?'

'I'm here,' came the solemn, deep-toned reply.

Bold now saw the meat dish close against the chain link fence. 'You haven't touched it!' he exclaimed in astonishment.

'No, I – I thought I'd wait for you,' replied the dog. 'It's more companionable to eat together.'

'Poor Rollo,' said Whisper as a fresh rumble racked the cavernous depths of his stomach. 'How you must have suffered!'

'Well, I'll do so no longer, now you're here,' he replied and took a gargantuan mouthful.

Whisper and Bold were able to hook pieces of meat through the wire with their paws, and all three made a good meal. Rollo was far too polite to take more than the two foxes did between them; neither did he tell them he could comfortably have eaten as much again. But he did ask them when they expected to leave.

'Not later than the new moon,' said Whisper.

'I shall miss you,' said the mastiff, looking at them with his great mournful eyes.

The foxes did not know how to comfort him, so said nothing on that subject. They talked for a while and then made their farewells.

'I'll be here waiting for you tomorrow night,' Rollo promised, 'with the same supplies.'

'Don't starve yourself on our account,' said Whisper kindly. 'Eat what you want first.'

'Thank you, Whisper,' said Rollo, 'but it wouldn't be with the same relish.'

'He really is a friend to us,' Whisper remarked as they left him. 'We owe him quite a lot.'

'We do,' agreed Bold, 'and it makes me sad that we have to desert him so soon.'

But Whisper's resolution was final. 'As to that,' she said, 'we have no choice. For blood is thicker than water.'

—17—
Back to the Country

The day for their departure came sooner than expected. Bold had gone at daybreak one day to have a look round for Robber to acquaint him of their intentions. He did not find the crow but he did find a message left under the privet hedge: a piece of meat still sufficiently fresh to persuade Bold that it had been dropped there that very morning while he'd been looking elsewhere. What could it mean? The crow seemed not to be in the immediate vicinity, so what was he to do? Bold decided he would go and consult Whisper.

As he approached the familiar churchyard wall, which soon would no longer encompass his and Whisper's home, he realized what Robber's message had intended to convey. The gap in the wall made by their friend the

mastiff had been repaired again and so, once more, Bold
had no access to his earth. Even as he looked at this new
barrier there came several loud 'caws' from a nearby
treetop. Bold spotted the bird among the bare branches
and barked a greeting. Robber flew down.

'I think we're in need of your powerful friend again,' he
said to the fox.

'No-o,' Bold said dubiously. 'Not on this occasion. The
wall seals my entrance and my fate at the same
time.'

'Don't talk in riddles, Bold,' Robber urged. 'What are
you hinting at?'

'Oh, I've just been looking for you to tell you that
Whisper and I are to embark on a journey,' Bold said
casually. 'Now I can add to that piece of information. We
shall start today.'

Robber was full of questions.

'It's to be White Deer Park, my own birthplace,' Bold
told him. 'For the sake of my unborn cubs I'm returning
to the safe haven I turned my back on only last
summer.'

'Ah, so a family is in question,' said Robber. 'In that
case, your young vixen is behaving very sensibly.'

'She is – I don't deny it,' Bold averred. 'Yet I can't be
sanguine about my own chances of completing the
journey.'

'You look more robust now than you've done for
a long time,' the crow observed. 'If you take it
easily . . . .'

'Yes, I've gained some weight,' Bold admitted. 'But it's
an awfully long trek on only three sound legs.'

Robber re-arranged his wings and looked thoughtful.
At length he said: 'I'll keep you in sight as you go. Then, if
you ever should need help –'

'I'm most grateful,' said Bold promptly. 'I have to confess I was rather hoping you might say something of the sort.'

The two separated momentarily as they spotted some human figures walking close by. Robber flew back to his tree-top while Bold found cover amongst some undergrowth. When the coast was clear again the fox emerged to ask his friend to alert Whisper to their new situation. Robber flew to the earth's entrance hole and 'cawed' repeatedly until Whisper responded. She came at a run and jumped over the wall.

'Our cue to leave, it seems,' Bold said to her.

'Yes. We must hide up until dark.'

'We'll go to my old hideaway,' Bold decided. 'Robber, will you scout around and see if it's safe to proceed?'

The crow flew off at once and returned quickly. 'If you come now, you should be under cover before any fresh danger appears,' he announced.

Bold led his mate back towards the playing fields and the familiar tangle of shrubbery and undergrowth in the old waste-plot. Robber left them with a parting 'I'll look for you tomorrow'. The hours to darkness dragged by while Bold and Whisper tried vainly to sleep, their minds too aroused and full of thoughts of their undertaking. Only as the still-early dusk began to descend did they fall into an uneasy doze.

During the night they awakened to the screeches of a pair of owls calling through the trees. They looked at each other significantly.

'Time to go,' said Whisper.

'Time for one last sustaining meal?' Bold queried. He was thinking of Rollo.

Whisper knew it. 'Very well, dear Bold – if we're quick.'

Rollo's greeting was as boisterous as ever but the foxes' restraint told him the news he had been fearing. For the last time he silently pushed his meat dish across the yard. The three animals ate with glum expressions. There was no time to talk afterwards. They made hasty but warm farewells and the pair of foxes disappeared into the night. Neither cared to look back, for they both knew that poor Rollo would be standing by his fence, gazing after them with the wringingly forlorn expression he had been wearing ever since he had heard their plan.

They travelled steadily and noiselessly. Bold tried to ignore his bad leg and Whisper, of course, allowed *him* to set the pace. By dawn they had put the neighbourhood of the town behind them and were on the fringes of open country once again. A dark patch of woodland beckoned them to their rest. The murmurings of town life reached them still, but so muted as to enhance the new peacefulness of their surroundings. The night's frost, as yet undispersed, nipped at their skins and they huddled together for warmth. A delicious languor overcame them and they slumbered gratefully.

The next morning Robber followed their direction. He knew which route Bold would take. Unerringly he flew into the clump of trees that sheltered them, saw their sleeping bodies and vanished again. Now, for the bird, too, the sojourn amongst town-dwellers was over.

That night Bold and Whisper needed to hunt for food for the first time in many days. It was February and the last month of what had been a relatively mild winter. Food was still by no means abundant. The weight of their effort was necessarily undertaken by Whisper. Bold had passively to accept a lesser role and he did so almost thankfully. The difficulties of once more finding sufficient to eat meant that their travelling time was restricted. So their progress did not advance much before daylight threatened again. In this way, almost by fits and starts, the first week passed.

Bold was not displeased with their slow pace, as in that way his injured leg was not overtaxed. However, by the end of the week, Whisper was visibly fretting.

'We must make an effort to speed up a bit, Bold,' she urged. 'We've come such a little way!'

'Don't worry; there's no need,' replied Bold, who had the benefit of his knowledge of the distance to the Nature Reserve. 'We have to take time to eat.'

'It's not the eating, but the hunting, that takes the time,' she corrected him. 'If only there were some way of reducing it.'

'There isn't,' Bold said flatly. 'It was your decision to travel in the winter when food isn't plentiful.'

'I know. I know. There's no way round it, I suppose. But I can't help getting concerned.'

'Trust my knowledge – we shall do it.'

'Of course I trust you,' Whisper said tenderly. '*I* shouldn't complain when it is you who are finding it most difficult.'

The next night they were close to the farm where Bold had killed the bantam cock. There was no such rich fare for him and his mate on this occasion. They caught what small creatures they could, dug up some roots, and were glad to get them. Bold led Whisper to the hedgerow where earlier he had been dug out of his earth. He told her how he had only escaped death by a hair's-breadth of unaccountable human whim. They decided to lay up in the shrubbery during the daytime. Robber was still following them, but kept to his plan of not approaching while things went well.

Now that the pair of foxes were in an area of farmland, there were scraps and pickings to be had for a little less work. This pleased Whisper who then, naturally, tried to force the pace a little. Bold uttered no objection but simply gritted his teeth more firmly and hung on. Now, when

the time came to rest, he was prostrate with exhaustion.
Yet still he did not demur. As luck would have it, the
weather came to his rescue.

It was the middle of February and it seemed that only
now was winter about to release its worst on the countryside. The temperature had been steadily dropping and
now there was a savage, new bite in the air – such as had
not been felt all season through. It was as if it had been
held in reserve to inflict the greater hardship when it was
most unexpected. Ice formed on every small puddle,
each twig was rimed with white and, at last, the snow fell
in earnest. It began at night and continued around the
clock. Coupled with the strong wind, it was impossible to
withstand. Bold and Whisper found what protection they
could amongst some holly and shuddered miserably as
the wind moaned over the land. Snow was piled up
against any large obstacles in drifts, and overall its mantle
was spread to a depth daunting even to the largest and
longest-legged of would-be travellers – Man himself.

While the wind raged and the snow fell Whisper accepted the impossibility of moving. Indeed, she tried her
best to enlarge a rabbit burrow to give them more shelter,
but the ground was now so hard that she could not
manage to make more than a sort of depression in the
soil. Here she and Bold cowered, burying their faces in
their brushes, while their backs gathered snow enough to
bury them. When the blizzard abated at last, Whisper
was eager to press on, however tardily. Bold looked at the
scene before them with more than just misgiving.

'It would be madness at present,' he declared.

'But if there's no alternative?'

'There *is* an alternative,' he argued. 'We look for better
shelter and take cover until there's an improvement.'

'But think of the time we might lose,' Whisper
persisted.

'Better that than losing our lives,' Bold answered grimly, '*and* those lives not yet begun.' This latter remark tipped the balance as far as Whisper was concerned and she gave in.

'Perhaps you are right, after all,' she said. 'But it mustn't be a long stay.'

Bold didn't answer. He was content to let things take their own course while they were at the dictates of the weather.

'I'll see if I can find a more promising shelter hole,' Whisper volunteered. 'We do need to go underground.' She left Bold in the hollowed-out 'form' and went deeper into the little wood. Under the trees, albeit with their bare branches, the snow was less thick than in the open. Nevertheless her search was not an easy one. At each step, her feet sank about ten centimetres and moving around, even here, was laborious. She realized Bold had been more sensible than she. A deserted hole, not quite filled and disguised by snow, lay under the half-exposed roots of an oak tree. It was just about large enough inside for the two of them and, before returning to her mate, Whisper scooped out the unwanted debris from the interior.

She and Bold were soon esconced safely inside, heartily glad to be out of reach of the worst excesses of the winter elements. The main thing on their minds now was, of course, food. But first they slept.

When they awoke it was daylight. The wind had dropped but more snow had fallen and the wood was shrouded in silence. By the entrance to their hole, which was nearly blocked up, lay a few, poor scraps. Whisper was puzzled but Bold knew at once how they came there.

'Don't you see – it's Robber!' he exclaimed. 'Even in these conditions he didn't forget us. And I bet he went short himself to spare these morsels. He'll be facing the same difficulties as any other creature.'

'How on earth did he find us?' Whisper wanted to know.

'No doubt he's had his sharp black eyes on us all along,' Bold answered with amusement. 'I'll just go a short distance and see if I can spot him.'

Bold made his way to the edge of the wood and looked out. The sun shone; the air was fresh and very cold. The landscape spread before him was a sea of brilliant white. Trees and clusters of vegetation were festooned with sparkling decoration as bright as diamonds. He was dazzled. Against that gleaming array, even the smallest bird's movements were plainly discernible. Their dark, darting little bodies stood out in startling contrast. Bold looked for a larger black shape among the snow-clad branches. He saw it. He took a few hesitant steps into the open, hoping it was indeed Robber he had spied. As if he had been waiting for a signal, the bird came winging down directly towards his friend.

'Hallo, Faithful,' said Bold good-humouredly.

'Aha! You must have found my little offering?' Robber said and uttered a croak of pleasure.

'I want to tell you not to concern yourself with us,' Bold said, 'because, my dear friend, you will have your work cut out feeding yourself.'

'It's certainly become very difficult all of a sudden,' Robber concurred. 'Just when we looked forward to the spring, too. But I *do* want to help. Now you've come this far you can't turn back and – well, finding food in *this* situation is a pretty daunting task.'

'It is,' said Bold. 'But Whisper and I have holed up in the wood here whilst we can go no further.'

'I'm going back to the town,' Robber rejoined. 'It's safer to be near humans at times like this. Then, as soon

as I strike lucky, I'll be able to bring something for you –
and more worthwhile than this time.'

'No, Robber,' Bold said flatly. 'It's too far for you to fly
to and fro for our benefit. I couldn't allow myself to be so
beholden to any creature, and I know how Whisper
would feel about it.'

'A long way by foot, yes,' agreed Robber, 'but less far as
the crow flies!'

Despite the joke Bold remained serious. 'Please, let's
say no more about it,' he said. 'Whisper and I will cope.
It's different from when I was alone – she's not handicapped in any way. And I'd be far happier knowing you
have only the worry of looking after yourself.'

'So be it,' said the bird. 'I won't press the point. At least
I know where to find you while this weather continues.
And, once it's over, I shall return to open country – for
this must be winter's last fling.'

'Good luck go with you,' said Bold.

'The same to you,' returned Robber. 'I shall be thinking
of you.' Bold made his way back to Whisper's side. They
divided the scraps of food between them and tried to
sleep again. But their appetites had only been aggravated
by the little they had eaten and sleep was next to impossible. They lay in discomfort, sometimes cat-napping,
until it grew dark.

Then Whisper said: 'I'm going to see what I can
find.'

Bold said: 'I'll come with you.'

'No,' she replied. 'I can do more on my own. I'm
sorry,' she went on, knowing Bold would feel this deeply,
'but I really think there's more chance that way.'

'You're right, of course,' he said with resignation. 'I'd
only hold you up.'

When she had gone, he pulled himself out of the hole.
He scratched around in the snow and chewed at some

stalks of grass in a desultory manner, wondering about their chances of reaching his birthplace. Whisper came back quite soon.

'We're in luck,' she said. 'Follow me.'

Bold stumbled in her wake, his spirits raised. She took him to a glade in the wood which she had discovered was rich in bluebell bulbs. She had dug up quite a quantity of them. Bold looked at the little white bulbs with a sense of irony. In these conditions, such miserable fare could assume the proportions of riches unknown. Whisper had already started eating. She looked at him with irritation.

'Don't turn your nose up at them,' she said. 'They may be all that's standing between us and starvation!'

—18—

A Lack of Patience

The halt in their progress enforced by the appalling weather proved to be a mixed blessing for Bold. His appetite, like Whisper's, was never properly satisfied, but his bad leg was rested. The lull in their activities was a good thing from that point of view. The leg had a chance to recover from the strains recently imposed upon it, and the pain seemed to subside. Five days passed with no let-up in the icy conditions. For Whisper, these were five more days lost. On the sixth day the temperature rose a few degrees. She went out of the wood to test the ground for travelling. The reverse of her expectations occurred. During the coldest temperatures the snow had frozen each night and become compacted and firm underfoot. Now it was thawing ever so slightly and, consequently, was softer and more giving so that it was more taxing to walk on. Disheartened, Whisper reported her findings to Bold.

'We must be patient,' he told her.

'I've tried to be,' she answered, 'but it's difficult for me. I've seen a previous winter, Bold. You haven't. There will only be a gradual change each day. The snow might take days to disappear.'

'We needn't wait for it to vanish altogether,' Bold said encouragingly, trying not to think of himself. 'I'm committed to this venture as well, don't forget. I'm responsible for getting you to that Reserve.'

'I'm sorry,' said Whisper softly. 'You must forgive my anxiety.'

'Of course I do,' he said. 'And I do understand, Whisper.'

The next night they resumed their journey. The ground was sticky, slippery and toilsome. After only a short distance Bold's bad leg ached and, when he paused, the three good legs trembled from the strain. He licked his lips but said nothing. Whisper also refrained from comment. On they went again. Bold's pace grew slower and slower; his limp more pronounced. The beneficial effects of their five days' rest were undone in a couple of hours. Yet he struggled on grimly, and without complaint. They came to a slight rise in the land. Even for Whisper the task of pulling herself up it when, at every step, the slush caused her to slip back, was awesome. For Bold it was torture. He could exert no pressure on his injured leg to get a grip and so he was left to flounder on three. By a supreme effort of will he reached the crest of the slope where he promptly collapsed.

Whisper looked at him in anguish. 'Oh, Bold!' she wailed. 'What have I done? We shouldn't have started – I've been so foolish!'

Bold tried to put on a brave face. 'Just need a . . .
breather,' he muttered. But Whisper knew better.

'I shouldn't have forced you – oh! oh! we should
have waited.'

'You didn't force me,' he replied. '*I* said not to
wait longer.'

'No, no, it was my fault,' she insisted. 'My over-
anxiety . . . .'

'Whisper . . . no use being wise . . . after the event,'
Bold murmured. He tried to stand, staggered, and fell on
his side.

Whisper was beside herself. They couldn't stay where
they were, yet how could she assist him? She lay down
next to him and nuzzled him; then licked at his
face.

'You must take cover,' he said to her painfully. 'Before
daybreak . . . .'

'I can't leave you here alone, in this exposed position,'
she protested. 'Anything could happen!'

'I'll be all right. A bit longer to rest . . . then I'll follow
you,' he answered.

Whisper licked at his bad leg – at the hole in his thigh
left by the cruel pellets the previous autumn. It was a
vain but loving gesture, and Bold appreciated it. For a
while longer they lay together silently. There was no
wind. The air was mild. Presently the sky began, almost
imperceptibly, to lighten. Somewhere a solitary bird
uttered a few sleepy, burbling notes as if it were
talking to itself.

'Go!' whispered Bold.

The vixen stood up and shivered. Her coat was
saturated by the melting snow. She gave herself a shake
and regarded Bold anxiously. She looked around for the
nearest point of cover. There was a copse poking through
the greying expanse of snow on the horizon. She knew

Bold's chances of getting there were nil. 'I'll stay,' she told him. 'There's no cover.'

'I may be injured and exhausted but I'm not blind,' he answered her drily. 'You must head for that copse – for the sake of the cubs,' he added tellingly.

'But . . . but . . . .'

'It will be light soon,' he said emphatically. 'Whisper – you *must* go.'

'I shall come back for you at dusk,' she said hopelessly. She really didn't think she would see him again – alive.

Bold said: 'I'll join you when I'm ready.' His voice sounded hollow.

Whisper went, with many a backward glance.

When the sun was fully up, Bold again hauled himself to his feet and tottered a few steps as he tried to estimate the distance to the copse. He knew he could never get across even a quarter of it. He looked around the wintry vista. Luckily, there was no sign of any large creature abroad. How long could he hope to remain un-threatened on that rather prominent knoll? It was essential for him to move from there to a place of greater safety. But where?

He slipped, slithered and stumbled down the other side of the slope. His body was miserably wet and chilled through with slush and mud. The bleak February sun had no warmth in it. He was hungry, but there was no chance of his finding anything to eat. Above all, he felt lonely. How long it seemed from the days when he had revelled in his solitude. Yet it was less than one whole season! Not only had his appearance changed over those few months, but also his attitudes and desires. And most of all, now, he desired company.

There was no hope of Whisper's return until the day was over – indeed, he had insisted she stay away from him. He wondered if the thaw in the weather would induce Robber to quit the area of the town again. How glad he would be to see the crow fly up. He lay down again at the foot of the slope, utterly dispirited. He would make no attempt whatever, he decided, to start for the copse. It would be senseless in his present state. Far better to wait for Whisper.

He awoke from a troubled doze with a strong sense of another's presence. The sun was now high in the sky. He turned his head – and there stood Robber!

'I didn't want to disturb you; you looked so weary,' said the crow. 'You're quite safe – nothing else has passed this way. But why are you lying out in the open like this?'

Bold's tail had been weakly thumping up and down in his pleasure at seeing his friend. Now it stopped. 'Easy to answer that,' he said abruptly. 'I can't get any further!'

'Why, what do you mean? What's happened?' Robber demanded.

Bold explained.

'Ah, you were ill-advised to try and travel through this!' Robber remarked with his beady, black eyes fixed on the fox. 'What are a couple of days? You should have been more patient, Bold.'

'I acknowledge it, and I myself would gladly have paused longer. But I tried to do what Whisper wanted.'

'Humph! She should have thought more about you!' Robber said shortly. 'Will she be back?'

'Oh, yes, she will try to get back to me. You see, she needs me to point the way.'

'I know all about parental care,' Robber said. 'I've helped to raise several broods in my lifetime. But you should have been more cautious, the pair of you. More haste, less speed. Now you've got to pause whether you like it or not, until you can walk again.'

'It may be too late,' Bold said pessimistically. 'I don't know if I can make a recovery this time.'

'Nonsense!' Robber croaked. 'There's warmer weather coming – I know it as sure as I know that night follows day. We'll get you some food – good food – and you'll soon mend.'

Bold sighed. 'What a comfort a good friend can be,' he said thankfully. 'And, Robber, you are as good a friend as any creature could hope for.'

Robber cawed a rather more melodious couple of notes than he was wont to do. He was delighted to be held in such high esteem. Perhaps this was the magic of the Farthing Wood pledge at work on *him*, this strange willingness to help another animal in need?

'I brought this – it's not much,' he said, pushing a small dark object towards Bold with his beak.

'Carrion?' inquired the fox.

'No. Stolen goods,' answered Robber. 'What the cat didn't want.'

Bold sniffed curiously at the item. It was certainly meat, but a meat he had never seen before. However, an empty stomach needs no second bidding to be filled, and down the morsel went.

'You said something about *good* food?' Bold hinted.

'I did – and it's as good as arranged,' said the crow. 'As you can't move, I'm going to have to leave you here for a bit. I'll be back as soon as I can. In the meantime, is there any way in which you can make yourself less conspicuous?'

'Not without immediately turning the colour of my coat to white,' Bold answered sarcastically.

Robber looked at him askance. 'You've hit upon something there without intending it,' he observed. 'Why don't you dig yourself more into the snow – you'd be difficult to spot except at close quarters?'

'I could try, I suppose,' Bold said without enthusiasm. 'But I don't want to freeze to death.'

'Don't be absurd, Bold,' Robber answered. 'There's no danger in it greater than that of feeling some discomfort. Well – I'll away.'

Bold was left alone again. For some time he didn't move. Then he heard some human voices and took Robber's advice to heart. He pawed at some of the firmer snow close to the ground until he had made a makeshift sort of tunnel under the slushy surface. This at least served to hide part of his body and gave him an added feeling of security. The voices disappeared and a hush returned to the countryside. Bold lay trying to ignore his misery, by listening to the beats of his own heart and telling himself that each one brought him close to the time when Whisper might return.

A sudden noise made his heart beat much faster. It sounded again – the noise of dogs following their quarry; excitable, savage and lusting for blood. It was horrible to listen to. For any wild creature it was terrifying. And Bold could not move. Instinctively, he flattened his body. He tried to make himself as small as possible, in the nature of all animals trying to avoid detection. He could see nothing, except what was immediately in front of him. A few moments later, a hare streaked across his line of vision – running, leaping, zigzagging this way and that as it tried to shake off its pursuers. Then two long, thin dogs raced past in the little animal's wake, their pointed faces agape, and their tongues lolling between cruel, laughing fangs. Bold shuddered at their eager, frantic barks. Angry human shouts tried to call them back, but in vain. It seemed the hare should have been allowed to escape; yet now the dogs were deaf to everything but its certain death. And the ghastly race continued. The hare doubled back on its course, back past Bold in his fragile igloo, its springy, elastic bounds flagging by a fraction. Desperate to outrun each other the dogs had increased their speed, and came on with their gleaming, murderous eyes. A scream – thin, childlike but shattering, rent the countryside. The hare was caught – and torn – by those ferocious jaws.

Bold had never seen such fearsome beasts. He knew nothing of greyhounds. Dogs that seemed to be uncontrolled by their human masters threatened the safety of any animal – wild or otherwise. Despite his sufferings, Bold simply could not bear to stay still any longer. He crawled out from the snowy shelter, intent on one thing: to move somewhere, somehow, away from those dreadful dogs. He started to walk blindly; mechanically. Had he remained where he was he would have been safe. The owners of the greyhounds had almost reached them. But the dog who had been cheated of the kill by its faster rival now saw the chance of another victim, as it spied Bold's halting movements in the distance. In a trice, it ducked the grasp of its frustrated master and launched itself on a fresh attack.

—19—
A Friend in Need

For a bird, and a large bird at that, the distance through
the air from the point where he left Bold – back to the
town, was modest. At their necessarily slow pace, the pair
of foxes had really come no great way. So Robber was
soon among human habitations again, and now he flew
straight towards Bold's other friend.

Rollo was napping, half in and half out of his kennel,
when Robber descended and perched on the fence. He
woke at once and sprang up. 'Have you seen them? Have
you seen them?' he asked quickly.

'Yes, yes, I've seen them,' Robber replied. 'At least –
I've seen Bold. He's in a bad way. He needs food.'

'Of course he does,' Rollo said. 'Can't find it out there
in these conditions, can he?' He went at once to his food

bowl to remind himself if he had left anything from his previous meal. It was licked clean. 'Hm. I can't seem to help at the moment,' he muttered with some embarrassment, 'but tonight I –'

'Tonight's no good,' Robber interrupted peremptorily. 'How can I find him in the dark? Haven't you *anything* left at all?'

'Well, no, you see I wasn't expecting –'

'Obviously.'

'Wait a bit, though. There might be a biscuit or two . . . .' Rollo put his great head in his kennel to look.

'*Biscuits?* Robber echoed derogatorily. 'That's no use. He needs something nourishing. Of all the greedy . . .' he started to mutter, then thought better of it. Luckily, Rollo didn't hear.

'I've found two,' the mastiff said with great satisfaction, and carried out similar bone-shaped biscuits to those he had given his friends before.

'What he wants is *meat*,' Robber said irritably. 'And Whisper too, of course,' he added as an afterthought. 'Those won't get him moving again!'

'Moving?' asked Rollo. 'Can't he move?'

'He's exhausted himself trying to travel in thick snow,' Robber explained. 'He hasn't even any shelter.'

Rollo suddenly gave a tremendous bark. The crow nearly fell off the fence with alarm. 'What's that for?' he screeched.

'I've just remembered,' said Rollo excitedly. 'My master gave me a huge bone some time ago, but I've hardly touched it.'

'Well, where is it then?' demanded Robber.

'I buried it – you know, to save for the future.'

'Can you find it?'

'Oh, yes, nothing easier,' said Rollo. 'Now, let me see, was it over here by the kennel or – no, I think I put it near the fence.' He went over to one of the fence-posts and began to sniff. 'Of course, I could find the spot at once if all this snow hadn't covered up my signs,' he told the bird. 'But, don't worry, I'll soon have it up again.'

Robber was nearly expiring with impatience. 'Can't you be a bit quicker?' he croaked. 'We have to be back with him in the daylight.'

Rollo paused in his search and looked up. '*We?*' he asked, his deep voice tremulous with excitement. 'Am I to come too?'

'Oh, really!' cried Robber. 'How do you think a bird could carry a bone selected for a great, stupid dog like you – in its claws?'

'Of course, of course,' the mastiff answered, ignoring the insult. He renewed his efforts. Slush and mud flew in every direction as he dug furiously for the treasure, spattering Robber liberally until the bird flew to a safer spot. Robber 'cawed' angrily and began to preen himself.

At last the bone was unearthed. Rollo gripped it in his huge jaws and ran over to the crow, dropping it at his feet. 'There!' he cried. 'What do you think of that?'

Robber examined the mud-caked object with disapproval. 'I don't think anything of it,' he announced. 'You could hardly describe it as edible!'

'Of course it's edible,' Rollo answered. 'Why would I have saved it otherwise?' He started to claw the worst of the mud off. 'You see – there's a lot of meat on it,' he pointed out. 'A lovely succulent bone!' He barked once or twice – quite deafeningly – in his appreciation. Then he grasped the bone firmly once more and ran at the fence with a great leap. Dropping the bone briefly he cried: 'Come on then! What are we waiting for?'

Robber flew down and tried to pick up the two large biscuits with his beak. After juggling unsuccessfully for a while, he abandoned one and flew off with the other without a word, leaving Rollo to follow his flight.

The mastiff's powerful legs covered the ground in great bounds as he watched Robber's direction through the air. Snow, slush, mud – none of these was a barrier to his progress. He ploughed through everything like a juggernaut. The crow flew as low as he dared and found perches along the way to enable the dog to keep him in sight. So they progressed on the trail of the foxes.

The sun was dropping imperceptibly as Robber heard the first sounds of the greyhounds. As he flew on he saw the field where they had been set to course the hare. He saw the men and he saw the hare's desperate flight, and how it leapt right over the low hedge bordering the field and into open country. He saw the dogs push through the hedge after it, furious at the hare's attempt to escape, and how the men failed to stop them. Then he saw the slope where he had left Bold earlier that day and, even as he looked for signs of his friend, he witnessed the hare's inevitable demise. The men were out of the field now, trying to round up the hounds. One was taken; the other avoided capture and turned to race away. Robber saw what it was aiming for and opened his beak to screech an alarm, dropping the biscuit. He flew round in a circle, cawing frantically as he saw Rollo in the distance, still running gamely but much slower now after his long journey. The greyhound had lost none of its speed, and was closing on Bold rapidly. Robber realized that any help the mastiff might give would arrive too late. So, as on a previous occasion, he flew forward to see if he could divert the attack.

Bold had taken only a few limping steps when he heard the dog's renewed clamour. He faced about hopelessly.

But he was no hare. He gritted his teeth, preparing to fight. The greyhound's advance was now impeded by the harassing tactics of Robber. The crow had flown right into the face of the fierce hound before flapping away, causing it to veer; then immediately repeating the manoeuvre. The greyhound's greedy jaws snapped furiously but closed on air. Meanwhile Rollo approached.

At last the greyhound's supple body succeeded in getting clear of the bird and the dog impelled itself towards its target. Bold lunged at the aggressor, caught a glancing blow, staggered, and fell. The greyhound swung round and bit deep into the fox's neck-scruff. Bold yelped and tried to struggle free. But he was held fast. The fangs sank deeper into his flesh.

In the next few seconds Rollo joined the fray. The great bone he had so faithfully carried all the way was dropped and forgotten. With a mighty bellow of rage he hurled himself on the unsuspecting greyhound. The weight of his huge body drove all the breath from its lungs, so that it instantly released its grip on Bold. Then Rollo's great jaws seized it by the neck and shook it as if it had been a ferret. The hound's eyes glazed over and Rollo cast it away, leaving it for dead.

Bold lay still. Dark blood flowed from his wound and collected in his fur, dyeing it a deeper red. Rollo and Robber stood over him and watched his gasps with concern. But Bold, for once, was lucky. The greyhound's teeth had only pierced the thick fold of skin at the base of his neck by which Vixen, his mother, had carried him when a cub. No real damage had been done. He recovered sufficiently to sit up. He looked at the black crow and the huge frame of the mastiff and murmured simply: 'My friends.'

The men came up and, quite timidly, went to examine the motionless greyhound. They dared not approach

Rollo, for he was more than a match for them. His presence loomed over the entire scene. One man bent to pick up the hound, then stumbled away, cradling it in his arms. He went, whispering to its limp form as it hung laxly, more dead than alive. His companion followed him, leading the other greyhound, now a morose and much subdued animal. The sun continued to sink down into the horizon.

Bold slowly bent his head and licked carefully at some snow. It seemed to revive him a little. Robber went off to look for the biscuit.

'That really was . . . the nick of time,' said Bold, referring to the mastiff's entry into the mêlée. 'But wait – I don't know yet why you're here, all the way from home.'

'Wait, and I'll show you,' boomed Rollo. He retrieved the bone and came back, swishing his tail. 'There wasn't any meat left, you see,' he explained, 'when your friend the crow came for food. It's the best I could do.'

Bold sniffed at it elaborately. 'It has a very rewarding smell,' he said with amusement, 'but it looks as if it's been underground for years.'

'Oh, no – not years,' Rollo corrected him innocently. 'I think I buried it last week some time.'

'I see. Well, it shall be eaten,' said Bold. 'But I'll wait until Whisper can share it.'

Now Robber came with the biscuit. 'Eat that, at any rate,' he said. 'You've got to eat, Bold.'

'Of course,' said Bold, and he ate the stale biscuit with great relish.

As the sun sank further Robber went to roost. Rollo remained where he was. Fox and dog watched the sky darken and waited for the return of Whisper. It had been night for two hours before they saw her figure approaching through the gloom. Her relief at finding Bold almost exactly where she had left him soon changed to alarm at his wounds. But he made light of them.

'I'm lucky to be alive, Whisper,' he said, and Rollo had the great pleasure of hearing himself named as Bold's deliverer. The mastiff could not contain his delight and gambolled around the re-united foxes like a puppy.

Whisper set about licking Bold's hurts. Her touch was soothing. Afterwards they lay down, just where they were, to tackle Rollo's bone. The mastiff himself was forgotten now that they were together again.

Rollo wandered a little way off, unmindful of their neglect. He was happy just to be near them and he felt he never would forget this wonderful time when he had been at hand to rescue his friend. He sprawled on the melting snow at a distance, still near enough to offer his protection if necessary. He had no thought of returning home until, at least, the sun rose again.

After the fretful events of the day, the night was peaceful and untroubled. Bold and Whisper were kept busy by the bone for an hour or so; but they realized they would have to move before it got light. After his long rest, Bold felt ready to test his leg again. He and Whisper shook themselves free of the worst of the wet snow and called to Rollo. He came up at once.

'We have to find somewhere to hide up in the daylight,' Bold explained. 'I can never thank you enough for what you did . . . .'

'I'll stay with you as you go,' Rollo offered. 'Then, if you need any help I'll still be around.'

'But what of your master?' Whisper inquired. 'Won't he be missing you?'

'No, no . . . it's not likely,' Rollo answered, rather sorrowfully. 'I'll return when it's daylight.'

So the three animals set off again through the slush and mire. Bold's bad leg had stiffened up again and he winced visibly for the first few metres. After that it loosened a bit, and they were able to proceed a little less slowly. The remaining snow was melting fast, revealing great patches of grass. Pools of water collected everywhere and new rivulets ran over the ground wherever it was not quite flat. Water seemed to seep into everything and soon the coats of the three beasts were soaked and matted with mud. But the night was mild and windless so that their discomfort was not extreme.

'We must try and find some piece of cover nearer than that copse,' Bold panted, 'and, in any case, we don't want that direction.'

'There doesn't appear to be much available except dead bracken,' Whisper remarked.

'Well, if that's all there is – it'll have to do,' Bold answered. 'We should at least be well camouflaged if we can find a thick clump. I really can't go very far, I'm afraid.'

'Of course,' Whisper reassured him. 'We must think of you now, first and foremost.'

They discovered a patch of soggy dead bracken, beaten almost flat on the ground. But it was just thick enough for them to crawl underneath and conceal themselves.

'Where's Rollo?' Bold asked suddenly.

'He's probably started on his homeward journey now we're settled,' answered his mate.

However, shortly afterwards, up came the faithful dog again, carrying something in his jaws. It was the remains of the dead hare. 'Why waste it?' he asked, after depositing it by his friends. 'There's a good meal for each of you in that carcass.'

'There certainly is,' agreed Whisper. 'Why ever didn't we think of it?'

As dawn approached Rollo sadly bade his friends farewell, and they watched his huge lumbering form trotting, with many a backward glance, in the direction of home. The mastiff retrieved his bone on the way, for most of it was still left and it was not in his nature to abandon such a choice morsel.

When he was close to his home yard it was broad daylight, and he received the surprise of his life. His master, who had noticed his absence, was combing the area for his huge pet in great concern. When he saw Rollo coming towards him he was so relieved he ran up to the dog and made such a fuss of him as he had never done before. The enraptured dog dropped his bone and danced around, covering his laughing master with mud and uttering the most vociferous bellows in his joy. Then Rollo leapt his fence, still barking, while his master prepared to give him a thorough scrub. Now it was the foxes' turn to be forgotten as man and dog renewed their friendship in a way that made them both realize that they could never ever lose it again.

—20—
The Parting

Each night thereafter Bold and Whisper continued their journey. When the last of the snow had disappeared, food became more readily available. Now that the approach of spring was heralded, more small creatures were on the move. Whisper no longer made any attempt to force the pace. She knew that she and her unborn cubs depended on Bold entirely. She was more solicitous than ever for his well-being and did not comment on the fact that his pace was becoming slower and slower. Of course, Bold himself was well aware of it. Every night he wondered if his leg could endure yet more strain on the morrow; yet somehow he managed to keep on. Robber still followed their stages by day and he, too, noticed how

the distances they covered were becoming progressively
shorter.

Gradually and very, very gradually, the foxes' destination grew closer as the month of March was ushered in.
They passed the ditch where Bold had first hidden after
his injury. He showed Whisper the actual place where he
had been shot and she looked very solemn. Then he told
her of the game coverts nearby that really had been the
cause of all his trouble and he mentioned Shadow the
sow badger.

'You've certainly not lacked for friends,' Whisper
remarked.

'No. I *have* been lucky.' Bold thought for a moment.
'You know,' he said, 'I'm obliged to admit that I wouldn't
be here now if I hadn't had their help. Each time I've
been in dire trouble one creature or another has come to
my rescue. First of all there was Shadow; then Robber
saved me from starving. Then, dear Whisper, you yourself came on the scene; and finally, poor simple Rollo.
I could have died several times over without you
all . . . .'

'But you yourself haven't been slow to do good turns,'
Whisper reminded him. 'And anyway, Bold, it wasn't
your fate to die too soon.'

'Fate?' he muttered. 'And what *is* to be my fate?'

'To lead me to White Deer Park and to see your young
ones born and brought up there.'

'I suppose so,' he replied, thinking how different it was
from the destiny he had planned for himself. By a strange
coincidence Bold at that juncture happened to be passing
a puddle of dark water where the moon and stars were
reflected like a handful of diamonds and pearl. He
stopped and looked at his own peering face. Shadow
would have been a fitter name for *him*, for shadow he was
of his former self. He saw himself as an animal dying of a

lingering disease, for which there never was, and never could be, a cure. He actually shivered at the sight of his own image and hastily passed on. He said nothing; neither did Whisper – but the moment was charged with their own recognition of its significance. Bold knew then – finally and incontrovertibly – that he would never enter White Deer Park again. If he didn't die in the attempt of leading the vixen to its borders, he would absent himself from her company when she was close enough to need him no more. For his re-appearance in the Nature Reserve would be, for him, an admission of failure. Only by living alone for as long as his blighted life might last could he retain his self-respect. And that was all that remained to him. He had not been independent; neither had he enjoyed total freedom. He had only survived to this point because others had succoured him when in need. But he would regain his independence at last. He could at least die alone.

Bold gave no utterance to his thoughts and Whisper was left to think her own. Something of his feelings communicated themselves to her but she dared not voice her fears. And so they continued.

They went close by the game wood but, this time, Bold had no intention of entering it. He did not care to renew his acquaintance with the female badger, neither did he wish to court the dangers of traps and gibbets. At length he and Whisper reached the open downland. Will-power alone had enabled Bold to keep going through pain, weakness and exhaustion. Now he knew that a few more stages would take them near enough to the Reserve for Whisper to manage alone. That night, after the vixen had caught their frugal supper, she started to question Bold again about their destination.

'It won't be long now,' he promised her. 'Patience and

caution have brought us this far and should see us through.'

Whisper looked at him penetratingly. 'Can *you* keep going?' she asked. 'I've been worrying and worrying about you.'

'Worry no more,' Bold said. 'I'll last the course.'

His cryptic remarks did not reassure her. She tried to probe his thoughts. 'Once we're in the Park you need do nothing but rest and eat. I'll find us a den – or I'll dig one myself.'

Bold remained silent.

'Will we see the Farthing Wood – er – your father?' she asked. 'And your brother and sister cubs?'

'If they're still alive,' he answered evasively. He thought of Vixen, his mother, with regret. How he longed to see her once more. But it couldn't be.

Whisper fell silent, but she continued to wonder about Bold's intentions. Five more days and nights passed. Then she wondered no more. She woke from an uneasy sleep amongst some budding undergrowth to find Bold gone. She jumped up and went carefully into the open. Although she scanned the landscape in every direction, there was no sign of him. The event she had dreaded had occurred. She searched the nearby wood, calling to him in the vixen's characteristic way. Then she started to explore further afield. Copses, undergrowth and even dead vegetation she searched, always looking for an earth where he might have hidden himself. She found nothing. Then she wondered if Bold might have returned to the spot where they had last been together, while she had been looking for him in vain. She went back to their hideaway.

When she again found no trace of him she lay down miserably. She decided to wait, for perhaps he would return at nightfall. Dusk fell and her hopes were raised. But the night wore slowly on and she remained quite alone. She ate nothing. She wanted nothing – except Bold's return. She slept.

In the daylight she knew he would not come back. But still she stayed. Then, when darkness came again she knew she had to move on. Her time was approaching and now her duty to her unborn cubs was paramount. She made herself eat for their sakes and, continuing resolutely in the direction she and Bold had travelled all along, she approached the Park. As she went she still looked for signs of her lost mate wherever she thought there was any chance of finding him. But she soon realized it was a hopeless task, for by now it was obvious to her that Bold had parted from her for good. Two nights later she stood before the boundary fence of White Deer Park. Safety and protection beckoned her inside, yet she hesitated. Added to the sadness and emptiness she had been experiencing for the past few days there was now a feeling of remorse as she thought of the choice she had forced poor Bold to make. He had succumbed to her entreaties for a safe home for their cubs, whilst all along he had had no wish to return to his birthplace. He had sacrificed his own chances of survival by ensuring that his mate should reach her destination. His struggles on the long journey had been only too apparent to her, and she had seen him grow weaker with each day. Now she had lost him – for Whisper knew in her heart that Bold had gone away to die.

She stood forlornly on the threshold of *her* new world with the most bitter regrets gnawing at her conscience. Yet she felt that Bold had accepted her wishes because he himself wanted his cubs to be born in safety, even if he had decided it would mean his own life was over. She found the selfsame gap in the fence from which Bold had left his old home, and entered the Park. Giving herself a shake, she set her mind to the task of finding an earth. There was not much of the night left.

As dawn crept over the Reserve Whisper took cover. She had encountered none of the inhabitants of her new home as yet, and now she automatically took her usual precautions. She was very tired and was glad to rest. During the day she woke briefly to see a herd of white hinds stepping daintily through the grass. She had never seen such large animals before but she knew there was nothing to fear from them. Bold had long ago described all the animals she might meet at her journey's end.

In the evening she resumed her explorations. A wooded part of the Park attracted her. Under an ash tree a small animal had built a hole. Whisper began to excavate with the intention of enlarging it into a den. As she halted once from her work, she found another fox watching her. It soon became apparent that the animal was another vixen; very young; and in the same condition as herself.

'I'm sure I've never seen you in this wood before,' said the vixen, in a not unfriendly way.

'No – nor in the Park,' Whisper added.

'Oh? You've come from the outside?' Her astonishment was obvious.

'Yes, from outside. You see – I'm soon to have a litter of cubs and I wanted protection for them.'

'Indeed! May I ask how you know of the Nature Reserve?'

'Why not?' Whisper decided to cast caution to the winds. 'Their father was born here.'

The vixen gasped. '*Born* here ... but ... but ...' she stammered, 'where is he now? Oh, tell me where he is!'

Whisper realized she might have encountered one of

Bold's relatives. 'I don't know,' she wailed. 'He parted from me whilst I slept. I don't know where he is now, but – oh! he's outside the Park somewhere. He didn't want to come back here ... in spite of his mate ... and his unborn cubs,' Whisper ended miserably.

'Describe him to me, do!' begged the other vixen. 'It's very important.'

Whisper bowed her head. 'I'm afraid that would serve no purpose,' she said with a sad expression. 'You wouldn't recognize the description. But I know he was known here as Bold.'

'Bold!' cried the vixen joyfully. 'I knew it! My brother cub!'

'Your brother? Then you must be –'

'Charmer,' interrupted the vixen. 'But tell me everything, please, everything! Oh, we must find him and bring him here. Our father and mother – and my own brother – all live here still. He must come back, he must!'

Whisper felt more downhearted than ever. How could she tell Charmer that her brother might be close to death? Before she could say anything, Charmer was asking her name.

'Bold gave me the name of Whisper,' she answered almost inaudibly, so great was her emotion, 'because of my stealth.'

Charmer's eyes shone. 'Our cubs shall be cousins, Whisper,' she said excitedly. 'They will grow up together.'

'Do you have an earth in this wood?' Whisper asked.

'Yes, just a few metres from here. Shall I help you prepare yours?'

Whisper declined her offer. 'You're very kind,' she

said, 'but I prefer to manage things myself as far as my family goes.'

'I understand,' said Charmer. 'You're quite right – and I'll leave you. Do I have your permission to inform my parents of your arrival here?'

'By all means,' Whisper answered sweetly. 'They and I – and you, too – have a mutual bond. They have a right to know.'

'I will come and see you again, Whisper, to hear your story,' said Bold's sister vixen. 'I hope we might be friends. My brother chose his mate well.'

—21—
The Farthing Wood Fox

Bold's last look at Whisper was one of tenderness as she lay dreaming. Her limbs twitched occasionally and from time to time a flicker passed over her face as she followed her imaginary adventures. Bold watched. He was glad he had been able to bring her thus far, though at such cost to himself. Now she would have no difficulty in completing her journey. He stood up shakily and looked out on the sunlit countryside. Spring was approaching. In but a few weeks he would have been one year old.

Bold knew he would not live that long now. But *his* cubs would be born and the whole cycle would begin anew. Now he must make himself scarce. He had not long to reach his hiding-place before Whisper might come looking. With one last affectionate glance at his mate, he hobbled away.

From a high, high branch of a poplar tree, Robber the Carrion Crow watched Bold turn his back on the vixen. He watched in earnest as Bold limped slowly over the wet ground. Where was he going? He decided to investigate. Maintaining a discreet distance to the rear of the fox, he flitted from one tree to another, always keeping him in view. Bold went towards a spinney of silver birch through which he and Whisper had passed the previous night. To and fro he went through the dappled tree-trunks. Robber surmised he was looking for something. He flew closer. Bold had found a hollow log – all that remained of an ancient beech tree. It lay on its side, encrusted with lichen, moss and fungi. As Robber flew up, the fox bent and slunk inside. Robber perched on top and waited. Bold did not re-appear. The bird assumed he had found something to eat inside – or that he was sleeping. He fluttered to the ground and strutted to the open end of the log. He could then see his friend quite clearly. Bold was lying with his head on his paws, but was still quite awake.

'Robber!' he exclaimed. 'Wherever did you spring from?'

'I didn't "spring" from anywhere,' the crow answered. 'I flew here – as usual. Bold, what are you doing?'

'That's my affair,' came the reply.

'Of course – if that's how you feel about it,' said Robber haughtily, and made as if to go.

'No – stay. Robber, stay,' Bold said hastily. 'I'm sorry. Why shouldn't you know?' He paused.

'Well?'

'I'm going no further,' said Bold slowly. 'Whisper must finish the journey by herself.'

'But why, when you've come so far?' asked Robber.

'Look at me,' said Bold, 'and look hard. How much do I resemble even the beast *you* once knew?'

Robber shifted his feet awkwardly. 'But I'm sure, once you reach the Reserve again you'll soon –' he began.

'I'll soon be dead,' Bold cut in harshly. 'Let's be realistic. I've brought my death closer forcing myself on and on, night after night. I've done what I promised –I've shown Whisper the way. Now her cubs – *our* cubs –will be safe. But I won't ever see them.'

'That is a very sad remark,' Robber said.

'It's true nonetheless. Even if I should continue from here, I should never survive long enough for that.'

Robber looked away uncomfortably. 'She'll come searching for you,' he said.

'I know she will. But she won't find me,' Bold answered. 'I'm going to block up this entrance.'

'How ever can you do that?'

'Oh, there's plenty of dead leaves and grass and such like I can rake together.'

'I don't like the thought of it,' said Robber. 'You might perish in there.'

'You know, Robber, by all the laws of Nature I should have perished already,' replied the fox fatalistically. 'Do you remember my boast of living the True Wild Life? Well, I haven't. My life has been as protected outside the Reserve as it would have been inside – only in a different way.'

'Not true,' Robber disputed. 'You wouldn't have been *shot* in a Nature Reserve.'

'Foxes have been shot – even there – by poachers,' Bold informed him. 'But what's the point of arguing? You've been a good friend to me.' He got up and stumbled to the end of the log. 'I've no time to lose,' he said, beginning to scrape together the leaf litter where

Robber stood, into a pile.

Robber noticed that Bold found even this a difficult task, although he was using his front paws. He was swaying from side to side in his weak state. The crow tried to be helpful by picking up leaves and grass in his beak and dropping them on the mound.

'Please don't trouble,' said Bold. 'I'll get it done, even if it is the last thing I ever accomplish. You should go now, Robber, before you give the game away.'

'Very well,' said Robber. 'But I shan't stray far. I fear for you.' He left the poor struggling fox reluctantly, convinced now that the end was near.

Later in the day he saw Whisper set off on her sad, fruitless search. Bold's precautions proved to be unnecessary as she did not go anywhere near the spinney of silver birch. The next day Robber saw the vixen waiting for him still. He yearned to fly to her, to greet her with the news of Bold's lair. Yet he baulked at such an act of betrayal.

The next day Whisper was gone. Robber knew she must have reached her objective. He waited no longer. Finding what food he could, he swooped down to the beech log. 'Bold! Bold!' he croaked. 'It is I – Robber!' He heard nothing. He 'cawed' loudly four times and then began feverishly to peck at the bundle that sealed the log's entrance. He cleared a space and peered in, his head on one side. Bold was there, lying quite still.

'Bold?'

'Yes, I'm ... still here,' came the animal's weak voice.

'Thank goodness! cried Robber, who had suffered a fright. He went back for the food and brought it inside.

Bold slowly raised himself. 'Can't ... eat that,' he muttered. 'No point now.'

'Yes, yes, there is,' beseeched the crow. 'Whisper has gone, but you can still live. You *must*.'

'No . . . appetite,' said Bold.

'Try. You'll feel better. Try!'

Bold licked at Robber's offering, then took it in his mouth obediently. Robber watched him with gratification.

'I'll fetch more,' he promised, and wasted no time in setting about it.

When he returned, Bold had quitted his hollow trunk and was stretched on the grass, blinking in the March sunlight. Robber pushed a dead fledgling towards him, still almost bald, that had dropped from its nest. Bold grunted. 'You crows have . . . catholic tastes,' he managed to say.

'Bold, it's not too late to change your mind,' Robber said urgently. 'I've seen the Park. It's not far away.'

'I know you mean well,' said Bold. 'But you are wasting . . . your breath. My mind . . . is made up. I can't hunt – I can barely walk – would you have me remain alive and pampered with food while I lie almost helpless, like a Queen Bee?'

'You make your point well,' said Robber. 'What do you intend to do then?'

'I shall stay here,' Bold answered. 'The log will be my home until –' He left the rest unsaid.

The fledgling still lay where Robber had left it. 'Won't you eat this?' he asked.

'No.'

'What shall I find for you then?'

'Find me nothing and I shall be content,' said Bold enigmatically. 'And why do you stay with me? You should be looking for a mate.'

'I shall do so,' answered Robber. 'Eventually.'

Bold knew what he was thinking. 'You haven't long to

wait, my faithful friend,' he told him.

The Farthing Wood Fox and his Vixen had remained together even when their cubs had grown and departed. Their inseparability made their relationship a unique one indeed among foxes. So when Charmer visited their earth with her startling news, they heard it together. In the darkness their faces were inscrutable, but their voices betrayed their emotion.

'I always believed he was still alive,' said Fox huskily. 'Bold had the mark of a survivor.'

'But why doesn't he wish to return here?' Vixen asked. 'Why has he left his mate before his cubs are even born?'

'Whisper didn't tell me that,' said Charmer, 'so you must ask her yourself.'

'There's no need to ask,' said Fox. 'Bold is a proud animal. To return to White Deer Park would mean a loss of face.'

'You are right, Fox,' said Vixen. 'I know you are – and yet I also know it to be an absurd notion. Pride can be stretched too far. How can loss of face be important when all his family long to see him?'

'Those closest to him would be the very ones to fuel his sense of failure,' said Fox who understood such things. 'And so it's necessary for us to go to him as he won't come to us.'

'How can we? Even Whisper doesn't know where he is,' said Charmer.

'If Bold led his mate to the Reserve he is still close at hand,' Fox remarked. 'And we shall find him. *We* must all go – and Friendly his brother too – to look. But first, we should make the acquaintance of the new young vixen in our midst.'

Whisper was a little abashed to see Charmer leading

the famed Fox and Vixen – as well as a strange young
male fox – towards her. But their unfeigned delight in
seeing her soon put her at her ease. When they explained
their plan she looked at their eager faces compassionately.

'I don't know how you will find him,' she said. 'But,
even if you do, you must be prepared for the worst. Even
now it may be too late.'

'Too late? Why, how can it –' Vixen began.

'Bold is not the animal you once knew. He is older and
wiser for his adventures, but he has suffered a great deal.
His energy and physique are severely depleted. He
received a terrible injury, long before he and I encountered each other, and he has never recovered from it.
The journey he undertook at my behest to bring me to
safety was – I freely admit it – too great an ordeal. During
the last few days we were together he was failing
visibly . . . .'

'Are you telling us, Whisper,' Vixen asked, barely
audibly, 'that Bold is . . . dying?' The last word came out
as a long sigh.

Whisper groaned. 'Yes,' she whined, 'I believe that to
be so.'

'Then we must go at once!' cried Friendly. 'Father,
Mother, we must leave now!'

'Can he be so close and yet . . . so far . . . from us?'
Vixen whispered.

'We can save him, surely?' Friendly asked hopelessly.
'We're not too late?'

'I fear . . . the worst,' Whisper muttered.

Bold's family looked stunned. To have received such
unexpected good news and then for their hopes to be
dashed almost at the same moment was awful. Vixen
made the first move to go.

'Whisper – you will come with us?' Charmer asked.

Whisper looked away, into the distance, as if she were picturing Bold as he now might be. She drew a deep breath. 'No,' she answered at last, in a low voice. 'I don't think I could bear it.'

Charmer hung her head, sensing, but not wishing to see, her anguish.

'We must trust that we can bring you good news,' Fox said, much moved.

Vixen led her family away in the direction of the Park's boundary fence. Whisper stood to watch them, unmoving. Then, with a toss of her head, she turned to finish preparing her earth.

Outside the Reserve the four animals divided, the two foxes taking one course; the two vixens, another. It was a black, cloud-covered night and, for the two young beasts, Friendly and Charmer, quite an adventure. Neither of them had ever been beyond the Park's bounds, and each kept close to its parent. Fox and Vixen knew the terrain from of old and began systematically to comb the area. The hours of darkness passed with no clue found.

Charmer watched the grey dawn break with misgiving. 'Should we remain here to be seen?' she asked her mother nervously. 'Wouldn't it be better to return home until the next night?'

Vixen nuzzled her gently. 'I understand your fear,' she answered. 'But there will be no danger if we are careful. We can't afford to lose many hours in idleness.'

Friendly was experiencing the same qualms but preferred not to let his father know.

The early morning light took on a pearly quality as the birds began to sing in greater and greater numbers. One solitary bird saw Vixen and Charmer and wondered at their activity. As he wheeled on the wing in search of his breakfast he saw the other two foxes behaving in the same busy manner. Ignoring his empty stomach, Robber alighted on a branch and pondered. The more he pondered, the more he became convinced that he knew who the animals must be and what they were doing. He croaked to himself, wondering if he should become involved. He was not sure of Bold's wishes. And yet, and yet . . . if one of these animals was the Farthing Wood Fox, he, and he alone of all the creatures around, had the chance of reuniting father and son. He hopped up and down the branch in his anxiety. If he did nothing, they might never meet again – or, worse still, the meeting might be too late . . . . He simply *couldn't* allow such a sad event to happen when he might be the one means of preventing it. He 'cawed' twice to steel himself and flew down towards Fox and Friendly.

The animals looked up but paid him no attention. A crow was a commonplace enough sight, even in the Reserve.

Robber croaked nervously. 'Er – er – are you searching for someone?' he asked with awkwardness.

Fox looked at the bird in surprise. For a moment he said nothing. Then, ever cautious, he answered: 'Who are you, that you ask such a question?'

'A friend, I hope,' Robber muttered, still very much in awe of the Fox. 'I think I may be able to help you.'

'Do you have a message for us?' asked Friendly.

'No. But I must identify myself,' Robber pulled himself together. 'I am called Robber by my friend the fox – the one whom I think you must be seeking?'

'Ah!' Fox and Friendly exchanged glances.

'You are the Farthing Wood Fox?' Robber asked the senior animal.

'Yes.'

'Then I *can* help you. I can take you to Bold.'

'Do so,' Fox answered at once. 'We shall learn your history later.'

Robber signified the direction. 'You must run fast,' he said. 'I'll point out the way. You've still quite a distance to cover.' He took to the air. The two foxes ran underneath his flight path. Robber led them to where Vixen and Charmer were located and kept flying on, leaving the explanations to the foxes. He dipped and turned once to make sure they were following. The four animals were running as hard as they could. Robber kept on to the birch spinney.

Only a metre or two away from the great log, Bold lay amongst the sprouting grass and the remains of the winter's dead leaves. He was in no pain now. He felt calm. He had no desires. He was now too weak to move and he knew he would die where he lay. He saw Robber alight close by on a birch sapling and was glad. Despite his decision, he was glad he would not die entirely alone. He closed his eyes gratefully.

When he next opened them he saw, as through a mist, four familiar and beloved shapes and faces. He blinked slowly, thinking he was a cub again back in White Deer Park. Vixen came forward, sniffed, and nuzzled him with a very real tenderness. Bold blinked again.

'You're alone no longer,' Vixen whispered, 'my brave, bold cub. We will stay with you.'

A feeling of peace – almost of happiness – engulfed the stricken animal. He saw his father and his brother and sister cubs. 'Is Whisper. . . .' Bold tried hard to speak.

'Whisper is well,' Vixen said soothingly. 'Rest now. She will soon be a mother and we shall keep watch for her and bring food for her when necessary.'

Now Fox came closer. 'Your cubs will be fine, sturdy youngsters, Bold, with you for a father. My, what a stout, plucky cub you were!' Then he lowered his voice so that only Bold could hear his words. Not even Vixen overheard. 'You are a courageous animal,' he said, 'and your adventures will be remembered as long as mine. *I'm* proud to be *your* father.'

A sigh escaped Bold's parted lips. He felt a sense of release. All had not been in vain. He looked joyfully towards the black, watchful figure in the birch tree, and prepared to leave, at last, the real world.

Epilogue

In the spring Whisper's cubs were born. There were four of them – two male and two female. Charmer produced her litter, too, and so the blood of the Farthing Wood Fox renewed itself in the third generation. But Whisper had another reason to be proud, for in her cub's veins was mingled also the blood of Bold, her chosen mate. Only now could her regret at losing him be effaced by seeing his image reproduced in her offspring. As her cubs would mature and grow up, it would be Bold's history they would hear as they nestled around her in their earth. They would remember the father they would never know as the heroic creature she believed him to be, who had sacrificed himself for their well-being.

Robber came to tell her he had found a mate and, before he bade her farewell, they reminisced a little. They talked of Bold, and of their adventures, and remembered Rollo. They parted with affection.

And Whisper was never to feel lonely. Apart from Bold's family, there were new friends to be made all the time – Bold's friends and his father's friends from their old home. She soon learned that life in White Deer Park was quite unlike her previous existence.

Two months passed; her cubs gambolled in the sun and grew bigger and stronger and learnt how to hunt. One night Whisper's special friend – Charmer – came to talk. They lay on the ground by Whisper's bolt-hole, watching Tawny Owl swooping silently through the summer evening.

'My cubs wanted to know what's outside the Park,' Whisper remarked. 'I tried to explain but couldn't find the right words. I have to find a way of justifying their father's actions without persuading them to copy him.'

'This Park can be a paradise,' Charmer said. 'That's what they should learn.'

'*I've* learnt it,' Whisper answered. 'There are creatures here on the best of terms who would be tearing each other to pieces anywhere else.'

'It's a friendship that's rooted in the old Oath and worth preserving,' Charmer said.

'And a means of persuasion, perhaps, for any animal who might develop itchy feet,' Whisper added.

'I think you and I between us, Whisper, can find a more telling cure for that problem,' said Charmer humorously. 'When our cubs are a little bigger they must be encouraged to mingle. And the rest can be left to Mother Nature!'